THE SISTERS OF SUGARCREEK

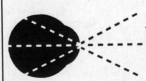

This Large Print Book carries the
Seal of Approval of N.A.V.H.

THE SISTERS OF SUGARCREEK

CATHY LIGGETT

THORNDIKE PRESS
A part of Gale, Cengage Learning

GALE
CENGAGE Learning·

Farmington Hills, Mich • San Francisco • New York • Waterville, Maine
Meriden, Conn • Mason, Ohio • Chicago

GALE
CENGAGE Learning·

LIBRARY OF CONGRESS CATALOGING-IN-PUBLICATION DATA

Names: Liggett, Cathy, author.
Title: The sisters of Sugarcreek / by Cathy Liggett.
Description: Large print edition. | Waterville, Maine : Thorndike Press, 2017. |
    Series: Thorndike Press large print Christian fiction
Identifiers: LCCN 2016055516| ISBN 9781410498243 (hardcover) | ISBN 1410498247
    (hardcover)
Subjects: LCSH: Large type books. | GSAFD: Christian fiction.
Classification: LCC PS3612.I343 S57 2017b | DDC 813/.6—dc23
LC record available at https://lccn.loc.gov/2016055516

Published in 2017 by arrangement with Tyndale House Publishers, Inc.

Printed in Mexico
4 5 6 7 8 9 21 20 19 18 17

To Pete
Even in the midst of your own battle,
you never stopped encouraging.
Thank you!

ACKNOWLEDGMENTS

Psst!

I'm talking to you, Pat Edgar and the ladies of First United Church of Christ in Sugarcreek, Ohio. You women don't know this, but if it weren't for you, it's doubtful this book would have ever come about. Years ago you invited me and Jennifer Davis, the founder of Beaded Hope, to come talk to your group about the nonprofit and my novel *Beaded Hope.* We also got to be a part of your church's Christmas sale that December, organized to benefit others. And the fact is, at the end of our time that weekend, neither Jennifer nor I wanted to leave. You made us feel that welcome, warmed by your hospitality and instant friendship — enchanted by you and your town. As we reluctantly got into our car to head back to Cincinnati, I mentioned to Jennifer that I wanted to write a book set in Sugarcreek someday just so I could come

7

back to visit you again. Well, here that book is. In the meantime, over the years you have continued to inspire me with news of the countless charitable things you ladies bond together to do for your town and even abroad. I feel privileged to have met you, and I really do hope to see you again very soon!

I not only want to thank the ladies of Sugarcreek and the charming town itself for inspiring *The Sisters of Sugarcreek,* but I'm also most grateful to the group of people who have brought this book to life. Thank you, Karen Solem, for being the best kind of agent for me — for always believing but never posturing; for always being honest but also incredibly encouraging. My only wish is that you lived closer so we could do more girl-days-out at the art museum (or any other place in town you'd like to visit!).

Once again, I feel so blessed to have the good fortune to work with the special people at Tyndale House Publishers. Jan Stob, a very heartfelt thank-you to you for giving this book a chance and for your insights and kind support as it took its time falling into place. Sarah Rische, how I appreciate your eagle eye, your sense of timing, and your ideas on deepening characters! It has been such a great pleasure to work with you; thank you so much. Thank you, too, to Kathy Olson and Shaina Turner for your time and input. And to all the others at Tyndale whose names I don't know but who have made huge contributions to this book in the areas of art design, copyediting, marketing, and sales — I appreciate your efforts very much.

I also want to thank my real-life sisters (and brother), my extended-family sisters, my writing sisters, my sisters at work, my ladies' Bible study sisters, and my sisterhood of friends for encouraging me and helping me through this writing process — and even more importantly through life. I shy away from listing all of your names for fear this will get far too long.

But as I type this, please know I smile (hugely!) as each of your faces cross my mind and sweet thoughts of you bless my heart.

To my children, Kelly, Michael, and now son-in-law Matt, you are the absolute joys of my life, and I love watching you strive toward your dreams. It amuses me, too, how the tides have turned. Whenever I'm writing, you're the ones asking me if I've gotten my work done yet! Thanks, guys, for keeping me on track.

Mark, if there was ever a reason to believe

in God's timing, you are certainly it. After all the decades together, I never stop being grateful for the day He brought you into my heart to walk beside me all these years. That was the very luckiest day of this girl's life!

And finally, dear Father in heaven, I praise You and thank You from the depths of my heart for all the dear and special people I've mentioned here. I am also humbly grateful for the glorious, ever-constant gifts of Your greatness, Your grace, Your caring, and Your love, which hard as I try, I can never quite put into words.

Therefore encourage one another and build each other up, just as in fact you are doing.

1 THESSALONIANS 5:11

Kindness, when given away, keeps coming back.

AMISH PROVERB

CHAPTER ONE

Be strong.
Be strong in the Lord, Lydia.
Strong in the Lord . . .

With not a tear in her eye, Lydia's *maam* had whispered those parting words eight years earlier as she gave Lydia's teenaged shoulders a hasty hug and sent her off in a buggy with Henry, the husband she barely knew.

Too shy and bewildered to have much to say to the far older Henry Gruber, Lydia had focused on her mother's words instead. She'd repeated them over and over, trying to ignore the homesickness seeping into every part of her. Trying to be as brave as she could, she had kept her head raised and her eyes fixed on the black roads that wound all the way from Pennsylvania to Sugarcreek, Ohio.

Now, as Lydia sat in a chair at the farthest end of the white canopy tent set up on her and Henry's property, her mother's chant came back to her. Just as she'd needed to hear the words at the beginning of her life with Henry, she needed to hang on to them again as she watched *Englischers* traipse in the drizzling rain across her lawn to their cars, clutching her deceased husband's belongings.

She'd been trying so hard to contain the emotion welling up inside her, not wanting to do the unthinkable and break down, that she hadn't even noticed the auctioneer who approached her.

"Mrs. Gruber?"

She turned at the sound of Mr. Cohen's voice. He tilted his head in a kindly way toward her.

So it really was time, wasn't it? The auction she'd been dreading was over. Could it really be so?

Mr. Cohen stood holding a bulky, cream-colored envelope in his hand, and there was no denying it. The empty tent was full of empty chairs. The auction was finished. Complete. The last public rite of Henry's passing was done with. Nearly all his life's possessions carried away by others. Mostly strangers.

The finality of it all brought on another wave of dread, more weighty and numbing

14

than the first. Although she was much too young for her legs to feel so weak, her limbs felt as unsteady as a newborn foal's as she strained to push off the folding chair to stand face-to-face with the stout-bellied auctioneer.

"Everything's here. In the envelope," Mr. Cohen said softly, slowly, his rapid-fire banter gone as if it never existed. "Mostly cash, but a few checks too."

Days ago, sitting across from Henry's empty chair with her Bible in her lap, the Scriptures all a blur, she'd imagined this moment and how it would unfold. But she'd never imagined how losing all of Henry's belongings would feel. Could've never known how it would feel.

The span of years had linked her to Henry more than the small confines of the buggy ever could in their first days together. Her heart wrenched sorrowfully and a sick taste rose in the back of her mouth. How was it possible? The measure of her husband's life on earth reduced to a small envelope of money?

She swallowed hard, wishing she could put off the moment forever. Even paused to smooth the wrinkles from her long black skirt, as if erasing the toll that hours of sitting had taken on the freshly ironed dress

15

were so vitally important. And yet she knew she couldn't hesitate any longer. Long-held-in tears burned the back of her eyes as she forced herself to reach for the manila envelope the auctioneer held out to her.

Even in the damp stuffiness of the air beneath the canopy, the envelope felt notice-ably cold in her hand. Lydia tightened the shawl around her shoulders and tried to find her voice. A *danke* stuck in her throat along with the lump of emotion lodged there. The best she could manage was to bow her head in silent thanks, her *kapp* shielding her face from his gaze.

"There aren't many items left. Just a few that didn't sell," Mr. Cohen went on to say. "Your husband's tools from the lumberyard and the lawn ornaments he made all went very fast. I'm sure you noticed."

But she hadn't noticed at all. She'd forced herself not to watch or to listen, not want-ing to know which of Henry's whatevers went where. Or what things left their prop-erty with whom. She'd only been on hand to answer questions about his belongings if need be. But there hadn't been any ques-tions from the few Amish and mostly *En-glisch* who had dropped by.

If there were any questions at all, there were hers. All the whys and the hows that

16

kept taunting her mind. Torturing her heart. Interrupting her sleep for the past weeks. And as of yet, *Gott* hadn't seemed to be filling in the answer to a one of them.

"I can take the remainder of your husband's things to Goodwill if that would help," he offered. "I've got my pickup truck here."

"*Nee, nee,* Mr. Cohen." She quickly found her voice. "I appreciate it. But I shouldna be having you do that. I should do it myself."

Drawing in an uneasy breath, she wondered how many trips it would take to haul the remaining items to town. She wasn't much accustomed to driving the buggy. Henry had typically taken the reins, as he had done with most all things in their marriage.

But the job had to be done. It had to. The living weren't meant to hold on to the possessions of those who passed. Weren't meant to treasure them. Or store them. For fear of turning their loved ones into idols. Though it wouldn't be easy on her nerves — or her heart — she would just have to manage.

"Well, if you're sure . . . Josh and I will move the remaining items into your barn." The auctioneer nodded to his older son, who was already gathering up the rest of

17

Henry's things. "Then we'll take the canopy down and be out of your way."

"That would be *gut,* Mr. Cohen. Thank you."

The auctioneer nodded in reply, his eyes offering one more look of sympathy before he turned to walk away.

"Oh, Mr. Cohen!" she blurted, suddenly realizing Henry wasn't there to take care of business anymore. "You did take your fee out of the money, *jah*?"

"Honestly, Mrs. Gruber, under the circumstances . . ." The auctioneer paused to rub his chin. "I just wouldn't feel right about taking a fee. It's the least I can do. I mean, your husband — I didn't know him. But, well, he was out there volunteering with the rest of those firefighters. Trying to help. And if the fire had gotten beyond the church . . ." He puffed out a relieved-sounding sigh. "We're all just thankful it didn't."

She'd heard someone say that if the fire had spread, it could've set the entire Main Street of Sugarcreek aflame. But even so, she wasn't used to getting something for nothing. It didn't feel right.

"But you've spent your entire day here," she reminded. "And we agreed on a fee, and —"

He held up his hand to stop her. "It's all good."

It was a very kind gesture, and one she should've felt at peace with. Yet her mind and insides twisted with indecision. Henry had never been one to do such a thing. He would have protested and would've demanded to pay. But at this minute she was beyond tired. Far too weary to argue. "Then thank you again for your services, Mr. Cohen."

"If you need anything . . ."

His parting offer brought another sting of tears to her eyes. People had been saying that to her since Henry died. People she didn't know. People who had shown up on her doorstep with a meal or condolences, whose faces weren't familiar to her. So many strangers after living in the small town all this time.

But in all honesty, she didn't know what she needed. Besides Henry. He'd organized every minute of her days. Every year of her life. And right now, all she knew how to do was to figure out a moment at a time.

As the men began to take down the canopy, the rain started to come harder. And in that moment what Lydia needed couldn't have been clearer — she needed to get out of the rain. But the muted sound of car

19

engines stopped her legs from moving. As she watched the last of the *Englischers* pull away in their vehicles, a deep, gnawing yearning tightened her chest.

Oh, if only she could be one of them. If only she could drive. If she could, she'd drive far away. So far, to some place where there might be comfort for her hurt. Where the unbearable aching inside her could flutter right out the car window and be left behind.

But then . . . that was a silly notion, wasn't it?

Because no matter where she went, Henry wouldn't be there. He was gone from her forever. Forever gone. And no matter where on earth she was, no matter how far she went, there was no escaping that truth.

Be strong, Lydia.

Be strong. . . .

Finally letting the pent-up tears flow freely down her cheeks, she turned from the sight of the cars. Making her way over the wet grass, she headed back to the only place she knew. To the house she used to share with Henry.

Chapter Two

Without a doubt, Jessica Holtz knew Liz Cannon was full of the best intentions. And just as sweet as the vanilla-scented cologne she wore, which lingered inside the older woman's car. Jessica remembered sensing those things about Liz even when she'd been a young girl, growing up with Liz's daughter. She was sure all of Liz's kind-hearted qualities were why her aunt Rose and Liz had become fast friends. Both of them were so much alike.

It was also why Jessica was doing everything she could to hold her tongue. And to be polite. Even though Liz's driving — and the "twinge" of night blindness she admitted to having — was scaring Jessica beyond belief.

For the last eight miles or so, she'd been holding her breath. Not to mention digging her nails into the underside of the leather seat. All while Liz weaved and careened her way over one dark country road after another, searching for the Gruber homestead.

"I'll tell you what —" Liz gave her blue-rimmed glasses a push up the bridge of her nose — "things certainly look different on these country roads at night." She leaned forward and squinted through the windshield.

Jessica couldn't argue with that. She'd thought the same thing many times. By day, all along the roadside, stretches of lush farmland and hillsides rolled out invitingly as far as the eye could see. But on a dark, starless night, the looming blackness could be notably disorienting and intimidating.

Making her wish she'd offered to drive in the first place. She really was a much better driver, plus her eyes were at least twenty-five years younger.

"Well, just take your time, okay?" she said as calmly and soothingly as she could. While her insides twisted into a dozen kinds of knots. Their excursion had already taken far longer than it should have. She just wanted to get home safely to her son!

Jessica pulled her phone out of her jeans pocket, ready to text her sitter if they didn't come across the Grubers' home soon. Hopefully Marisa wouldn't have a problem with her being late. Much later than she'd hoped to be.

It was a rare thing for her to be out on a weeknight to begin with. Or any night, for that matter. As a single working mom, her babysitting budget wasn't the healthiest, and most evenings were all about spending as much time as she could with her little guy, Cole. Unless something unusual came up, of course. Something out of the ordinary, like Liz's plan.

She gazed into the darkness beyond the car window, remembering how easy Liz had made her idea sound. . . .

All they needed to do was stitch a "Simple to Make in a Weekend" quilt for the recently widowed Lydia Gruber. Using material from Henry Gruber's shirts, which Liz had bid on at the widow's auction two weeks ago. Then they'd sneak around in the night to anonymously drop off the gift. Just to give the young widow a sprinkle of hope. To let her know someone cared.

Jessica had readily agreed to the plan. She'd wanted to say yes for so many reasons. Yet nothing about Liz's plan had been simple for Jessica, especially not where her emotions were concerned.

With every crooked, knotted, messy stitch, she'd wished she could do anything right and pretty and even with a needle and thread. She wished she'd spent more time learning from her aunt Rose, who had made knitting and quilting her life and her livelihood. Oh, how she missed her aunt, who had loved her unconditionally. Who had raised her like her own daughter.

Her heart couldn't stop hurting, couldn't stop yearning with the greatest wish of all: that there'd never been that day of the fire . . . at their church, of all places. That it hadn't claimed the life of a man named Henry. And mostly — most selfishly — that the fire hadn't taken her sweet aunt Rose's life too.

Familiar tears of disbelief sprang to Jessica's eyes. She turned from the window and her thoughts, hoping to control them. Liz's voice seemed to help.

"The drive sure didn't take this long when I drove out for the auction," Liz shared.

Jessica cleared her throat and took a moment to process Liz's words, to focus on the present. "Um, yeah, you said it was just up the road from town."

As Liz suddenly jerked the car around another corner, the gift for the Gruber widow went sliding across Jessica's lap. Grabbing onto it, she nestled it closer. "Uh . . . I think I'm going to text Marisa to let her know we're running behind."

Marisa had always been a great sitter for Cole, but in the past weeks, she'd been even more than that — she'd been a godsend, helping Jessica however she needed her to. Jessica sure didn't want to abuse the high school senior's willingness to work.

She had just tapped in her first words of apology to Marisa when she heard rustling coming from Liz's side of the car.

"Oh, my!"

"Oh, my, what?" Jessica looked up from her phone to see Liz sitting up straight, peering over the steering wheel.

"Over there." Liz pointed to movement on the side of the road. "Oh, goodness! It's a deer!" she exclaimed. "Now, don't you go jumping out in front of my car, you precious creature. No jumping, okay?"

Jessica could feel Liz easing her foot off the accelerator — right before she jerked the wheel into the oncoming lane. Causing Jessica's body to sway right then left as the gift and her phone bounced in her lap.

"Liz, I hate to tell you —" she grabbed the dash to steady herself — "but that's not a deer. It's an Amish man. Riding a bike."

"Oh? Well, no worries, then. For sure he's not going to dart out in front of me."

Liz's shoulders went slack while Jessica's definitely tightened up around her neck. Yes, she was an animal lover. And yes, she would never in her life want to bring any deer to harm. But the possibility of running over a man — a real live human being — well, it just seemed a tad more serious. At least to her way of thinking.

She braced herself and held her breath again as Liz slowed the car to a near crawl. It seemed to take Liz forever to skirt around the man on wheels, coming a little too close, in Jessica's humble — and unuttered — opinion.

"He should have a taillight on that bike," Liz commented once she'd passed him safely. And Jessica could let out her breath at last.

"Uh, he did," Jessica replied softly.

"Really? Well, it must've been awfully dim. Or small."

"I suppose the light could've been larger," Jessica agreed — actually just tried to placate the older woman. "You know . . . I'm happy to drive," she offered. "It might make more sense. I mean, that way you could look for the street since you've been there before." She worked to hide the nervous timbre in her voice.

"Oh, no. I've got this, honey. Besides, I have a feeling we're close," Liz said, her tone reassuring. As always.

Jessica didn't know when she'd ever learn that some things — and people — were simply out of her control. She sighed and sat back, attempting to relax. Trying not to think about all that had happened over the past weeks. Trying to focus on the moment and the surprising things Liz had shared about her aunt. Things that shouldn't have been a surprise to her at all.

"I can't believe you and Aunt Rose used to go on nighttime escapades like this. What I really can't believe is that I never knew about them."

"Well, how could you?" Liz smiled into the faint light of the car, the tufts of her trendy spiky hair silhouetted in the dimness.

Jessica laughed softly. "Yes, that's right. Those escapades were supposed to be secret, weren't they?" Although she thought she knew everything about the aunt who had mothered her, obviously that hadn't been altogether true. " 'The Secret Stitches Society, dedicated to bringing a stitch of hope to others.' But still, you'd think I would've figured out that Aunt Rose was behind all that good in town. Well, and you too, Liz," she added hastily.

"Oh, no. It wasn't so much me." Liz shook her head. "Like I told you, Rose is the one who started the whole thing. I was just lucky that she invited me along on a few of her jaunts so I could feel a bit like Santa Claus all year round."

Soon after her aunt's funeral, Liz had shared with Jessica how years earlier, Rose had come up to her after a church service one Sunday, out of the blue. Almost as if she knew that Liz needed someone at that moment. Liz's husband had been gone for three years that very day, and though that was old news to everyone else, Liz was still trying to find more and more ways to fill that void in her life.

That morning Rose invited Liz to a free knitting class at her shop, and after Liz had gone more than a few times, Rose also let her in on the secrets of the so-called society of which there was only one member at that point — Rose.

"It sounds like you and Aunt Rose did a lot of good and had some memorable times," Jessica said, recalling the stories Liz had already shared with her.

"Definitely. We did a lot of giggling on those nights." Liz chuckled. "Doing for others felt good. Getting my mind off myself felt even better. She was one special lady, that aunt of yours." Her voice faded with an undeniable note of sadness.

Jessica reached out to gently pat Liz's shoulder just as Liz had done for her so many times over the past weeks. There really were no words. Or if there were, they were lost on her at the moment.

Losing her aunt and inheriting Rose's Knit One Quilt Too Cottage at the same time felt all too strange. Too unreal. Like she was living someone else's life and had no handle on her own.

"I still can't believe Aunt Rose left her shop to me." She didn't mean to murmur the words out loud.

"Honey, you were her only family. She loved you and she loved the Cottage," Liz soothed. "Why wouldn't she have wanted you to take over the shop?"

"I know. But . . ." To Jessica's way of thinking, the situation was logical and unbelievable all at the same time. Her? Owning a knitting and quilting shop? She was so not that person. Not a crafter at all. And it wasn't like her aunt didn't know it. Regretfully, growing up, Jessica also hadn't made it her business to get to know her aunt's business.

Yet in her heart of hearts, she knew she wouldn't have it any other way — and she guessed that's the way her aunt had felt about the matter too when she'd drawn up her will. Jessica had grown up having the Cottage in her life. Like Rose, it had always been like family to her too. "I just hope I can learn everything and make it work," she said to Liz, fearful of botching it all up.

"Hey, you didn't do so badly on our quilt for Lydia Gruber," Liz said.

Or rather, blatantly fibbed. Causing Jessica to look over at her and smile. "It's okay, Liz. You don't need to lie. I'm well aware of my limitations." But she'd vowed to try to turn into a crafty person yet.

"No, really. You said you'd barely ever held a needle in your hand, and I believe you."

Jessica laughed at that. While Liz's face crinkled like a raisin, appearing baffled by her own statement. "Something about that didn't come out right. What I meant to say was —"

"Oh!" Jessica cut her off. "There's Quarterhorse Road." She pointed at a small sign posted on their left. "That's what we're looking for, right?" she asked hopefully.

"Yes! Finally." Liz made a sharp left turn. "We're nearly there. The Gruber place is only a little ways up the street," she said, quickly turning off the headlights.

Unable to help herself, Jessica shot a glance at the woman. "Liz, seriously. What are you doing?"

"It's okay. This is how it's done. No lights." Liz shrugged. "It's a secret mission, remember? Besides, we'll be pulling in the driveway in five seconds."

"I hope we pull in the driveway and not a ditch!"

Again Liz reassured her. "Oh, now. Here we go. Five . . . Four . . . Three . . . Twooooo . . ." She drew the word out as long as she could while Jessica held her breath once more. "One!"

Liz sounded rather victorious as she turned off the main road onto the Gruber lot. Jessica's torso flung lightly against the seat belt as Liz slammed the car into park at the end of the driveway and cut the engine abruptly.

Jessica had thought she'd feel a surge of instant relief, just being stationary and safe at last. But as she and Liz both sat, staring at the Gruber house, surges of bewilderment mounted all over again.

She'd had a theory as a young girl. A theory that only one devastating thing could happen to a person in their lifetime. She'd come up with that theory after the one unthinkable, tragic thing had happened to her: losing both of her parents in a fatal car accident when she was only eight years old.

With that horrid event, she was sure she'd

be exempt from anything else so awful. Yet here she was at twenty-seven, and even though a mother herself, with her aunt's untimely death, a part of her felt orphaned all over again. Proving her theory all wrong. Proving her theory was just a fantasy.

Gazing at the windows of the widow's house, she hated knowing there wasn't any place safe from things that tore your heart and your world in two. Not for her. Not for the widow she didn't even know. Not for anybody.

She hugged the wrapped package to her chest, wishing once again she'd been able to do a better job of sewing and stitching. Wishing the gift wasn't as flawed as her theory. Liz in her typical positive way had said that the funky stitches on the front side of the quilt and the loopy threads on the back side would go unnoticed, that sentiment would override the mistakes. Jessica had to hope that was true.

"The auction was here?" she whispered in the hush of the car. "In the yard?"

"Yes, over there." Liz nodded beside her.

How strange that must've been for the woman — Lydia Gruber — Jessica thought. Such an ado. The invasion of people. An auctioneer's yodel. Cars parked in the grass. And now all of that gone. All so hushed and quiet with barely a star in the sky.

"Did you meet her?" Jessica asked quietly. "The day of the auction?"

"No," Liz answered. "But I feel like I know her."

Jessica nodded, knowing how Liz had gone through the same situation several years earlier. And of course, Jessica had suffered her own losses too. "I sure hope finding this quilt on her doorstep makes her feel a little better."

"That is the hope, as your aunt Rose would always say." Liz paused before asking, "Are we ready?"

As Liz started to open her car door, Jessica couldn't help but reach out and lay a hand on her arm to stop her. She'd hesitated to say anything earlier, but thinking of her theory . . . her son . . . Liz's grandkids . . . the dark night and even darker country roads . . . made her rethink that decision now.

"You know, Liz, as we were talking tonight, it made me realize that some people really are better at some things than others."

Liz gave her a puzzled look.

"So how about you take this —" Jessica handed her the gift package — "and I'll take those." She pointed to the keys in Liz's hands, then plucked them away before Liz could react. "For the trip home."

"I scared you that much?"

"Well . . ." Jessica offered up an apologetic smile. "Kind of."

For a brief second, Liz looked a bit befuddled. Then, true to form, she bounced back to her bright-as-ever self. "We can't have that, can we? Not on a special night like tonight."

And for just a moment as Liz said that, Jessica did feel something special. A whirl of emotions that brought a sting of tears to her eyes . . . hopefulness, devastation, kindness, empathy, wonder, loss. But through it all, mostly an overwhelming feeling of gratitude — a profound thankfulness — for the gift of the aunt she'd loved so dearly. And who had loved her.

This one is for you, Aunt Rose!

She was too overcome to say the words out loud. But she felt them with all her heart as she and Liz got out of the car and quietly headed toward the widow's house in the still of the night.

Lydia gasped into the darkness of the bedroom. Her entire body froze beneath the bedcovers, stiff with fear. There it was again. The sounds. The sense that something was

34

near. That she wasn't alone.

"Oh, dear *Gott.*" She winced, wanting to break down and cry. "I need to sleep. To rest. I need to feel safe."

Not once in her life could she ever remember being so tired. She'd tried to keep the schedule Henry had set for them — the one he claimed resulted in a healthy, productive life. Off to bed by nine thirty, awake at five thirty. But night after night, it was the same — the unease that kept her awake. Had Henry's breathing as he lay next to her all those years hidden every sound of the darkness?

Staring at the ceiling, she waited and listened. Something scraped overhead. Or was the sound coming more from the sitting room? Rigid with fear, she slowly turned her head on the pillow, trying to listen for something more over the heartbeat pounding in her ear. All the while, hoping not to hear a thing. But there it was again. A muffled noise . . . and the sense that something was close. Inside? Or outside? And the feeling that she was not alone.

Glancing at the lantern on her nightstand, she willed her hand to move from under the covers to turn it on. She couldn't do this another night. Couldn't cower like a frightened animal in her own bed.

Forcing herself to get up, she felt her heart beat wildly in her chest as she wrapped her shawl around her shoulders, grabbed the lantern, and tiptoed into the sitting room. Her eyes drifted around the room, looking for anything out of place. But she couldn't see a thing. Couldn't hear a thing. Nothing.

She stood there in the silence, feeling her body weave, light-headed with exhaustion. Still, she couldn't return to her bed. Didn't want to feel the empty space beside her.

Instead, she turned off the lantern, and as a slender beam of moonlight shone through the window, she settled into Henry's chair. The armrests felt cold to the touch and the cushion more rigid than she ever imagined it would be. Even so, she could almost sense him there. Could almost imagine his presence, offering her protection. At least for a few nights that's where she'd stay, she decided. Where she'd try to get her rest.

CHAPTER THREE

Despite the coolness of the morning air, beads of perspiration formed along the edges of Lydia's hairline and *kapp* as she stood staring, bewildered by the collection of leather straps and reins that she'd dragged outside from the barn.

"If only you could talk, Flora," she muttered to the skittish horse that was dubiously appraising her with large brown eyes. "If only you could remind me how this all works."

She felt so overwhelmed. And anxious. So angry at the unfairness of it all.

Especially on a day like today.

The morning was crisp and clear, with a slightly cool breeze, and the sky such a bright shade of cornflower blue, a person had to almost close her eyes to look at it. It was the kind of morning she used to savor and offer up audible praises to the heavens for. The kind she'd always found so perfect

37

for hanging Henry's freshly washed charcoal broadcloth pants and cotton shirts in a row on the clothesline as she squinted into the glorious sun.

But that wasn't so any longer. Not any of it. Not since *Gott* had taken Henry away.

There were no more peaceful musings . . . no more idle thoughts of what to make her husband for supper that night as his shirts flapped lazily in the breeze. Instead her insides warred constantly. Hating *Gott* for taking her husband away . . . then begging for His help with all she had to learn and do.

But He didn't seem to be much help at the moment.

It was also clear as the day that Flora wasn't going to help hitch herself to the buggy either.

Very much used to Henry's care and his knowing touch, the creature was noticeably perturbed by Lydia's sudden attention. Clomping backward. Shifting sideways. Wriggling restlessly from head to tail, as if deciding whether to stay put or to run for the hills.

Oh, how Lydia wished she could run too. Flora's nervous behavior made her feel even tenser and more bedraggled than she already had. Not only was she as nervous around the horse as the horse was around her, but she was so stiff and bone-tired from dozing in Henry's chair all night, she could barely stand up straight.

"I don't blame you, Flora. I don't, girl." She sighed as she rubbed at her aching lower back. "You're mighty mistaken if you think I want to be doing any of this. And I sure don't wanna go to town, either."

In fact, as she said the word *town* out loud, tingles of apprehension pricked her cheeks. The hair stood up on her arms with anxious chills as if she were headed for the other side of the world, not several miles down the road.

Because it felt that way, didn't it? After spending so many years, day after day after day at their house alone, that routine was all she knew. Doing chores — and waiting for the end of each day when Henry would be coming home, of course. As for town, she couldn't even recall the last time she'd gone on her own.

But supplies all around were running low. Flora needed feed, and then there were items to pick up from the grocery. Certainly more milk, for the stray cat that she'd let become dependent on her since Henry was gone. It had come mewing expectantly on her doorstep for days.

"I'm only trying to help you, Flora. You do like to eat, don't ya, girl?"

Flora snorted loudly in reply, catching Lydia off guard. Causing her to jump back in shock, her heart racing all over again.

There'd been a time as a young girl when she'd spent hours playfully braiding the manes of her father's horses, fluffing out their tails with a comb. But ever since the one day when she'd taken her *daed's* favorite horse for a ride, wanting to show off her handiwork, she'd shied away from the creatures. Nothing had ended well that day. Not for her when the horse got spooked by a car and she was thrown into a ditch and suffered a concussion. And especially not for the horse when the creature slipped down the embankment, broke its leg, and had to be put down for good.

The accident that long-ago day left her with plenty of scars and fears — a distrust for horses and even more than that, doubts about her ability to handle them. Plus, whenever she caught sight of one of the four-legged creatures, there was always that dull ache — the pain of knowing she'd been responsible for the demise of one of them.

She'd told Henry about the incident, but he'd never seemed to have much to say about it. He'd been clear that the only things she needed to conquer were the kitchen and the garden. He'd taken care of all the rest. He'd been in charge of everything else in their lives.

Which certainly didn't help matters right now.

Lydia drew in a deep breath and tried not to think about that day in the past or her discomfort in the present. What she needed to do was focus on what was right in front of her, or she'd never get to town and back before the afternoon traffic picked up.

Making an effort to concentrate, she studied the leather pieces at her feet once more, until her eyes finally landed on something she recognized. Of course — the harness. That was the place to start.

Bending down, she picked it up and carried it over to Flora. But Flora wasn't having any of it. Wagging her head vigorously, she whinnied up to the skies. Every movement, every sound causing Lydia's courage to crumble.

"Please, Flora, please," Lydia begged the creature, knowing for the horse's own sake she couldn't back down. "You need to settle," she said, then remembered the slice of apple in her apron pocket.

She was far too nervous to let the horse take the treat from her hand. Instead, she tossed it on the ground in front of her. As Flora's head dipped to snatch it up, Lydia quickly slid the harness over the horse's muzzle and face. With tentative fingers, she worked to settle it into place.

One piece down! She stepped back and wiped her brow.

Heartened by her minor success, she could feel a twinge of relief ease the tightness in her stomach. Until Flora began to snort and shake her head. Lydia's insides seized all over again.

It wasn't like she didn't know the next set of leather straps she needed to put into place. But she could hardly move, frozen in place by the sound of Flora's unease growing louder and louder as she shifted left hoof, right hoof. Left hoof. Right . . .

Added to the feel of Lydia's own heart thumping one beat, two beats, one beat, two . . .

"Looks like you've got a jittery horse on your hands."

Lydia's entire body leapt at the sound of a man's voice behind her. Her hands flew to her chest, and she gasped out loud as she turned to a face she'd never seen before.

"I'm sorry," the stranger apologized, jerking his head back. "I didna mean to startle you."

Clutching the neck of her dress in fear, she felt like all the breath had gone out of her as she glanced around for something or someone to protect her. But all she could see were the empty fields. No people. No help. Not for miles around.

"What do you want?" Her voice rasped in a way she didn't even recognize.

"Ah, well . . ." The man's head dipped. "I wanted to . . . give you this."

As the man raised his arm, she flinched. She'd been so caught off guard by him showing up out of nowhere, she hadn't even noticed the package dangling by his side.

Confused, she stared at the parcel wrapped in a deep-purple paper, then eyed the Amish man suspiciously. "Are you a friend of Henry's?"

Soon after Henry's passing, some of his male acquaintances, mostly Amish and *Englischers* from his work and volunteer job, had made a point of contacting her, offering their regrets and condolences. A few of the men's names were familiar to her from Henry speaking about them, and she could finally put faces to those names. But most of the men she didn't know. Had never heard of. It was almost as if her husband had had a life other than the one they shared.

For her safety's sake, she hoped this man was a part of that life of Henry's. But his forehead pinched under his straw hat, telling her it wasn't so. Another wave of fear washed over her.

"Henry?" His light eyes shadowed in confusion. "*Nee.* I don't know a Henry."

"No?" Tendrils of fear shot up the back of her neck. Her hands tightened into fists at her sides.

"No, I just moved back to town a couple of days ago. I live next door. I'm Jonas. Hershberger." He turned slightly, pointed to the property sitting to the left side of her home. A stretch of scraggly shrubs separated her house from the old O'Malley home, which had been vacant for so long that the place barely existed to her anymore. She rarely even thought to look in that direction.

"I'm guessing Henry's your husband?"

Her mouth opened, but no words came at first. She didn't need to tell a stranger her business, did she?

"*Jah,*" she said. Lord help her, she lied. "*Jah,* he is."

"*Gut.* I'll get to meet him later then," the stranger said, sounding as if he was actually looking forward to it. Causing her to bite her tongue to hold back the truth. "In the meantime," he added, "like I said, this is for you."

She shook her head decisively. "I canna take gifts from strangers."

His brow tilted and he eyed her curiously. "Oh, *nee*. It's not from me. Is that what you're thinking?" The slightest smile tugged at his lips. "My dog has a habit of snooping around other people's houses. And a really bad habit of dragging home things that don't belong to him."

He might've had a decent sort of face, much younger than Henry's, and his eyes might've even held a glint of kindness. But even so, his explanation seemed mighty questionable. Especially with no dog at his side, and not one she could see anywhere in sight.

"He's in the house, napping." The man — Jonas — must've read her mind. "Worn out after all his gallivanting very early this morning. I have a feeling he must've found this on your doorstep." He held out the package to her once again. "I'm sorry he chewed up the wrapping some."

After all the weeks that had passed since Henry died, she couldn't imagine what a gift would be doing on her doorstep. But the sooner she accepted the package, she considered, the sooner he'd go away.

45

Wouldn't he? *"Danke."*

"You're welcome." He tipped his hat and took a step back, but to her dismay, he didn't leave. Instead, he pointed toward Flora and the buggy. "She seems jumpy this morning. Let me finish that for you, okay?"

"Well, I . . ." She was torn between wanting him to leave and wanting his help. Just as torn as she'd been with the Lord lately, she realized.

But at this point, she needed help more than she needed to be left alone. Maybe that's why *Gott* had sent this kind soul her way. Maybe she shouldn't be so quick to send him away.

"That would be mighty kind of you," she finally acquiesced.

She watched as Jonas deftly hooked up one leather strap after another and at the same time began to win over Flora's trust and affection. Between each fitting, he'd stroke Flora's neck with his strong-looking hands. Little by little, the horse began to lean into his palm, as if she'd been missing a man's touch and his was feeling just fine.

Lydia couldn't help but gape at the change in the creature and was also surprised at Jonas, who finished tending to the buggy in less time than it had taken her to drag all of the equipment from the barn. He gave Flora a final stroke before he turned to her. "You're all set here."

"You certainly got Flora to calm down quickly." She couldn't hide her amazement. "Thank you *verra* much for your help. *Danke.*"

"You're welcome . . ." He paused, and she knew from the way he inclined his head toward her that he was waiting for her to fill the space with her name.

After a moment's hesitation, she let out a breath and complied. "Lydia."

"Lydia." His eyes smiled at her. "Nice to meet ya."

He held out his hand and she stared at it for a moment before she realized he meant to shake her hand. She reached out and met his clasp and knew instantly why Flora had been so easily subdued. Even with a brief shake, she could sense his touch was firm and assuring, somehow making all feel well.

"You have a *gut* day, Lydia." He started to step away but didn't get very far. He stopped and turned with one last thing to say. "Oh, and I promise you, I'll have a serious talk with Jeb about staying out of your yard."

She figured he had to be teasing her. But she flushed, not sure how to respond. She wasn't accustomed to anyone being playful with her. Henry had never been that way in

47

the least.

Cradling the gift to her chest, she kept watch on Jonas Hershberger as he retreated from her yard. Mostly everything inside her believed he truly was her new neighbor. But as vulnerable as she felt lately, she had to make sure he crossed over her driveway and then into his. A small, wary part of her still had to be certain he wasn't some impostor or drifter.

It wasn't until he was out of sight that she even remembered the gift she'd been holding in her hand. Who in the world had left something on her doorstep? She couldn't begin to imagine.

Tearing at the already-tattered paper, she hoped to find a card inside. What she discovered instead tugged greatly on her heart.

The square blocks of the small quilt might've been plain, and the patches of fabric not so vibrant, with only muted blues, worn-looking whites, and a subdued yellow here and there. But she knew where each and every one of those fabric swatches had come from. She'd made all of Henry's shirts and she'd washed them over and over again. Some days as she'd hung them up, before shutting his closet door, she'd even reached out to press the fabric against her cheek, longing for something she wasn't sure of, something she couldn't express. The same hollow feeling came to her now, bringing with it a surge of fresh pain to her heart.

"Oh, Henry," she whispered.

Hugging the quilt to her chest, she touched a corner of the fabric to her cheek. "Oh, Henry," she whispered again. "I can't believe you're gone!"

As her tears fell on the quilt, she pulled it from her cheek and wiped the moisture away. Oh, but she wasn't supposed to keep such a thing, was she? She shouldn't keep it, should she?

Torn for yet another time that morning, she covered the quilt with the purple paper, not even wanting to look at it. It would make a nice, warm lap cover for someone. But that someone couldn't be her.

She could barely see through her tears as she made her way to the rear of the buggy. Opening the storage box there, she placed the wrapped package with the load of Henry's other things that she'd resigned herself to take to Goodwill. Buried it in there, so she wouldn't be tempted to take it back out.

Hopefully she'd never know who the gift was from, and hopefully whoever stitched the thoughtful gift would never know what she'd done with it.

She forced herself to close the black box, then through tear-blurred eyes made her way around to the side of the buggy. Taking a deep breath, she turned back to the task at hand, willing herself to step up into the driver's seat and take hold of the reins.

Tears dried on her cheeks as she shifted on the hard seat, attempting to find a grooved-out, comfortable spot. Her tongue felt thick as she clucked to Flora and tapped the creature's backside with the reins, signaling her to move. But of course, after all she'd gone through to prepare the horse for their outing, and all her neighbor had done as well, the stubborn animal wouldn't budge.

"*Jah,* Flora? This is how it's going to be?" she said, exasperated. "I know I'm not Henry, but you still have a job to do."

Even with her badgering, Lydia couldn't get Flora to step an inch. Frustrated, she looked up to the heavens and sighed in despair. She needed patience. Lots of it. Her hands were so tightly clenched around the reins she wondered if maybe her tension was fueling Flora's obstinate behavior.

She let go of the leather straps, and the two of them sat in silence while she closed her eyes and let her head drop back on her shoulders, attempting to calm herself and muster up enough patience to try again. As she did, a gentle waft of air drifted into the buggy and cooled her face. With the air and the quiet seemed to come the reminder of her husband's ways . . . how he always let the reins fall slightly on Flora's back not once but twice before they'd start out.

Opening her eyes, Lydia lifted the reins again, held them loosely in her hands, and did just the same as her husband had, trying to duplicate his touch. One light flick. Two light flicks. Finally, Flora consented.

The horse's hooves clapped slowly down the gravel drive, now seeming to relax, seeming to know what to do. But Lydia couldn't unwind. With every step the sure-footed horse took, her body tensed more and more. As they passed the side of the yard where she should've been hanging Henry's clothes. As they passed the garden where she should've been picking vegetables for dinner.

Passing by all of the sameness that would never be the same again. Now every day was a surprise. Every day she had to find her own footing. And every day she didn't like it. Didn't know what to make of it. How to cope or survive it.

Only knew that somehow she must.

As Flora came to the end of the driveway, Lydia pulled back on the reins, startled to see how different everything looked without Henry by her side. The fields across the street sprawled in every direction, going on and on, all the way to the horizon. And to her right . . . the black length of road leading north to town dipped and swelled over and over again until it disappeared into an ominous haze.

Without her husband, her buffer, the world beyond her house appeared all too large. Too wide. Too much to handle. Clutching the reins in her hand, she sat, her heart pounding. Not wanting to venture out into it all, but wanting the trip to be over just the same.

Oh, but maybe if I just get started . . .

Maybe if she could just hear the steady clip-clop of Flora's hooves on the pavement once again. Maybe the calming sound would ease her senses the way it used to. Lull her into a soothing daydream the way the motion always had with Henry at the reins. Let her forget the fears of the past like a clueless child. Not let her think about the present . . . being a young woman all alone.

Determined to at least try, she turned her head to the left, searching the road. All was clear. Veering Flora to the right, toward town, she signaled for the horse to go.

To her relief, Flora readily obeyed her command this time and sauntered onto the road. As the creature trotted in a steady rhythm, Lydia could feel the tension in her shoulders relax ever so slightly.

Be strong . . .

She could do this. She *would* do this.

"Good girl, Flora." She found her voice. "Good girl."

CHAPTER FOUR

"Marisa will be here to take you to practice any minute, Cole," Jessica said, looking up from straightening a bin of teal-colored yarns. "Are you sure you brushed your teeth?"

Cole sat on her aunt's old oak bench in the middle of the Knit One Quilt Too Cottage, heavily concentrating on a video game. Or at least appearing to. His slight frame barely filled the seat, making it easy for Jessica to see most of the words carved into the back planks of the bench. Not that she needed to see any of the words. She'd sat on that bench plenty of times herself as a young girl — and as an older one too — and knew her aunt's favorite adage by heart: "Friends are like quilts. They never lose their warmth."

"Cole," she repeated when she didn't get any response from him. "Your teeth. Did you brush them?"

Most likely noting the hint of sternness in her voice, her son responded. But only with a nod. Without looking up.

She pursed her lips, knowing it was silly to ask what was wrong with her typically talkative son. Why wouldn't he be acting out and sulking some? Inwardly, wasn't she too?

They'd been through a lot of changes recently. Changes in the amount of time they spent together since she'd inherited the shop and he'd started first grade. And the kind of time they spent together too. Instead of enjoying free hours in the evenings the way they used to, often dusk found them at the kitchen table, Cole with schoolwork or reading and her catching up on shop work.

From Cole's perspective, there had been a major change in their living arrangements as well. It hadn't been easy on him moving into Aunt Rose's tighter living quarters above the shop, leaving behind their spacious apartment. Not to mention him having to give up his very own man cave — an awesome bedroom with outer space decor, complete with glow-in-the-dark stars, which Jessica promised she'd try to replicate soon . . . just as soon as things slowed down.

And of course, there was the huge void in

their lives these days — the empty spot that Rose used to fill. Great Rose, as he'd called his great-aunt, who had been like the best kind of grandma to him.

"You know . . . you haven't had a joke for me the past few mornings," she tried again.

Cole shrugged as he continued to thumb at the pad in his hand.

Many mornings he'd have a joke or riddle for her, something silly he'd found in one of the joke books his Great Rose had made a part of his birthday gifts for the past two years.

"So I'm getting the hint you're thinking he might grow up to be a comedian one day, Aunt Rose," she'd teased her aunt this past birthday, his seventh.

"Actually, no, I was thinking more like a doctor," her aunt told her. "One with a deep heart and a lighthearted bedside manner."

Which Jessica had realized in that moment was exactly how her aunt lived her life. The way she'd always rolled.

"Well, Colester," she addressed her son once more, "since you haven't had any jokes for me lately, I have one for you."

Finally. He tore himself away from his game. And glanced up, eyeing her curiously.

"Ahem." She cleared her throat dramatically, stalling. Now trying to recall the joke she'd found online earlier that morning. "Do you, Cole, um . . . Oh! Do you know what's smarter than a talking bird?"

She could tell his little mind was whirling, sifting through possible answers. Until he gave up and shook his head.

"A spelling bee!" She grinned, proud of the clever nugget she'd found.

"Mom, that's not funny," her son informed her. But despite what he said, a smile twitched at the corner of his mouth.

She sighed. Well, at least that was an improvement. Worth the time she'd spent online looking for first-grade jokes.

"You know, sometimes a joke is only as funny as the person who tells it." She shrugged, nudging the last skein of yarn back into place. "You're a much better joke teller than I am." She deferred to him, but he wasn't taking the bait.

"When is Marisa coming?" he asked instead.

The shop wasn't supposed to open for a half hour yet. But she'd unlocked the front door anyway so Marisa could fetch Cole from there, instead of making her sitter and lifesaver these days climb the wooden stairs that ran up the side of the building to the apartment. Plus, there was never an end to things she could straighten up in the shop while the two of them waited.

"I'm sure she'll be here any second."

No sooner had the words left her mouth than the bell tinkled over the front door. She and Cole both looked that way expectantly. Her son, she was sure, was hoping it was Marisa since he was anxious to get away from all the "girl stuff," as he kept calling the bins of yarn and material in the store. And Jessica, in true Pavlovian mode, felt a certain degree of anxiety each time that little bell chimed. True, she'd been used to dealing with the public as a receptionist at one of the town's dental offices. She'd also enjoyed being a sort of publicist for the practice, overseeing their social media and implementing some marketing ideas. But now there wasn't a dentist or higher-up to confer with or defer to. Now she wasn't just a greeter and marketer. She was large and in charge, completely.

But it wasn't Marisa coming in the door for Cole. Or a customer for Jessica. It was Liz.

Jessica barely got out a hello as Liz sailed into the shop, waving a white paper bag in her hand.

"I believe I just snagged the very, very first pumpkin muffins of the season from Good for the Soul Bakery. They're still warm, in fact," Liz informed Cole, who was looking at her — and the bag — wide-eyed. "But, oh, dear." Liz's expression changed like the tide. "It looks like you're headed off somewhere." She nodded to his feet.

"Soccer practice," Cole replied, glancing at his own soccer shoes and shin guards.

"Well, how about we save these until after soccer practice then?" Liz bobbed her head as if Cole had already agreed to the suggestion. "You don't want to be doing a lot of running with muffins stuffing your stomach."

"Thank you for bringing them," Cole replied, and Jessica felt warmed that even in the midst of his terseness with her lately, he wasn't being that way with Liz.

"You're very welcome, Cole, and I appreciate your good manners."

Cole beamed as Liz gushed over him, as if she were speaking to one of her grandchildren. But then, even the few times Jessica had been in contact with Liz, she'd thought that everything about Liz was effusive in one way or another. The older woman's plump cheeks appeared to be continually stained cherry red, as if she was always excited about what was to be or what had been. Her eyes rarely stopped twinkling behind those blue glasses of hers.

"I have something for you, too." Liz handed Jessica the bakery bag and then fumbled around in the purse hanging from her shoulder. "I believe this is yours." She drew out a lipstick tube. "I found it in the car from the other night. It must've fallen out of your purse. I didn't want you to be without it."

"Oh, my Raspberry Rhapsody. Thanks, Liz. I was wondering what I'd done with that." She took the tube with her free hand. "But you didn't have to make a special trip over here. I could've picked up the lipstick from you."

"Not a big deal. The shop is on my way to work."

On the occasions Jessica had seen Liz, she'd been in everyday street clothes or even a casual dress on Sundays at church. Now she looked so official and professional in her white blouse and navy Regency Real Estate blazer topping her khaki skirt, almost like a different person.

"Do you have an appointment today?"

"Just going to the office to scare up some business. I hope." She tugged at a spike of hair at the back of her head. Jessica always thought Liz's hair looked adorable and in style. Cropped short and dyed the color of molasses, it stuck up and out in some places, sprung to life with the help of mousse. "But actually —" Liz grimaced — "do you mind if I use your facilities before I head out? I've had too much tea this morning."

"Sure. Come on upstairs. Cole, we'll be down in a minute," she said to her son, who after the removal of the muffins was already absorbed in his game again.

Jessica led Liz across the hardwood floor of the Cottage, Liz's one-inch heels clacking behind her. Even though she'd never had much interest in knitting or quilting — which her aunt had never tried to push — Jessica had always been proud of her aunt's shop. On the outside the shop resembled a chalet like a few of the other stores along Main Street, indicative of Sugarcreek's nickname, the Little Switzerland of Ohio.

The inside of her aunt's store, however, couldn't have been truer to its name. Every inch of the interior had a cozy cottage feel. Bins and baskets of vibrant yarns, chunky yarns, sparkly yarns, and pastel ones, too, decorated the left side of the shop. Row after row of bolts of plain fabrics, patterned fabrics, silky fabrics, and textured ones were displayed along the right side. Knit sweaters, shawls, and scarves hung from the shoulders of burlap floor mannequins. Quilt samples, displaying a variety of patterns, hung from available walls and parts of the ceiling.

Once they reached the midsection of the shop, the staircase to her aunt's apartment was off to the right, hidden behind a closed door so customers would never suspect it was even there. As Jessica made her way up the staircase with Liz in tow, the old wooden steps squeaked beneath their weight, and she couldn't help but think of all the times she'd traveled up and down the stairs.

As a young girl, it'd been a heady experience to strut her friends through the colorful store and to impress them with the mysterious "reserved for owners only" staircase.

At twenty years old with a newborn, she'd walked those steps plenty too. Trying to soothe Cole, attempting to get him to sleep, while wondering how and when she'd manage to get a place of her own, even though Aunt Rose promised all would work out fine.

Now she was here again . . . another phase of her life. Climbing the steps with Liz, a woman she'd never suspected she'd become so familiar with.

And every time she climbed those stairs, no matter what, she wished her aunt Rose were waiting for her at the top.

"Watch yourself," she warned Liz as she opened the door to the apartment. "It's a little crowded in here."

As Liz gingerly made her way to the bathroom, stepping around boxes and misplaced end tables, Jessica headed for the kitchen. She was wrapping the muffins in plastic wrap when Liz joined her.

"Thanks again for the muffins, Liz. Cole loves them — and I do too."

"No problem at all." Liz waved a hand, then glanced around at the conglomeration of furniture behind them, and Jessica knew everything she was thinking but was kind enough not to say.

"I know. I've still got some work to do. I've already gotten rid of a few things. But not enough obviously."

It was funny that when she was a little girl growing up over the shop, the apartment had seemed so spacious. Now that she was on the other end of the spectrum, she was having a hard time making sense of the small area she had to work with.

"I have to figure out what to keep of mine and Cole's, and what to keep of Aunt Rose's." She sighed, thinking about the dilemma all over again. "It hasn't been as easy as I thought it'd be. I either feel sentimental because there's something Cole grew up with or sentimental because of something I know Aunt Rose was fond of."

"It all takes time, honey." Liz nodded understandingly. "You'll figure out what makes you and Cole most comfortable."

"Some things have been easy to part with, though. I mean, I obviously don't need two toaster ovens or blenders or mixers, and I don't feel particularly attached to any of them." She nodded to a box she'd packed a week ago that was still sitting against the kitchen wall. "I've packed some of those up to give away since it's not like Cole will be getting his own place anytime soon."

"Let's hope not." Liz smiled.

"If our church was still there, I could donate Aunt Rose's things to their fall collection drive," she said, then shook her head. "I can't believe I just said something so stupid. If the church was still here, she would be too." She could feel the familiar dull sorrow begin to rise inside her.

Liz reached out and touched her cheek. "Hey, it's okay. It's all still unbelievable to me, too." She paused and bit her lip. "Listen, honey, I'll be going right by Goodwill if you want me to take that box of kitchen stuff for you."

"I would've done it myself, but I kind of

feel chained to the shop right now. Really, you wouldn't mind?"

"I wouldn't have offered if I did."

Knowing Liz as she did at this point, Jessica didn't think that was altogether true. But it would be good to get one more box out of the way. "I appreciate it, Liz. I really do. I'll carry it to your car."

"And what about this bag?" Liz tugged on a green garbage bag next to the box.

"Yeah, that one can go too. It's just place mats and napkins and tablecloths," Jessica told her. "There's not enough room for all of it."

As Liz picked up the bag and Jessica grabbed the box, Cole's voice shot up the stairs with more energy than she'd heard from him all morning. Lifting her heart a bit.

"Mom, Marisa's here."

"Hey, Jessica," the sitter called up to her.

"Hi, Marisa. You two guys stay put for a minute, okay? I'm coming right down to say good-bye."

If the past weeks had her son feeling apprehensive about where they were living, they'd left her feeling apprehensive and more protective than ever about him leaving her side.

No way was she going to let him head off

anywhere without kissing him, hugging him, and telling him she loved him.

Suddenly wanting to be near her, the stray cat purred and strutted in and out of the folds of Lydia's skirt as she knelt over the garden bed at the side of the house.

"I'm sorry. Not now, Kit."

She gently shooed the sleek gray cat away with the back of her hand before turning her attention to the sad-looking patches of lettuce again. Most of the greens were overgrown with leaves spiking upward and outward in every direction. She could only spy a few heads of lettuce that might even still be edible.

Reaching over mounds of greens gone haywire, she cut off the top two-thirds of a head that still looked contained and normal. Turning it over in her hands, however, she was disappointed. A milky white substance oozed from its center, meaning that head of lettuce had also bolted and would be bitter for sure.

Sitting back on her heels, she grimaced at the tacky mess of a garden that had once held a beautiful, tidy bounty of vegetables. A sting of shame pricked her cheeks. She'd neglected the bed of plants for far too long.

Not only had most of the greens wasted

away, but she had a bucketful of tomatoes that had fallen from their vines and been prey to whatever critters had chomped on them. Also, with the unexpected upheaval in her life, understandably the time had long since come and gone for planting rows of turnips and beets to gather later in the fall.

It wasn't so much that she needed the harvest from the garden. Living all alone now, she could manage on a pot of soup for a week. Plus, it wasn't as if her cupboards were bare. Canned tomatoes and beets lined her pantry, and the freezer was stocked with peas and beans.

But after counting and recounting the envelope of money Mr. Cohen had given her, and after getting an idea of what her monthly needs and bills would be, she discovered there wasn't as much of a cushion as she thought there might be.

She'd hoped selling some fresh vegetables might be that cushion. At least until she found another way to get by. Considering the mess her garden was in, there wasn't even the slightest possibility of that now.

Still . . . the area did need to be cleaned out, and she needed to salvage whatever she could since so much had already gone to waste. Hopefully dear *Gott* could forgive her for being so wasteful with His provision.

Getting back up on her knees, she'd decided to start with the lettuce again when a shadow came over the row of greens.

"Oh!" She looked over her shoulder, tightening the knife in her hand.

"I need to stop doing that to you, don't I?" Jonas stood over her.

"It would be a *gut* thing if you did. My heart can't take many more surprises," she said, even though as she looked up into her neighbor's face, she could already feel her pulse settling down to its normal rhythm.

"I thought for sure you'd hear my footsteps this time. Or notice Jeb's panting." He nodded to the tan-and-white collie at his side.

"Oh, so this is Jeb? Jeb the snoop, *jah*?"

The animal stood nearly as tall as she was on her knees and apparently was as friendly as he looked. As she reached out to pet him, Jeb moved past her hand, coming right up close to lick her face instead. Taken by surprise, Lydia lost her balance and toppled backward. She had to catch herself with her hands to keep from falling to the ground.

"Jeb, down," Jonas commanded. "Down, Jeb. That's enough." When Jeb didn't seem to hear him, he pulled the dog off her.

"Sorry about that," he apologized.

"He certainly makes friends quickly," she said as she straightened her *kapp.*

"He must like you."

"Ah, well . . ." She took off her garden glove to wipe the dog's slobber from her face. "I'm sure in time we'll get to be good friends, Jeb." *Just not so close so fast,* she thought. "Are you two out for a walk?"

"*Nee.* I needed to ask a favor, but when I knocked on your front door, neither you nor your husband, Henry, answered. Then I saw you around the corner here."

Feeling like she'd been caught in a lie at the mention of Henry's name, Lydia asked, "What favor do you need?"

"Ah, well, my rake broke and I tried wiring it together —" he scratched at his forehead — "but it won't hold."

"That's all? You want to borrow a rake?"

"*Jah.*"

"That's not a problem." She got to her feet, relieved his favor was simple and that it had nothing to do with him needing Henry's help with something. "I'll get the rake from the shed."

He nodded his thanks, and when she looked into his kind eyes, she thought maybe she should tell him about Henry, but somehow she didn't want to. It was only the second time she'd seen him, and she just wasn't ready to talk about it with him. Like Jeb's friendly but overbearing introduction, it felt too close too fast to be talking to another man about her departed husband.

"You don't think your husband would mind?" he called after her as she crossed the yard to the shed.

Lydia didn't even turn to answer. Instead, she shook her head feeling thankful he couldn't see her face. That she didn't have to look into his eyes again.

As she stood in the shed, grabbing the rake from its spot on the wall, she realized that, at least, was the truth. Henry wouldn't mind Jonas borrowing the rake — or anything at all for that matter. Her husband had always been generous with everyone. Even strangers. He'd been talkative with everyone too.

Everyone else, except for . . .

Lydia's body froze. Her heart jolted when she realized the place her thoughts were running off to. She shouldn't be questioning such things about Henry . . . and her. The two of them together. What they had shared . . . or hadn't.

She shouldn't.

She wouldn't.

CHAPTER FIVE

If you can't be big, don't belittle.

Liz sat at her kitchen table, amber rays of late-afternoon sun seeping through the window, and smiled over her cup of tangy pomegranate tea as she read the snippet of Amish wisdom topping the lined ivory page of her purple suede-covered organizer.

Even though she'd lived in Sugarcreek almost all her life, she never tired of Amish proverbs and had been thrilled at the beginning of the year when she'd laid eyes on the pretty organizer at the Mim's on Main gift shop. Even beyond the thoughtful precepts for living, not surprisingly the Amish creators had thought of everything to make the organizer perfect — or at least perfect for her and all of her lists of things to do.

There were two full pages designated for each week, with large blocks for each day. A blank page following each week for notable notes. And also a two-page spread for each month, not to mention an Amish recipe at the beginning of the month — more than half of which she hadn't tried before.

There had been a time in her life when she was so busy being a working mother and wife that she felt completely pressured and overwhelmed by scads of to-do lists and all the Post-it notes lying around her kitchen or attached to the wall calendar or stuffed in her purse. It seemed life rushed by and was such a blur that she could never get close to the bottom of any list. And as soon as she scratched one item off, ten others took its place.

But now on Sundays, with her golden retriever, Daisy, settled at her feet, she looked forward to sifting through the Post-its, scraps of papers, and appointment cards she gathered throughout the week and posting them in her book with her blue gel pen. She loved seeing how her entries gave shape and structure and purpose to the week ahead, listing all the very important things she needed to do regarding work, errands, calls, e-mails, appointments, meals to make, and knitting to do.

She had just started to jot down a reminder on Monday's section to check in on Mr. Herman, the elderly widower down the street, and see if he'd finished the chicken and broccoli casserole she'd made for him, when her cell phone vibrated against the tabletop.

Peering through her glasses, she found herself smiling at the photo of her grandkids lighting up the screen.

As Liz picked up the phone and got up from the wooden chair, Daisy perked up her head and rose too, toenails clicking on the tiled kitchen floor and then going silent as she followed Liz across the family room carpeting.

Curled up on her overstuffed sofa was the best place to savor the call from her one and only daughter, Amy. Liz clicked on the phone as Daisy jumped up alongside her, most likely preferring the cushier spot to her previous one on the kitchen floor.

"Hey, honeypot." Even though Amy was all grown up, married with two children, Liz still often greeted her by her childhood nickname. "What's going on?"

"Oh, nothing much. Just calling to check in."

"Check in on me?" Liz gave a slight chuckle, settling back into the deep comfort of the cushions. "Ames, you act like I'm some feeble old woman, honey. You don't need to 'check in' on me. Haven't you heard? Fifties are the new forties."

"I know you're not feeble, Mom, trust me. I just, you know . . . worry about you sometimes."

"Nothing to worry about on this end. I'll let you know when to fret."

"Well, not worry exactly. It's just . . ." Amy paused long enough for Liz to pick up on the fact that her daughter was trying to find a delicate way to say whatever was on her mind. "I'm just wondering, how are you *really* doing, Mom?"

"*Really* doing?" Liz was at a loss as to what to say exactly.

"Well, yeah. I mean, you used to be so busy at the church, 24-7 when you weren't working your real estate. You were always there, cooking and baking for who knows who all. They gave you some kind of award at church, didn't they? For most meals cooked last year?"

"It wasn't just last year, and it really wasn't an award per se. It was a mention in the bulletin." A half-page write-up on her that had made her blush but feel good about herself. Now Liz frowned, wondering where this conversation was going.

"Oh. Well, I was just thinking about that and . . . You're not going to go nutty, cooking and inviting strangers to your house for meals or anything, are you?"

"I don't believe that's called 'thinking,' Amy. It's more like you're stewing, honey. Worrying. Fretting."

"Not really," her daughter countered. "Not when I could see you doing that. Driving around looking for lost, hungry people. There was a crazy lady on the news here doing just that thing." Her words tumbled out in a rush, her voice sounding frantic. "She ended up in the hospital, all beat up by the strangers she was trying to help. So please don't be doing that, Mom, or I'll never sleep at night."

"You really think she was crazy?" Liz bit her lip.

"Mom, that's not the point."

"You've been living too close to big cities for too long, and you should turn off the news. Who wants to see all that awful stuff anyway?" Liz cringed. "Really, Amy, you don't have to worry."

For one, according to Jessica's opinion, she didn't see well enough at night to go driving around looking for strangers to feed — although she wasn't about to mention that to Amy and give her something else to fret about. Instead she just said, "I'm in Sugarcreek, remember? Hardly anyone is a stranger here."

"Sugarcreek or not, I have to say, I was

relieved when they figured out the origin of the fire was an electrical malfunction in the furnace room," Amy replied. "I can't believe there was even talk of arson at first." She added the dreadful reminder before asking Liz to hold on. "Mom, I have another call. Just one second, okay?" Amy clicked the phone, assuming consent.

Meanwhile, Liz remembered how upset she'd felt a week after the fire, standing inside Miller's butcher shop, hardly able to tear her gaze from the front window and the sight that lay just a half block up on the other side of the street. The place where crime-scene tape was strung around the perimeter of the ashen grounds. The grounds where Faith Community Church used to stand. The very spot where her friend Rose, always in charge of seasonal decorations, had gone to search through the supply closet in the bowels of the church . . . and had never come out.

"It must be very hurtful for you," Martha Miller had said in a hushed voice from behind the meat cases, nodding understandingly in her cotton *kapp*.

"Oh, Martha, you're so right," she'd replied. "Every time I pass by and see it in ashes, it's just . . . I don't know. . . ." She shook her head at her Amish acquaintance.

"It makes me feel so sad and so . . . lost."
And violated when the investigators hadn't
readily been able to come up with a cause
and the gossip about arson had started buzz-
ing.

It was the first time she'd put words to
the way she'd been feeling. Even just running errands and driving over familiar wind-
ing roads past rolling farmlands didn't seem
the same to her. Nothing felt right with the
world. Or whole. Not with the loss of her
dear Rose, whom she'd gotten so close to in
the past few years. Or with the loss of her
church, which had been so much a part of
her and her adult life.

"Feeling lost in a town the size of Sugarcreek is not a *gut* thing." Martha had sighed
sympathetically, and Liz had to agree.

"It's a foreign feeling, for sure." Liz nodded. "It's been very kind of some of the
other churches in town to invite us to their
services, and I've tried, but . . ."

"It's not the same, I would imagine." Martha had finished the sentence for her.

And it wasn't.

Faith Community was where she and her
husband, Karl, had been married, and
where they'd baptized their precious baby
girl. Amy had walked down the aisle of the
church as a beautiful young bride six years

ago. Just a year later, the pastor had delivered Karl's eulogy and many people were there to hold Liz and comfort her and not let go until she was on her feet again.

She'd felt lost then, too, for a long stretch of time, her daily life no longer bearing any resemblance to the titles that defined her. Karl wasn't there to be a wife to. Amy and her family were on the East Coast, slimming the opportunities to be an active mom and grandmother. So she took on the title of active member of Faith Community Church — "uber-active," as her daughter would say. The hours she wasn't at work, she'd been at church. But then with the fire, it had been like a grenade had gone off, fragmenting the congregation and her place of purpose and worship in all directions — and that role of hers had been eliminated too.

As a result, her kitchen had become her comfort zone. The place where she spent most of her time on Sundays, baking and preparing a dinner or two for anyone who had a need.

"Mom, thanks for letting me get that." Amy's voice interrupted her thoughts. "Like I was saying, as much as I worry about you out by yourself, I also hate having a vision of you sitting there watching Food Network.

All alone."

Raising her brows, Liz immediately reached for the remote and turned down the volume before Amy could hear how right she was about Food Network — even though she'd only turned it on for background noise. Then she glanced at Daisy, snuggled up against the apricot afghan Liz had hand-knit, hanging over the arm of the sofa. "I'm not alone, Ames."

"You're not?"

Was that excitement or relief she heard in her daughter's voice? Liz couldn't be sure. Amy had become such a worrier since becoming a mom.

"Oh. Should I let you go then?" Amy asked. "Who's there?"

"Daisy's here. Right by my side." Liz reached out to pet the creature that had wandered into her yard — and heart — several years earlier. Just a puppy back then. Liz had tried to locate the dog's owner, and when all her attempts failed, she had to admit she was thankful. So quickly, almost overnight, she'd come to love the animal that had found a path to her door and fit into her life so easily.

"Well, I guess she's better company than some people I know," Amy said offhandedly, and then she sighed in that longing mother's way — wishing all were perfect in the world of those she loved but feeling helpless to make things that way. "How's Jessica doing, by the way? Have you seen her?" she asked about her former classmate.

"I'm definitely keeping tabs on her. She's got a lot on her plate right now." She paused and frowned. "I told you she took over the Cottage, didn't I?"

"Yes, you did. A few times," Amy answered with a slight snicker that Liz knew was aimed at her memory and had nothing to do with Jessica's abilities. "That can't be easy for her, and she's got to be missing her aunt so much."

"She is. She and Cole also moved in over the shop, and that's a big adjustment. She's still sorting through Rose's things, and —" *Goodwill!* She'd forgotten to go to Goodwill yesterday! She truly had to write everything down anymore — or at least everything she hoped to remember.

"That's a lot to do on her own. It's nice you're trying to help, Mom. Will you tell her I'm thinking of her?"

"I'll do that," Liz replied, and before her daughter could start to mother her any more, or worry about Jessica or anyone else in Sugarcreek, she quickly shifted to her favorite topic of conversation. "So how are my grandkids? Besides adorable, I mean?"

Her eyes lit on one of the many framed photos of her precious grandbabies, Ellie and Jack, displayed all around the house. It was a photo she'd taken in the spring when the kids had visited from New York. She'd trekked them up the road to Kingfisher's petting farm to visit a newborn goat there. In the photo the kids were hunched together, wide-eyed in amazement, so delighted to be petting the fuzzy creature.

For a while, she'd had the picture sitting on the mantel. But that didn't last long. It was just too far away. Instead, she moved it to the coffee table, where she could see every little dimple on her grandchildren's faces and the brightness in their eyes as they smiled at the camera. The two of them may have gotten their chestnut hair from their father's side, but their oval-shaped brown eyes were definitely from the Cannon side.

"Did I tell you Ellie is playing on a basketball team?"

"Basketball? At four years old?"

"It's an instructional league," Amy explained. "They mostly just fall over each other running up and down the court."

"And how do you keep Jack sitting still through all of that?" Liz asked, picturing her rambunctious two-year-old grandson.

"We don't. Brian and I take turns playing ball with him behind the bleachers."

"You'll have to send me pictures of Ellie in her uniform."

"Oh, don't worry. She's so excited about her player cards. They're due back from the photographer's next week. I'll be sure to get one in the mail to you." Her daughter's tone softened. "By the way, Mom, you remember we're not going to be there for Thanksgiving, right? We go to Brian's parents' house in Connecticut this year."

"Oh, sure. Yeah. Of course I remember." Liz managed to keep her voice light, though her insides suddenly felt dull and heavy. Not that Amy's reminder came as a surprise. Not by any means. The kids switched off each year for the holiday.

Jumping up from the couch, she padded into the kitchen with Daisy on her heels and headed straight for the cookie jar. Maybe one or two oatmeal cookies wouldn't be so bad. A little appetizer before dinner? Something to help that sudden empty feeling not feel so empty?

But as she lifted the lid, she remembered that her khaki work skirt had been fitting a bit too snugly lately. She willed herself to close the container and walk away — far away, over by the kitchen window, where she could she see it wouldn't be too long until the sun would begin its descent for the day. By then only silhouettes of the trees in her backyard would be visible, whereas right now their branches still shone with hints of crimson brilliance here and there.

"How's the foliage in Connecticut by Thanksgiving?" she asked absentmindedly. "Are there still lots of leaves on the trees then?"

The only response she got was a thump over the phone, followed by a dog's yelping.

"Huh?" Amy sounded distracted. "What were you saying, Mom?"

"The foliage in Connecticut. Is it — ?"

"Mom, can you hold on a minute?"

More indistinguishable noises sounded in Liz's ear — and then one she recognized. A burst of crying. From Jack? Or Ellie? She wasn't sure which.

"Mom, can I call you back in a — Brian, can you get the dog, please?"

"Amy, honey, it sounds like your family needs you. You don't need to call back. You all have a good week, you hear?"

"Oh, okay! You too, Mom."

"And give my —"

. . . *grandbabies kisses,* she'd wanted to say. But Amy had already hung up.

For a moment, Liz stared at her phone,

wishing the call hadn't ended so abruptly. But that was life with little ones, as she knew from experience.

Meanwhile, everyone in Amy's family was well and healthy, and that was a lot to be thankful for, she told herself as she walked to the stove and peeked into the pot of chicken and rice soup. She was making the soup for her friend Lucy from church. Or rather, she was making it for Lucy's aunt's daughter Denise, who had been hospitalized for stomach issues and had just been released but still wasn't totally up to par. The recipe was a miracle worker when it came to gastro problems. And while she might not exactly know Denise, she had met Lucy's aunt once before, meaning she wasn't cooking for a complete stranger on the street, as Amy was so fearful of.

Giving the pot a quick stir, she glanced at the clock on the stove. It was still early enough to get to Goodwill and get that errand taken care of instead of adding it to her list. Afterward she could come home, simmer the soup a bit more, and she and Daisy could settle back in and finish filling in her planner for Friday, Saturday, and Sunday.

Turning off the stove, she was just about to go in search of her shoes when — *plop!*

— something dropped into her cup of tepid tea on the kitchen table. Followed by another *plop* and splashes of tea flying.

Walking to the table, she picked up the cup and examined it more closely, somewhat surprised by what she saw inside — white plaster turning pink as it floated in the reddish tea. Was her kitchen ceiling really as bad as all that?

Looking up, she gazed at the cracks running across the ceiling, which didn't look all that alarming given the fact that the house was quite old and something or other was constantly in a state of repair or disrepair. Plus, she didn't think the lines in the plaster looked much different than they had been lately.

But luckily Lou Hager was already scheduled to come to her rescue. She'd written his name down in the first slot for Thursday morning. Picking up her blue pen, she opened her organizer briefly and underlined the handyman's name twice.

CHAPTER SIX

"I hope we're not making a huge mistake, Liz," Jessica sighed. And she hoped they weren't wasting time riding out to Lydia Gruber's house again.

At least on this mission, she'd insisted on driving, so she wasn't afraid for her life as the car wound over the unlit country roads. This time, too, she'd waited to have Marisa come by after she'd already said Cole's prayers and put him to bed. She hadn't wanted him to think she was leaving him again.

"I really don't think we are, honey." Liz sounded hopeful and determined. As usual. "At least that's not what the clerk at Goodwill led me to believe, like I told you."

Jessica had been enjoying a quiet sort of Sunday. She'd just set the spaghetti sauce on to simmer and was glaring at her knitting needles, knowing she had to start practicing soon, when she heard footsteps shuffling up the outside staircase.

At the first sound, her heart dropped, thinking it was Tad Lyon's dad bringing Cole home early because something had gone wrong with the end-of-the-season fishing outing that he'd been kind enough to invite Cole to. But it hadn't been Tad, or his dad, or Cole at all. Instead it had been Liz. With the Secret Stitches quilt they'd made for Lydia Gruber. Along with an explanation of how Liz had discovered it at Goodwill and why they needed to return it to the widow.

When Liz had first arrived at the apartment, she'd been so wide-eyed, her words tumbling over one another so quickly, that Jessica had instantly herded her into the kitchen and put on water, thinking Liz could use a cup of her aunt's chamomile tea still left in the cupboard. But the calming brew didn't help much as Liz gave a rousing explanation of how she'd gone to Goodwill to drop off Jessica's things, and lo and behold, when she stopped to look at some yarn and fabric remnants, what did she see next to them? A stack of blankets with their special quilt right on top.

In her own words, Liz had been so paralyzed with disbelief that a clerk had stopped and asked if she needed help. Evidently he'd been the same clerk who had come to Lydia Gruber's aid just days before when the widow was having trouble getting her horse under the awning of the drop-off area. It wasn't until later, when he was sorting through her things, that he'd found the quilt with the wrapping paper half on and half off. Naturally, he'd wondered if she'd meant to donate the quilt, but the store didn't have any way of getting hold of her to ask. All of which seemed to make sense. Sort of.

"Still, Liz . . . why would the quilt be in the trunk of Lydia's buggy?" Jessica questioned for at least the third time that evening.

Liz finally seemed to hear her question, and she didn't have a quick answer. "Hmm," she drawled while Jessica slowed to a near stop and made a right turn. "Well, maybe . . ." Liz paused again. "Maybe she was taking it to show to friends."

"I guess that could be." Jessica wanted to believe the quilt — or at least the thought behind it — had been worthy enough for Lydia to keep and to share with friends. But why not put the quilt inside the buggy and make sure there was no mistake? No leaving it behind?

"Wait a minute." She glanced at her Secret Stitches partner. "You didn't have to pay for the quilt, did you?"

"Well, I . . . no. Under the circumstances, the nice people at Goodwill weren't going to charge me when I said I'd return the quilt to its owner."

"Oh." Jessica grinned, knowing what was coming next. "But you paid anyway?"

"I had to," Liz confessed. "I mean, I felt funny just taking it. Especially when they could've made money from the quilt."

Jessica couldn't help but smile at Liz's unending positivity and to wonder at the woman all at the same time. To Jessica's way of thinking, the jiffy quilt they'd not-so-expertly sewn might not have had the general appeal Liz believed it did. It was possible that Lydia Gruber hadn't even liked it. Maybe their first Secret Stitches gift had been a dud. A reject. She certainly couldn't blame a recipient for thinking so. Her aunt Rose would've done a better job on it for sure.

Without real proof, however, Jessica agreed they had to make the trip to the Gruber homestead again on the off chance that Lydia hadn't meant to unload the quilt. If that was the case, then Lydia would have the quilt back safely. They could believe their first Secret Stitches gift was a success — a memorable success to say the least.

Lydia Gruber would also know someone had been thinking of her. Not just once, but twice.

Afterward, Jessica could go home, feeling all was right with the world while she cleaned up the kitchen, made Cole's lunch, folded the last of the laundry, paid bills, got ready for the week — all before her bedtime.

She glanced at the clock to see if she was still on schedule. So far, so good.

"You keep looking at the clock," Liz noted.

"I do?" Jessica feigned ignorance but deep down felt caught, knowing, of course, it was true.

Liz smiled at her. "Yes, you do."

"Oh, I just have some things to do when I get home."

"There's never enough time when you're a working mom, is there?" Liz sympathized.

Jessica shook her head. "Doesn't seem to be."

"You're always being torn in lots of different directions."

Jessica glanced at Liz, appreciating her insight. "No matter what I do, or how much I do, I never feel like I'm doing any of it well enough. Or right enough. Not with Cole and now not with the shop. I don't know how Aunt Rose did it all. Actually, it's a good thing I'm not married, come to think of it. I'm sure I wouldn't feel like I was doing a good job at that either."

Liz chuckled beside her.

"Sorry. I must sound like a ranting lunatic."

"No. Just like a mom who cares."

"Oh, I do." Jessica focused on the road. "Hopefully I can do better, though. My poor little guy has been having bad dreams."

"Things will get better. He's had a lot of adjustments lately with the move and all," Liz offered.

"I know." Jessica had been telling herself the same thing. Still, there seemed to be something more going on with Cole. She couldn't put her finger on it, and he wouldn't open up and say. Not yet anyway. Her mind had started to drift to the night before, when he'd climbed into bed with her, when Liz spoke up again.

"That's it, isn't it, Jessica? Quarterhorse Road?"

"Oh, you're right." The road going off to the left did look familiar.

As she made the turn, she hoped for the hundredth time that the Goodwill clerk was right, so that in the end, all would be good with Lydia Gruber and the mystery of the not-so-well-put-together but well-meaning traveling quilt.

"Jessica . . ." Liz leaned toward her, interrupting her thoughts.

"Huh?"

"I think you're forgetting something, honey."

"Yeah?"

"The headlights. You need to turn them off."

"Oh. But —" She started to protest, but she couldn't. Not when Liz's voice began to hum.

"S-S-S. Secret Stitches Society, remember?"

Jessica groaned. But true to being an SSS member, she dutifully flicked off the lights. Then hoped that they'd be safe.

The screen door snapped closed behind Lydia, sounding like a thunderclap in the still of the evening. She stood on the porch and wrapped her shawl around her shoulders, not sure what to do with herself. Simply being in the cool air felt mighty good. And a relief. Far better than being trapped inside the house, where she also hadn't been sure of what to do with herself. For hours.

Once again, her early supper had been easy to clean up, especially since she'd been eating on the same pot of carrot soup all week. Holding a ready dishcloth in her hand, she'd purposefully looked around the kitchen more than once for something — anything — else to scrub. Sadly, one bowl, one spoon, and one glass didn't take time enough to wash.

Aching from loneliness, she had then tried to find refuge in the sitting room. The place she and Henry had spent nearly all of their evenings. The two of them had barely acknowledged each other, rarely ever talking. Him reading, her stitching. Still, he'd been there all those nights, sitting across from her as the stars began to dot the sky. She'd hear the steady sound of his breathing. Occasionally, on some evenings, he'd even read aloud.

The modulation of his voice, clipping along with the clicking of her knitting needles or with the rustling of the quilt in her lap, had created a pleasant rhythm. But mostly, he was quiet. Still, sitting in that quiet room together was the closest she'd ever felt to her husband.

As hard as she tried to sit and stitch, the silence was much too much for her tonight. Her fingers fumbled; her hands trembled. She knew she couldn't stay in the hushed house one minute longer.

As she made her way to a wicker chair in

the corner of the porch, even the noisy creaking of the wooden slats beneath her feet sounded like heaven to her ears. Settling into the padded seat, she closed her eyes, took a long, deep breath, and listened. To chirping crickets. Singing cicadas. The distant shriek of an owl.

Oh, Lord, thank You! Thank You for the sweet, noisy sounds of these! Her eyes welled up with gratitude. *Thank You for letting me know that You're near.*

Her anxious heart slowed to a relaxing rhythm as she continued to sit and listen to the comforting sounds all around. They soothed her like a baby's lullaby, filling her with a peace she hadn't felt in a long while.

Which only made it all the more startling when she heard a new sound — at close range. The crunch of tires on her gravel driveway.

Her eyes shot open. In an instant, the pleasant noises of the night faded far into the background. She stared into the darkness expecting — hoping — to see headlights. Maybe a driver who had lost their way and was pulling into the drive to turn around.

Pounding replaced the peacefulness in her heart when she realized there were no headlights. More sounds drifted through the darkness. One car door closing. Then another.

As two figures came closer, emerging from the shadows, her body stiffened. Oh, why had she trimmed the rose of Sharon bushes along the porch rail? There was nowhere to hide from the pair of trespassers sneaking up the steps.

Gripping the armrests of the chair, she tried to bite back her fear and stay silent. Maybe they wouldn't see her. Maybe they wouldn't —

"Lydia!" the first intruder gasped.

"Lydia Gruber!" the second woman confirmed. "What are you doing out here?"

There wasn't any question in their voices about who she was; they sounded as if they knew her well. But even with the light from the sitting room lantern glowing onto the porch, helping her to see, she couldn't place their faces. Not the young, thin one with the long dark hair. Or the older, rounder woman with the short brown hair. They were as unfamiliar to her as the constellations in the sky.

"You, uh — you weren't supposed to be sitting here," the older woman said, clarifying her comment.

Lydia narrowed her eyes, confused. "But I live here."

"Well, I know. We know. But what I mean is . . ." The woman scratched at the back of her head while the younger woman offered a concerned look.

"I hope we didn't scare you, Lydia."

"I might be less scared if I knew who you both might be."

The *Englischers* looked at each other, then glanced at her, then looked at one another again, perplexing her even more.

"We're . . . um . . . ," the older woman murmured.

"Uh . . . ," the younger woman hedged.

"Oh, we should just tell her," the short-haired woman sighed.

"I know. You're right." The long-haired woman pointed to herself. "I'm Jessica. And this is —" She nodded to the other woman.

"I'm Liz. Liz Cannon. I sell real estate."

"Real estate?" That confused Lydia even more. "I'm not planning to sell my house right now." And she certainly wouldn't hire an agent who went out snooping around at night.

"Oh, no." Liz shook her head. "I just said that because sometimes people will think they know me from somewhere, and that's because they may have noticed my picture on a For Sale sign in someone's yard at some point. But that has nothing to do with why we're here."

"That's not why we're here at all," the other woman chimed in.

"Who did you say you are again?" Lydia asked.

"I'm Jessica. Holtz. I own Rose's Knit One Quilt Too Cottage."

"Oh, goodness." Lydia put a hand over her heart. "The Rose who —" She faltered, unable to even say the words out loud.

"Yes." Jessica nodded slowly. "She was my aunt."

Lydia rose from the chair and stepped close enough to look into Jessica's eyes. So this was who she'd prayed for? Those times she'd prayed for healing for Rose's family? "I'm *verra* sorry for your loss, Jessica."

Jessica gave her an appreciative half smile. "Thank you. We're very sorry for your loss too, Lydia."

"Yes, I've been there. I know what you're going through," Liz shared. "That's why we're here."

"Again," Jessica added, and then looked like she'd said something wrong.

"You've come here before?" And she hadn't been home? "I'm surprised I wasn't here."

"Oh, well, you . . . we . . . sort of . . . ," Jessica stammered, and the Liz woman piped in.

"The important thing is we made something for you, Lydia, and we think maybe you lost it."

"Yes, that's the important thing." Jessica's expression brightened, looking relieved at the turn in the conversation. "We thought if you did lose it, you might want it back."

"*Jah?*" Lydia had absolutely no idea what they were talking about.

"Yes." Liz nodded as she reached into the bag on her shoulder. "Lydia, this is for you. From us."

Even in the dim light of the porch, as Lydia took their gift, she could tell it was the quilt she'd taken to Goodwill. Stunned, she felt torn all over again, the same way she had the day she'd first seen it. Wanting to have a keepsake of Henry's, yet wanting to do what was right. Although now that she'd been introduced to the ladies who had made the quilt, wasn't sparing their feelings the right thing too?

"Oh, the quilt!" she exclaimed. "I'm so glad you found it!"

She didn't feel like she was very good at pretending, but evidently she was better than she thought. The two women glanced at one another and seemed to heave dual sighs of relief.

"That's great news to hear," Jessica said.

"It sure is." Liz clapped her hands. "You see, I was at Goodwill earlier and —"

"You saw the quilt," Lydia finished her sentence.

She could feel her face heat and was thankful the ladies couldn't see her red cheeks in the dark. She'd been so lost in her own pain at the time she'd tossed the quilt into the rear of her buggy that she hadn't even considered the time and effort it had taken for someone to come to the auction and then to also make the quilt. Since the quilt definitely looked like the work of beginners, it had to have been difficult for Jessica and Liz to make.

"Yes, I saw the quilt," Liz continued, a sweet lady but talkative for sure, "and the clerk said you'd been having trouble with your horse when you stopped there."

"Flora." Lydia remembered the horse's apprehension well.

"Actually, no." Liz shook her head. "The clerk's name was Nick."

"I was speaking of my horse. Flora."

"Oh, right." Liz laughed. "Anyway, Nick said he didn't think you meant to donate the quilt with the rest of your things because it was still in the gift paper we'd wrapped it in."

"*Jah.* Well . . . ," Lydia stammered, bent on trying not to tell another fib. "This is all *verra* kind of you both," she said because that really was the truth.

The three of them stared at each other for a moment longer while a moth flitted between them and bumped noisily against the window. Jessica rubbed her arms, as if she was chilly. Liz shifted on her feet as if she didn't know if she was staying or going.

Not used to having company, Lydia wasn't sure what came next. "Do you . . . would you want to come inside?"

"Thank you, Lydia, but it's getting late," Jessica spoke up. "We should get going."

"But before we go, can we ask you a favor?" Liz added.

Lydia shrugged and nodded even though her stomach stirred, apprehensive about what was coming next. "Sure."

"Please don't tell anyone we were here, okay?" Liz peered over her glasses.

"Yes, that would be very helpful," Jessica agreed.

"Oh, I . . ." She started to say that she didn't have a long list of people to tell, or even a short one, but decided to keep that to herself. "I definitely won't," she said. "Thank you again, Jessica and Liz. Thank you for thinking of me. I know quilts take a lot of time and effort."

"Do you quilt?" Jessica asked.

"Oh, *jah.*" She smiled. "Since I was a young girl. I know it's not easy, so *danke.*"

The ladies looked pleased with themselves as they turned to go, which made Lydia feel pleased too. As the pair started down the stairs, Lydia spied Jeb — the friendliest dog in all of Sugarcreek — waiting for them at the bottom.

"What a cute dog you have." Jessica held out her hand for Jeb to sniff.

"Oh, Jeb's not mine. He's my neighbor's. He likes to visit quite often."

"*Jah* — he likes to visit whenever he can get away with it." Jonas suddenly appeared from around the rose of Sharon shrubs. "I hope he didn't scare you ladies," he addressed Jessica and Liz. "Or cover you with too much drool."

"Oh, no," Liz cooed, petting Jeb behind his ears. "He seems to be like my Daisy. A real sweetheart."

"*Jah,* he's everyone's sweetheart," Jonas repeated and Lydia watched as he hooked his thumb in Jeb's collar. "Okay, sweetheart, it's time to head back home," he said to Jeb, making the women laugh.

"See you, Jeb." Lydia waved. "And thank you again, ladies," she called out, now oddly wishing that the two of them had decided to stay.

"You're welcome, Lydia." Jessica waved back. "We hope the quilt brings good memories of your husband."

"He was a brave man," Liz added.

Lydia could feel her heart drop at the mention of her departed husband. But this time it didn't have as much to do with Henry as it did with Jonas. Even in the shadowy moonlight she could see him. His head turned swiftly and his eyes locked with hers. Questioning her. Maybe even looking slightly hurt by her and the way she hadn't been truthful with him.

Lydia tried to settle down after everyone left, but as she sat staring at the quilt she'd refolded and laid over the arm of Henry's chair, all she could see was her neighbor's eyes.

For sure, it was time to be honest with Jonas, the man who'd been so friendly and open with her. She just needed to do it and not think about it. Because if she thought about it, then she wouldn't do it, and things would be even more uncomfortable the next time she saw him.

Not to mention, she'd be awake half the night again.

After fetching a flashlight from the kitchen drawer, she closed the front door quietly behind her. Cutting across her side yard, she thought about all the times she'd wished for a well-worn path leading to her neighbor's house. That would've been a sure sign that she had a good female friend close enough to visit on days when she could've used some company — or on evenings when Henry was running late coming home from work and his volunteer job. Instead, Mr. O'Malley had lived there by himself until he'd left the place vacant over a year ago.

As she shone the flashlight on the shrubs, looking for a spot to cross through, she realized she'd only been to O'Malley's house a couple of times by herself when the older man had lived there. Once when she had to wrangle one of his baby goats that had gotten loose and was feasting on her garden. The other time when a letter had come for him in her mail. Certainly neither of those times had been after dark.

Finally making her way across Jonas's yard and up his walkway, she knocked on the door and waited for him to answer. She felt odd and far too bold. So unlike the reserved person she knew herself to be. Jonas looked as surprised as she was at herself when he opened the door.

"Lydia?" Half of his face stayed in the shadows, making him look sterner than she'd ever seen him. Or was he really that upset with her?

She crossed her arms over her chest and stood bravely. "I'm sorry to bother you, Jonas."

"It's awful late. Is there a problem?"

"*Jah,* Jonas. There is."

"What's going on?"

"I lied to you," she said simply.

He looked down at his feet, then raised his head and looked into her eyes. She realized it was the first time she'd ever seen him without his straw hat. His dark hair was cut short and outlined his forehead neatly. His left brow rose a slight fraction as he asked, "Do you want to come in?"

"Nee." She shook her head, not feeling right about going inside. He seemed to sense her feelings and stepped out the door.

"Okay, then." He motioned to the cement stoop. "Want to have a seat in that case? It's big enough for both of us."

"Danke." She felt relieved by his understanding as she tucked her skirt under her and sat down on the step. In a matter of seconds, Jeb came to sit as well.

"Actually, it's big enough for the three of

us," Jonas added, amusement coloring his voice.

Somehow having the friendly creature sitting between them gave her more confidence. "Jonas," she started.

Her neighbor raised his hand. "Lydia, you don't owe me any explanations about anything."

"Well, if we're going to be good neighbors, I think I do." She folded her hands in her lap and found herself looking everywhere but at him. "You see, it hasn't been so long since my husband — since Henry's been gone. He died in the big church fire, and I haven't completely gotten my bearings. I haven't gotten my bearings at all. And the first day you came by, well —"

"Lydia, I know about your husband."

"You do?" She dared to steal a glance at him.

He nodded. "And I'm real sorry for your loss." Even in the dim porch light, she could see the sympathy in his eyes. "I learned about it from some people at church just this morning. But I didn't want to say anything to you. I thought I'd wait till you felt comfortable to say something to me first." He paused, his expression just as strained as he added, "I'm also real sorry cause I must've made you mighty nervous showing up at your barn the way I did."

"Well . . . *jah*. But you already apologized for that, Jonas, and it wasn't anything you could help," she said, though she vividly recalled how scared she'd been. "I'd been so wrapped up in my own situation, in my sorrow, I hadn't even noticed that someone had moved in over here. Then, the day you found me in the garden, I started to tell you but at the time, my mind — well, I had it on something else." With all of that confessed, she finally felt like she could breathe again and let out a sigh.

"Anything you want to talk about?" He plucked a prickly leaf off a holly shrub next to the step and rubbed it between his fingers.

"Oh, I . . ." She wasn't sure what to say. Or how much he wanted to hear. "Not really." She shrugged, glancing out into the hushed darkness. "There are just a lot of changes with Henry gone, and things I'm not used to. He took care of everything. Now I have to find a way to do all those things and to make money too. Even handling Flora is new to me," she admitted. "You'll never know how much you helped me with her, Jonas. I've had a fear of horses for a long time, and I know my nervousness makes her nervous too. I'm guessing I should've worked to overcome my fear long ago, and Henry should've let me get used to horses again. But he liked to take things over and do them his way. That's how things were." Her cheeks suddenly flushed at the realization of how much she was talking. Why was she saying so much? Surely he was tired of listening to her.

But as she started to apologize, hoping she hadn't made him uncomfortable, he reached out and patted her hand. "If it helps to know you've got neighbors you can call on for anything — well, Jeb and I are here."

"Oh, *jah,* Jeb is always everywhere. Ain't you, pup?"

She chuckled slightly as she put her arms around the creature and nuzzled her face into his neck. Before she knew what was happening, tears sprang to her eyes. She hadn't realized how raw her emotions were, but she couldn't stop herself as all of her feelings came tumbling out onto the willing, furry Jeb. The simple comfort she found burying her sorrow in the pet's warm, silky coat made everything seep out of her. Crying for Henry. Crying for herself. Crying for what was and what might have been. Crying for the sweetness of the night filled with the kindness of strangers and a neighbor's consoling touch.

It was minutes before she released Jeb from her hug and sat up, wiping the tears from her cheeks, emptied and embarrassed by her outburst. "I'm sorry, Jonas."

"Sorry for having feelings?" he said softly. "Don't ya be."

"Sorry I got Jeb all wet too." She sniffed.

"Aw, I think he can handle it. He's been through worse."

They sat together quietly for a bit. She realized she could hear the comforting sounds of the crickets and cicadas once more.

"*Gott* is *gut,* Lydia," Jonas said, words that seemed to come out of nowhere but oh, how they fit the moment.

"*Jah.* I know." Her voice cracked. "You're right." Giving Jeb one last pat, she stood and straightened her skirt. "So . . . do ya forgive me?"

"There's nothing to forgive. All is well between us, neighbor." He smiled up at her.

"I should be going then."

"It's mighty dark. Jeb and I will walk you back."

"That's okay. I have a flashlight." She took the light from her apron pocket and flicked it on. "I'll be okay," she said, treating the flashlight as if it were protective armor.

She could see the hint of a smile reach his eyes. "All right then, if you say so. I hope you get a good night's rest, Lydia."

"*Danke,* Jonas."

"Come on, Jeb. We need our rest too." With that, Jonas got up from the stoop and stepped onto his porch. "Oh," he called out to her. "Lydia, I don't know what kind of job you're looking for —"

She chuckled at that. "I'm mighty sure I don't either."

"Well, just to tell you, I saw a sign in the bakery last week. They were looking for help."

"*Jah?*" A flutter of hope lifted her heart. "Thank you. I'll be sure to check it out tomorrow. Good night, Jonas."

He waved his good-night, and even though her flashlight lit the way, she could feel her kind neighbor watching out for her as she crossed into her yard and into her house. Closing the door behind her and on all that had taken place, she felt like she really might get a good night's rest for a change.

CHAPTER SEVEN

"I promise I'll make it happen, Mrs. Grisham." Jessica cradled the phone on her shoulder as she jotted down notes and at the same time rang up four skeins of bulky yarn for a customer. "I'll get the correct yarn here as quickly as I can. I apologize for the mistake."

She covered the phone with her hand as Mrs. Grisham prattled on. "Thank you for stopping in," she said, handing the bag of yarn to the white-haired woman leaning over the counter. "Please come back."

"Oh, we always do." The lady brightened at her attention. "Many of us love visiting the Cottage when our group comes to town. It's been a little too hectic in here today, though. The pen to sign the guest book isn't even working. Usually the place runs much more smoothly than this." Uncertainty filled her gaze as she glanced around.

"Well, I —"

Jessica couldn't even begin to explain to the woman about her aunt Rose and the reason for all the delays and hiccups. For one thing, she was afraid she'd break down in tears if she started talking about her aunt. For another, the line at the register was growing longer, and Mrs. Grisham wouldn't stop harping on the phone.

"We sure hope to see you again," she said to the woman instead.

If only someone would've told her about the busload of women visiting town from a senior center in Columbus, she might've been better prepared for the barrage of chattering ladies. At least she would've made the effort to try.

As it was, she was stuck behind the counter at the cash register, unable to bring order to the chaos around her. She couldn't do a thing to help the women throughout the store who were digging through supply drawers and bins, searching for yarns and needles and threads. She also couldn't help Marisa, who was at the cutting station at the other end of the counter, doing her best to take care of customers as quickly as possible. How could Jessica help with anything when she was ringing up sales with a phone to her ear, trying to calm down one of the Cottage's biggest customers?

"I know your group needs the yarns for your project as soon as possible, Mrs. Grisham." She shifted back to her phone call. "That's why I'm willing to pay for overnight delivery."

"Yes, we do need the yarns, Jessica — like yesterday." Mrs. Grisham's voice rose. "Which is when you said they'd be ready for pickup."

"And with overnight delivery they'll be here promptly," she offered again, still wondering how she could've messed up the order so badly. Had she been helping Cole with his math homework at the same time and somehow transposed dye lot numbers on the order form?

"Well then . . ." Mrs. Grisham paused, seeming to consider the offer. Jessica would've crossed her fingers for good luck if her hands hadn't already been in motion. "You need to call me the moment they arrive," the other woman acquiesced.

"Absolutely. The very moment." Jessica smiled into the phone. "Thank you, Mrs. Grisham. And . . . that mistake won't happen again."

It had been a fifteen-minute battle working her way back into Mrs. Grisham's good graces, but feeling triumphant, Jessica clicked off the phone. How had her aunt ever been so adaptable with everyone and everything?

She was just about to ring up the next sale when Marisa sidestepped toward her. With her naturally curly hair tucked behind her ears and her face void of makeup, Marisa looked young for her age but as pretty as ever. Her olive complexion was creamy and flawless, but her blue-green eyes were apologetic. "You remember I have to leave early, right? Like right now, actually."

Jessica had been feeling fortunate that Marisa only had a few classes that morning and had been able to come in early to help. But she'd totally spaced out about her having to head back to school for a college-prep presentation.

But then again, she could hardly keep her and Cole's schedules straight lately. "Hmm . . . are you sure, Marisa?" She edged closer, whispering to her teasingly. "Do you really want to go away to college and miss all of this?"

Laughter bubbled up from her helper. "You're kidding, right?" She glanced out from the counter, shaking her head at the line of ladies that seemed to never end. "I do hate to leave you like this, though."

"I'll be fine. You need to get going." Jessica signaled her release by pulling at the strings of the apron tied around Marisa's waist. Marisa always liked to wear Aunt Rose's ivory apron, thinking she looked official and crafty when she was measuring and cutting. "Now scoot, girl. Get out of here."

Even though she'd been given permission, Marisa looked sheepish about leaving, taking her time pulling the apron over her wavy mane. It really was the worst timing ever. But how could Jessica be upset with her? She knew how fortunate she was to find such a conscientious, hardworking teenager, a mature young girl who wanted to save money for college — and just as importantly for a prom dress, even though the event wasn't until spring.

A whiff of cherry blossom trailed behind her helper as Marisa handed the apron to Jessica and went to grab her sweatshirt and backpack from the closet at the back of the store.

Standing in the middle of the counter, Jessica took a deep breath and looked to her right toward the line at the register, and to her left toward the one at the cutting table. "So, who's next?"

The ladies at the head of both lines held up their fragile-looking hands.

"Okay, then." She was just about to revert

114

to a quick round of "eeny, meeny, miny, moe" in her mind when the phone rang again. She took it as an out and held up a finger to the ladies in front of her before she answered.

"Jessica." Mrs. Grisham's voice was completely familiar by now, plus she was one person who rarely bothered with formalities. "I've changed my mind."

"You mean you want me to order a different color?" Jessica grabbed a pen and pad by the register, ready to write down the woman's request.

"No, I changed my mind, meaning you don't need to reorder the yarn."

"But it's no problem, I promise you."

"Yes . . . well . . . the shop in Coshocton has what our group needs, and we're going to purchase it all from there."

Coshocton? Over fifty miles round-trip? The woman would drive all that way rather than deal with Jessica?

"But you don't have to go that far for the yarn you need. I can have it here quickly," she promised once again. "Please give me a chance to make it right."

"I can't trust that will happen. I think Coshocton will work out best."

"Well . . . if that's really what you need to do, Mrs. Grisham." She could feel her heart sink, but she knew any more pleading would be a waste of her breath. The woman had her mind made up. "You take care."

Dazed by the call and loss of a huge sale, she hung up the phone and tried to concentrate on the business at hand. She was just about to ring up the customer directly in front of her when a woman at the cutting station interrupted.

"Can you cut three yards of this for me, honey?" she asked, patting the bolt of material she'd laid on the table. "I want to get to the cheese shop before our bus leaves." Jessica noticed the woman's cane and thought it might take her some time to get to the other shop, so she started over to that end of the counter.

"What about me, Millie?" The bespectacled lady waiting at the register put a hand to her hip. "At least you already got to go to the gift shop. I haven't even made it there — or to the cheese shop."

"Oh, you must get over to the gift shop, Lucy," another woman in line chimed in. "They've got the cutest frames. Forty percent off."

Jessica looked from woman to woman, then over their heads to the grandfather clock at the front of the store. How many more hours did she have to endure? How many more hours *could* she endure? At the moment thoughts of all she had to do at the end of the workday — picking up Cole from after-school care, making dinner, doing homework, and taking him to soccer practice — almost seemed like a picnic in comparison.

Just as she was lamenting and trying to regain her strength, she spotted a familiar face walking by the front window.

"Ladies, I know you're all in a hurry. But give me one second, will you, please? I think help may be on the way," she announced. Rushing from behind the counter and out the front door, she certainly hoped it was true.

"Lydia!"

Lydia felt a tap on her shoulder at the same time she heard her name.

Startled — and shocked that someone recognized her — she turned to see one of the women who had stood on her porch the night before.

"Jessica?" She blinked, not believing her eyes.

"I know this sounds crazy, but . . ."

Lydia almost smiled at that. Seeing Jessica at her house the night before hadn't seemed very normal either. *"Jah?"*

"Would you possibly have time to help me out in the shop? Just for a little while?" Jessica's eyes pleaded. "A huge busload of women got dropped off in town, and I'm completely over my head." She gestured with her hands. "Actually, I'm drowning."

"I don't know how much help I'd be." If Jessica was the owner of the shop and over her head, wouldn't Lydia be too?

"From what you said last night, I know it won't be hard for you. I'll pay you."

"It's not that, Jessica, but I have to . . ." She glanced down the street at the bakery, hesitating.

Eager to act on Jonas's suggestion from the night before, she'd gotten up early, eaten a light breakfast, and spent her usual quiet time with the Lord. But then realizing most shops in town didn't exactly open at the crack of dawn, she busied herself with chores for a few hours. Following that, she got cleaned up, put on a neatly ironed navy dress, and after mustering up her courage with Flora, which took less time than it had before — but more time than she thought it would — she'd driven the buggy to town, still enthusiastic about her plan.

Yet, admittedly, as she walked up Main Street, her excitement began to wane. In all the years she and Henry had lived in Sugarcreek, he'd rarely taken her to town with him. She felt like a stranger in a strange town. Plus, the closer she got to the bakery, her stomach tightened more and more. Her steps grew slower and her heart beat faster as reality sunk in. She'd never looked for a job before. She wasn't at all sure what to expect, questions tumbling over and over in her mind.

She was beginning to feel just as anxious and desperate as Jessica looked.

Maybe it would be good to work in Jessica's shop for a bit. A few minutes might be all she needed to get her stomach settled and her nerves quieted before she headed to Good for the Soul.

"Okay. *Jah,* I'll do my best to help," she answered.

"Oh, Lydia, you're a lifesaver!"

She couldn't remember anyone ever calling her such a thing. Before she knew it, Jessica had looped an arm through hers and led the way to the Cottage. In an instant, Lydia realized why her new acquaintance had looked so frazzled — she couldn't believe the number of women swarming in the shop. Many stood at the counter with bolts of fabric in their arms or baskets of yarn in their hands. Others roamed the store or sat on the bench, resting their feet.

"How about I ring up people and you cut fabrics?" Jessica suggested.

Since Lydia didn't know the first thing about checking out customers, that was more than fine with her. She followed Jessica's lead and stepped behind the counter, feeling completely out of her element and off balance.

When she'd first rolled over in bed that morning, the familiar heaviness in her heart had still been there, just as she expected it would be for a long, long time. The prospect of employment, however — of having something to do with her time and a way to make ends meet — had woken her up with a bit of hope fluttering through her veins for a change. But she'd never imagined she'd be thrown into a situation like this. Even a temporary situation like this.

Smiling timidly, she nodded at the woman who was next in line, feeling shy and awkward. "How — how can I help you?" Even though she'd heard shopkeepers and clerks ask the same question plenty of times before, the words felt strange coming from her own lips.

"I'd like five and a half yards of this cotton." It was obvious the frail woman was having trouble heaving the bolt onto the counter. Lydia leaned over as far as she could, taking it from her, quickly realizing the woman was too caught up in her own needs and thoughts to even notice her shyness. Even so, her hands trembled as she smoothed out the fabric along the yardstick. The scissors wagged in her hand. What if now, of all times, she couldn't cut a straight line?

"I'm making a sweater for my daughter," a woman interrupted as Lydia tried to concentrate on her cutting. "Can I mix these two different brands of yarn?" she asked, holding out the skeins.

Lydia hesitated and glanced at Jessica, hoping she'd hear the woman and chime in with an answer. But Jessica was busy ringing up an order. She was on her own. "Well," she stalled, wanting to make sure she gave the right answer. "Are the yarns the same weight? If so, that will be a *gut* — a good thing. But you'll have to test your gauge and make sure it's the same for both," she warned.

The woman at her other side edged closer. "I have a question too. I'm making a quilt for my granddaughter's wedding, and now the backing is showing through the white background of the quilt top."

"*Jah?*" Again Lydia looked Jessica's way. Jessica was handing a woman change. "It's showing through, you say?" She had to think about that for a bit. "That's probably due to the kind of batting you're using."

As she continued to cut the fabric as carefully as she could, she made a suggestion for a brand of batting she always used, hoping she wasn't wrong in saying so.

"Oh, dear." The customer in front of her sighed. "I forgot to get a pale-green thread for the fabric you're cutting."

"I can get it for you if you'd like."

"Would you mind?" The older woman glanced toward the floor. "My feet aren't used to all this walking. My legs are swelling, and I'm starting to get worn out."

When Lydia got back to the counter with the thread, Jessica called out, "Lydia, what do you think of this yarn for an afghan?"

Lydia could feel Jessica and the customer staring at her while she studied the pile of medium-weight yarns Jessica was referring to. She noted the pastel colors. "Is it for a baby?"

"A great-grandson." The customer nodded.

"In that case, you may want a lighter weight. That's more common for a baby blanket."

"Can you help me pick something out?"

"Well, I —" She wasn't familiar with the

layout of the store. Typically, Henry had taken her to discount stores on the outskirts of town to get whatever she needed for her knitting or quilting. But Jessica and the woman were looking at her as if she knew everything there was to know. "*Jah,* sure. Just let me finish up with the person I'm waiting on."

It seemed like only minutes had gone by when the shop began to clear out, the crowd trickling down to a pair of ladies browsing some seasonal fabrics. Glancing at the clock, Lydia was shocked to realize she'd been at the Cottage for over two hours. Time had flown by!

"I didn't mean to keep you this long," Jessica apologized.

"Oh, it's fine," she said. She was tired but felt pleased about the work she'd done. "It was a different sort of experience, for sure. It was good for me."

"It was good for both of us. I honestly don't know what I would've done without you." Jessica stepped over to the cash register. "I hope you don't mind if I give you cash." She opened the drawer and pulled out some bills, handing them to Lydia before she could even respond.

Lydia quickly noted the twenties in her hand. "This is way too much, Jessica," she protested.

To which Jessica held up her hand. "You earned every penny of it. I would've lost most of the sales this afternoon if it hadn't been for you. Half of the women would've gotten frustrated and walked out the door."

"I've gotta say, it sure was busy." She felt like she was just catching her breath from all the commotion. "The women were buying up everything."

"One lady even asked if she could buy the 'All You Knit Is Love' plaque Aunt Rose made." Jessica shook her head, smiling in disbelief. "But I wasn't about to sell that."

"I don't blame you." Lydia couldn't believe how easy it was to talk to this new person who had entered her life, but she needed to get going. She still had other business to take care of. "Well, I best go and get to the bakery."

"Thanks again, Lydia." Reaching out, Jessica hugged her, surprising her. She couldn't remember the last time she'd been hugged . . . by anyone.

"You're, uh, you're welcome," she stammered.

As she tucked stray hairs into her *kapp* and headed up Main Street once more, she felt good about the way the day had gone. It had probably been best she hadn't gotten

124

to the bakery earlier. Surely they would've been overrun with the customers off the bus too.

The chimes above the bakery door greeted her cheerily, making her feel welcome right away. She'd only been to the bakery a very few times and had forgotten how much she loved the vanilla scent of the place and the layout of the shop. Decorated in hot pinks and vibrant greens that reminded her of the peonies that bloomed in her yard each spring, it had plenty of places to enjoy a sweet treat or rest from the day. Tables topped with vases of flowers graced the middle of the shop, and filled-to-the-brim bookcases and cozy chairs were off to the right.

She almost felt like she deserved to sit and rest for a few minutes after the hours she'd put in at Jessica's. She even might have done so if she hadn't been on a mission.

"Can I help you?" a lady asked in Pennsylvania Dutch from behind the bakery cases.

Lydia almost felt like she was looking into a mirror. The two of them appeared to be the same age, with the same *kapp* and same navy dress. Except for this woman was wearing an apron as green as grass — which protruded over her pregnant belly. "We don't have much left, I'm afraid. But what we have is still fresh from the morning."

Even after all she'd managed to accomplish at the Cottage, now when it mattered most, her voice faltered. "Ah, *nee*. I, uh . . . I'm Lydia. I'm here to ask about a job. Is there a job you might have?"

"Oh, I'm so sorry. That position has been filled."

"*Jah?*" Disappointed, she forced a weak smile.

"It's for my position, actually. I'm Rebecca, by the way. I'll be leaving to have my baby, though not for a while yet. But the owner of the shop wanted to make sure she had a replacement. She posted the job never expecting to find the right person so quickly."

"I guess I'm a little late, then."

"You should stop back in the next few weeks, though, in case something changes with the other person." Rebecca smiled kindly. "People do change their minds, you know."

"That's true. *Danke.*" She felt a bit heartened by her new acquaintance's suggestion. "*Danke* for your time."

Lydia started to walk away, then turned and studied the bakery cases again. She hadn't baked anything for months and couldn't remember the last time she'd had a sweet. She stepped back toward the counter. "You know, I'd like one of those crullers you have left."

"Would you like that for here or to go?"

She glanced around at the inviting-looking shop but knew she couldn't stay. She had to see how Flora was doing. "I'd like to take it with me, please."

Rebecca bagged up the donut quickly. "That'll be ninety-five cents."

Lydia pulled the bills from her apron pocket and stared at them. It was the first money she'd ever made. The first time she'd worked and been paid. It felt like a good start and something to be mighty grateful for. If Flora seemed all right, she'd poke her head into a few more shops and see if anyone else was hiring.

Needing to catch her breath, Jessica sat down on the oak bench in the middle of the Cottage, still reeling from the whirlwind of women.

A glance around revealed that the visitors had taken a toll on the shop too. Bolts of fabric were piled up behind the counter. Others were leaning haphazardly on shelves or lying everywhere they shouldn't have been, left by women who'd changed their minds just as women were wont to do.

Bins that had once held one color of yarn were now mostly multicolored messes, and the worktable was covered with more work for her to do — putting away all the items ladies had considered and left lying there.

Surely Aunt Rose had seen her Cottage as messy as this some days. Oddly, Jessica couldn't ever remember it being that way. She'd been too caught up in her own world to notice, especially as a young girl, playing games and dress-up. It hadn't ever mattered to her what disarray the Cottage was in, or what cleanup there was to do, had it? She was simply happy scuffling around the place in her aunt's sparkly gold cape and cherry-red high heels.

"Can I wear these shoes to school tomorrow?" she remembered asking more than once.

"Not tomorrow." Aunt Rose always smiled. "But someday. Someday you'll fill my shoes . . ."

The memory jolted Jessica, causing a surge of unexpected tears. She could almost hear her aunt's voice, her aunt's promise. But it just wasn't true. It wasn't. She couldn't fill her aunt's shoes when she was a little girl, and she still couldn't fill them now.

"Oh, Aunt Rose, I'm already making a

mess of things." She sputtered the words out loud, looking around the shop, wishing she would see her aunt there. Needing her encouragement. Her absolution — Jessica realized she may have already lost the shop's biggest client for good. Not to mention a portion of sales that she could've consistently depended on.

She couldn't even answer any of the women's questions today. And there was no chance she could offer any classes or workshops — she needed help herself. With the holidays coming quickly, things in the shop were only going to get busier and worse.

True, she needed to hire someone. But also true, her funds were tight. She'd had to use her aunt's savings for funeral costs, and sadly, being the sole supporter of her son, Jessica barely had any savings of her own. That left little extra money to employ anyone on a steady basis. But if she didn't, where would that lead? She couldn't do this on her own as Aunt Rose had. If she tried, she might lose it all. For good.

She needed help. She needed expertise. She needed someone her customers would trust.

She needed . . . Lydia.

Jessica shot up from the bench.

Where had Lydia said she was going? To

the bakery?

Moving behind the counter, she grabbed the keys to the shop and ran out, locking the door behind her.

Feeling somewhat anxious, Lydia knocked on Jonas's door, then stepped back down onto the porch step, waiting for him to answer.

Muffled sounds came from inside. A scooting chair . . . footsteps. She'd probably interrupted his supper. But if she had, he gave no clue of that when he opened the door and saw her standing there.

"Hey, Lydia," he greeted her with an easy smile. "What's going on?"

"You don't have to worry," she said earnestly. "I won't make a habit of coming here every day."

He chuckled. "I can honestly tell you that's the very least of my worries."

She could feel her face flush as she held out the bag from the bakery. She couldn't remember the last time she'd given anyone a gift, except for Henry on his birthday. "I brought home some sugar cookies for you, Jonas."

"Ah, my favorites." His eyes lit up as he took the bag from her hand.

"They're my way of saying *danke*," she

explained.

"*Jah?* Does that mean what I think it does? You got the job?"

She shook her head. "*Nee,* I didn't. The position was already filled."

"Oh." He frowned.

"But —" she couldn't contain the huge grin spreading across her face — "I got a job at the quilting and knitting shop instead."

"You did? Really?" His grin looked pretty uncontainable too. "Well, *gut* for you, Lydia!" He chuckled as if he was sincerely tickled. "*Gut* for you!"

"*Jah,* I start tomorrow." She couldn't believe her own ears. "And I wanted to thank you because I wouldn't have even gotten to town today if you hadn't made that suggestion last night. And there couldn't have been a better time to go because today there was a bus full of women from Columbus who invaded the quilt shop." She paused to explain. "The shop is owned by the lady who was here last night — Jessica."

"*Jah?* That's a mighty big coincidence."

"I know, and she saw me through her shop window when I was headed to the bakery, and she asked me to help in her store because she was so busy, and —"

"And it was all *Gott*'s perfect timing."

131

"*Jah,* you're right. That's what I've been thinking too. It was all *Gott*'s perfect timing — including your suggestion, you know."

"Then I will enjoy these cookies even more than I usually do. In fact —" he began to dig into the bag — "I think I'll start celebrating right now."

She laughed as he rambunctiously bit a big chunk out of a cookie, leaving flaky crumbs dangling from his lips.

"You make that look *verra gut,*" she said.

"It is mighty tasty. Want to try one?"

"*Nee.* I'd best go." She shook her head, backing down the steps. "I have work in the morning, you know, and that will certainly be a long day for me."

"*Gut* luck on your first day." He held up the half-eaten cookie. "You'll do great, Lydia."

"Thank you again, Jonas . . . for everything."

As she cut through the place in the shrubs where she was beginning to wear a path, Lydia thought about how Jonas wasn't the girlfriend next door she'd always wished for. But all the same, Jonas Hershberger was a mighty good neighbor. And for that, she felt blessed.

CHAPTER EIGHT

Liz peered into the pot of stew with a critical eye to make sure it was simmering just right. Giving the chunky meal a stir with a wooden spoon, she refrained from adding another dash of pepper or salt. It was perfect as it was — she'd already given it a taste test, twice.

She definitely needed to leave well enough alone. But she was so excited to have Jessica and Lydia coming for dinner that she'd found herself fussing over everything, even the simple mixed-greens salad she'd put together to accompany the stew. She'd also taken the time to cook up homemade applesauce and had made a special trip to town to buy a loaf of Amish bread.

Her cottage-style home didn't have a dining room, so she'd set the farm table in her kitchen using her cobalt-blue linen, "for company only" place mats and blue paisley napkins to brighten her white French countryside dinnerware. Adding the last item to her table — a small clear, round vase of burnt-orange mums — she stepped back to take a look at everything and decided that she'd done all right. The overall effect was cozy and warm and friendly, just the way she'd hoped. Certainly a setting her guests would feel comfortable in.

That thought had her relaxing — until her cell phone rang. She didn't even want to look at the caller ID, hoping Jessica wasn't cancelling or having trouble picking up Lydia. Not only was she looking forward to sharing a meal with the pair, but as the Cottage's new employee, Lydia had offered to share knitting and quilting tips with her and Jessica after dinner. Liz couldn't wait to learn from a true, experienced Amish woman.

Holding her breath, she picked up the phone from the island.

"Hello?" she said apprehensively, expecting to hear Jessica's voice.

"Liz? It's Lou Hager."

"Oh, Lou. It's you." Her shoulders loosened at the sound of her repairman's voice. "My kitchen and I are looking forward to you coming tomorrow."

"Uh, well, that's why I'm calling. I actually should've called earlier, but I didn't think of it till now. I'm at a hospital near Youngstown. They admitted my mom yesterday. She's been real sick, and my dad isn't in the best condition either. I had to head up here to take care of them."

"Oh, Lou, I'm sorry to hear that."

"Yeah, well, obviously I'm not going to make it to your house to start on that ceiling of yours tomorrow. Honestly . . . I can't tell you when I will be there. It could be a few days or it could be weeks."

She'd already scratched Lou's name from her organizer the week before when he'd had to cancel due to other issues, something about his ailing dog. Apparently he'd been having a run of tough times. She could certainly sympathize with him.

"Of course, Lou. I understand," she told him. "Your parents need you. They definitely come first."

"Liz, if you have to get someone else —"

She cut him off. "This old ceiling has hung in here for this long. I'm sure it'll last awhile longer."

She didn't even know who else she could call, or whom to trust to do good work. Plus, Lou had been a classmate of hers and Karl's way back when, and they'd used him for most repair jobs. Lou's name was one of the first to come up whenever anyone in town needed repairs.

"Well, I'll be there as soon as I get things under control here. But seriously, Liz, like I started to say, if you need to get someone else, I totally understand."

"I hear you. I'll keep your family in my prayers, Lou."

"I know you will, Liz. Thanks."

She slipped the phone into her jeans pocket and eyed her kitchen ceiling more seriously. She was glad that Jessica and Lydia were both so easygoing — and not people she needed to impress. Unfortunately, she'd grown so accustomed to the cracks in the plaster that they'd become a part of her scenery. She hadn't thought about how awful it looked when she'd invited the ladies over.

But actually, now that she was really looking, the ceiling was quite a sight. In fact, was she imagining it, or were there a few more cracks than there had been the last time she looked? She racked her brain, trying to remember which cracks had been where. Her eyes were still turned upward when the doorbell rang.

Daisy had been lying in a corner of the kitchen, keeping her nose attuned to the myriad of food scents. She also was taking every opportunity to beg Liz for a sampling or two with her big, brown, drooping eyes. But the sound of the doorbell trumped the scent of the stew, at least momentarily. Daisy hopped up and fell in behind Liz.

"Our company has arrived, Daisy Duke," Liz hummed to her companion as the two made a path to the front door, Liz eyeing every cushion, pillow, rug, and afghan along the way, seeing that they were fluffed, angled, and lying just so in their particular places.

"Hey, you two, come on in." She greeted Jessica and Lydia with hugs, thinking that the pair coming through her door may have been about the same age but couldn't have looked more different.

Jessica was dressed in jeans and appeared taller than usual as a result of the tan boots she wore. Her nearly black hair fell in neat bangs across her forehead, then in long, soft waves around her face and past the collar of her waist-length olive-green corduroy jacket. A caramel-colored sweater hung out from below the jacket, completing her casual, trendy look.

Lydia, meanwhile, had her hair tucked beneath her *kapp* as usual, only hints of its beautiful auburn shade visible from wisps that had escaped at the nape of her neck. The dark-gray jacket she wore over her plum dress was a twill fabric, much longer and boxier than Jessica's. The only thing that appeared remotely similar between the two was that they both had their hands full.

"Goodness, what all did you gals bring? I told you you didn't have to bother."

"Well, after working all day, somehow Lydia still found the time and energy to go home and make blueberry fry pies from scratch." Jessica deferred to her new employee, her eyes glistening with astonishment.

"Fry pies!" Liz clapped a hand to her chest. "I haven't had a fry pie in forever. My Karl loved them, and I have to admit I never once tried to make some for him."

"Henry didn't care for them. He always thought they were a shortcut to a real pie," Lydia said, then flushed as if she'd shared too much personal information. "But, um, they're not so difficult. And I'd already rinsed the berries before I left for work this morning."

"I've quickly learned Lydia is very modest too." Jessica grinned. Then, holding up a rose-colored bag from the Cottage, she added, "The best I managed to do was bring goodies from the shop for the lessons Lydia has so kindly offered to give. Oh, and I also made a quick stop at Skinny's Ice

Cream Parlor for some vanilla ice cream." She nodded to the parcel in her opposite hand.

"You two are the best." Liz smiled. "Jess, you can just leave your bag right there." She pointed to the black painted bench sitting at her entryway. "Then let's get all of the yummy stuff put away," she said, leading her guests into the kitchen.

"I didn't realize you lived on this street," Jessica chatted as she trailed behind her. "I've always loved the homes here. They're so quaint."

"For nearly five years now," Liz answered as she stored the desserts in the refrigerator.

By the time she'd closed the refrigerator door, Jessica was shrugging out of her jacket. Liz saw Lydia glance at Jessica before she started to do the same.

"Here, I'll take those." She held out her arms for the coats and noticed that as soon as Lydia's hands were free, she smoothed out the skirt of her dress, then stood rubbing one hand with the other. Liz thought she appeared nervous and her heart went out to the younger woman — she was feeling slightly anxious herself.

In all the years she'd lived in Sugarcreek, as much as she came in contact with Amish acquaintances each day, and as much as she appreciated their culture, she realized she'd never invited an Amish person to her house. She certainly wanted her home to be as welcoming as possible for Lydia. And Jessica, too, of course. But Jessica already seemed to feel quite comfortable.

"Whatever you're cooking smells delicious, Liz," Jessica said.

"Thank you for saying that, but it's only stew."

"She says it's *only* stew," Jessica explained to Lydia in a confiding tone, "as if it's not a big deal. However, Liz is one of the best cooks and bakers around. She's like Paula Deen and Betty Crocker all rolled into one."

"Jah?" Lydia's brows arched. "Paula who?"

"Oh." Jessica bit her lip. "It's just this lady who's on — well, it doesn't matter." She blinked and Liz found herself biting her lip too. "The fact is Liz used to make nearly all the dinners for events at church. And as for baking, let me tell you, all of us kids at school were thrilled when it was her daughter's birthday. Amy always brought in the best cupcakes ever. We gobbled them up in seconds."

"Well, thank you for those kind words, Jess." Liz smiled. "But I just meant I'd made stew — and not anything fancy. It really is one of my favorite comfort foods, especially at this time of year."

"A comfort food can be a very *gut* thing, I think," Lydia said a bit shyly, ducking her head. "*Danke* for asking me here."

"Yes, Liz, thank you," Jessica chimed in.

"I'm really glad you both came," she said sincerely. "And actually, if you both are hungry, everything's ready. There's no need to wait. Why don't you take a seat at the table, and we can visit while we eat."

As Jessica and Lydia settled around the table, Liz quickly took the coats to the office off the kitchen and laid them on the love seat there. When she came back to the kitchen and saw her guests sitting and talking, and Daisy right between them at their feet, she couldn't believe the warm feeling that came over her.

It brought a tear to her eye, thinking how it would've made Rose so happy to see them that way. And as for herself . . . it made her happy too. Ever since the fire she'd been trying to get her footing, feeling displaced. But right now her house felt full and her heart did as well. Maybe following Rose's lead and performing the simple act of kindness where Lydia was concerned had been more than a good place to start.

Heartened by the thought, amid their chattering, she set the applesauce and salad bowls on the table, followed by the basket of bread. Then she ladled the stew into a large white porcelain soup tureen. A wisp of steam swirled over the huge bowl as she brought it to the table. The sight of the main dish seemed to quiet the conversation.

"Well, ladies —" Liz slid down into a chair and glanced around the table at her guests — "should we say grace silently, to ourselves, before we eat?" she suggested, knowing it was the Amish custom.

She'd scarcely asked the question when a sound crackled over her head. As they all glanced up, a few chips of plaster fell from the ceiling. Followed by a sprinkle of more plaster. Until suddenly a shower of the stuff trickled onto the table. Plopped into the stew-filled tureen. Onto the applesauce. Over the bread. And throughout the salads. Then, without warning, while the three of them sat gaping, the brushed-nickel light fixture dropped from the ceiling like a leaden weight. Dangling just a foot above the table, it swung back and forth like something out of a spooky movie.

While more spurts of white were still splattering onto plates and splashing into the stew, the three women jumped up from the table and fled to the family room, Daisy scurrying close behind them, tail between her legs.

"It's okay, Daisy. It's okay." Liz bent down and looped an arm over the creature's neck, hugging her protectively. Yet as they all watched from the adjoining room, Liz couldn't believe her eyes. Tremors rippled across the ceiling like an overhead earthquake, sending more chunks clattering to the floor. The grand finale finally came when a block of plaster the size of her stovetop fell, smacking onto the tile floor, causing the three of them — and Daisy — to jerk back simultaneously.

In a state of shock, Liz was sure she looked just as wide-eyed to Jessica and Lydia as they did to her. "Oh. My. Goodness. Did that really just happen?"

With white dusty stuff spewed everywhere, the potentially heartwarming evening had turned into a heart-stopping nightmare. As Daisy shook herself to be rid of the flying debris, Liz turned to her guests, more concerned about them than her destroyed kitchen. "Are you two all right?"

"No worries, Liz," Jessica reported, brushing off the front of her lightweight sweater. "I'm fine."

"*Jah,* me too." Lydia gazed at the mess.

"But your poor kitchen . . . and dinner."

"At least your fry pies and ice cream are safe in the refrigerator. I hope so anyway." Taking in the totality of the mess, Liz wasn't even sure if that would be true. "This place looks like a disaster area," she said, to which Jessica started laughing.

"What?" Liz grimaced. "Did that sound funny?"

"No. Not at all. I'm sorry. . . . it's just . . . well, you look like — I don't know — the ghost of Christmas past or something. There's so much white stuff in your hair. And your face . . ." Jessica giggled some more as she stepped closer and started to pluck plaster from Liz's hair. "How did you get so much white all over your face?"

"Hmm . . . let me think how that might have happened," Liz answered mockingly, then began to relax a bit and chuckle as well.

"You know —" Lydia tilted her head and grinned — "you actually look good with white hair, Liz."

"Oh, I promise you, this hair of mine will not be turning white anytime soon — at least not until I'm so old that my hairdresser absolutely refuses to cover up the gray for me."

"I'm glad I don't have to worry about those things." Lydia pulled at the strings of her *kapp.*

"Yes, well, maybe your hair is fine, but let me tell you there's enough plaster up there to start your own ceiling," Liz teased, reaching up to get at the debris stuck in Lydia's *kapp.*

Standing taller than either of them, Jessica glanced at the tops of both of their heads and chuckled. "Yeah, you two are a sight."

"You're laughing —" Lydia smiled — "but you haven't seen the back of your sweater."

"Really? What's wrong with my sweater?" Jessica tried to look over her shoulder to see.

"Don't worry; I'll get it for you," Lydia offered.

Standing in a less-than-perfect circle, while Jessica plucked fragments from Liz's hair, Liz worked on the back of Lydia's *kapp* and shoulders. At the same time, Lydia picked away at the white flecks stuck to the back of Jessica's wool sweater.

"Isn't this what they call social grooming in the animal kingdom?" Liz wondered out loud. "I feel like female lions, cleaning each other."

"Or apes." Jessica snorted.

"I think I'd rather be like baboons." Lydia brushed over Jessica's back. "They're much cuter than apes, don't you think?"

"Oh — like the baboons at the Farm at Walnut Creek, you mean? They're Cole's favorites of all the exotic animals there. They're adorable."

"I, uh, I've never been to the Farm, actually," Lydia said softly. "I've only seen pictures of baboons in a book once."

"You've never been to the Farm? Right down the street?" Liz was surprised to hear that, and as Jessica's eyes met hers, she could tell Jessica was too.

"*Nee,* I haven't." Lydia's voice grew quieter. "Henry always promised to take me. But he was usually mighty busy. Somehow it never worked out that way."

"Well, like I said, Cole loves it at the Farm," Jessica spoke up. "We'd love to have you go with us one day."

The three of them grew quiet as they finished ridding each other of plaster and dust as much as they could.

"We should've done this outside." Jessica shook her head and ran a hand through her hair. "Now we've made a mess in this room too."

"It doesn't matter." Liz brushed off one more speck from Lydia's shoulder. "I've got all night to clean this place up."

Jessica looked at her. "You mean *we* have all night."

"No. No. And no. I'm going to grab your coats from the back." Liz started to tiptoe through the debris on the kitchen floor. "Then you two are going to get out of here and go get something to eat." She wobbled precariously on the piles of plaster.

"Liz, you're not getting rid of us because of a measly kitchen ceiling caving in. We're not leaving you with this mess."

"*Nee,* we're not." Lydia rolled up the sleeves of her dress. "Where do you keep your broom?"

"And your trash bags?" Jessica asked.

"Girls, really . . ."

She kept trying to change their minds, but she could tell it was useless. Within moments Lydia had found a broom in the pantry, and Jessica had discovered trash bags underneath the sink.

"All right," Liz conceded. "But I'm sure not sending either of you home hungry. I'm calling to order a pizza right now."

"Twist my arm," Jessica said as she pulled a bag out of the box.

"*Jah.*" Lydia put a hand to one hip. "You can twist mine, too."

Liz wasn't sure if the idiom was exactly common in Lydia's vernacular, but it didn't matter. She couldn't believe she was smiling over the evening — instead of wailing

147

— as she tapped in the number for Antonio's.

CHAPTER NINE

After hours of cleanup at Liz's place, Jessica didn't think she could be any more tired as she laid her purse and keys on her kitchen table and slid the box of leftover pizza into the refrigerator. She felt like she'd been gone for a hundred years.

Thankfully, everything appeared quiet on the home front, all except for a low murmur coming from the TV. Following the sound into the family room, she found Marisa wrapped in Aunt Rose's chocolate-colored afghan, curled up on the couch asleep. The teenager must've had quite the day too, Jessica decided. She hadn't even stirred when Jessica came in.

"Hey, Marisa." She gently rubbed the girl's shoulder. "I'm home."

"Huh?" Marisa opened one eye slowly but didn't move, taking a moment to get her bearings.

"You're at Cole's," Jessica reminded her.

"Oh . . . yeah. Right." Both eyes opened and she pushed back the knit throw. "Is it really late or something?"

"Later than I thought I'd be. I should've texted you but I got so caught up in the drama at Liz's, and then I had to take Lydia home, and honestly I just forgot." She felt like she was the teenager and Marisa the parent as she tried to explain her lack of communication throughout the evening.

"Drama?" Marisa blinked.

Jessica smiled. "Liz's kitchen ceiling came crashing down. It scared us half to death."

"Her ceiling fell?" The news was enough to make the teenager bolt upright. Her eyes grew wide. "Like the whole ceiling? Seriously?"

"Most seriously." Jessica nodded. "It was quite a shock."

"I don't get it. How does a ceiling fall?"

"Very messily, I can tell you." By the time they'd gotten Liz's kitchen tidied up the best they could, the pizza had been cold. But the three of them had each gobbled down a piece anyway. "Liz has tried to have someone over to fix it for weeks, but the guy kept having different issues and never showed up. So the ceiling just kept getting worse and worse and . . ."

"That's crazy."

"You're not kidding." She bent over to straighten the piles of books, yarn, mail, papers, and games on the coffee table, which seemed to keep getting worse and worse too. "How was Colester tonight? Everything go okay?"

"Yeah," Marisa said around a big yawn. "We did his homework, then played a few games of cards. We took turns reading a story after he got in bed. He seemed happy to go to sleep. No drama on this end."

"I can't tell you how thankful I am to hear that. I'm beat."

"Me too." Marisa yawned again. "And I've got a test tomorrow I still have to study for." She started to push up from the couch, but then stopped. Her face brightened. "Oh — do you want to see the prom dress I'm getting?"

"Of course I do." Jessica sank down on the couch next to her sitter, feeling a bit like her older sister. Her much older sister, actually, as tired as she felt. But still, the prospect of looking at a fancy dress did sound fun and perked her up a bit.

"I'm really excited about it." Marisa fished her phone from her jeans pocket. "I refuse to wear a borrowed dress like I did for last year's prom. I want my last dance here to be awesome, and I plan to look awesome too."

"I guess it's never too early in the school year to be thinking about prom, huh?"

Marisa shrugged her shoulders. "It's the last big thing for everyone to remember you by, you know? Then we graduate and go our separate ways. Or at least I'm going mine."

The teenager was so full of plans . . . and hope. Just as Jessica had been. "You're a hard worker, Marisa. Smart, too. I'm sure you'll go far."

"I plan to," Marisa said. She pushed on the phone screen, then swiped at it till she came to the picture. "Wait till you see this dress. It's, like, amazing."

And the price was too, Jessica noticed when she peered at the phone. "It's gorgeous, Marisa. It really is, and that red will look incredible on you."

"Right? I thought it would be a good color for me. It looks slim-fitting, though. But I'm thinking that's a good thing. It'll force me to lose some weight." She glanced down at her body, which was closer to chubby than slender, but not overly so. "Which means I've got to cut down on sweets."

"Don't we all?" Jessica said guiltily, still full from Lydia's blueberry fry pie à la mode. "Which reminds me . . . it was sweet of you to help me out in the shop that one crazy day." She pushed up from the couch. "I still owe you for that and for tonight, too. Let me get a check for you."

"Oh, and we're having our powder-puff football game next week, so we're practicing after school a lot," Marisa said as she followed Jessica into the kitchen. "But if you need me for anything, just text me, okay? I'll try to work it out."

"You're first on my list." Jessica nodded. "Actually, you're the only one on my list," she added as she fished through her purse for her checkbook — Marisa's preferred form of payment so she wouldn't spend the money so easily.

"Good. I've got to pay for the dress, you know."

"The dress . . . and shoes."

"Oh, yeah . . . shoes."

"And earrings."

"And a necklace?" Marisa's face scrunched.

"With the neckline on your dress, I'd say so."

"You're probably right. I need a cute little clutch, too."

"I may have one you could borrow."

"Really? That'd be great. . . . Oh!" Marisa's eyes suddenly opened so wide, Jessica thought for sure she was about to relay some juicy gossip from her aunt's Hair and Now Salon. "I can't believe I forgot to tell you the big news of the evening."

"This evening?" Jessica looked at her quizzically.

"Yeah, some guy showed up here."

"Some guy?"

Her sitter's head bobbed vigorously. "Yeah, I thought it was you coming back for your keys or something because the doorbell rang like right after you left. But then I opened the door and it wasn't you," she said all in a rush. "It was a guy. A really hot guy."

"You keep saying 'guy,' Marisa. Who was he? Did he say what he wanted?"

"He just wanted to know if you were home. His name was Drake. Or Dirk. Or — no. Derek."

"Derek? Derek was *here*?" It was crazy how Jessica's heart stopped at the mention of his name. But then, it had to be because she was so surprised. Or maybe *stunned* was a better word for it, she thought as she reached out for the back of a kitchen chair to steady herself.

"So you *do* know him," Marisa concluded from her reaction.

"I, uh — well, I used to, yeah."

"Well, you might want to get to re-know him, Jessica. Like I said, he was really —"

"Hot."

"Yeah, even for an old guy."

"I'm sure," she said, slowly coming out of her shock and forcing herself to concentrate on the task at hand. Nine dollars an hour times eight and a half hours . . . "Did he, uh . . . did Derek mention if he was going to stop back?"

Marisa shook her head. "And he didn't leave a number either."

"Okay. Just wondering," she said as casually as she could while she wrote out the check. Tearing it from her checkbook, she handed it to Marisa. "Here you go. More money for your prom fund."

"Awesome." Marisa folded the check and put it in her back pocket. "Every bit helps."

"Yeah, it's a much more expensive proposition than when I went to prom. I can't imagine what it'll cost when it's Cole's turn to go."

"Plus, I just remembered, if I go with a group instead of a date, I'll have to pay for my ticket and meal, too."

"Even more money." Jessica cringed. "Well, at least it's still a long way off. And who knows? You could be crazy in love by that time." She smiled.

155

"Were you crazy in love with your prom date?"

"Me? Oh, I . . ." Jessica felt her cheeks heat and was surprised at the involuntary reaction. "That was eons ago, Marisa." But even as she said the words, the unforgettable image of Derek Reeves as an eighteen-year-old decked out in the tux her aunt had rented for him flashed across her mind. Even then he'd caught the eyes of most of the other girls with his startling good looks. Apparently he hadn't changed much if Marisa's reaction to his visit was any indication. "Actually, you've met my senior prom date."

She could tell Marisa's brain was on overload, trying to connect the dots. "I have? It's not the UPS guy who comes in the shop, is it? He flirts with you constantly."

"Paul Haskell?" Jessica laughed. "He flirts with everyone. No, you met my prom date tonight."

"No way. The hot guy?"

Jessica nodded. "But don't get too excited. We went as friends."

"That's all?" Marisa looked crestfallen, her eyes and mouth drooping simultaneously.

"Pretty much," Jessica replied, knowing she was hedging as she crossed her arms

156

over her chest, unwilling to say more. The truth was, she and Derek had never been "just friends." Ever since junior high, they'd been the very best of friends. And maybe they would've been something more if graduation hadn't come along. After high school, good decisions took him one way. Bad decisions took her another. Time passed, things changed — and as it turned out, they weren't the best of friends anymore.

"So you weren't dating anyone your senior year, then?" Marisa asked, apparently not short on questions.

"Not steadily," Jessica admitted. She'd never needed to with Derek around, always available.

Back during her school days, her friends had called Derek "Go-To," as in Jessica's go-to guy, and were sort of envious he was in Jessica's life. But had he really had a choice? After all her aunt had done for him?

Even though Derek's parents were both alive, he'd been more of an orphan than Jessica was. It was no secret that his dad was the town drunk, abusive and completely irresponsible. It was a wonder his mother put up with it. And a mystery why she took her husband's side over her son's.

Which always tugged at Rose's heart.

Aunt Rose had welcomed Derek into the shop anytime he wanted and found repair jobs he could do to earn some money. She also took him to church and fed him so many dinners that all of his favorite dishes were ones she made.

"What was prom like way back then?" Marisa asked, then quickly bit her lip. "Sorry. I mean, I'm not, like, saying you're old or anything."

Jessica had to grin. "You're right. It was a while ago. But I can still remember way back then, believe it or not." Without even having to stop and close her eyes, she could easily recall the night in May so many years ago. Quite vividly.

"Well?" Marisa's mouth gaped.

"Well . . . ," Jessica drawled. "We were all dressed up, of course. My dress was long and a shimmering blue satin. I really liked it, I remember, just like I'm sure you'll love yours."

"Could you tell if he — Hot Guy Derek — liked it too?"

"I think so. He mentioned that he did."

Truthfully, the moment Derek saw her in the spaghetti-strap gown, he'd appeared instantly anxious. A side of him she'd never seen before. Having to be a survivor as a result of his home life, he'd always been the kid who could talk to any adult and handle any situation. But that prom night he seemed nervous simply opening the car door for her and awkward trying to lead her with his hand on the small of her back. Even when he was holding her hand to help her along as she wobbled in her heels, his palms were clammy and sweaty.

But as the night developed and the hours flew by, an unexpected pull began to surface between them. She couldn't get over how Derek seemed to grow so mature and manly in one evening. He must've felt the same because he kept looking at her like she was the most amazing thing he'd ever laid eyes on — and that was even before she was crowned prom queen.

"So then you danced, of course." Marisa started to tell her own version of Jessica's prom night.

"We did. Which was fun. And then, you know, he took me home." She cut directly to the chase.

"Oh, no." Marisa sounded truly disappointed. "He didn't even try to kiss you good night? After the great dress? He didn't want to be more than friends? That's a bummer."

"Well, let's say he tried to kiss me," Jessica admitted.

"And you didn't let him?"

"Did I say that?" She made a fuss of putting her pen and checkbook back into her purse, remembering how it had been just the opposite.

She hadn't hesitated a second when she and Derek reached her friend's house, where all the girls were spending the night after prom. Instead of saying good night on the porch, she let him pull her back down the steps and around the side of the house.

There, underneath a trellis, surrounded by the sweet fragrance of first-bloom lilacs, with a full moon beaming, they'd stood holding hands, gazing at each other in a way they never had before.

She could still recall how her full heart felt near to bursting in anticipation of a first real kiss, all her years of innocence blending with a curious passion she hadn't ever really given in to before. She parted her lips in preparation for his mouth on hers. He bent his head and started to step closer. But then —

"What happened?" Marisa asked.

"Huh?" Jessica blinked, jogged from the memory.

"I said, aren't you going to tell me what happened?"

"Uh, yes. What happened is that we were

standing at the side of a friend's house holding hands and he was just about to kiss me. But as he moved closer, he tripped over the garden hose lying on the ground and came flying at me." She snickered, remembering. "All five feet eleven inches of him. Instead of our lips meeting, his teeth crashed against mine."

"You're kidding." Marisa winced sympathetically, but her eyes were twinkling with amusement.

"No, I'm not. The jolt knocked us to our senses and out of the mood, of course. We just stood there rubbing our mouths, laughing like crazy."

"That's funny. Sounds like you had some kind of special friendship." Marisa paused, looking thoughtful. "So then did you two, you know? Ever try it again? Ever hook up?"

"Hook up?" Jessica pretended not to understand.

"Well, I mean, did you end up liking each other — or was it just prom?"

"You sure are nosy tonight, you know that?" Jessica frowned at Marisa, who only giggled. "And unlike you, this girl needs to get her beauty sleep. Plus, didn't you say you need to study for a test?"

"Okay. I get it." Marisa smiled. "Private stuff." She grabbed her jean jacket off the back of the kitchen chair and started for the front door.

"By the way," Jessica called after her, "did Derek say how long he'll be in town?"

"No. But if he shows up again and I'm here, do you want me to give him your number or anything?"

Jessica nodded. "Sure, you can."

"Like I said before, maybe you should get to re-know him."

Jessica chuckled. "Thanks for the advice, Mother Marisa."

"I do my best." Her sitter shrugged as she reached for the doorknob. "My grandma always tells me I'm an old soul."

"But not too old to text me and let me know you got home okay."

"Will do." Marisa waved assuredly as she slipped out the door.

Jessica's hair was still partially damp when she crawled into bed. She'd been too whipped to dry it all the way and figured she'd deal with the frizz and flyaways in the morning. Her down comforter had never felt so soft and gratifying to her weary bones as she curled up underneath it. But even though her body was crying out for sleep, her mind wouldn't stop racing. Wouldn't stop thinking about Derek, wondering about his visit.

Was he still in town? Would he stop back again? Why hadn't he let her know he was coming?

She hadn't laid eyes on him in three years, and even then his visit to Sugarcreek had been a short one. He'd come from Wisconsin to close on his parents' house after his mom had passed away. He'd stopped by to see Aunt Rose and had taken time to play T-ball with four-year-old Cole that weekend. The four of them had also enjoyed a pot roast dinner — one of his favorite meals — compliments of Aunt Rose.

But then, after that, Jessica hadn't heard from him again. Not until his card arrived around the time of Rose's funeral. He'd sent his sympathies, explaining that he would've been there if he could've taken time off. Unfortunately, he'd been the arresting officer in a trial that was going on and couldn't get away.

Though she would've liked to see him, to her way of thinking, he didn't need to make the long trip to Ohio to pay his respects. She knew what he felt for her aunt was undeniably special. He'd have to have changed a whole lot not to grieve and remember her aunt in his own way.

Still . . . now that he *had* made the trek to

Sugarcreek, she found her mind going to weird places. Places where there was no reason for her thoughts to go. Wondering if he still looked the same. Wondering if she would look the same to him. Wondering what if things had been different once upon a time . . .

Which was silly to even think about. And besides, she needed to get her rest.

Snuggling deeper under the comforter, she closed her eyes tightly and tried to concentrate on something calming, soothing. Maybe something green and lush? Or, no, something blue . . . like the blue ocean underneath a sunny blue sky with the sound of the waves going in and out, and in and . . .

"Mom?" Cole suddenly cried out from across the hallway. "Mommy?"

Jessica's eyes flew open and her feet hit the floor. She'd dashed out of her room and into his before she even knew what she was doing.

"I'm here, Cole. Everything's okay, honey."

She hated seeing her poor little guy cowering in his bed, blankets all the way up to his chin. His eyes were as wide as the full moon beaming through the window, his lips thin and trembling.

"You're okay, honey," she said, rubbing

his covered shoulders as soothingly as she could. But he certainly didn't look as though he believed her. "Was it a bad dream?"

Stiff with fear, he was barely able to nod, and her heart went out to him. By day, he always tried to be her funny, brave guy. But lately the nights had him scared in a way he'd never been before. Settling down onto the bed, she lay next to him and wrapped her arms around him, hoping to help his rigid body relax.

"I dreamed there was a fire." He turned his head, his breath warm on her face. "Sparky couldn't get out of his house."

"Sparky?" Was that a character on one of the shows he watched? She couldn't recall.

"The fire dog. He came to our school for fire week. We all got to pet him."

"Oh, that Sparky." How could she forget? "Hear the Beep Where You Sleep" had been the slogan from fire prevention week and had prompted the testing of all the smoke alarms throughout Aunt Rose's place. They'd also come up with an exit plan in case of fire. "Cole, I'm sure Sparky is just fine," she assured him. "Really, honey."

But he acted like he didn't even hear her. "It wasn't beeping where Sparky was sleeping."

"It was just a dream, Colester. You know the firemen at the firehouse always make sure the smoke alarms beep anywhere Sparky sleeps. Just like it beeps in your room." She gently pushed back the hair from his forehead. "We did the test, and it beeped," she repeated, figuring fear for Sparky's safety was a manifestation of fear for his own. "You heard it, remember?"

"Mm-hmm."

"And see the light on the smoke alarm? It looks like a little green button?" She pointed to the ceiling.

"Uh-huh."

"That means it's working just fine."

With all the proof presented to him, relief flooded his expression. She could feel him start to relax in her arms. "So all is good, my son, and you can get started on lots of sweet dreams now." She kissed his forehead and got up from the bed.

But instead of settling in, he suddenly felt brave enough to come out from under the covers. Tossing them back, he turned on the lamp on his nightstand and stood up on the bed.

"Cole, what are you doing? This isn't playtime," Jessica said, thinking he was going to start jumping up and down. "It's sleep time. Now," she said a bit sternly.

"I know. I just want to see this," he said as he reached for the dream catcher she'd hung at the top of his headboard. Snatching it from the hook, he made a raucous bounce down onto the mattress with the dream catcher in his hands. Holding it under the lamplight, he studied it closely.

Jessica had gotten the dream catcher for him the week before, and one night at bedtime they'd read about Native Americans and how they believed the air was filled with good dreams and bad ones. They also learned how, according to legend, the dream catcher would allow good dreams to pass through the center hole to the person who was sleeping. The bad dreams, however, would be trapped in the web around the hole, where they would perish in the light of the dawn.

Cole had been sold on the idea that night and seemed soothed by the lore as they ceremoniously hung the dream catcher on his headboard. But now he didn't appear so sure.

"I can't see any bad dreams that it caught," he said, examining every part of the circular web.

"Well, you really can't see a dream," Jessica tried to explain.

"Uh-huh." Cole looked at her like she was

ten kinds of crazy. "I can see them when I'm sleeping. That's why I get scared."

She couldn't deny there was some kind of strange logic in what he was saying. She just wasn't sure how to respond to it.

"Well . . ." She paused, feeling far more weary than wise. "Maybe . . . it's like . . . when a person plays baseball."

He gave her a puzzled look.

"Do you catch every ball that's thrown to you?" she asked.

He shook his head.

"But it helps you catch better when you practice catching, doesn't it?"

He nodded agreeably.

"Maybe the dream catcher just needs more practice."

He stared at the leather-covered circle in his hand and stroked the attached dangling feathers, as if considering her explanation. He must've taken it to heart because he got up on the bed and placed the dream catcher back onto the hook.

"Okay. Time to settle in," she said as he got under the covers again. "And time to tuck you in."

"Real tight," he said.

"Real tight." She scrunched in the blankets all around him just the way he liked, then bent over, did a quick Eskimo kiss, and then kissed his forehead good night. "Love you, Colester."

"Love you, Mommy."

She started to turn off the light, but even with all the tucking, he quickly drew out his hand from under the blankets and clutched her arm.

"Will you stay?" He looked at her plaintively, his eyes searching hers.

"Oh . . ." She didn't know if it was bad parenting to cave in this instance. If it was, she supposed she wasn't going to win a best mommy award anytime soon. Because she couldn't help but think how he wouldn't be a little guy for long. Couldn't help but think how he might not need her for long either. Certainly the years would fly and soon enough he'd have fears and feel like he was too old to talk about them — especially with her. Soon enough he might even think guys shouldn't act like their fears existed at all.

Besides that . . . he sure knew how to use his baby blues on her.

As she retrieved the afghan from the bottom of the bed and settled in next to her son, wishing him sweet dreams once again, she found herself thinking of someone else's baby blues too. Remembering that special night in May so long ago all over again. And

how she'd stood under the trellis waiting . . .
for the kiss that never came.

CHAPTER TEN

Lydia stood in the center of the Cottage, waving good-bye to a pair of customers. The women had come into the shop as strangers to her and weren't feeling quite that way as they were leaving. "Thank you for coming in, ladies."

"Thanks for helping us find easy afghan patterns, Lydia."

"You're *verra* welcome," she replied, touched that one of them had remembered her name.

"If we have trouble, can we come back to see you?" the other woman asked.

"*Jah,* of course," she said, beaming even more. "Please do."

Lydia watched the ladies depart with their bags full of yarn, still not quite believing that Jessica had left her in charge of the shop for the past couple of hours.

When Jessica had mentioned she was leaving to go to Cole's soccer game and then to

171

drop him off at a friend's birthday party, Lydia had felt her heart lurch. She'd never been in charge of anything in her life. Not anything beyond her kitchen and vegetable garden, anyway. That's the most Henry had ever let her manage on her own. And even with those things . . .

She could feel her smile fade as she remembered how he always had a remark to make: The rows of greens in the garden weren't quite straight enough. There were too many jars of tomatoes in the pantry and not enough beets. When would she learn how to cook eggs the way he liked them?

He'd said he was trying to be helpful. And she'd wanted to believe him. But if he only meant to help, why had his words always made her feel worse about herself?

Trying hard not to think about how weak those words could make her feel sometimes, she glanced around the shop, reminding herself how well things had gone so far in Jessica's absence. Surely the good Lord must've heard her prayers. She hadn't had any trouble with the register or the credit card reader, and thankfully He'd only sent friendly customers her way.

Sighing with pure relief, she wound her way to the mid-section of the shop. Before she did anything else, she needed to straighten the mess she and her most recent customers had made at the worktable. Scooting the padded chairs back in place, she was gathering up the pattern books strewn across the tabletop when Jessica came up from behind, startling her.

"I'll take care of this, Lydia." Jessica patted her shoulder. "You've already done enough today. Go get some fresh air and relax before Liz shows up and we put you to work again."

Since the evening at Liz's house had turned into a cleaning event instead of a knitting night, Lydia had offered to help Jessica and Liz at the Cottage after the shop closed. But that wasn't for another twenty minutes or so.

"I don't mind working till closing time."

"I know you don't mind. But I do." Jessica laughed. "I mean, look at this place. The bins are all neat. The windows are shiny. I just saw a pair of women leave here looking totally happy," Jessica rattled off a list. "And the best part is, I got to go to Cole's soccer game. This is the first Saturday that's happened for me all season. You're making me feel guilty. You deserve to take a break." She smiled.

"But . . ." Lydia balked. Where would she go? What would she do?

173

"Just get out and take a walk," Jessica suggested. "Trust me, you'll be glad you did. The weather is awesome."

Before Lydia knew what was happening, Jessica slipped the pattern books out of her hands, leaving her with nothing to do but what her boss had suggested. Getting her jacket from the closet in the back, she wrapped it around her and went out into the street.

Jessica was right — it was a beautiful day, for sure. The late-afternoon sun still gleamed brightly, canceling out any chill in the air. But even so, she had a hard time relaxing. The sidewalks of town still didn't feel altogether like a natural fit for her. Outside the haven of the shop, she felt somewhat displaced. Not sure which way to turn, she finally chose to go right, which felt more familiar. Minutes later, she found herself in the place she knew second best in town — the Good for the Soul Bakery.

"Hey, you're back."

It was nice to see Rebecca's familiar face. Lydia hadn't been sure if her new acquaintance worked Saturdays or not.

"*Jah.* How are you doing, Rebecca?"

"I'm sorry to say the person taking over my position hasn't backed out yet. We still don't have any openings."

"That's okay. Believe it or not, I was lucky enough to get a job at Rose's Knit One Quilt Too Cottage."

The afternoon Jessica had caught her leaving the bakery and offered her a job, she'd been in such a state of shock, not believing her good fortune, that she hadn't mentioned it to Rebecca when she'd gone back into the bakery to buy thank-you cookies for Jonas. In too much of a stupor, she'd left the bakery without saying a thing.

"That's wonderful!" Rebecca looked truly excited for her. "The lady who runs the Cottage comes in here sometimes. She seems *verra* nice. I heard she was Rose's niece, right?"

"Jah." Lydia nodded solemnly.

"Aw . . ." Rebecca sighed. "It's such a tragedy the church fire took those two lives. I feel sorry for that girl losing her aunt, and my heart goes out to the widow of that volunteer firefighter too."

Lydia hesitated, not sure whether to share or not. But the incident with Jonas and how she'd put off telling him flitted across her mind. She decided it best to say something. "That widow . . . is me."

Rebecca looked stunned at first; then quickly her expression turned apologetic. "I'm sorry, Lydia."

"It's all right. You couldn't have known."

"Did you and your husband — do you have any *kinner*?"

"No, we didn't." Even now as she spoke the words, a familiar melancholy settled over her, leaving her feeling empty. Leaving her with a void in her heart where she'd always believed love for her child should have been.

But Henry had never wanted children. Not that she would tell that to Rebecca because as sure as anything Rebecca would want to know why. Wouldn't she? Wouldn't anyone be curious? Just as Lydia had been . . .

Quickly as she could, she changed the subject. "I forget. When did you say you're having your baby?"

"Somewhere near Christmas." Rebecca smiled, looking relieved to be speaking of more pleasant things.

"That's not so far off."

"*Nee,* it's not, for sure," she said as she slid open the back of one of the bakery cases. "I'm not sure what kind of treats you came in for. But since it's Saturday and nearly closing time, I have some lemon squares you can have for free. Oh, and some caramel chocolate bars too. Otherwise they'll go bad before Monday comes around."

"*Jah?* That would be a nice thing, *danke.* I'm helping Jessica and another woman with their knitting tonight. I'm sure the ladies would appreciate some sweets."

"Do you know how to make baby booties?" Rebecca asked as she gave shape to a pink-and-green box and began loading it up with treats. "I need to learn how to make them."

"I've never tried booties before," Lydia confided. "But I've made socks, so I'm sure I could figure it out. Would you like me to show you how?"

"*Jah.*" Rebecca's eyes lit up. "Maybe we could get together on our lunch break sometime. My husband would like me to make as much as I can for the baby. His job is going well, but we already have three other *kinner* to feed. And let me tell you, my little Matthew already eats like a teenage boy. Actually, sometimes he even eats more than my husband."

In a haze of thought, Lydia barely heard a word Rebecca was saying about her children as she chatted on, packing up the bakery goods. She didn't notice a soul on the sidewalk, either, as she left the bakery and walked up the street toward the Cottage.

All she could hear was the roar of Henry's

voice when she'd asked him about having children. All she could feel was the hurt from his reaction again and again.

All over again.

She'd never questioned him about other things. She'd done everything just the way he wanted. She had listened to him — always. But had he ever heard her? Had he ever heard her when she said how she yearned for a child?

During their first several years together, when she'd told him about her disappointment in not having a family, he'd seemed to take her wishes in stride, acting as if the day would come soon enough and there was no need in her rushing things. But as more years passed and she expressed her desires and concerns again, his reaction changed. Almost like a man who had something to feel guilty about, he didn't seem able to look her in the eye or to offer a reassuring word or two. Instead he became quiet and seemed anxious to retreat from her, as if there was something in the barn or in town far more pressing that he needed to do. Something more important than her needs and wants.

And maybe she would've stopped asking if he'd only given her an answer. Never once had he given her a reason. Never once did he seem to care how much she wanted a baby. How much she wanted to hold and nurture and make a home for a child — just as she'd been happy to make a home for him. When she turned to reach for him at night, he rarely ever reached back. She had no blushing stories to tell like the new brides she'd sometimes overhear talking to one another.

The last time she'd questioned him was a year earlier, and he hadn't just grown silent or withdrawn. Much to her surprise, he became explosive and angry. His face twisted up in the ugliest way as he commanded her never to ask again. With the harshest tone, he reminded her that he was the head of the household. That he was her authority. And that he was never, ever to be questioned.

His cruel words were so jarring, so unlike him, they silenced her for good. She never questioned him again. Until now, she'd pushed aside the memory the same way he'd pushed aside her desires.

Now she wished once again she could've known his reasons. Now she wished she didn't have to wonder why.

As she reached the entrance to the Cottage, Lydia took a deep breath and tried to get ahold of her emotions, not wanting Jessica and Liz to know all that was going through her mind. But apparently her attempts didn't work. The moment she walked through the door, the two women exchanged glances.

"Are you okay?" Liz asked.

"Nee."

"What happened?" Jessica asked.

"I . . . I . . ." How could she say all that was wrong?

"You need to come over and sit down." Liz took her by the elbow and led her to the worktable.

Less than an hour earlier, she'd been busy and happy at the worktable with customers, but now she wanted to collapse into one of the chairs. The memory of Henry — of him raising his bitter, angry voice to her in such a hurtful, frightening way — made her feel weary, taking all the energy from her just as the incident had that evening.

She definitely did want to sit. To crumple into the chair.

As Jessica helped Lydia out of her jacket, Liz took the container of sweets and set it on the table.

"I don't understand. Did something happen at the bakery?" Jessica asked, glancing at the box.

"Oh, *nee. Nee.* Rebecca gave those to me for free, in fact."

"Well, do you feel all right?" Jessica eyed her. "You look pale."

"I'll be all right, *danke.*"

"You're really not feeling sick?" Liz felt her forehead.

"No. I was . . ." She glanced between the two of them, not sure of what she wanted to share. "I was just thinking . . . about Henry."

"Oh, Lydia . . ." Jessica groaned, making a heartfelt, hurt-filled sound that was everything Lydia was feeling inside herself. "You know what?" Jessica reached out and squeezed her hands. "I'm going to make us all some chamomile tea. It's just the thing you need. It will help, I promise."

Lydia could tell Jessica wasn't sure at all that the tea would do any good. But Jessica's efforts did make her feel a little better.

As Jessica ran up the stairs, Liz pulled up a chair next to Lydia. Reaching out, she took Lydia's hands in her own. "Oh, honey, how I feel for you. I do. I know just what you're going through." Her touch was warm and reassuring, and she let the silence surround them for a moment before asking, "How long were you and Henry married?"

"Eight years."

Eight years of asking a question he would

never answer.

She began to tear up. In response, Liz let go of her hands and in a motherly way pulled her into a hug. But it was so much more than the hug her mother had given her eight years earlier as she was sent off from her home. Clearly Liz understood and wasn't afraid to show how much she cared.

"That's just not enough time, is it?" Liz said. "Though it never seems like enough time when you lose your best friend. Karl and I dated in college and were married for over twenty-six years before he passed away five years ago. It still didn't feel long enough."

Pausing, Liz tucked a stray hair back into Lydia's *kapp* for her. "And losing your husband . . . Well, it's more than losing your best friend. He's supposed to be there all your life to grow with. I mean, even when we didn't agree on things, Karl and I still grew together in our differences."

"You and your husband didn't always agree on things?" And they'd still been good friends?

Liz laughed. "Are you kidding? But communication is the key, don't you think? Communication, compromise, and caressing. That's what my mother told me. And of course, whenever we'd have a disagreement,

Karl couldn't stand it."

"You mean he got angry?" Lydia had to ask. Maybe she'd misjudged Henry?

"Oh, sure." Liz nodded. "But many times Karl got mad at himself — which was nice for me. Because after we'd argue, he'd bring home a huge bouquet of flowers for me, asking my forgiveness. Guys think flowers are the answer to everything." She smiled. "They don't hurt, that's for sure."

Obviously Liz assumed the same kind of things had gone on in Lydia and Henry's marriage. But their time together hadn't been like that. Henry wouldn't have even had to give her flowers. She would've been happy if he just would've held her hand. If he just would've told her why. Why he didn't want her to be the mother of his children. Wasn't she smart enough? Didn't he like the way she looked? They may have shared the same bed, but did he find it too distasteful to be close to her in that way?

Lydia could feel the sting of tears in her eyes start all over again. She was thankful when Jessica came down the steps, carrying a tray of steaming mugs along with napkins, forks, and plates.

Jessica looked at her so sympathetically, though, that it was hard to hold back those tears. Plus she almost felt guilty Jessica was extending her compassion so freely. Without a doubt, Jessica thought she was mourning a love . . .

But even sadder than that . . . she was questioning the very existence of it.

Appreciative of Jessica's caring heart, Lydia tried to muster a smile. "*Danke* for the tea, Jessica."

"Oh, how Rose loved her chamomile tea," Liz commented as she scooted her chair up to the table. "You're getting to be just like your aunt, Jess."

"Ha. Don't I wish," Jessica replied as she distributed mugs and plates all around before sitting down at the table.

Lydia had to admit she felt oddly soothed simply holding the warm cup in her hands. "I feel bad because I'm supposed to be helping you with your knitting and here you both are spending the time helping me." She sniffed.

"I don't feel bad at all." Jessica smiled. "The longer I can put off knitting, the better."

"You don't like to knit?" Lydia blew into her cup.

Jessica shook her head. "But even so, I don't want to give up on this shop. Aunt Rose was the only family Cole and I had, and this shop is a part of that family. It was my aunt's baby, and it's the only roots we have left. So I'll do anything to help it survive. Even if that means learning to knit." She smiled.

It was easy for Lydia to understand what Jessica was saying. The Cottage was like a living, breathing thing — even to her. So quickly it had become a cozy nesting place, a healing place where she was getting more accustomed to the camaraderie of women, little by little. She thanked *Gott* every morning for the blessing of working there.

"And do you girls want to know the best part of all this for me?" Jessica eyed Lydia and Liz. "With you two, I don't have to pretend to like knitting or be good at quilting or anything else. Thank goodness for Aunt Rose's Secret Stitches Society, or I never would've gotten to know you both so well."

As soon as Jessica had mentioned the word *baby*, Lydia found herself wishing she could open up the way Jessica had. Tell the truth about all she'd really been thinking that evening. But she couldn't. She wasn't ready. She didn't know if she ever would be.

"What is that? What's the Secret Stitches Society?" Lydia picked up a napkin and dabbed at her eyes, thankful to have something else to focus on.

"We were actually going to tell you all about it during dinner at my house," Liz spoke up. "But then after the ceiling caved in, we never got around to it."

Lydia blinked. "I almost forgot." She searched her apron pocket for a piece of paper. "I don't know if you've found anyone to fix your ceiling yet —"

"If I want to wait a month or two, I can find a lot of people," Liz answered.

"Well, when Jonas returned a rake he'd borrowed, I happened to mention your ceiling to him." She took out a piece of paper and handed it to Liz. "He wrote down his uncle's name and address to give to you. He said his uncle can fix anything. He also said to use his name if you go to see him."

"Jonas, your neighbor? He seems like a pretty good guy."

"*Jah,* from what I know he's very hard-working." *And kind,* she wanted to add but didn't say the words out loud.

"He's also a godsend," Liz said. "Tell him thank you."

"I will."

"Have either of you tried one of these caramel bars?" Jessica asked. "They're awesome."

Lydia turned to her. "Can you eat and tell

186

me about the secret society at the same time?"

"Actually . . ." Jessica paused. "Liz is the one who told me about it. She and Aunt Rose went on a few missions together. Something I never got to do with my aunt. Do you mind explaining all about it, Liz?"

"I'd be honored," Liz said.

Lydia watched expectantly as Liz laid down her fork, folded her hands on Rose's old, nicked oak table, and cleared her throat. "Once upon a time," she began, "there was a wonderful woman named Rose. She was named after a flower, which was most fitting because Rose made everyone around her blossom." Liz paused to smile, as if remembering something she and Rose had shared.

"Rose had a very special cottage where women came when they wanted to make things for people they loved," Liz continued. "It was the right place to come, too, because Rose made things for people she loved . . . and for people she barely knew. No matter what was going on in her own life, she never forgot that there were others around her who hurt and needed hope. A stitch of hope, Rose would always say, was just the thing that could get a person through. . . ."

As Liz talked on, her sweet words about

Rose filling the quiet, Lydia glanced up at Jessica, hoping to share a smile. Instead, she saw tears brimming in Jessica's eyes, then spilling over onto her cheeks.

Lydia hesitated . . . but then she couldn't stop herself. Before she knew what she was doing, she reached out and patted Jessica's hand as consolingly as she could.

She felt odd at first. And awkward.

It was the first time in her life she'd ever had a friend she could do that for.

CHAPTER ELEVEN

Following Liz's touching explanation of Aunt Rose's Secret Stitches Society, Jessica attempted to get her emotions in check. As she did, Liz was still talking, promising a receptive Lydia that they'd have a secret outing soon. Then the three of them grabbed their needles and settled in with their individual knitting projects.

Or at least Liz and Lydia settled in. Just not so much her.

Instead, Jessica watched helplessly as a ball of rosy pink yarn slipped from her lap, slid noiselessly off the seat of her chair, and made a pastel trail as it rolled across the dark hardwood floor of the Cottage.

She thought about reaching out and retrieving the pink ball of fuzz. But her hands were already occupied, each tightly clutching a size ten knitting needle, which felt as awkward and clumsy to her as the pair of chopsticks she'd once tried at the town's Chinese Wok. She was afraid if she let go of the metal sticks, she might drop a stitch or lose a stitch to whatever place it is that lost stitches go.

Clearly, knitting was not her thing.

Her aunt, so artfully skilled at knitting, quilting, and most any craft, had tried to teach Jessica when she'd been a young girl, time and time again. But the rhythm of it never sunk in. She'd find herself twisting the yarn in front of the needle when the strand should go behind it. She'd take up a stitch from the right needle instead of the left and lose any number of stitches along the way while her hands grappled with the needles, trying to correct her previous mistake.

Honestly, she had always thought it was silly, spending hours being tortured that way, especially when she could go to any number of stores in town and buy the same things already made. And made better.

That is, she always thought it was silly until she inherited her aunt's business. Until she'd been put in charge of the very thing that her aunt had given life to. Like she'd told Lydia and Liz just a little while earlier, she was going to do all she could to make the shop work. Even if it meant going through more than a few growing pains.

"Argh!" she groaned as another rebellious runaway stitch slid off her needle.

"Here, I'll get that." Lydia put down her needles and reached over for Jessica's. Pro that she was, within seconds she picked up the stitch and had Jessica back on track.

"You know, maybe it would help if you sat back in your chair and tried to relax a bit," Lydia suggested softly as she handed the needles back to Jessica. "Your shoulders look so tense hunched over like that."

"They probably look that way because they are that way." Jessica smiled at her mentor. "I told you, you didn't know what you were getting yourself into with me."

"Oh, now, you're doing a good job, Jess. Isn't she, Lydia?" Liz said as her needles clicked double, triple, actually quadruple time compared to Jessica's.

"Thanks for the encouragement, Liz. But I'd hardly say this is going well," Jessica countered. "Or even halfway well."

She'd decided her project would be a young girl's scarf — something simple and quick. Only nothing about knitting was simple and quick for her. It was all laborious. Even trying to remember how to cast on had taken some time for Lydia to explain and re-explain to her. Once she got started knitting, things didn't get better. It was plain to see her tension was uneven with bumps and lumps all along the way.

After earnestly slaving over an entire row of stitches, Jessica dared to take her eyes off her own needles long enough to look up to see how everyone else was coming along. Lydia was working on some baby booties using such tiny needles Jessica couldn't even imagine being able to hold them in her hands. The binding on Liz's vest was coming along rapidly too. Unfathomably, it had already grown another half inch or so.

"And look at you," she countered, dipping her head toward Liz's hands. "You're a speed demon with those needles."

"Oh, honey, I've made this vest so many times. For my dear husband. And son-in-law. Even Amy and my grandkids. I practically have the pattern memorized." She shrugged off the compliment.

"But you're going to let me help you with a new sweater pattern one day, right?" Lydia asked.

"Oh . . . I'm thinking about it," Liz hedged.

"So right now you're just here for moral support?" Jessica asked her.

Her friend nodded with a smile. "There's no place else I'd rather be."

It wasn't so long ago that Jessica would've

countered with a smart remark about all the other places she'd rather be, but she wasn't thinking — or was trying not to think — like that any longer.

"Well, I need all the help I can get," she admitted.

"Just take your time, Jessica. Find your own rhythm," Lydia said, sounding like the true guru she was.

"Trust me, I would love to." She sighed.

She tried to sit back and relax as Lydia had encouraged her to do. That only lasted seconds until she was hunched over the stressful mass of yarn in her lap again. She was happy for the distraction when the bell jingled over the Cottage's front door.

"I must've forgotten to lock the shop."

Liz and Lydia barely looked up as she set her knitting on the table, jumped up from the chair, stepped over the string of pink yarn on the floor, and made a beeline to the front of the shop.

And then an abrupt stop at the sight of him.

At the sight of Derek.

She'd been thinking about him ever since Marisa said he'd stopped by. She'd even wondered if he'd already left town until one of the moms at Cole's game had mentioned seeing him that morning and gone into a lengthy dissertation about how awesome he looked. Hiding behind a carousel of pattern books and eyeing him, Jessica had to agree the mom had been right.

Even though autumn had officially arrived, he hadn't seemed to notice or be in need of a jacket. Dressed in worn jeans and a short-sleeved olive-green T-shirt, he glowed like summer — from the sun-kissed amber tints in his light-brown hair to the golden residue of a tan on his brawny forearms. And just when had his arms gotten to look so muscular anyway?

"Anybody home?" he called out, glancing around the shop.

Eyeing him from afar was one thing. Hearing his voice was another, making his presence there seem even more real.

"I, uh, I'll be right there," she yelled back, stalling for time, realizing that in comparison to him, she must look a mess. She hadn't glanced in a mirror since early in the morning and had been on the run all day, not to mention outside at Cole's soccer game.

Because he hadn't spied her yet, she scampered back toward her friends.

"It's Derek," she whispered. At the sound of his name, the ladies' needles stilled in their laps.

194

"No way." Liz grinned.

"Derek?" Lydia frowned.

"Her senior prom date," Liz informed their new friend.

Jessica eyed Liz quizzically, wondering how she could possibly remember such a thing.

"Your aunt loved that boy like her own." Liz shrugged. "It was one of her favorite stories."

"Oh."

"Well, aren't you going to go talk to him?" Lydia got to the point as always.

"Of course I am. But how do I look? Is my hair a mess? I haven't put on lipstick since this morning."

"Just tuck the left side of your hair behind your ear. Lick your lips. And there's a little mascara smudge under your right eye," Liz pointed out.

Taking her advice, Jessica tucked, licked, and rubbed. "Any better?"

"You look very pretty as always," Lydia said.

Jessica knew her Amish friend would never out-and-out lie, but she also knew her version of pretty and Lydia's probably didn't quite mesh.

Nevertheless, taking a deep breath, she tucked her white blouse into her jeans. Then

195

she set out for the front of the shop once again, wishing Derek were standing there looking like the hyper kid she grew up with, trying to juggle balls of yarn in the air. Instead, he stood patiently with one toned arm crossed over the other as he scanned the room.

"Derek?" She pretended to be surprised. "Is it really you?"

"Jessica." His voice was moderately deep and easygoing as always as he held out his arms to her.

She slipped into them and into a hug that took her back years, feeling just as natural as it ever had.

When they both stepped back, he eyed her appreciatively. "You look great, Jess."

"And you're a charmer as always." She gave the left side of her hair an extra tuck.

"Hey, when could I ever charm you? I had to be straight with you. You were onto my ways."

She laughed. "Someone had to be."

"I'm glad you're here." He glanced around the shop. "When I first walked in, I wasn't sure if anyone was around."

"Oh, well, yeah." She slipped her hands in her pockets and made a conscious effort to stand straighter, tummy pulled in the way her aunt had taught her. "The shop is actually closed, but I forgot to lock the door. I was in the back with some friends — knitting."

"You were knitting?" His blue eyes flickered with surprise.

She shrugged. "It's true. I'm trying to learn."

"Hmm. I figured all you'd need to run the shop would be your marketing and social media knowledge. Last I heard, it sounded like your expertise sure helped that new dentist in town get his practice up and running, full gear."

"Well, I . . ." She didn't know which to be more flattered by. His compliment of the skills she'd learned from evening classes and put into practice at Pro Dental in past years or the fact that he'd remembered those details from a conversation they'd had the last time he visited Sugarcreek years earlier. "I figured knowing how to knit can't hurt . . . much." She smiled weakly.

He nodded as if she didn't need to say more. "So, how are you doing? And how's Cole? I got a glimpse of him when I stopped by the other night."

"We're doing okay. It's been hard with Aunt Rose gone." She took in a deep breath. "But we're making it, you know?"

Taking a step closer, he raised his arm.

She thought for sure he was going to reach for her hand. But instead his hand traveled all the way up to his chin. He rubbed at his day-old whiskers. "I really felt bad about not being able to make it back for the funeral. I wanted to be here, Jess. For Rose. For you."

"Derek, there's nothing to feel bad about," she said as sincerely as she could. "Even if you weren't here, I know how much you cared for Aunt Rose. You didn't have to be present for a funeral service for me to know that. I can't believe you came now. You didn't have to, you know."

"Well . . . I did, actually."

"Really? Why?" She hoped not to hear any bad news from him. Anticipating the worst, she sank onto the shop's bench right behind them. "Is something wrong?"

"No. More like I want to make things right, I guess. With the past."

Looking up, she eyed him curiously. "Yeah? What do you mean? What's going on?"

"I've moved back to Sugarcreek."

Her mouth gaped open as her mind spun in a million directions. Had she heard him right? "You've moved back? Like — for good?"

"For as long as they'll have me." Derek

chuckled as he sat down on the bench next to her.

"That's incredible." The news began to sink in, and she began to gush. "It's awesome."

"I'm glad you're saying so. At first I couldn't tell what you were thinking."

"I'm sorry." She closed her mouth. "I was just so surprised. You've been gone a long time. And it's weird to think . . . I mean, I had no clue. But it's good." She reached over, giving him a friendly hug. "Really good."

"Yeah, well . . ." He rubbed his hands together. "Ever since my last visit here, I've been thinking about coming back. All along I've been inquiring about deputy jobs at the sheriff's department. Obviously for a long time there haven't been any changes. But now that Sheriff Blackwell is retiring, Sam Lane is moving up the ranks and his deputy spot is open. So . . ."

"It's all worked out."

"Yeah, and I'm glad because I feel like I owe something to a lot of people in Sugarcreek. A lot of people who helped me grow up and survive."

She was touched by his sincerity. "Derek, how could they not help?" She looked into his eyes. "I mean, you're just too likable."

She smiled as he laughed off her compliment.

"I'm not sure about that, but . . ."

"Plus, you were always grateful, never took any of it for granted," she added. "And you were quite a survivor on your own. Who doesn't want to be part of a story like that?"

Glancing at him, she could tell he'd come to terms with all he'd gone through, growing up the way he did. The peace of that etched a certain degree of composure and dignity into his face. Still, he lowered his lids humbly. "Rose sure was one of those people, Jess."

"I know, and it's really sweet of you to say so, Derek."

"Well, it's true. Anyway, I wanted to stop by and tell you before you heard about my move from anyone else."

Looking at the man next to her, she was glad he still felt close enough to her that he'd want her to hear the news straight from him. But she also felt a twinge of sadness for all the years gone by that they hadn't shared anything with one another. Back in the day, they had never made a decision without consulting each other. As she remembered, that included something even as minor as when he'd helped her decide on a basket for her bike a few lifetimes ago.

"Thanks." She patted his knee. "I appreciate it. I really do."

With that all said, he leaned back, placing his arms along the top of the bench. "Boy, does this bench bring back memories."

"You stained it back in high school, didn't you?"

"I did. Even though it didn't need it." He chuckled. "It was Rose's way of keeping me busy and out of trouble. Plus, a way she could pay me and show me the benefit of a job well done."

She noticed he didn't mention the time the two of them had sat there talking into the night, until she'd finally fallen asleep with her head in his lap. She wondered if he even remembered that. Or any of the talks they'd had.

"Well . . . ," he said after a pause. "I should go. I don't want to hold you up from your knitting."

"Oh, I wish you could hold me up all night." As soon as the words left her mouth, her cheeks flushed.

He glanced at her and grinned. "Don't worry, Jess. I know you didn't mean that the way it sounded. You're far more circumspect than that."

"Circumspect?" She arched her brows. "You make me sound calculating."

"See, you always go to the dark side. I meant circumspect as in discreet."

"Oh . . . discreet. Like sneaky?" She pretended to be appalled. "Don't even go there, Derek, not when you were the one who was always pulling a fast one on the librarian with your overdue books. Oh, and on the cashier in the school cafeteria. Those women let you get away with anything."

"You don't forget a thing, do you?" He laughed. "Maybe we can get together sometime soon and reminisce."

"I'd like that. Do you want to come for dinner?" she asked on a whim as they both stood up. "I can't promise anything as good as what Aunt Rose used to make."

"You used to fix a mean grilled cheese sandwich."

"Well, hopefully I can do better than that."

"Why? It's a good memory."

He was right. It was a good memory. And one she didn't want to lose. A memory of a time when she was a lot more innocent and hopeful about the future.

It had been a winter night when Derek had been locked out of his house once again. Not knowing where else to go, he'd thrown stones up to Jessica's bedroom window to wake her. Without even hesitating, she'd let him inside. While she made a midnight grilled cheese sandwich for him, she told him about the acceptance letter she'd gotten from Ohio State University that day.

She'd held off until then, reluctant to tell him, knowing when she did say the words, it would all become too real. She'd be leaving him in the fall. Every concern she'd been struggling with internally registered on his face when she told him the news. But supportive as ever, he quickly recovered, offering his sincere congratulations. Then he glanced out the window, where the first snow of the year was falling.

Without even bothering with coats, he grabbed her and they scampered down the outside steps. Dancing and swirling with him in the midst of the huge flakes, all her anxiety about leaving him seemed to dissipate. Just being with him felt like a promise. An unspoken promise that no matter what, everything would be all right.

"Okay," she agreed. "Grilled cheese. That sounds perfect."

"It does." He nodded, then leaned forward and placed a light brush of a kiss on her cheek. She felt an unexpected tingle course its way along the curve of her jawline.

" 'Night, Jess."

"See you soon, Derek," she managed to say.

As he reached the front door of the shop, he turned around to look at her. "Lock the door behind me, will you?"

"Yes, Deputy." She smiled at his concern. "I'll be sure to do that."

She could've said more as he left the Cottage. Could've told him how just being around him made her realize how much she'd missed him. But why say anything else? As it was, she knew she was going to have an even harder time concentrating on her knitting than before.

CHAPTER TWELVE

In the past couple of weeks, pumpkins had started to dot the sidewalks and storefronts of Main Street. Some were wholly intact, having escaped the knife, while others had been carved with faces ranging from menacing to humorous. Usually Liz would have delighted in taking some time to pull her car over and amble up and down the walkway, checking out many of those faces, relishing the time of year the way she did. But today wasn't one of those days.

What had looked like all the makings of a positive week when she'd written down everything in her organizer on Sunday surely wasn't ending up that way.

Not only was her ceiling crumbling and falling more each day, but when she'd stopped in at the office earlier in the morning, she found out that a major sale had fallen through too. Quite disappointing, since she'd been working with the young couple for over a month, showing them all kinds of properties, only to find out they'd decided not to move to Sugarcreek at all.

After that, she'd still managed to get to her dentist on time for her cleaning, and sad as it was, she'd almost enjoyed sitting quietly and listening to the soft, relaxing music while the hygienist did her job. But after learning she needed a new crown to replace the one that was only two years old, her frustration mounted all over again.

Luckily, Lydia had given her the name and address of her neighbor's handy uncle over the weekend. Since Lydia seemed to think her neighbor was a hardworking, trustworthy man, maybe his uncle would be too. Feeling hopeful of that at least, Liz headed north on Main Street, then turned right at the end of the strip before the road fed into the major state route. After that she drove a block and turned right again onto Trader Lane.

Having lived in Sugarcreek all of her life, and having been in real estate for years, Liz would've thought she'd have at least noticed the small shop that shared the block with Tuttle's Garage. Although in her defense, there was no sign above the door and nothing in the window to disclose whatever the shop might be selling. There wasn't even any indication as to whether it was open to the public. In a way she was surprised to find the door unlocked, but not at all shocked when she walked into the establishment and didn't find anyone manning the store.

But she didn't mind in the least. In a glance she could see the shop was filled with handcrafted furniture, and at once she felt at home, immersed in the smells of fresh-cut wood and furniture oil that clung to the air. The combined scents had been longtime favorites of hers ever since she was a young girl visiting her grandparents and her grandma would send her out to her grand-dad's workshop with a glass of iced tea or a plate of oatmeal cookies.

Happily distracted, she took her time strolling through the shop, dipping in and out of the sunshine that poured through the windowpanes. Like spotlights, the warm rays shone on the gleaming surfaces of one-of-a-kind tables, chairs, desks. Stopping to run her hand over the smooth top of a cherry side table, she stood admiring the beautiful wood and flawless craftsmanship. She was just wishing she had a need for a new table when a male voice came up from behind, startling her.

"Can I help you?"

She turned to see a man close to her own age, brushing at the sleeves and chest of his flannel shirt. He seemed more concerned with the sawdust gathered there than with her.

"Oh, yes. Yes. I'm looking for . . ." She fumbled in the pocket of her Regency Real Estate blazer for the piece of paper Lydia had given her. "Daniel Kauffman," she read from the wrinkled scrap of paper. "Jonas Hershberger sent me to see him."

"Ah, Jonas." The man's eyes lit, and he appeared to give up on the specks of sawdust. Instead, he pulled a bandana from the back pocket of his jeans. "I haven't seen him for a while." He grinned openly, rubbing his hands with the cloth. "How is he doing?"

"Good." Liz assumed Jonas must have visited the shop from time to time for the man to know him. "All seems well with him . . . I suppose." At least from what she'd seen of him at Lydia's house, he seemed to be all right.

"I'm glad to hear it." The man stuck the rag back in its place. "That's a good thing."

"Yes, it is." She politely paused a beat. "So do you know where Daniel might be?"

"Ah, yes, I do."

His direct answer gave her hope. "You do? Can you tell me where to find him?"

"He's right here," he said.

"Great! Do you mind getting him for me?" she asked, glancing around him toward the workshop at the rear of the store.

"It's not necessary."

Ah, this had all been too easy up to this point, hadn't it? Much too easy. Liz sighed and took a deep breath, ready to assert herself. "Look, if the furniture in here is any testament to your skills, I'm sure you're a great craftsman, sir. It's quite exquisite."

"Not all of it is my work," he admitted. "I'm in partnership with some other furniture makers part-time. But thank you for the compliment." His eyes shone. "It's nice of you to say so."

"You're most welcome." His sincere appreciation took her aback, causing her to lose track for a moment. "But, um, anyway, Jonas said I should specifically ask for his uncle. For Daniel. Said he can make and fix anything. And, well . . . if you wouldn't mind getting him for me? Please?"

The man nodded. "Like I said, it's not necessary to go get him. Because I am him. I'm Daniel."

"Oh. Oh?" She blinked. "But I thought —" She didn't even pretend to be discreet as she glanced up and down at the man's — at Daniel's — clothing once again. She couldn't have been more confused. Loose-fitting blue jeans. A red plaid flannel shirt. Clean shaven. Clipped hair. How could he be Jonas's uncle and not have on black broadfall pants, a plain shirt, and suspenders? "Are you . . . sure?" she asked, which made him laugh in such an open, friendly way that a smile crept onto her own lips.

"Yep. Quite sure. Sorry I kept you going like that. But it was kind of fun."

"Well, I just assumed that Jonas's uncle would be —"

"Amish." He finished the thought for her. "And rightfully so." He paused and added more seriously, "Would you prefer an Amish for your job?"

"You know . . ." She relaxed into a full grin. "I really don't think my ceiling will know the difference."

"Ah, I know where you're coming from. It's been my experience that ceilings usually don't."

Already she liked his sense of humor. "I'm Liz Cannon, by the way." She held out her hand, and he grasped it lightly before letting it go.

"And how may I be of service to you, Liz?"

"Oh, Daniel Kauffman, that may be a question you'll be sorry you ever asked."

"That bad, huh?" He winced.

210

"It's my kitchen ceiling. And pretty bad. I can't even cook."

"Some people would be happy about that." His mouth curled upward.

"Well, not me."

"Any burst pipes from an upstairs bath or anything?"

"Unfortunately, no." She shook her head in dismay. "Nothing that's covered by my homeowners' insurance."

"That is unfortunate. What street do you live on?"

"Trellis Lane. Why?"

"The cottage homes built in the thirties?"

"Yes," she said, feeling as if she were in her doctor's office, going over a list of symptoms.

"That explains it, then. Those ceilings weren't built to last forever."

In her line of work, she'd been in enough homes to know what he was saying was true. Many of the houses also hadn't been built to code, or at least the codes mandatory for builders today. She should've been more proactive and updated the kitchen years earlier. But something else always seemed to get in the way. "Well . . . can you help?" she asked tentatively.

"I'm fairly certain I can. But of course, I'd need to check out the problem first."

"And when is the soonest that would be?"

He glanced around the shop, and she was sure he was thinking of all the other projects on his docket. She couldn't help but hold her breath, waiting for his reply.

"I'd say as soon as I put away some things in the back and lock the doors. Would that be soon enough?" he asked, a twinkle in his eyes.

She wanted to reach out and hug him, but of course she held herself back. She hugged her purse to her side instead. "I'll be waiting outside," she said excitedly. "You can follow me over to my house if that's all right."

"Great. The surest way to get somewhere is to know where you're going," he said, repeating an Amish proverb she thought she'd read in her planner.

Liz eyed him quizzically as he walked away, wondering about his past and his heritage. But more than that, she simply felt thankful she'd found help for her kitchen at last.

CHAPTER THIRTEEN

The lantern cast a glow upon the mantel clock, making it easy for Lydia to see the time from where she sat on the love seat.

Nine forty.

Ten minutes past bedtime.

Or at least it was ten minutes past the bedtime Henry had imposed on her during the years of their marriage. Would there ever come an evening when she'd look at the hands on the clock and think differently?

Henry certainly wouldn't have approved of her sitting in her jacket, staring out the front window, waiting for Jessica and Liz to pick her up, as she'd been doing for the last twenty minutes. More than his disapproval, he would've *forbidden* her to go traipsing out into the night with her friends, sneaking onto someone's property — no matter if it was for a charitable reason or not.

Bedtime was an indisputable time, written in stone. No arguing. For her own good.

Or . . . had he imposed the routine because it also kept him from having to interact with her?

The thought had been weighing on her mind a lot lately.

Each time she glanced around the room, she had slowly come to realize what their time spent together had really been like. Oh, how she'd romanticized their hours together. But it hadn't been like that at all, had it? She had been such a small part of Henry's daily life.

An early bedtime didn't leave much time for him to spend with her in the evenings after getting home from work, eating a quick supper, doing chores, reading the Bible, and then getting ready for bed and the next day.

Now that she really thought about it, how many nights had she gone to bed wishing that she had someone to talk to into the night . . . someone to pray with when old fears kept her awake . . . someone to hold her close simply because he wanted to?

Beginning to feel her emotions get the best of her, she took in a deep breath. A long, cleansing breath to muster her strength.

Well, she certainly had not been ending her day at nine thirty for a while now, she thought a bit defiantly, and she wished she could tell Henry she was feeling just fine. More than fine, actually. She was feeling excited and useful and necessary. Especially tonight, anticipating the venture ahead of her.

Oh . . . and maybe slightly nervous, too. As a girl who'd never taken part in *Rumspringa,* she was about to embark on the most adventurous thing she'd ever done.

Suddenly hearing the crunch of Jessica's tires on her gravel drive, a rush of heart-ticking adrenaline shot through her veins, replacing her sad thoughts. All at once, feeling like a young, giddy schoolgirl, she picked up the brown paper bag sitting alongside her chair and rushed out to her friends, locking the door behind her.

Liz waved to her from the passenger window and Jessica apologized the minute she slipped into the backseat of the SUV. "I'm sorry we're so late."

"I was hoping you were still coming." Lydia settled in with the bag on her lap.

"I didn't want to leave until Cole went to sleep, which seemed to take forever." Jessica eased down the driveway. "And then Marisa was slow getting to the apartment."

"And I had a showing tonight," Liz turned around to inform her.

"Did you make a sale, I hope?"

"Not even close." Liz grimaced. "I spent practically all afternoon with a couple, then most of the evening. At the end of it all, they informed me the wife has a cousin who's in real estate and their family's upset they're not using him. So they're switching on me, midstream."

"That sounds *verra* disappointing." Lydia felt for her. "I'm surprised you still wanted to do this tonight after a day like that."

"Trust me, the thought of a nice, hot bath did cross my mind," Liz admitted. "But I couldn't back out. This was my idea, and I shouldn't be complaining. My circumstances can't even compare to poor Norm Fletcher's. He's got to be devastated about his son."

"Wait a minute." Jessica tapped the steering wheel. "Now I remember the Fletchers. They used to go to our church, right? Ryan was a few years younger than me?"

Liz nodded. "Their family went to our church for the longest time until Norm's wife ran off with a fellow parishioner. Once that happened, Norm never showed up again."

Lydia could certainly understand that. *Gott* forgive her, she'd barely been able to make herself go to Sunday services without Henry, and her circumstances weren't anything like that. "How did you find out about Mr. Fletcher's son?"

Liz twisted around to look at her again as she explained. "I ran into one of Norm's neighbors at the grocery store. I'd sold her a house down the street from his many years ago. She's the one who told me about Ryan being in intensive care at a military hospital in Germany."

"Where had he been stationed?" Jessica sounded curious.

"I have no idea." Liz shook her head. "All she said was Norm was having a rough time of it, understandably. He's retired, all alone, and not in the best of health. He's just waiting for Ryan to be okay and to get back home."

"I sure hope all is well with him. . . ." Jessica's voice drifted. "I ended up bringing a scarf for him."

"You knit an entire scarf?" Lydia asked in shocked unison with Liz.

"I wish! You guys are great mentors, but that hasn't turned me into a world-class knitter — not yet anyway." Jessica laughed. "It's a taupe-and-gray striped scarf that Aunt Rose made. I found it in her treasure chest."

Lydia smiled, remembering the morning she and Jessica had gone through the antique cedar chest at the back of the shop, filled to the brim with incredible hand-knit pieces and quilts Rose had made and stowed away. Most likely for times just like this.

"What did you girls bring?" Jessica asked.

"Well, when I was on the hospitality committee at church, Norm was always one for a hot drink," Liz said. "So I brought a basket of teas and coffees and flavored creams."

"Oh, that'll go nicely with my contribution," Lydia spoke up. "I wasn't sure what to do, so I brought a jar of my strawberry preserves, and then I made peanut butter spread and a loaf of sourdough bread."

Jessica gave a thumbs-up signal with her right hand. "That sounds yummy, Lydia."

"You really know how to make peanut butter spread?" Liz asked.

"You can be mighty sure I do." Lydia laughed. "My *maam* started me on chores when I was *verra* young, growing up in Pennsylvania. Making the spread is one of the first things I wanted to learn to do."

"I can never get enough peanut butter spread," Liz confessed. "That's another thing you'll need to teach me to make as soon as my kitchen gets fixed. Oh, my. Fry pies and peanut butter spread. There go my weight-watching efforts again."

Lydia laughed. "I'll be glad to show you how anytime you'd like, Liz."

"You told me your mother is still in Pennsylvania, right, Lydia?" Jessica asked.

"*Jah,* in Lancaster County. My younger sister is there too."

"How did you end up in Sugarcreek, so far from home?" Liz wanted to know.

It was odd how for so many years Sugarcreek had seemed a long way from her home in Pennsylvania. But now it was beginning to feel just the opposite — Pennsylvania seemed a long way off. A place she didn't know anymore.

"My *maam* sent me here with Henry after my father died," she said bluntly.

Liz and Jessica grew quiet, too polite to ask questions, but Lydia could sense their curiosity. Maybe it was the intimacy of the car, or the anonymous darkness outside the window — whatever it was, she felt compelled to open up and share with them.

"My *maam* thought it best if I married and went to live with him. One less mouth to feed, I suppose." She'd always thought she could've been a help to her mother, but obviously her mother had looked at it just the other way around. *Maam* had gone on a husband hunt for Lydia so quickly that she'd felt like she'd lost her father and her

219

home all at the same time. She'd mourned for both of them simultaneously for a long while. "I had just turned eighteen and Henry was twenty-nine."

"Do you hear from your mom very often?" Jessica asked.

"Oh, *jah.* I get a letter from her once in a while." Not nearly as many letters as she sent to her mother. "My younger sister writes sometimes too. She's in love every other week. I hope she waits to get married. She's only nineteen."

"I was twenty-two when I got married, and I definitely thought I knew everything there was to know," Liz said.

"You must've married Cole's father when you were young too, Jessica."

"Oh, me?" Jessica nodded. "Yes, I was young, all right. Nineteen to be exact, and more immature than you can imagine. As it turned out, I may have had one of the shortest marriages in recorded history."

"Jessica, I'm so sorry. I didn't know." She'd only been trying to draw Jessica into the conversation. She hadn't been trying to be nosy or bring up an awful memory.

"You don't have to be sorry, Lydia. It was all my fault. None of it was very smart of me." Jessica turned to Liz. "I'm sure Aunt Rose told you all about my foolishness."

"No." Liz shook her head. "Rose and I talked about a lot of things, but I'm guessing she thought it was your story to tell. If you ever wanted to."

"Oh, my poor aunt." Jessica sighed. "I sure put that woman through a lot." Her voice drifted as she maneuvered the car over the empty road. "But she was always full of grace. That was Aunt Rose."

A silence fell over the car and Lydia felt uncomfortable, wishing she'd never asked Jessica about Cole's father in the first place. She was hoping Liz in her open, funny way would fill in the gap, but she assumed even Liz wasn't sure what to say.

She was surprised when Jessica began talking again. It was almost as if she needed to.

"You know, I don't know that I've ever said this out loud . . . but the night of my parents' accident, I'd been fussing and fussing before they left home." She turned on the blinker and eased left onto another dark road. "So much so that I had good reason to believe — as a young girl might — that because I'd acted up, I'd been punished, and that's why my parents never came home to me again."

"Oh, Jessica." Lydia's heart immediately went out to her friend.

"You poor thing," Liz sighed.

"Yeah, well, when Aunt Rose took me in, I was nothing but good. Good behavior all the time. I minded, never got into trouble. I did well in school and in sports, I worked hard, and I did everything as right as I could. But by the time I got to college . . . Aunt Rose had always said, 'Remember who you are. Remember you're a child of God.' But when I got away from Sugarcreek, when I got on that campus, it's not like I forgot I was a child of God. It was more like I didn't want to remember I was."

"That happens to all of us at times," Liz offered.

"Yeah, and it happened to me big-time." Even in the dimness of the car, Lydia could see Jessica shaking her head.

"When I met Sean my sophomore year," Jessica continued, "I let all of the good in me go bad. That boy was like a drug to me. Little by little I grew more and more addicted to him and his ways. I gave up so much for the thrill of being with him. I did things I never imagined I'd do. Skipped classes, let my grades drop, drank far too much, gave up my body to him . . ."

"Don't you think a lot of kids go astray at that time of life?" Liz interjected.

"*Jah*," Lydia agreed. "Even sometimes a

teen's *Rumspringa* years can get a bit wild and get the best of them."

Jessica chuckled sardonically. "Yeah, well, I took it one step further. Actually Sean and I took it one step further. During spring break we took off and drove to Las Vegas with another crazy couple I hardly knew. Our big plan? To get married. The crazy couple was going to be our best man and maid of honor. I called Aunt Rose with the good news once we got there," she remarked caustically. "Understandably she barely said a word, just offered to buy me a plane ticket home, which of course I refused."

Jessica grew quiet for a moment and Lydia could just imagine how the memory of that call made her feel.

"But anyway . . ." Jessica kept her eyes focused on the windshield as she continued. "Sean and his friend went out to have a bachelor sort of party the night before the impromptu wedding was supposed to happen. It was all pretty sad, really, him with a hangover at our so-called ceremony the next day and me with a maid of honor whose name I couldn't quite get right." She paused, as if remembering. "A month and a half later when I found out I was pregnant, Sean immediately dropped out of college and out of sight. The next thing I knew I was getting annulment documents from his family's lawyer, and poor Aunt Rose had to take me in again." Shaking her head, her voice sounded strained as she continued, "I know it was all for the best, but even so my poor choices meant Cole never had a father. No man in his life to ever love him, which is the worst part of it all."

Lydia could feel the pain in Jessica's words. "What about the boy's parents? Cole's grandparents?" she dared to ask.

"Sean's mom and dad? My goodness, no," Jessica said definitively. "Ironically, they thought I was the devil and that I had been the bad influence on their son. That I'd *forced* myself on him. Come to find out, though Sean never acted like it, he was from some well-to-do family from the northeast. And they certainly weren't going to let me — a 'hick' from Ohio — and a baby who they assumed wasn't even Sean's ruin their son's future. After a couple of times trying to contact them, I let it go." She sighed. "I didn't want Cole to know there were people who could've been in his life but didn't want to be. I never had to grow up that way. I certainly didn't want him to."

Lydia wondered what Jessica would tell him one day when he got old enough to ask about such things.

"Despite everything, you've raised a good boy," Liz said reassuringly.

"*Jah,* he was helping me unpack some boxes the other day," Lydia chimed in. "He's a sweet one, for sure."

Jessica glanced at her in the rearview mirror. "I think he's starting to get more comfortable with all the changes lately."

Detecting a lift in Jessica's voice, Lydia felt relieved.

"Goodness, I'm embarrassed," Jessica said as she turned the car around a corner. "I've talked all the way here."

Lydia hadn't really noticed. The driver who took her to work most days — an older man named George — seemed to talk a lot too as he wound his car over the roads to town. George was a bird-watcher, and she was fascinated by everything he had to share. He'd told her she was a good listener, but after all the years of near silence with Henry, she had to admit she liked to hear what was on people's minds.

Looking out the window to see where they were, she was surprised that the streets and houses looked somewhat familiar to her. "Isn't this near where you live, Liz?"

"Yes, my street is just two blocks east."

Lydia leaned forward in the seat to get a better view. "I can't believe you both came

225

all the way out to pick me up just to have to turn around and head back to town."

"You don't think we'd do this without you, do you?" Jessica asked.

"You're officially a part of the Secret Stitches Society, Lydia." Liz looked over the seat and smiled.

Warmed by their words, she hugged her parcel to her chest as Liz directed Jessica to turn off the headlights and park on the side of the road. As soon as Jessica cut the engine, the other women began gathering up their gifts. They were just about to exit the car when Lydia blurted out, "Wait."

The two of them turned around to look at her. "If you're nervous, Lydia, I totally understand," Jessica said. "I was so nervous my first time with Liz."

"I am a little nervous, *jah*," Lydia admitted. "But I also thought — well, maybe we should say a prayer. Even a silent one."

"That's the best idea yet," Liz said.

As they bowed their heads, Lydia not only asked for healing for Norm and Ryan Fletcher, but she gave thanks for the clear night and for these new women in her life too.

Seconds later, Jessica lifted her head. "Okay, are we ready, ladies?" she asked.

Closing each of their car doors as gently

and quietly as possible, Lydia followed behind Jessica and Liz as they tiptoed across the silent street toward Norm Fletcher's property.

Creeping onto the man's driveway, she was just giving thanks for the moonlight illuminating their way when two lights encased in brick stands at the base of the drive flickered to life. That didn't seem unusual at all — not until they dared to take a few steps more. Halfway up the drive, a row of spotlights flashed on over the garage, causing each of them to freeze in place.

Not sure what move to make next, they glanced at each other apprehensively. Finally, Liz took charge, waving Lydia and Jessica toward the walkway. Hopeful, the three of them pranced in that direction. But even there, with each step they took, lights burst on, alternating one side of the walk and then the other.

"This is crazy!" Jessica hissed.

"I know, but we're almost there," Liz encouraged.

The front stoop was definitely in sight, and Lydia had switched her prayer of thanks to a plea not to be caught. Because as they each took turns laying their gifts on the porch, more lights sparked and gleamed, beaming in their faces from spotlights above the front door.

"This place is booby-trapped!" Jessica whispered.

"Motion sensors everywhere." Liz waved again. "Quick, before Norm comes to the door and sees us."

Lydia felt like she was running for her life as the three of them flew across Mr. Fletcher's yard and out onto the empty street.

Luckily, they didn't have to wait for Jessica to unlock the car. The doors were open, and Lydia's heart was pounding wildly as she fell into the backseat. "Oh, my goodness." She tried to catch her breath. "That scared me. The next time I'm going to pray there aren't any secret lights."

The other ladies were trying to catch their breath as well, but around their puffing and huffing, they laughed.

"Amen to that, Lydia," Liz said as Jessica started the car, and with their good deed complete, they escaped into the night.

CHAPTER FOURTEEN

Liz had just sat down at her antique writing desk and clicked on her laptop, ready to check e-mails the same way she did first thing every morning, when she saw the new message. Unfortunately.

"Oh, Daisy. This is not good. Not good at all."

As any close friend would do, Daisy instantly seemed to pick up on her dire tone of voice. The dog got up from her spot by the sliding glass door and lay down at Liz's feet, crossing her paws over her muzzle.

"Certainly not the way I wanted to start my day," Liz sighed to her furry confidant.

But there it was, an e-mail from one of her clients with news that was similar to what she'd received the day before.

. . . And while we appreciate all your dedication and legwork over the past few months, we've decided it's best to stay in our current home after all. Therefore, thanks so much, Liz, but we won't be in further need of your services at the present time.

At the present time. Which just happened to be an awful time, considering she had no sales pending. No new clients on the horizon. And not to mention her world had come crashing down on her. Well, at least her kitchen ceiling had, which was a big part of her world and an expensive undertaking. Bad timing, too, when her savings were crumbling as quickly as the plaster from her ceiling.

"And why don't people have the decency to pick up the phone and call anymore? But no. It's texts or e-mails. That's how we learn our fate these days," she lamented some more to Daisy. "Really, are there any decent people left in this world?"

As if on cue, her doorbell chimed.

Liz had fully expected to see Daniel Kauffman standing on her front porch when she and Daisy heeled to the sound of the bell. He'd scheduled himself to report for his first full day of work on her pathetic mess of a kitchen. But what she hadn't expected was for the all-around handyman to greet her with a white bag from the bakery and a Styrofoam cup that wafted the aroma of coffee.

"Good morning, Liz Cannon." He smiled, offering up his handfuls of surprises. "I brought you a little something."

"Oh, Daniel, how nice of you!" She looked up into his eyes, which were a clear hazel and sparkling, even in the early-morning hour. She shook her head, genuinely touched by his thoughtfulness. "You didn't have to do this." Yet at the same time she said the words, her heart lifted with gratefulness at his gesture. Her lips curved upward as she took the cup and bag from his hands. "However, I appreciate it more than you could know." Which was absolutely true, considering the way her morning had started.

"I was already at Good for the Soul getting a muffin for myself." He shrugged. "Knowing the state your kitchen's in, thought you might like one too."

"Well, thank you for thinking of me," she said, not wanting to put a damper on his kindness by mentioning that earlier she'd boiled some water in her teapot and made instant oats, which she ate in the family room. It also didn't seem necessary to mention that while she loved the smell of coffee, she actually preferred to drink herbal teas.

"Again, no problem," he said. "I'm just going to grab some things —" he pointed over his shoulder to his truck parked in front of the house — "and then I'll get started."

"But you have to let me pay you for this." She held up the bag and coffee cup. "How much was it? I'll go grab my purse."

His smile was slow and easy, just like the tone of his voice. "Not necessary, Liz. It's my treat. Besides, you're going to be doling out quite enough in the weeks to come."

"Oh, I know, I know! And that's the thing —" She started to blurt out her worries all in a rush. Then stopped herself. And bit her lip. "I mean, that's something I, uh, I need to speak to you about, Daniel. Before you get your things from your truck. Do you mind coming in so we can talk first?"

"I don't mind." He glanced down and checked the bottom of his work boots before he stepped into her entrance, which suddenly felt small with him standing there. "Is there a problem?"

"Well, I hope not. But to tell you the truth, I haven't finalized things with the bank yet. I'm supposed to go back and do that today. But it's not their fault that everything isn't approved. It's mine. I keep debating on which way I want to go," she explained. Or more like which way she could afford to do things — with a line of credit or a home improvement loan. "Anyway, I just want you to know that I'd like to do all the suggestions you made. You had so many wonderful ideas for remodeling my kitchen, and I'd like for you to be the one to do them, but —"

Daniel held up his hand, stopping her. "It will all work out the way it's supposed to, Liz."

He appeared calm and composed, in major contrast to how she felt inside. "Excuse me?"

"I'm not worried about the project, and you needn't be either," he said matter-of-factly. "We know the ceiling has to be redone. That's a given. So that's where I'll start. And I know you said you'd like new flooring, new cabinets, fresh paint, and so on. If there's extra money, I can do all of that too. If there's not, you can hold up on those things. Or as I mentioned before, there are other ways to cut costs and still accomplish a good deal of what you'd like to have done."

When Daniel had come to her house yesterday, he'd been efficient and taken control, which was just what Liz had needed. First, he'd pulled down more chunks of ceiling, researching the root of the problem, and discovered what they'd both suspected. The original nails weren't long enough, and over time the plaster didn't have sufficient support. Then he went on to explain how he'd do the repair and gave her estimated costs.

After that, she'd fully expected him to be on his way, but instead he reminded her that the area — as well as her home office, which lay off the kitchen — was mostly going to be off limits for some time. So then he went about the business of helping her rearrange her family room.

They worked seamlessly together as if they'd been doing it all their lives, moving her antique writing desk from her home office to the family room so she'd have a spot to work from. Daniel even brought in a small refrigerator, left over from Amy's college days, from the garage and placed it at the edge of the family room so Liz could have easy access to a few drinks and fruit.

At that point, once again Liz thought he'd say his good-byes. But instead, they stood for another hour talking about her dream kitchen. All the while, Daniel made suggestions about how she could get close to fulfilling that dream, seeming as interested in the project as if it were his own property.

"But, Daniel —" she looked up at him — "I'm sure you have other clients and other projects. I'm sure you need to figure out a work schedule for yourself."

How could the man work without a schedule? She certainly couldn't.

"Look, Liz." His eyes narrowed with kind concern as he spoke to her. "You strike me as a bright and capable woman. I'm sure you'll figure out what's right for you and your finances. Actually, you probably already know what's best. You just need to trust yourself and your decision more. So, first things first. Let's get started on today. And let's see how it goes from there."

"But I . . ." She was so taken aback by his words she could barely find any of her own. She couldn't remember the last time a man had complimented her that way. And it especially meant a lot coming from someone like Daniel.

The moment she'd met him at his shop she'd seen what an accomplished and successful craftsman he was. Beyond that, she'd also readily sensed that he was an upstanding, kindhearted man.

With just the bolster she needed, she squared her shoulders. "I, uh . . . Okay then. I'll let you know about things as soon as I can, Daniel."

"I know you will." He leaned his head to one side. "Now if that's all you wanted to talk about, Liz, I should probably get the day started. Like my Amish ancestors would always say, 'Planning your work is important, but doing it is better.' " He smiled.

She hadn't heard that particular maxim before, but she had to muse at the truth in it. As Daniel made his way to his truck, she knew she had to get started on her day too, and all the decisions that were going to come with it.

But as Daniel had also just said — first things first. For her, that meant taking a few minutes to enjoy her treat from him.

Setting down the coffee cup on her desk, she peeked inside the bakery bag and couldn't believe what she saw. A morning glory muffin. Of course Daniel couldn't have known it was her very favorite. And of course he'd never know how he'd made her smile once again that morning.

Thankfully the route to the bank was a familiar one because Liz could barely keep her mind on her driving. Instead, her thoughts volleyed back and forth between comforting memories of the past and the realities of the present.

Undoubtedly, she'd been luckier than

many women. She'd been quite spoiled in her marriage. Not that she didn't always work hard, whether it was inside or outside their home. Not that Karl treated her like a china doll and tried to protect her from everything.

No, she was fortunate because for decades she'd had a true and loving partner. Someone she shared everything with. The ups and downs of life, all the good times and all the bad. And whenever there was a decision to be made, she and Karl would discuss the pros and cons of the situation and come to a resolution together. They also had each other to rely on when it came time to celebrate — or weather — the outcomes of their decisions.

And although Karl had been gone for years, she still missed that. Still wasn't keen on making decisions all on her own. Certainly, she always took time to garner as much information as she could from as many professionals as she could. But when it came time to decide on something, ultimately it was all up to her. And no one else.

Which was stressful at times. Especially when it came to money issues.

Obviously, she didn't know Daniel well enough to fully discuss her finances, or her lack thereof, with him. But in a strange way, simply hearing his vote of confidence echo in her mind and recalling his reaffirming statement about her capabilities released a sense of calm inside her. So that the closer she got to the bank, the more clearly she could assess her options. And by the time she pulled into the institution's parking lot, she'd made a decision to go with the line of credit. Daniel was right. Her gut instinct had been to go that route since the very beginning, thinking she'd only use small amounts of the funds as she could afford to.

Less than an hour later, all the financial papers were completed. The autumn air didn't seem quite as chilly as she left the bank and walked to the rear parking lot. She felt lighter, at peace with her decision, and momentarily at peace with herself. And there was no doubt why. It was because of Daniel, who with one insightful comment had helped her feel especially confident.

She warmed, thinking of her new acquaintance. Reflecting on his thoughtfulness. His encouragement. And the muffin from Good for the Soul, which brought an even wider grin to her face. If only she could thank him in the best way she knew how: cooking, of course. But how could she cook something special for her handyman with her kitchen out of commission?

No sooner had the question crossed her thoughts than the answer came in a flash. Excited by the possibility, she practically skipped to her car, got in, and pulled her phone from her purse.

"Hey, Jessica," she said in a rush the moment her friend answered. "Can I stop by and use one of your cutting boards?"

There was a pause on the other end of the line. "You just want to use a cutting board?" Understandably, Jessica sounded puzzled.

"Well, that and a mixing bowl. Also a skillet. Oh, and do you know if you have a wee bit of Worcestershire sauce I can borrow?" Liz's mind rifled through the list of items she'd need.

"Borrow?" Jessica raised an eyebrow.

"Well . . . use."

"Liz, my kitchen is your kitchen," Jessica said graciously. "Although if I were you and had a kitchen out of commission, I'd use it as an excuse not to cook. But I know that's nearly impossible for you, Betty C." She took a breath before adding, "You missed your calling, you know."

It wasn't the first time someone had said that to her. Liz was never sure if she was supposed to feel glad that someone thought she had a calling or sad that she'd supposedly missed it. But no time to dwell on that now.

"I'm going to stop at the office for a couple of hours, and then can I come by?" Liz started the car, looking left and right and to the rear before backing out of the parking space.

"Sounds good. Lydia and I will see you when you get here," Jessica replied.

With a semblance of a plan in place, Liz stopped by the Regency office, hoping to make some calls that might drum up new business. But after a few hours without much luck, she left, wanting to keep her prior good mood intact. Plus, she wanted to think about happier things, like cooking for Daniel. After a quick stop at the grocery for ground turkey, buns, and produce, she made her way across town to the Cottage.

True, being at Jessica's wasn't the same as being at home in her own kitchen. But she readily found all the utensils and spices she needed along with her rhythm. She was chopping away at onions and red peppers when Jessica and Lydia took a minute from the shop to come up and visit.

"What are you making there?" Lydia peered over her shoulder.

"My special turkey burgers."

"Ahh . . ." Jessica nodded to the piles of

red and white on the cutting board. "How many burgers are you planning to make? Enough for your entire street?" she kidded.

"Only four," Liz replied, holding her breath, anticipating the questions her friends would have next.

"Four, huh? Are you freezing them? Are they all for you?"

"No." She gave an honest, one-syllable answer. But knew it wouldn't suffice.

"Who are they for, then?" Jessica prodded with a smile.

Liz kept focused on her chopping and answered as casually as she could, "Daniel."

"Your handyman?" Jessica acted shocked.

"Jonas's uncle?" Lydia sounded surprised.

"Only he's really not like Jonas's uncle, but then he is."

Jessica and Lydia exchanged puzzled glances, and Liz found herself anxious to explain.

"What I mean is, Daniel isn't Amish, but he still has so many wonderful Amish characteristics."

"Well, that's mighty nice of you to say." Lydia smiled.

"It is surprising he's not Amish." Jessica stole a sliver of red pepper from the cutting board and crunched into it. "And you're making him burgers because — ? Is his kitchen out of commission too?"

Again Lydia and Jessica traded glimpses, their eyes twinkling all the while.

Surprising to herself, Liz could feel her cheeks heat as she tried to decide how to answer. Should she tell her friends about his compliments and his help with her financial decision? Or make things simpler than that? She chose the latter scenario. "Well, because he brought me a muffin."

Suddenly Jessica coughed, choking on the piece of red pepper. And coughed some more.

Liz hurried over to the cupboard, pulled out a glass, and filled it with tap water. She handed the glass to Jessica, who hacked a few more times before she was able to take a drink. It was a long minute before all seemed right with her.

"Are you okay?" Liz asked.

"I think so." Jessica lifted her chin, cleared her throat. "But oh my goodness, Liz, what about you and your handyman? It sounds serious already."

"You're a funny one, Jess." Liz waved a hand. "I barely know Daniel."

"And yet . . . you are feeding each other," Lydia needled with a sparkle in her eye.

"We are not really feeding each other. He made a kind gesture, and now I'm returning that kind gesture. And it's different with him, anyway, since he's related to your neighbor, Lydia. I feel like I already know him. As a friend."

"Uh-huh. Don't try to explain your way out of this, Liz," Jessica teased.

"There's nothing to explain." Liz opened the package of ground turkey, put it in a large bowl, and started to add the minced onions and diced peppers.

"Whatever you say. Whatever you say." Jessica chuckled to herself, and Liz felt her face grow warm again at the girls' unspoken implications. Which was silly. But somewhat understandable. After all, there'd always only been Karl. She hadn't had a male friend since she was a teenager.

"If you're worried about me coming over and cooking here some more, you don't need to be. I'm thinking about buying a hibachi."

"A hibachi, huh? At this time of year?"

"I don't know. I'm just thinking about it. They're not expensive, and I could make it an early Christmas present for myself."

"And you could also make kebabs for you and —"

Liz interrupted before Jessica could say Daniel's name. "Don't you two have a shop to run?"

"We're going; we're going." Jessica linked her arm through Lydia's.

But even when Jessica and Lydia headed back downstairs and Liz was left alone with her thoughts, she could feel herself flushing all over again.

It was late afternoon before Liz arrived back home, her car filled with the scent of turkey burgers and sweet potato fries. She was relieved to see Daniel's truck still parked in front of the house. It would've been a letdown to impose on Jessica — although she could tell Jessica and Lydia had enjoyed her impromptu visit — only to have him already gone.

Daisy's tail wagged vivaciously in greeting, though Liz was certain the pup was more eager to sniff the plastic bags full of containers of food than to see her. After setting the bags high up on a bookshelf out of Daisy's reach, she coaxed her forever pup outside to do her business, then came in and studied the plastic sheets covering both entrances to her kitchen.

She imagined the sheets had been seethrough and clear of debris when Daniel had started his work that morning. Now they were streaked with white like a smudgefilled chalkboard. So clouded with whiteness that she could barely make out his frame on the other side. She literally jumped inches when he suddenly pulled back the plastic curtain.

"Oh!" she gasped. Her hands flew up.

"Sorry. Didn't mean to scare you." He pulled down a pair of dust-covered goggles from his eyes, letting them dangle around his neck. "I thought I heard something."

"You did. Me." She grinned. "How are things going in there?"

Lines crinkled at the sides of his eyes as he smiled back at her. "Actually I just finished for the day. Want to see?"

"I'm sure it looks like something out of the blitzkrieg."

"Slightly." He drew back the curtain to a sight that looked nothing like her kitchen at all, with an exposed ceiling, chunks of white piled in the corner, more plastic covering, and snow-like dust settled virtually everywhere and on everything.

"Wow. You've got your work cut out for you, huh?"

"It's not as bad as it looks."

"That's good because it looks horrendous," she said as he eased the curtain back into place. "Did Daisy give you any trouble while I was gone?"

"None at all. She's a great girl," he said as

245

he tugged the now-familiar-looking bandanna from his back pocket to swipe his face.

"You still have some up there." She pointed to his hairline. "It's all white."

"That's my hair."

"Oh, it is not." She laughed. She'd never noticed any white and had barely seen any gray in his dark hair. Just a few lighter, distinguished patches at his temples.

"I think I know where I'm going to spend the evening."

She looked up at him, questioningly.

"In the shower." He glanced down at his clothes, covered in plaster dust. "In fact, I need to get out of here now, or I'm going to get this stuff all over your entryway and family room too. I'll just be leaving my tools and equipment in the kitchen if that's okay with you."

"That's fine. Oh!" She held up a finger. "One more thing." She stepped over to the bookshelves to retrieve the bags of food. "I have something for you." She handed one of the bags to him. "A bite to eat."

"*Jah?* Really? Dinner?" His words rang with pleasure. He stuffed the kerchief back in his pocket before taking the bag from her.

"Well . . ." She shrugged as casually as she could. "I was cooking dinner at a friend's house, and it wasn't a problem to make a little extra," she said, using his same logic from the morning.

"It smells good, whatever it is. I appreciate it, thanks."

"No problem."

"So I'll be back tomorrow, then." He dipped his splotchy white head.

"Sounds good." She smiled and walked him to the door, realizing how much she was starting to look forward to her handyman's visits.

"Oh!" He was halfway out the door when he stopped and turned around. "We don't have to talk specifics right now, but overall how did things go at the bank today?"

"They went well."

"See, I told you," he replied. Did she see a glint of admiration in his eyes? "I had no doubt you'd get it all figured out the way you needed to, Liz."

"Thank you, Daniel," she said simply. Although as she closed the door behind him, she wished she would've said more. Said what she also hadn't mentioned to Jessica and Lydia. She wished she could've told him how much his words had meant. How good it felt to feel like there was someone on her side again.

And how she wished he'd stayed to eat dinner with her.

CHAPTER FIFTEEN

"Cole, could you get the door, please?" Jessica called out to her son.

She was just in the process of adding the last batch of ghost-shaped cookies to the tin she'd been filling for the Creepy Carnival when the doorbell rang. Knowing it had to be Derek, her cheeks grew as warm as the baking sheet in her hand.

She couldn't remember her cheeks tingling years ago when Derek would come knocking on her door, but they sure did now. Actually, every time a thought of Derek had run across her mind throughout the week, she'd reacted the same way.

Trying to shake off the feeling, she glanced into the family room where Cole had been patiently watching cartoons, waiting for the day's festivities to get under way. Sure enough, he'd heard her request. He'd already flipped his Spider-Man mask over his face and bolted for the front door, his red-webbed superhero shoe covers muting the sound of his sneakers.

"Wow! It's Spider-Man!" Derek did a great job of sounding genuinely surprised and taken aback when Cole opened the door. "Sorry to bother you, Spider-Man. I must be at the wrong house. I'm looking for Cole Holtz."

"It *is* me." Her son gave a muffled giggle from under his mask, the sound of it making Jessica smile. "I'm him." More muffles. "Cole."

"Are you sure about that?"

Jessica closed the lid on the tin and stepped into the family room, watching as Derek leaned down for a closer look at Cole. Shifting to the left. Then to the right. Hemming and hawing all the while he was scrutinizing her son. She had to cover her mouth with her hand, trying to hold back her laughter over his spot-on theatrics.

Finally, Cole lifted his mask.

"Oh, you're right." Derek jumped back, flinging his hand to his chest in mock surprise. "It is you."

"I told you it was." Cole playfully swiped at Derek's leg, but Derek was quick with his hand to deflect the blow.

"Hey, be careful with those superpowers of yours, buddy," he said. "You could hurt

250

someone. Right, Mom of Spider-Man?" He glanced over at Jessica. "I didn't realize you were raising a superhero."

"He's my super superkid, all right."

Derek had always been good with adults when he was a child. It was fun to see him being just as successful with her child as an adult. Not only that, she felt grateful he was giving Cole so much attention. All morning long it had felt like there was something missing. And of course, there was. Not a something, but a someone. Grand Rose. Every year since Cole had been in preschool, she had gone to Creepy Carnival with them.

"Cole is really excited about the day," she informed Derek. "He's been ready to go since early this morning."

"Ah . . . well, I guess he takes after his mom."

She looked at him quizzically, and he shot the look right back at her.

"Seriously, you don't remember? All the days before Halloween?" His eyes grew openly amused. "Your mom would put on whatever scary costume she had," he said to Cole, "and jump out from behind doors and furniture, trying to scare me."

She didn't know whether to be embarrassed or entertained. "Oh . . . I did used to do that to you, didn't I?"

"I think she was trying to scare me away," he said in a side whisper to Cole.

"Mommy tried to scare you?" Her son looked confused.

"Yeah, but I guess it never worked. I'm still here." Derek chuckled at his own joke.

"I wasn't trying to scare you away — it was just . . . you never seemed to mind."

Which was the truth. Whereas other friends of hers back then might've thought she was weird or uncool, and not understood she was just having fun, Derek simply accepted everything about her. Always.

Just like her messing up on her dinner invitation to him. It wasn't until the week was nearly over that she'd looked at the calendar and realized Creepy Carnival was the same day she'd scheduled dinner and couldn't be missed. She'd asked if she could push back dinnertime, and Derek had taken it in stride. He'd even asked if he could come along for the festivities.

"So are you guys ready?" Derek clapped his hands. "Maybe we'll stop and have you climb some tall buildings along the way to school, Spider-Man."

Her son's eyes lit up at the wild suggestion even though it was all pretend. And that did it. Her old best friend was suddenly

Cole's new one. He chatted nonstop all the way to the school, even sharing some Halloween jokes with Derek, which in the past he'd always reserved for his Grand Rose.

Meanwhile, as she listened to Cole prattle on, Jessica felt thankful he seemed so comfortable and more back to his old self.

"Why doesn't Dracula have any friends?" he asked Derek.

"I don't know. Why?"

"Because he was a pain in the neck."

"Ha, that's a good one," Derek said, which encouraged Cole even more.

"Why didn't the skeleton cross the road?"

"I don't know, but I bet you do," Derek said.

Cole nodded vigorously. "Because he didn't have any guts."

She noticed Derek was wise — and kind — enough not to give an answer even if he knew it, which pleased Cole even more. But after the fourth joke she had to speak up, suggesting that Cole save the rest for the ride home.

Derek looked over at her and smiled easily, as if they'd shared moments like these with Cole dozens of times before. She looked out the window, trying to put her thoughts to rest, trying not to imagine what it'd be like if they had. Or could . . . She was thankful when he pulled into the school lot and she could busy herself helping him search out a parking space.

If the school parking lot had been wall-to-wall cars, the inside of the school was wall-to-wall parents . . . along with ballerinas, ghosts, brides, monsters, and many more superheroes.

After dropping off the cookies at the concession stand, she stood in the lengthy line at the reception desk to buy games tickets while Derek and Cole went off to the side to wait for her. She could see them pointing out different costumes to each other, keeping themselves amused until she finally got back to them with a strand of tickets as long as Cole was tall.

Eager to use the tickets all up, Cole grabbed one of her hands and one of Derek's. Then their threesome worked their way through the crowded corridors as best they could, dipping into classrooms along the way so Cole could play games, try to win prizes, and best of all get a Spider-Man "tattoo" painted on his cheek.

"I want to guess the pumpkin seeds in the jars next," Cole declared.

"I think that's usually in the library," Jessica told him. "At the end of this hallway, we should head to the left."

She didn't know if he heard her; he was too busy talking to Derek. "Mommy guessed the seeds right last year," Cole informed Derek.

"Oh, yeah?" Looking over Cole's head, he lifted a curious brow. "What did you win?"

"You mean besides the admiration of my impressionable son?" She smiled. "Why, I won cotton candy — and not just pink cotton candy. I won blue, too."

"But you don't even like cotton candy." He leaned closer. "Could you switch up the prize?"

She couldn't believe he remembered such a small thing about her. "No, it was cotton candy or nothing. But aren't you impressed with me too?"

"I always have been."

His gaze rested on her, and his eyes seemed to shine with something even more than approval. But assuming it was nothing more than the customary Derek Reeves charm, she shucked off his comment as they continued heading toward the library. They hadn't yet made the turn around the corner when a former classmate, Rob Mitchell — a rather large, burly man with a large, booming voice to match — called out to them from across the hallway.

"Derek! Jessica!" he yelled.

Both she and Derek waved and were happy to leave their hello at that. But Rob cut across the wave of people, not seeming to care whom he bumped into or nearly tripped along his way.

"Well, this is something you sure don't see every day," he boomed as he eyed the three of them.

"Yes, this is Cole." Jessica put her hands on her son's shoulders. "He's quite the Spider-Man, isn't he?"

"Naw. I'm not talking about Spider-Man. Plenty of them around." Rob waved a fat-fingered hand. "I'm talking about the two of you — when did you bring your relationship back from the dead?"

Obviously it was Rob's stab at Halloween humor. He laughed as if he'd said something uproariously funny, then asked again, "Seriously, when did you guys get back together?"

"Uh, we . . ." Jessica shook her head and glanced at Derek just as Cole bit his bottom lip, a sure sign that he was confused.

"We're just making the rounds with Cole today," Derek told Rob, and then being the pro that he was, having had much practice deflecting questions all through his growing-up years, he began asking questions that got Rob off the subject of them and onto himself.

Yet throughout the afternoon, Rob wasn't the only one who made an assumption that the two of them were an item. By the time they left the Creepy Carnival, they'd run into other former classmates who talked to them as if they'd been a couple forever — even though they'd never been one before. Or others who gave them knowing, covert looks, as if her and Derek's secret was safe with them — when there was no secret to be safe about.

Derek seemed completely unaffected and easygoing about the situations, turning the conversations back around to whomever they were speaking to. But Jessica couldn't be so relaxed about all the inquiries and supposition. She had to say something to him.

Waiting until they'd been home long enough to eat dinner and get Cole settled on the couch with his *Big Hero 6* movie — which he proclaimed would be his costume for the next Halloween — she met Derek back in the kitchen. He was already clearing the table.

"Derek, you don't have to do that." She tried to take bowls from his hands, but he beat her to the sink with them.

"It's not a big deal." He shrugged. "Your chili was really good, by the way. As good as the grilled cheese."

"Yeah . . . well, I'm sorry we ate so late." She leaned against the counter, not sure yet how she was going to broach her concerns with him. "It was such a disruptive day with the carnival and all."

"Are you kidding? Cole's a great kid, Jess. I had lots of fun," he added, giving her the perfect lead-in.

"Even with all the people acting like we were together? I mean, you know —" she joined her hands in the air — "like, *together* together."

His face broke into a curious grin. "That really bothered you?" He crossed his arms over his chest, then leaned against the sink as well, facing her. "I thought you had fun too."

"I did have fun. But all the talk — I just wish people would mind their own business."

"It's a small town, Jess. You know that. People need something to talk about." He shrugged off the fact. "We were the something du jour."

"But why talk about us anyway?" she questioned. "Sure we were great friends, but we were never anything more. And now . . . all of that has changed. We're so different now."

"Yeah? You really think we're different?" He pushed off the counter and stood up straight.

"Well, of course we are, Derek. Why wouldn't we be? Just look at us. Look at our lives."

He glanced at the floor and then back up at her. "I don't know, Jess. I think you may be overreacting some, don't you?"

"Oh, I'm sure you won't be thinking that in the next month or two. Because today won't be the end of all the talk." She shook her head even though she wished otherwise. "I feel like people are thinking now that Aunt Rose is gone, you've come back here to save me. And I . . ." Her voice faltered as she was suddenly caught off guard by her emotions. "I don't want you to feel that way, Derek. That's not fair to you. You're just starting a new life here and already people are trying to dictate how it's supposed to be."

And all their meddling could very well have him moving on.

But even as she was thinking that, he took a step forward and reached for her hands, clasping them in his own.

"Hey, Jess, it's okay," he said gently,

squeezing her hands. "You're getting yourself worked up over nothing." He waited a moment for her to calm down before he spoke. "You know, a long time ago — I'd say about the age of eight, to be exact — I learned that people are going to think what they want to. There's no way I can have absolute control over that. And there's no way you can either."

She nodded, knowing he was perfectly right. That had been especially true for her after she'd come back to Sugarcreek, unmarried and pregnant. How the gossip had flown then! Not that she didn't deserve it.

"And I promise you, you don't have to worry about me." He tightened his grasp. "I came back here not because I had to, but because I wanted to."

She nodded again, whispering a hoarse "Okay" as a tear slid down her cheek.

"And your last issue — the one about saving you . . . Well, you might think we're so different, but I've always thought of us — of you and me — like that one bumper sticker."

"A bumper sticker?" His comment caught her so by surprise that she giggled through her tears.

"Uh-huh. You know, the one that's shaped

260

like a dog's paw and says, 'Who rescued who?' "

"Oh, Derek!" Laughter floated up her throat, and she wanted to fall into his arms, so happy he was back in her life. But she restrained herself, folding her arms over her chest. "You're right. That's so true."

Even though her aunt Rose had given her what most would've considered a charmed life, and a life she'd been thankful for, a part of her childhood, like Derek's, had been marked with misfortune. Something they'd always understood about one another.

"I've missed you so much," she gasped, caught between tears and the humor of it all. "You're so — so —" She looked up at him, trying to find the right word.

"Awesome? Wonderful? Handsome?" He grinned boyishly.

"I'd say all of the above if I knew it wouldn't go to your head."

"I promise I won't let it. Say all you want."

"I do want to tell you, you were really good with Cole today. Sometimes little boys can be a handful — even more than big boys."

His eyes flickered with amusement. "Well, to tell you the truth, I've had plenty of practice. In Wisconsin I worked with underprivileged kids at a kung fu center near my house."

"You know kung fu? Doesn't that bother your shoulder?"

"What do you mean? My shoulder?" He looked perplexed.

"Your, uh, right one — the one you used to have girls rub Bengay all over every chance you got. You know, the one that gave you so much pain after the last game of the football season that you claimed it would never be right again."

His face was suddenly flooded with a pink glow.

"Oh, Derek Reeves." She shook her head and audibly *tsk*ed. "You are so bad."

"Was," he corrected. "Was bad. And I should probably get going now before we take any more trips down memory lane." He zipped up the gray fleece he was wearing. "Besides, like Spider-Man, I need my sleep. I've got an early shift tomorrow."

Jessica followed him out of the kitchen. They both stopped for a moment to watch Cole slumbering peacefully on the couch.

"Your Cole's a keeper, Jess," Derek said once they reached the front door.

"He is indeed," she agreed. "Thanks again for going today, Derek."

"Like I told you, I had a great time. But

—" he lightly tapped her nose with his index finger — "you do owe me now."

"Owe you?" She chuckled. "Oh, I should've known. So what is it? What do you need me to do for you?"

"Blackwell's retirement party is next Saturday."

"And you need help with what? Picking out a suit? A tie?" She couldn't imagine what else he'd need.

"No, believe it or not, I've been dressing myself for a while now," he scoffed playfully. "Actually, I need a date."

"A date?" Her head rocked back on her shoulders. "You mean you haven't had time to get back in the good graces of half the girls in town?"

He waved away her comment. "Bottom line, you owe me. Are you in?"

"Sure." She gazed steadily into his eyes. His clear-blue eyes. "What are friends for?"

"Great." He opened the door, and a rush of chilled air swept in, cooling her warm face. "I'll give you a call and let you know what time."

"Sounds good." She nodded, rolling back on her heels. "You be careful out there, Deputy Reeves," she said, meaning every word.

"Always am." He tipped his head good-bye.

Locking the door behind him, Jessica padded back into the family room and settled onto the couch with her sleeping son. After the day they'd had, she was sure her little guy was dreaming of super feats and superheroes. Meanwhile she closed her eyes and smiled.

Simply smiled.

CHAPTER SIXTEEN

Lydia was glad she'd given herself plenty of time before church service to get Flora hitched up to the buggy because the creature certainly wasn't making things easy. In fact, Flora seemed quite put out with her.

"Flora, girl, I know you don't believe it, but I really have been missing buggy rides with you," Lydia said as she stood with the harness in her hands. She'd certainly been doing her share of sweet-talking for the past few minutes. Meanwhile, Flora shook her head vigorously as if she understood every word Lydia was saying but wasn't buying any of it.

"Truly, I have, girl," Lydia tried again. "I thought you understood by now. I can't be taking you to town every day while I work. You'd be mighty angry if I did. Being tied up in a parking lot all day long is no place for a pretty girl like you." She reached up and attempted to gently stroke Flora's mane. "Now it's Sunday, and our day to be together. Don't ya want to do that?"

Little by little, her honeyed words were beginning to quiet Flora's fidgeting. But it wasn't until she and Flora both heard horse hooves coming up the drive that the creature stilled completely.

"How's Flora behaving today?" Jonas called out from his buggy. "I thought you might want to share a ride to church."

"*Danke,* Jonas, but I think we girls need some alone time this morning. No offense to you boys." She nodded at his stallion.

Good-natured as always, Jonas laughed. "Need any help getting her hitched?"

"*Nee,* thank you, though. As long as both of our patience holds out, I think we'll be in good shape."

"Okay, then." She could see his dark eyes held a bit of concern for her, but instead of belittling her efforts, he took her at her word and dipped his black felt hat. "We'll see you girls at the Keims' house," he said before turning the buggy around and heading back down the drive.

Lydia didn't know if it was the sight of Jonas's horse leaving and Flora's instinct to follow the stallion, but Flora seemed finished with her balking. She stayed calm the entire time Lydia harnessed her, letting herself be hitched to the buggy in no time at all.

Contrary to her earlier behavior, the horse even seemed to enjoy their early-morning outing, clip-clopping leisurely down the road while crisp golden leaves fluttered and floated across her path. In contrast, Lydia could feel her stomach tighten the closer they got to the Keims' property. By the time she turned Flora into the family's driveway, she was unbuttoning her jacket and tugging at her *kapp* strings, suddenly feeling uncomfortably flushed, flashes of heat surging up her neck.

It wasn't right, this feeling she'd developed — dreading the time of worship, feeling awkward around people who believed just as she did . . . She felt so miserably out of place she wanted to break down and cry. And it wasn't because of anything her Amish neighbors had done to her. No, she'd done it to herself.

Actually . . . it had all started with Henry's way of doing things, hadn't it? He'd never let them stay after service to have lunch and visit with the others. Or on the rare occasions when he had, their stay had only been for a very brief time.

And yet, when it'd been their turn to host church at their house, no one could have faulted Henry for his open-armed congeniality. But then the very next Sunday, when Lydia thought she'd finally be allowed to stay for lunch and get to know her fellow worshippers better, Henry had the final word once again. He'd tug her back to the buggy right after church and drive them home so they could "enjoy a quiet Sunday afternoon."

And those Sundays had been quiet, for sure. With him puttering around the barn doing whatever he found to do, and her in the house wishing she had someone to talk to.

But I have to tell ya, I can't do it your way anymore, Henry.

Now the Sunday afternoons were far too long and even lonelier. All because she'd never gotten to know the others she worshipped with in the way she'd always wanted to. She hadn't gotten to feel a part of what was going on. No one had bothered her much — she was sure they thought they were only doing what she wanted. That she preferred to be left to herself. They didn't expect her to stay long. Or to say much. Or to smile much.

But today all of that was going to change. Unless she lost her nerve and needed to leave, of course. That's why she'd declined

Jonas's invitation and driven herself.

After tying Flora alongside the other buggies, she made her way to the Keims' barn. At least the Keims had hosted church many times before so she was familiar with their arrangements and didn't have to guess how things would be laid out. As usual, their barn had been cleared for prayer time, with benches on one side of the space for women in their *kapps* and benches on the other side for the bare-headed men facing them. The minister preached from the area left in the middle while a few young boys sat on the steps that led up to the loft, looking down on him.

As Lydia slipped into an empty spot at the end of a bench, the lady to her right was busy talking to another woman and didn't seem to notice her. But a moment before the service began she caught sight of Jonas in the cluster of men. Her neighbor smiled and she could feel the warmth of his gaze all the way across the wide space that separated them.

The kind gesture was all she needed to stop focusing on herself and begin concentrating and praising their mighty and generous *Gott.* After all, He had gotten her there safely, hadn't He? And she was among friends — if only she'd let them be. Beyond that, He was always with her. And today, *Gott* help her, she wasn't going to run home early. She was going to stay and start getting better acquainted with the people who loved and worshipped Him just as she did.

Yet three hours later as service ended and the men began moving tables into the barn to set up for lunch, the butterflies in her stomach started all over again. Steeling herself, Lydia took a deep breath and approached one of the tables, where a lady whose name she wasn't sure of was already setting places.

"Can I help you?" Despite her nervousness, luckily the words came to her as naturally as if she were addressing a customer at the Cottage.

"*Jah,* that would be a very *gut* thing. *Danke* for asking." The woman smiled. "How about you take one side of the table, and I'll take the other." She handed Lydia plates and napkins. "Together, we'll have the tables set in no time and everyone can eat. I think I heard some stomachs growling during church."

"I believe one of them was mine," Lydia said as she distributed plates. "But don't tell anyone."

The woman laughed. "I won't tell on you

if you don't tell on me. I'm Sarah, by the way."

"Hi, Sarah. I'm Lydia." She paused before adding, "I have a sister named Sarah."

"Jah?" Sarah paused over the table. "Is she younger or older?"

"Younger."

"I have a younger sister too." Sarah smiled, and with that, the two of them were as busy at talking as they were at arranging the lunch plates.

When they finally finished their designated tables, Sarah went to check on her children and Lydia knew just what she needed to do next. It was exactly what she'd been dreading.

Putting one foot in front of the other, alternating one bold step and then one timid one, she followed the curved path that led from the barn to the Keims' house, where the other women would be preparing lunch.

The door to the house was already open when she got there. Even so, she hesitated. How awkward it was going to be once she stepped inside! Women would be bustling around, knowing one another, knowing what to do and where they belonged. She, on the other hand, was going to feel mighty uncomfortable.

Or . . . she could skip the discomfort and head home right now.

Where she would feel alone and discouraged and mad at herself for not trying.

After weighing the options once again, she finally went inside the house. The scene was everything she'd been envisioning. Stepping around the groups of busy women, she wound her way to the hub of the kitchen to see what there might be for her to do.

She fully expected even more women there, scooting in all directions, taking care of all kinds of preparations. The only thing she wasn't anticipating was the greeting she received.

"Lydia?"

She'd barely been in the kitchen for ten seconds when Ruth Keim looked up and noticed her. Right away, the older woman put down the bowl she'd been stirring and came toward her. "Lydia!" she said again, her tone turning from surprise to glee as she wrapped her arms around Lydia. "You are really staying for lunch, *jah*?"

Lydia nodded.

"Oh, *danke,* dear *Gott,*" Ruth cried as she hugged Lydia once more. "Your being here is just what we've been praying for. Isn't it, Abby?"

Ruth's daughter Abigail happened to be

standing at the sink, peeling cucumbers, when Lydia had walked into the kitchen. Hearing the news from her mother, Abigail hurriedly laid her work aside, drying her hands on her apron.

"We're so glad you're here, Lydia." Abigail caught her up in a hug too.

Touched that these women had even been thinking of her — let alone praying for her — Lydia felt a surge of emotion well up in the back of her throat. She could barely get out the words that had become so familiar to her. "Can I . . . can I . . . help you?"

"Can you help?" Abigail took her hand. "Why, of course you can. You don't think you're going to get out of here without us putting you to work, do ya?"

With her arms around Lydia's shoulders, Abigail drew her to the kitchen table, pointing to the platters sitting there. "For starters, do you mind cutting the sandwiches in halves so there's more to go around?" she asked.

Did she mind?

"I would love to." Lydia smiled up at Abigail. "Really love to," she said, meaning the words with all her heart.

Because of the late lunch she'd had after church and still feeling full from sharing the company of others, Lydia hadn't been hungry for much of a dinner. After scrambling a couple of eggs and quickly cleaning up the mess, she settled into a chair in the sitting room with her knitting.

The second pair of booties she was working on was even more adorable than the first. Being at the Cottage all the time, she kept coming across patterns she liked and was eager to try. With her friend Rebecca getting closer to delivering, she knew the booties would go to good use. Not only that, after stopping in at the bakery often to visit Rebecca, her friend had grown dearer and dearer to her. She wanted to do something nice for her and the precious little one who would be arriving soon.

Yet every time she glanced at the printed sheet to see what directions came next, out of the corner of her eye she kept noticing the same thing. The quilt. Draped over the arm of her husband's chair. The one Jessica and Liz had made from Henry's shirts.

The quilt was all she could see.

Stilling the needles in her hands, she stared at the blanket and wondered about her husband all over again.

The time she'd shared with her fellow worshippers earlier had been so special and enjoyable. Why hadn't Henry ever wanted to stay after church and join them?

Had he been that disappointed in her as his wife? Was he that embarrassed by her? Or was there something else?

So many things about Henry didn't make sense, didn't ring true. She'd never realized before how tired she was of the hurt and the mystery. Of having lived with a man — and still grieving a man — she never really knew.

Chapter Seventeen

Rolling over, Liz peeked at the clock on the nightstand with more than a little trepidation — 7:20 a.m. Her alarm had gone off promptly at 6:55, and ever since she'd been lying in bed, barely hearing the light patter of the drizzling rain, staring at the shadows on her bedroom ceiling. Which wasn't very inspiring. And held no answers for her.

Kind of like her life had felt the past weeks.

Unsettling. And so out of rhythm again.

At first she'd simply attributed the problem to the upheaval in her kitchen. Being unable to cook had left her feeling antsy and with far too much time on her hands.

But the thing was, Daniel had been there every day, pulling down the old ceiling and preparing for the new one. She had no worries and no doubts that he'd have her kitchen back in working order before long. He was every bit as competent as Lydia's neighbor Jonas had said.

Yet knowing that to be true still didn't alleviate the deep-seated anxiety gnawing at Liz — the sense that her kitchen ceiling wasn't the only thing in need of repair.

Too many nights she'd been waking up, lying there in the dark, pondering and praying, wondering if she could continue to make ends meet selling real estate. In the past year, it seemed she'd been putting more effort into her job than ever before — doing more social media, making call after call, trying to solicit new business any way she could think of. And while all of those strategies proved to be effective for other salespeople in her office, for some reason they weren't working even half as well for her.

Overall, her sales horizon looked dreary and bleak. And yet . . . if she wasn't able to make a living selling real estate any longer, what was she going to do? It wasn't like she was getting any younger. Not like she had many options. At least not that she could think of.

Which was why she was still in bed thirty minutes after her alarm had gone off.

"I don't know, Daisy. I just don't know. Seems like these days the harder I try to put pieces of my life's puzzle together, the less they want to fit."

At the mention of her name, Daisy got up and moved from the foot of the bed up close by Liz, snuggling against her side.

"Oh, thank you, girl. Thank you." She sighed. "And don't you worry. Everything will be all right. I'll snap out of it. I always do."

But instead of popping up, she kept lying there. Trying to think of a solution, yet feeling as blank as one of the pages in her organizer lately. Until she looked at the clock again and realized Daniel would be at her house, ready to work, in fifteen minutes.

"Time to rise and try to shine," she told Daisy. But as she climbed out of bed, she wasn't sure how to dress or what to "shine" for. Had absolutely no idea what she was going to do with herself for the entire day — besides maybe stop in at the Cottage for a quick visit.

Feeling indecisive — and completely unlike herself — she grabbed a pair of black exercise pants from the shelf in her closet along with a faded pink T-shirt. Then, shivering from the slight chill in the house, she pulled her favorite, nearly threadbare purple zip-up from a hanger too.

Making a beeline for the bathroom, she startled at her own reflection in the mirror.

If anyone actually could look like they'd been wrestling a bear all night and lived to tell about it, she certainly did.

After hurriedly brushing her teeth, she splashed cold water on her face, thinking it might jump-start her features. But patting her face dry, she realized it hadn't helped much at all.

That's when she tried moisturizer. Lots of it. And then color. Five dots of beige foundation, blended in. A streak of grape lipstick to her lips. A swash of pink blush to brighten her cheeks. Followed up with a quick gliding of brown/black mascara sifted through her lashes before hiding them behind her glasses. Then using both hands, she tugged and fluffed at the ends of her spiky hair. She hadn't yet gotten to the back of her head when the doorbell rang.

Daniel!

Daisy eagerly loped ahead of her down the stairs, having grown as happily accustomed to their daily visitor as Liz. Standing in the entry, the dog wagged her tail expectantly, and Liz knew just how she felt. The day got better the moment she opened the door and spied Daniel's sweet grin and friendly face.

"Hey, Liz."

"Hey there!" she said, taking in his fresh

look for the day. Shaven, dressed in a green plaid shirt and jeans and smelling like something fruity and outdoorsy all at the same time, Daniel looked a far cry from the plaster-covered guy who had left her house most evenings.

Daisy, however, didn't have quite as much of an attention span. Scoping out a squirrel in the front yard, she scooted around their legs and bounded out of the house.

"Whew! Let me try that again." Liz chuckled, thankful Daisy hadn't knocked either of them over in her excitement. "Good morning."

"It is a good morning." Daniel's smile was like a conduit illuminating every feature of his face as he stood there holding a cardboard carrier with two coffees instead of the usual one for her. "I thought I'd bring something different this morning." He lifted a large white bag in his opposite hand. "It's a quiche. I hope you like sausage."

"I do. It sounds wonderful!" she said, wishing so badly that instead of lying in bed stressing she would've gotten up and done more to fix herself up. But he didn't appear to notice her haphazard makeup job.

"Good!" he replied, then paused, surprisingly apprehensive for him. "The only thing is I, uh, I couldn't eat quiche on the fly like

I usually do the muffins from the bakery, so —"

"You could join me while I eat mine."

He looked relieved. "I was hoping you wouldn't mind me doing that."

Was he kidding? Her heart leapt at the chance. If she couldn't share a cooked breakfast of her own, at least she could share her hospitality. "Why don't you set all of that on the coffee table while I grab a couple of things from the kitchen?"

She made her way to the kitchen and tiptoed across the dusty floor, gathering up all she needed. In a matter of minutes she returned to the family room and set the coffee table with her best blue place mats, creamy white plates, two juice glasses, and her better silverware, along with a wedged pie cutter. That, of course, was after rinsing and shaking everything out, making sure the items were all plaster and dust free.

Daniel eased onto the floor, stretching out his legs as he leaned against the bottom section of her sofa. Before she joined him, she retrieved a small carton of orange juice from the mini fridge across the room and filled both of their glasses. Then also filled their plates with the delicious-looking quiche.

Bowing his head, Daniel offered up a silent prayer before he lifted his fork. Liz felt moved to do likewise before they began to sample the special treat he'd brought.

If it hadn't been spitting rain all morning, the sight outside the patio door to their right might have been more inviting. But currently the bird feeder was void of any fine feathered friends, and the yellow and bronze chrysanthemum blooms around the perimeter of the patio had been beaten down by the rain, looking more like eyesores than eye-catching at the moment. Even so, inside Liz's family room all was good. Very good.

"This is nice." She looked up from her plate. "And the quiche is incredible. Delicious."

"I agree on both counts," he replied in between bites.

"Where did you get it? And how have I missed knowing about something this tasty?" she wondered out loud.

"You haven't overlooked anything. It's from Annabelle's in Millersburg. You probably just don't head that way too often."

"You're right; I don't." She stopped and sipped at the coffee — which, she realized, like her new friend, she was getting more used to and enjoying more all the time. "So what are you up to in the kitchen today?"

"Well, today is a big day in the life of your kitchen. It's the end of phase one, getting everything ready before the new ceiling goes up."

"You sure have been working hard on it, Daniel."

"It's definitely getting there." His eyes shone with appreciation. "How about you? What's on your agenda for the day?"

She'd been enjoying his company and the breakfast he'd brought, but suddenly his question brought on the same heavy, lost feeling that had kept her lying in bed too long that morning. She could feel her heart sink at the thought of what the rest of the day held — or more like, didn't hold. "I'm not sure — which, I have to tell you, feels very strange."

"You're not going to the office?"

She sighed, dangling her fork in midair. "I don't know. Here it is Thursday and I was there yesterday and all the days before that, as you know. But nothing seems to change. Or not for the good anyway." She shook her head, repeating some of the bleak news she'd already shared with Jessica and Lydia. "I had a sale pending that fell through. Then was waiting for a client to make a bid on a house, but now that couple is hedging. I know I have to scare up some business, but going into the office doesn't seem like the answer. I don't know what is."

She shrugged, feeling helplessly confused. "I have to admit it's beginning to worry me. So much that I've been waking up in the middle of the night," she admitted and would've been embarrassed that she'd said so much if he hadn't answered her with one of his gentle, empathetic smiles.

"It's hard being self-employed. Waiting for things to fall into place is tough," he offered. "But you know, one way or another, things typically do."

"I usually think the same thing. I do. But this time . . . I don't know. I'm not getting that feeling." She sighed. "I feel like the more I pray for things to fall into place, the more they keep falling apart."

"It does seem like that at times." He nodded agreeably. "And in the meantime, it's hard to do what we need to do. To trust in God's plans and to wait on His timing. We're generally not as patient with Him as He is with us," he quipped, causing her to smile.

"You're absolutely right about that." She poked at her quiche self-consciously. "Daniel, I'm sorry I blurted all of that out. Thank you for listening. It's sweet of you."

"We all have our days," he acknowledged easily. "At least you'll feel better about life after your workout." He nodded to her outfit. "Looks like you're going to the gym at some point today, right?"

"I could if I belonged to one. No doubt, I could use the exercise." She glanced down at her front side, which, along with her backside, had never been smaller than a size 12, but at one time at least had been a fitter version.

"Oh, I just thought seeing your outfit maybe that was the case. I mean, I wasn't suggesting anything," he backpedaled. "You look fine to me."

She smiled, thinking how sweet he was to say so even though it wasn't true. At all. Which reminded her she'd never finished spiking the hair at the back of her head. Reaching up, she daintily fluffed the flat spot there, pretending to scratch an itch.

"Yes, well . . ." Her eyes drifted to the glass patio door. "I suppose I could get some exercise with a walk in the rain." She took her last bite of quiche and laid her fork aside.

"True. Or . . ."

"You can say it. I'm open to suggestions," Liz said as she started to cover the remaining quiche with the plastic pie lid and gather up their silverware.

"You could help me."

"Really? I could?" At last, a purpose to

her day?

"I could sure use an extra pair of hands and eyes."

"And you're certain you want those hands to be mine? I mean, I know my way around a kitchen, but not when it's under repair."

Dipping his head slightly, he answered, "I think you can handle it."

"Then I'm your girl!" she blurted.

When he chuckled, she suddenly realized how her words sounded. "I'm sorry, I just meant —"

He held up his hand to stop her. "No need to apologize, Liz." His tone was reassuring. "I'm glad you said yes. Though you may be thinking differently after a long day of working with me."

"And vice versa." She laughed.

The work was tedious and neck-breaking, and the hammer got heavy at times as Liz worked with Daniel, removing the hundreds of rusty nails from the overhead wood laths that had been exposed once he'd removed virtually her entire ceiling.

But even if the job was drudgery, being around him wasn't at all. They talked easily and shared comfortable silences too. Plus, he was sensitive to her needs, encouraging her to take breaks to save her neck. But she didn't quit until he did, wanting to be as much help as she could. Besides, it felt good having something to show for her efforts for a change. Even if it was only a pile of rusty nails.

Once they'd tackled that job together, they stopped for a quick peanut butter and jelly lunch. Then spent the rest of the day sweeping and cleaning the area the best they could, preparing it for phase two. The last phase.

"How much longer till it's all finished?" Liz asked as she and Daisy watched Daniel put away his tools for the day.

His brows knit together thoughtfully before he spoke. "I'd say there's maybe another week of work left. Not necessarily full days. Some of that will be downtime while I'm waiting for things to dry in between the different coats that need to be applied."

"Oh!" she said, completely unprepared for that answer. Not ready for the work to be completed so soon. Of course, she'd be happy to have her kitchen back. She'd been missing it so much. But at the same time, when the days were up, she knew she'd be missing something else. Daniel's presence. Which she'd so easily gotten used to. "That's no time at all."

She felt a strange ache in her chest and experienced even stranger thoughts in her head, wishing she'd close on a house or two in the next week so she could hire him on for more projects.

"No, it isn't long, is it?" He snapped his toolbox shut and stood up. "It'll be here and gone before you know it."

While he dug in his jeans pocket for his keys, Liz reached down to pet Daisy, more for her own comfort than her pup's. "Thanks for everything today, Daniel. For listening. For letting me help out. Oh, and for the quiche."

"Yeah, about the quiche . . ." He played with the key fob in his hand.

"Oh, right. You should take the rest of it home with you." She started for the mini fridge.

"No, Liz." He held up a hand. "That's not what I meant. Earlier I was thinking, well . . ." He looked away for a moment as if gathering his thoughts. "Since you liked the quiche from Annabelle's so much, you'd probably enjoy their dinners, too."

"You know, you're right. I probably would," she replied. "I'll have to go there sometime."

"I think you should," he agreed. "How about a week from Friday?" He gazed directly into her eyes.

His question completely surprised her, and she wasn't sure how to take it. Was he asking her on a date? Asking as a friend? Or thinking her ceiling might be complete by then, and it'd be a sort of celebration? *Does it matter?* her brain shouted. After all, it was dinner with Daniel. The nicest person ever. Why question why?

"That'd be great, Daniel."

"Yes, I think it will be, Liz." But even as he said it, she thought he looked a bit surprised at himself for asking too.

CHAPTER EIGHTEEN

"You're a great photographer, Derek," Jessica called out to him as she stood in her strappy black heels admiring yet another framed print hanging on his family room wall. "This sunset photo is incredible. So pretty."

"Not as pretty as some things I've seen," he replied with a low whistle as he came around the corner from his bedroom, buttoning the jacket of his dark-charcoal suit.

When she'd first arrived at his condo, he'd left the door unlocked for her since he was hurrying to get dressed. He'd run into complications at work and his shift had gone longer than expected. Instead of him picking her up for the sheriff's retirement party as planned, she'd offered to meet him at his place to save time. Now she was glad she had. She couldn't imagine what he'd look like if he'd had even more time to get himself cleaned up. As it was, the sight of him filling out his tailored suit was enough to heat her cheeks. And the way he gazed at her, a glimmer of appreciation shining in his eyes, caused her face to warm even more.

"I . . . uh . . . ," she stammered. "I hardly think a little black dress can outdo your beautiful shot of a snow-covered field at sunset."

"Eh . . . I think it depends on who's wearing the dress." He grinned. "And you've even got on your ruby earrings." He nodded, noticing the pair of gemstones her aunt had given her years ago at graduation.

"I thought they worked with the dress." Right away when she'd put them on, she'd liked the way the rubies and diamonds glittered with a subtle elegance.

"They do." He smiled. "You look great, Jess."

"Thanks, um . . . so do you," she stuttered shyly, as if the two of them had never exchanged compliments before. Dumbfounded by her lack of cool, she quickly spun back to the photo. "Was this a Wisconsin sunset?"

"That? Oh, no." He stepped close beside her, and she tried to ignore the way the scent of his cologne pleased and teased her senses. "I took that photo on vacation. When I was out in Vail, skiing."

291

"I didn't know you skied." She turned to face him.

"Mm-hm. It took me a while, but I learned it was a less dangerous hobby for me than mountain climbing." He laughed in a self-deprecating way.

"Mountain climbing too?"

"Oh, yeah. Don't you know, I'm quite the mystery man these days."

He was teasing, of course. But in her mind, what he was saying seemed to be absolutely true. Every time she was with him — or spoke to him — she seemed to learn something else about the guy she thought she knew everything about. Helping underprivileged kids, taking stunning photographs, trips out west . . .

As he went to pick up his wallet and keys off the coffee table, she wondered what else she didn't know about him "these days."

"What? You're looking at me funny. Isn't this thing straight?" He tugged at the knot of his tie.

"It was just fine until you messed with it. Come here and I'll fix it."

She waved him close and then felt foolish that she had. All week long, every time he'd called or left a message, just the sound of his voice had rattled her in an unexpected way. Made her forget whatever job she was in the middle of. Caused her thoughts to slip into memories of him. And now that he was so close — near enough that she could feel his breath on her face — she tried to steady her hands and not wobble in her heels as she worked to pull the tie back to center.

"I thought you said you could clothe yourself. Now I have to be your date and dress you too?" she kidded, attempting to lighten the moment for her own sake.

"You *do* owe me, remember? After my day with you at Spooky Festival."

"Creepy Carnival," she corrected as she smoothed his shirt collar over the tie.

"Right, Creepy Carnival."

"I guess we *are* even then." She shrugged in mock resignation. "And I'm all done here." She patted his lapel dismissively and felt the surprising hardness of his chest underneath. He caught her hand, keeping it pressed against him, before she could step away.

"Well, actually — I wouldn't assume we're even until the night is over. I could be the one owing you again." His brow tilted apologetically. "I forgot. Rob is going to be at the party tonight."

"Big-mouth Rob? Oh, Derek . . . ," she groaned.

"Yeah, sorry about that. I know how you dislike being the topic of conversation. And I have to agree, Rob has always had a big mouth."

It had slipped her mind that Rob was on the city council so, of course, he'd be at the event. Once he saw the two of them again, he'd have half the town believing that she and Derek were not only "together" but that they were engaged to be married by the time the evening's festivities came to an end. More awkwardness. More gossip to overcome. More of a chance that Derek might start shying away from her in the future.

At the present time, however, he didn't seem disturbed by the possibility of more talk. And if that was the case, she needed to get past it too.

"You're right." She slid her hand out from under his. "You *are* going to owe me, Deputy Reeves. Big-time." She shook her finger at the handsome man in front of her.

"I think I can handle it." His blue eyes smiled into hers.

As Derek ushered her out of the condo and down the walkway to his car, she realized once again that he certainly wasn't the shy, awkward guy who had picked her up for the prom so many years earlier.

But once they were in the car and headed

toward Manor Lake's reception center, everything about him felt much the same. He was the same easy person to talk to that he'd always been. The same person who seemed to understand everything she had to say — even the times when she didn't completely finish a thought.

"So did you go out to Vail very often?" She found her mind drifting back to the topic of his vacations — not because she was interested in where he'd gone but because, silly as it was, she suddenly felt nosy and proprietary and was very curious to know who he'd taken with him.

"Just a few times," he said nonchalantly, not sharing any details before turning the subject back to her. "Has Cole ever skied?"

"No, we've never gone." For a moment she wondered what it must've been like for Derek. Always being so free — actually, still being so free — to do and go whenever and wherever he wanted. For a guy who'd come from nothing, he'd already seen a lot and done so much. Far more than she ever had.

"I think it'd be good to get started with it when you're young. I consider myself to be fairly athletic, but I had a heck of a time learning. It took a lot of lessons — and nerve." He smiled. "We could take Cole to Mansfield sometime. Maybe over his Christmas break?"

"You mean to Snow Trails?"

"Yeah, it's only an hour or so away. He might really like it. You might too."

"That'd be great, Derek. But then, of course, I'd owe you again, right?" she said in jest.

"That's my devious plan," he teased before they launched into another dozen subjects to talk about, reminding her of the times she'd return from a week at summer tennis camp and they'd barely take a breath, so eager to catch up with one another. It seemed like only minutes later when they pulled up the drive to Manor Lake's event center.

"Our old stomping grounds," Derek murmured.

"Yeah. It doesn't look much different, does it?"

Each window of the oversize cabin shone with a warm, golden glow, not to be outdone by the sparkles of moonlight reflecting off the bed of water that lay next to it. Silhouettes of pine trees flanked every corner of the center. She'd always thought they looked like large, caring gatekeepers, protecting the place.

"I'm glad some things don't change," he said.

"I know what you mean. Me too."

As they got out of the car, beds of fallen pine needles unseen in the darkness offered up their welcoming aroma. Smoke curled from the cabin's stone chimney with its own familiar, inviting scent.

"Ready for this?" Derek crooked his arm in a friendly, gentlemanly way.

"Ready as ever." Jessica slipped her arm in his. But with every step they took, she couldn't help feeling uncertain. Manor Lake may not have changed. But something inside her kept feeling like it had. And she didn't have a clue what she was saying yes to.

"I hear you have a really nice Amish lady working for you at the Cottage," one of the girls in the group standing around Jessica was saying.

The party had been more bearable than Jessica had first thought it would be. Having dropped out of college and jumped into life as a single mom, she'd rarely had much time to reach out to the girls she'd gone to high school with. The few who were still left in town had come to her aunt's funeral, and that was the last time she'd seen them. There was a lot to be said for catching up with them under happier circumstances.

"Oh, she's more than nice," Jessica replied. "Lydia knows everything about knitting and quilting that I can't even pretend to know, even gives classes just like Aunt Rose used to do — which lets me take care of the business of running the place. I feel extremely fortunate the two of us came together, for sure."

"Speaking of togetherness . . ." Her friend Beth glanced over her shoulder in Derek's direction, where he was talking to a group of guys. "It seems Rob has been spreading rumors about you and our new deputy."

Not surprised by that news, Jessica answered in as firm and friendly a tone as she could. "And that's pretty much what they are, Beth: Rob's crazy rumors."

"He *is* a strange one." Another old friend laughed. "He'd have his own gossip column if the newspaper would let him."

"I don't know." Beth's eyes twinkled. "You and Derek still seem to have that thing."

"If you mean we've been friends for a long time, that's true; we have." Jessica shrugged off her friend's comment.

Beth snickered and the other girls offered up polite smiles. "No, I mean a thing. A definite thing."

"Honestly, I don't know what you mean. . . ." Without even realizing what she was doing, she glanced across the crowded room at Derek. As if he could feel the heat of her gaze in that very instant, he looked up and smiled at her. What else could she do but smile in response?

As she turned back to the group of girls and realized they'd all witnessed the exchange, Jessica could feel her face flush slightly.

"Uh, yeah." Beth chuckled knowingly. "You two have always had a connection. I always noticed how you and Derek could connect just like that — across a room, or a gym, a party like this. With just a glance. Or a smile."

Jessica shook her head. "You've been reading too many romances, Beth," she objected, although she knew exactly what Beth meant. She'd always been able to feel Derek's presence anywhere . . . and obviously from his smile, he could feel hers, too.

"Oh, come on, Jessica, it's not a bad thing." Beth smiled, repeating the word. "It's a good one."

"And obviously it's not as serious as you think. Not as serious as your thing with Jason." She took a lesson from Derek, turning the conversation around. "Did I hear you guys just celebrated your eighth anniversary? Almost a decade — that's amazing. How's he doing, by the way? And your girls?"

As Beth launched into updates about her family, Jessica felt pleased she'd recovered so nicely from the speculations about her and Derek. With the topic behind her, she was glad to settle into the conversation. Until the Sugarland song came on.

At first she didn't hear the melody through the din of conversations floating around her and the room. But then the chorus came on, and suddenly — as childish as it seemed — her body responded in a way she couldn't seem to control. All at once she needed air. Lots of air. And some distance from the past. Something to make sense of the present.

"Would you girls excuse me? I need to grab my phone," she fibbed in the middle of Beth's monologue. "I just remembered something I forgot to tell my sitter."

She slipped away from the clusters of people and, without bothering to grab her wool jacket, stepped out the back doors into the chill of the November evening. Trying to get as far away as possible, she stole across the upper deck and descended the stairs to the lower one.

But what had she been thinking? How could she escape the past with the lake right there in front of her? It was a place that had been too much a part of her growing-up years. A place that had an undeniable hold on her.

How many summer evenings had she ended up there with a gang of girls, innocently scaring off geese with their giggles and shrieks as they tentatively dipped their toes in the water?

And then there were the few guys who had taken her to the lake at the end of a date. Guys who'd wanted more than she was willing to give at that particular time in her life. She'd had to demand to be driven back home — unless they wanted their moms to find out where they'd taken her.

But the times she and Derek had driven out to the lake had been the ones she remembered most vividly. How often had they gone out there to escape? To do for one another what best friends do best — listen, laugh, fill the quiet, and ease the hurts. Just be there for each other while favorite country songs played on the car radio . . .

Songs like Sugarland's "Want To."

Every time the melody sifted over the airwaves, circling them like a lasso, corralling them together, they'd teased each other over the lyrics. All about staying friends on the shore . . . or jumping into something more.

More often than not, one of them would push the other into the lake and that would end any tension that the suggestion in the song might've created between them. Had they just been too scared of messing it all up? Of possibly losing each other?

Or . . . had Derek never wanted more between them?

Jessica crossed her arms and rubbed at the goose bumps covering them. How often after sending her splashing into the chilly water had Derek stood behind her on the banks, rubbing her arms to take away the cold? He'd rub so vigorously, leaving her shrieking over an Indian burn he'd given her.

A fond smile playing on her lips, her thoughts continued to drift back in time. Until, the next thing she knew, she could sense his closeness. He really was behind her, placing his suit jacket over her shoulders. Warming her as he always had — only this time much more gently.

"You okay?" he asked softly.

"Yeah . . . I just . . ."

Pulling the coat closer around her, she looked up at him. Seeing his raised brows, she knew he was waiting for her to say something more. But she could barely say the words she wanted to say, let alone say them to his face. She turned from him and wished she had a rock to skip across the dark lake. He'd taught her how to skip a stone, many years of summer nights ago. The simple action always seemed to allow them to talk about even the most soul-searching things. Except for maybe . . . whatever they had or hadn't had between them.

But there would be no rock skipping tonight.

"Do you ever wonder about if things had been different?" she asked softly, looking out across the water, as if tracking an imaginary stone she'd just thrown.

As she said the words, immediately her thoughts went to Cole. Of course, she'd never change having Cole in a million, zillion years. But before she could add that disclaimer, Derek answered.

"I used to," he said quietly. And even though he admitted it, she realized she didn't know what he wished might've been different. His dad? His mom? His place on earth? Them?

Once again, she'd purposely left the question of the two of them open-ended, hadn't she?

"In some ways I still do." He leaned against the deck railing, his clasped hands hanging over the wooden bar as he looked out onto the water. She wondered if he was feeling like he wanted to skip a stone too. But he didn't sound like he needed one as he said, "But right now, Jess, I'm thinking things are good. Just being here." He gazed up at the crescent moon, hanging like a slice of lemon in the sky.

She studied him, his handsome face a profile of contentment, and realized she wanted to kiss him more than she ever, ever had before. But always, as before, she had no idea if he was feeling the same way. In all their years, he'd never said anything. Now as then, she was too afraid to ask.

And if she tried to kiss him — if she started, this time she knew it would be real. All of her. It wouldn't be a friendly peck on his forehead. It wouldn't be a brush of her lips on his cheek. It would be a kiss she wouldn't be able to stop. Wouldn't want to stop, leading to another kiss and more kisses and all the moments and moments after that . . .

Suddenly she shivered, stopping her from imagining more.

"Are you cold?" He pushed away from the railing and, as always, protected her, wrapping his arms around her.

Not now . . . not with you.

She wanted to say the words. Wanted to nestle closer. But she fell back into the rhythm, the song, of their past. For fear of complicating the moment. Of ruining them "just being there."

"I'm good," she said instead as she gazed up into the sky too, trying to be at peace with the present.

CHAPTER NINETEEN

Lydia lay in bed almost wishing it had been a frightening sound that awakened her while the pre-dawn sky was still so black outside her bedroom window. But it hadn't been a sound at all. It had been the clamor of thoughts about Henry that kept insisting she get up to do the only thing she knew that might make them stop.

Still, she resisted. It was only after tossing and turning for a half hour more that she finally surrendered to the racket in her head. It was clear she wasn't going to get any more sleep, and her mind wasn't going to get any more rest if she didn't take care of the very thing she'd been thinking about for the past few hours.

Lighting the lantern atop her nightstand, she found the pair of thick socks she kept by her bedside and pulled them onto her feet, one by one. Then she wrapped a shawl around her shoulders before making her way to the kitchen.

Gathering up her writing basket from the kitchen counter, she carried it to the oak table. Sitting down, she took out a blank sheet of paper and stared at it. Until finally she felt moved to pick up a pen and begin the letter that had been forming in her mind ever since she'd opened her eyes before dawn.

Dear Henry,

Once again I have spent another night wrestling with thoughts of you and our marriage. Once again I am starting the day feeling guilty for all that I've been thinking — all that has been going through my mind. I'm saying this because it seems with each passing day, I have a harder and harder time recalling any sweet memories of us at all.

I have no memories of the two of us laughing or working together, side by side. No recollections of your arms wrapped protectively around me. No memories of your lips curving into a smile when you'd wake up in the morning next to me or when you'd come home in the evening and see me.

All I have are questions. More and more questions. Wondering why you didn't choose to be close to me. Why you couldn't accept my love. Why you didn't want to raise a child with me. Why it seemed you wanted to be my ruler instead of my lover and friend.

I wanted to share a life with you, Henry. A happy, blessed life as one. I wanted to share everything about me with you — and yet you

All at once her hand froze on the page. The pen lingered over the last word as another surge of guilt shot through her. What was she doing being accusatory with a deceased man?

As she lay in bed, the letter to Henry had seemed like a good idea, something she felt compelled to do to get her feelings out. But now that she'd started writing it, it didn't hold any comfort for her at all. In fact, it felt somehow wrong and even futile. She had never been able to get responses from her husband when he'd been there to ask; did she really think she'd get any answers now?

Tossing the pen aside, she yanked the piece of paper from the tabletop and crumpled it with both hands. Then she sank back into the chair and peered out the window.

Remnants of frost covered the edges of

the four panes. Soon it would be gone, melted by the sun, which was slowly rising over the frost-tipped fields. It was a pretty sight to behold outside her window for sure. Yet she could barely feel moved by the view. Because inside her house on this morning, the kitchen felt too empty. Too quiet and chilly. And inside her heart, she yearned for the day it wouldn't feel that way ever again.

Would that day ever come, *Gott* willing? When she would have a house that would be a home she shared with a man who loved her and their children? When she'd rise before the sun and before her family, busily baking in the kitchen, just as her *maam* used to do?

How easily she could remember those winter mornings as a young girl. Waking up to the scent of a coffee cake baking. Of a fire already roaring in the fireplace. Starting the day with the gratifying comfort of being safe and warm.

Oh, how she missed those mornings. If her *maam* only knew!

Sitting up, Lydia took another piece of paper from the basket, and without hesitating she began to write again.

Dear Maam,
    I am up early this morning, sitting in

my kitchen, remembering the times I would wake to the sweet scent of your applesauce cake baking in the oven. It is a memory that made me miss you and home, so I thought I'd write a note and tell you so. I think of you and Sarah so often! I hope this letter finds both of you doing verra gut.

I would say things are going gut here too, and I am thankful for that. As I told you in my other letters, I've been blessed with new friends and a job I enjoy verra much. I also have a good neighbor right next door who is kind and helpful, and I'm making better acquaintances with the women and families I worship with.

I'm saying this again because, Maam, I don't want you to be worrying about me in any of those ways. Gott has been gracious and good and has made sure I am not alone.

But — is this so awful of me to say? — I'm finding even with the blessing of these people, there is a hole in my heart that I don't know how to fill. Jah, I realize this would be a normal feeling for anyone who has lost a loved one. I know when Daed passed there was a hole left inside all of us too. Yet with our dear Daed, I'm grateful to say I have sweet memories to remember him by. And. with Henry . . . well, I don't feel like I have anything to fill that hole.

In fact, as time goes by the hole seems to get a little bigger. I think it's because recently I've had the chance to be more social and meet more people. My friend Liz — she's a widow, too, and she has memories of her husband that bring a sparkle to her eyes. And with the married couples at church and couples I see in love, I notice how they smile and laugh together. How their eyes light up when they look at each other. How they touch and talk and respect one another. Seeing them makes me sad because I have to wonder why Henry and I were never that way. If he would've ever talked, I would've listened. If he had wanted love, I was ready to open my arms to him. I cannot understand why Henry never chose to be close to me, but I suppose it's nothing I can change.

She paused momentarily, long enough to wipe droplets of tears from the page.

Oh, Maam, have I gone on too much? If so, I'm verra sorry. I really don't mean to burden you with this. Deep in my heart I know in time and with prayer Gott's love will fill this hole. He will lift this hurt from me. He will bring the answers that will make my marriage to Henry feel like less of a mystery to me.

Just know, Maam, that I don't believe you did anything wrong when you hugged me that day and sent me away with Henry. I know you were only doing what you thought was best for me after Daed passed away. So please, don't ever think I blame you for anything. I surely don't.

You have been a good maam and have taught me well to stay strong in the Lord. No matter what, that is what I plan to do. You can be sure I will stay strong in Him.

Love,
Your Lydia

Lydia stilled the knitting needles in her lap long enough to reach up and cup her hand over a yawn. After getting up extra early and writing to her *maam,* her day's work at the Cottage felt like it had taken forever to end. Plus, the hours had been made even longer than usual since it was the night for her to meet with Jessica and Liz for their weekly knitting session at the shop.

"Oh, Lydia." Jessica's lips parted in a yawn as her needles came to an abrupt halt. "You need to stop doing that. Now you've got me started too."

"And me." Liz took in generous gulps of air and let out a robust yawn. "Goodness gracious — what a tired group we are tonight! I still don't think I've recovered from helping Daniel in my kitchen. I'm sore in places I didn't know existed on this old body of mine. I didn't realize how beat I am."

"Me neither." Droplets of moisture filled Jessica's eyes as she yawned again.

"Were you out late at the retirement party?" Liz turned to Jessica. "Did you have fun?"

As soon as Lydia had come back to work after the weekend, she'd noticed Jessica's eyes shining brightly. Even if her friend was bone tired, her eyes hadn't stopped twinkling yet. Jessica couldn't have hidden her pleasure at being with Derek even if she'd tried.

"We did have a surprisingly good time." Jessica's entire face lit up as she spoke of him, reminding Lydia that everything she'd said in the letter to her mother had been true. "It was also great to see so many people from town under happier circumstances, and . . . I don't know . . . It was just really nice being with him." She blushed, making Lydia smile.

"Your cheeks match the color of your scarf." Lydia nodded to the crimson skein of chunky yarn in her friend's lap.

"Oh, I know." Jessica's needles collapsed in her lap again. "What is wrong with me? I've never been like this before. Well, certainly not with Derek."

"He's a very nice-looking young man," Liz said approvingly.

"Jah," Lydia chimed in, "and he seems *verra* nice too."

"I know. You're both right. But . . . it's Derek," Jessica said, looking as hopelessly baffled about him as she usually did about her knitting. "I keep getting all jittery and silly around him. This is what I get for not dating much all these years. I'm like an impressionable schoolgirl all over again."

"Oh, goodness." Liz looked up from her nearly completed vest. "Talk about being out of touch . . . I hope I don't get like that when I go out with Daniel. I haven't been out with anyone except Karl for decades. Truly, ladies — I mean decades."

Lydia noticed Jessica straighten in her chair at the exact moment she did, both of them wide-eyed at Liz's news. "You have a date with Daniel?" Lydia asked.

"He asked you out?" A big grin settled on Jessica's face.

"To dinner." Liz nodded, and Lydia could see the beginning of a fond gleam shining in her eyes too. "But it's not a date," she added quickly. "Well, at least I don't think it's a date. Dating's more for younger people, isn't it?" Her forehead crinkled. "Oh, but poor Daniel. The moment the words came out of his mouth, he looked so nervous. Like he wasn't even sure why he'd asked. But then, I really can't blame him. I have to admit I'm a bit nervous too."

"But you're glad to be going with Daniel, *jah*?" Lydia asked.

"Well, sure," Liz said without a moment's hesitation. "He couldn't be any easier to talk to. From day one, I've felt totally comfortable having him at my house. He's been great in every way. You'll have to thank Jonas again for referring him to me."

"I'll tell Jonas the next time I see him," Lydia assured her.

"Is that very often?" Liz asked with a twinkle in her eye.

"Ahh . . ." Lydia shrugged. "Now and then. He brought by some firewood for me earlier this week."

Jessica had been fiddling with her needles,

getting them situated just right so she could start a new row. But Lydia noticed how her news now made Jessica pause and look up at her. "That's so sweet of him, Lydia," she said.

"*Jah,* I know. I hadn't remembered to put that particular item in my budget, so it was a blessing, for sure." She recalled how thankful she'd felt early one morning to find him placing a pile of wood at the side of her house. He wouldn't let her pay him for it either. He'd told her it was from a dead tree he'd had to chop down — a tree Mr. O'Malley had never taken care of when he lived there.

She worked a few more stitches on the heel of her bootie before she decided to share about the other times she'd been in the company of her neighbor. "I've also been letting Jonas ride to church with me."

Just as she imagined they would, Jessica and Liz exchanged glances and giggles. "You *let* him go with you?" Jessica asked.

"*Jah.*" She smiled. "Sunday is the only day I get to spend with Flora, and she gets cranky if we don't do some riding together. But I decided it's silly for Jonas and me to ride separately."

"And he doesn't mind you doing the driving?" Liz smiled.

"He hasn't complained so far." She shrugged, feeling slightly bashful. "I may let him take over the driving when the snow comes, though."

Both women nodded understandingly, but even as Lydia said the words, a small part of her felt uneasy. Even though she was afraid of driving on snowy roads, she was also leery of giving up the reins. Again.

As she took up her knitting once more, her thoughts strayed, idly comparing Jonas's personality to Henry's. But after a few minutes, her tired eyes were so bleary that she stilled the needles, rubbing her eyelids.

Jessica noticed and laid down her knitting as well. "You look tired, Lydia. We don't have to keep going, you know."

"*Nee . . . nee.* It's not the knitting." She shook her head, not wanting Jessica to think their sessions were too much for her. Their time together had become a precious highlight in her weeks. "I didn't sleep *verra* well last night, and then I was up early this morning, writing a letter to my *maam.* There was, uh, something I wanted to write to her about. Something I . . . I didn't want to put off."

She didn't want to mention the letter she'd started to Henry, but simply remembering it caused her voice to stress unexpect-

317

edly. Her friends' expressions went immediately from interested to concerned.

"Is your mom okay?" Jessica's brows dipped.

"I hope nothing's wrong." Liz bit her lower lip.

"Oh, *nee*. Nothing's wrong with her," she hurried to say. "It's . . ." She hesitated, looking at them. "It's me, actually. It's me that's not okay."

Both women put down their needles.

"Lydia, what?" Jessica asked.

"Is there anything we can do?" Liz's eyes shadowed with worry. "Anything at all?"

It wasn't until that moment with both of her friends looking at her so tenderly, so anxious to listen, that she realized how she'd stopped sharing her feelings over the years. It was only because Henry never acted as if what she felt mattered much. Nor did he ever attach much importance to what she had to say.

But the women sitting around her were different. They cared. She could see it in their eyes, feel it in the way they poured every bit of their attention on her. And though she barely had any tears of sadness left for what she and Henry had not shared, her friends' kindness was something else. Their caring brought on a surge of emotion, causing her eyes to well up.

"Do you remember the day you first told me about the Secret Stitches Society?" She flicked away the droplets in her eyes. "I'd come back from the bakery and was all upset?"

"Of course we remember," Jessica said. "We had some tea and talked awhile."

"You'd been thinking about your husband. A memory had caught you off guard." Liz offered her account.

"*Jah,* but . . ." Lydia looked down at her hand, where a wedding band used to be. "What I didn't say was that it wasn't a *gut* memory that had me grieving so awfully much that day. It was a terrible memory. One I'd tried to stow away and never think of again."

She glanced at the nearly completed bootie in her lap. "Ya know, ever since Henry passed, I feel like each day has been *verra* similar to my knitting. I pull out one memory or have one question about us, and it's as if I've tugged on a strand of yarn. The memories and questions only seem to lead to more, and right before my eyes, our marriage just keeps unraveling and unraveling, breaking my heart over and over again. Sometimes I wonder . . ." She swallowed hard. "I wonder if the day will come that it will finally unravel so much I'll have nothing to show for the years we spent together."

She looked up at her friends and noticed their misty eyes filled with sympathy. "There's nothing to say except that Henry and I didn't have a *verra gut* relationship. When I see you with Derek —" she glanced at Jessica — "or when you talk about the way you and Karl were together —" she looked at Liz — "well, I can't even begin to relate."

Liz cleared her throat before she spoke softly. "Not all relationships are the same, honey."

"Oh, I know. I'm sure you're right," she said. "But as a wise woman once told me, 'communication, compromise, and caressing' — those should all be a part of a relationship, and with us, none of those things existed. So how could we have learned to be close to one another? We rarely spoke to each other . . . or held each other. And all through the years, I barely questioned Henry because I was so afraid he wouldn't love me if I did. But . . ." She shook her head, disbelieving the irony of it all. "Even though I went along with the way he wanted things between us — all the while trying to earn his love and respect — it seems he never loved me anyway."

Jessica sighed deeply. "I don't know what to say, Lydia. Some people . . . Well, maybe he just had a hard time showing his love."

"*Jah,* well . . . I'm not sure what to think. But for sure, in the note to my *maam,* I didn't say all the things that I'm telling you. I wouldn't want to concern her with so much."

Yet, earlier in the day, the very moment she'd slipped the Pennsylvania-bound letter into a mailbox on her way up Main Street to the Cottage, she'd almost wished she could get the envelope back, fearing she'd still said more to her *maam* than she should have.

"I hope you know we're here for you, Lydia." Jessica reached out to pat her knee. "Whenever you want to talk."

"Or whenever you don't want to. We're here then too." Liz nodded with half a smile. "I'm also old enough to be your surrogate *maam* if you ever need me to be."

Liz's use of the Amish term brought a smile to Lydia's lips. "I appreciate it for sure," she said, genuinely touched.

They all bent over their knitting again, but she could feel the mood of the room had changed. Their eagerness to work on their projects had waned and passed. She wasn't at all surprised when Jessica spoke up.

"Since we're all so tired, maybe we should call it a night," her friend suggested. "You and I have to be back here at the shop before you know it." She glanced at Lydia and then around the room.

"Sounds good to me," Liz chimed in.

"But didn't you have something you wanted to show us?" Lydia asked Jessica. "You said you'd been working on a new kind of scarf?"

"Oh, yeah, that." Jessica laughed. "It's not actually new. It's more like I've revamped one of my awful scarf attempts." Bending over the side of her chair, she pulled a scarf out of the burlap bag sitting there and laid it on the table. Lydia and Liz both stared.

Made with a warm, plum-colored yarn that Lydia was familiar with, the scarf was also dotted with pretty sparkly bows in a lighter shade of lavender.

"It's darling, Jessica," Lydia said honestly.

"Just adorable," Liz agreed. "Where did you get the pattern?"

"It's the same pattern I've been using. But as you both know, hard as I've tried, I can't get the knitting right. I keep making mistakes. And that's when I remembered Aunt Rose's special ribbon."

"We sell it at the shop." Lydia recalled the small display of glimmering ribbons in a variety of colors, but she couldn't remember having a customer buy any.

"Right. Aunt Rose always kept sparkly ribbon around." Jessica nodded with a smile. "Until recently, I'd forgotten how she had it handy for times when shoestrings broke without notice. Or when a headband got lost. Or when she couldn't get the stain out of one of my tops, she'd make a pretty bow and pin it over the stain." Jessica smoothed her hand over the scarf. "When she first tried to teach me to knit, I stressed so much about all the mistakes, she pulled out a roll of her ribbon then too. I can remember sitting together with her, making shiny bows to tack on over the bumps and lumps I'd made."

"Aww . . ." Liz sighed. "She certainly was one sweet lady."

Lydia was moved by the story as well. "She did all of that to cover your mistakes?"

"I don't know that she was exactly trying to cover them." Jessica's voice drifted as her expression turned thoughtful. "No, I really think she was simply trying to turn them into something better. Something pretty to look at."

"It's very shabby chic, your scarf is," Liz

commented, "which is quite in vogue these days."

"Yeah — have you seen some of the furniture that's in style right now?" Jessica asked. "Not that I need any, mind you."

As the two women talked about fashion and trends, Lydia listened, not feeling one bit left out. Simply being in their company, and being their friend, was enough for her most times. Just the kind of hug she needed. They were part of what made her "off" days better and her good days seem more right.

They were, she decided, much like the sparkly ribbon in her life.

CHAPTER TWENTY

Once the waitress took their orders, Liz relaxed in her seat across from Daniel at the table for two. As she gazed at him, his kind face illuminated by the candlelight, she wondered why she'd felt anxious about going to dinner with him in the first place.

Not only was he easy on the eyes, but with his calm demeanor and accepting ways, he was also easy to be around. Yet even though she already knew those things about him from his working at her house, it'd still taken her forever to get ready. She'd expended enormous effort and hairspray to get her hair just right. At least five minutes to choose the best shade of lipstick. And then there were several trips to her closet and many try-ons until she finally decided on black slacks, an emerald-colored top with just the slightest bit of sparkle, and stiff black heels that had never seen the light of day.

But then, in her own defense, just like she'd told Jessica and Lydia, it had been over thirty years since she'd had dinner with any man other than Karl.

"I still can't believe I'd never heard of Annabelle's," she said. "But like I mentioned before, I rarely go as far as Millersburg to eat. Not that it's such a long ride from Sugarcreek."

"You've probably always done most of your own cooking."

"True. But it's a treat to get out and see what real live chefs come up with. And I love the atmosphere here, Daniel. It's so homey with the fireplace and warm, stained wood. I really like it."

She'd been delighted the moment they'd pulled up to Annabelle's. The eatery looked more like someone's home they'd been invited to than a restaurant. White rocking chairs dotted the wraparound porch of the two-story Victorian house painted a steel blue. Seasonal decorations — cornstalks, pumpkins, pots of yellow and magenta chrysanthemums — were tastefully displayed across the porch and up the wooden steps of the entrance, adding more color and a cozy ambience.

"Obviously it's a popular place," she said, looking around at all the filled tables.

"I believe it's been under new ownership for a while now, but it seems the proprietors have kept the place pretty much the same. I used to live out this way," he explained. "It's always been one of my favorite places to eat."

"Did your nephew Jonas live out this way too?"

"Oh, no. My sister's family lived closer to town — until they moved to Indiana. Jonas just moved back to Sugarcreek recently." He gave her a crooked smile. "And I'm sure your next question is, why is Jonas Amish and I'm not?"

"Well, I did give you a brief synopsis of my life when we were yanking out all of those nails together." As they'd worked side by side, she'd told Daniel about the people most precious to her — about Karl and Amy, about her son-in-law and grandchildren. He'd listened and asked questions, seeming genuinely interested as he always managed to do.

"I suppose it's my turn, then."

She fussed with her napkin. "Only if you want to share, Daniel. It's totally up to you."

"For some reason, you make it easy for me to want to do that, Liz," he answered softly, creating a warm sensation that coursed through her. She was pleased she could make him feel as comfortable with her as he made her feel with him.

"Although honestly it's not that interesting of a story," he continued. "Many people's lives take a turn for one reason or another. Mine took a different course because I liked basketball."

She had just started to pick up her glass of lemon water but stopped midcourse and set the glass back down. "Did you say basketball?" She crinkled her nose.

"Yes, and I understand how hard that might be to believe." He laughed. "But trust me, at one time this old body really was lean and mean."

"Oh, no, it's not that. To my way of thinking, you seem to keep yourself in very good shape. I mean your arms are so strong looking and your shoulders are broad and —" She stopped, biting back more compliments. Daniel had a way of making her feel she could say anything to him. Yet it'd been a long time since she'd complimented a man. She wasn't sure what sounded forward and what didn't. "But, uh, basketball, huh? That takes me by surprise."

"*Jah,* well," he said, falling into the Amish vernacular as she'd noticed he did from time to time, "it surprised my family, too. But I liked basketball so much that when the other Amish kids left school after eighth grade, I opted to continue on to high school. My dream was to play on the varsity team." He grinned. "Which I did."

"That's remarkable," she replied and was about to say more when the waitress appeared with their food.

"Ma'am, you ordered the pork loin and sweet potato casserole?"

"I did." Liz nodded as the young girl set down the plate.

"And, sir, medium rare steak with red potatoes and asparagus?"

"That's me." Daniel also nodded, and as the waitress walked away, he bowed his head in silent grace. Liz paused and followed suit before urging him back to his story.

"So, as you were saying . . . you were playing basketball and — ?"

"Enjoying it very much." He cut into his steak. "But then the closer it came to graduation, when everyone assumed that I'd had my fill and would want to be baptized Amish and go back to the farm, a few teachers had already planted another idea in my head."

Liz looked up from her plate. "College?"

He took a sip of water. "Uh-huh."

"You must've been a good student for them to care so much."

329

He shrugged modestly. "I enjoyed learning and I suppose they saw that in me. They paved a path for me that I could've never accomplished on my own. Helped me sign up for the ACT. Took me through the student loan process. Everything. I wasn't good enough to play college basketball, and I knew it. But I had a new dream by then. I wanted to be an engineer."

"That makes sense," she commented, completely caught up in his story. "You seem to like discovering solutions for problems. Fixing things and making them work. Like my awful old ceiling." She smiled. "Did you go on to college?"

"I did. I enjoyed it too. Well, until my father had a breakdown."

"And your mother needed your help?" Liz guessed.

"Actually my mom had already left us when I was in high school."

"Oh, my goodness, Daniel. I'm sorry to hear that."

"I don't know if it was my stepping outside of what was expected that led my mom to do the same thing or not." He shook his head and she could see how his mother's change of heart still puzzled him. "I never knew that she desired a life other than the one she had with us, but I suppose she did.

Apparently enough not to care that she'd be shunned when she turned her back on the Amish faith and left the community and her family. I've never seen her since."

"That's so sad, Daniel." She looked into his eyes, wondering how he'd managed to get through such a thing and still have such a caring heart.

"Well, what can one do except ask for God's help? Not every Amish family is the picture of perfection, ya know?"

"I'd say very few families are the picture of perfection, period," she said. Though she and Karl had rarely fought, she'd never forget how uncomfortable it was growing up with parents who squabbled day and night about nothing. She and Karl had promised each other that their daughter wouldn't grow up in that kind of atmosphere. "So then you left college?"

He gave a slow nod. "I'd hoped it would only be for a few semesters and then Dad would be back on his feet. But he was a lost man at that point and heartbroken. He'd started numbing himself with painkillers when my mom left, and when I moved home promised he'd stop. But that never happened. He only got worse. One day he had the tractor out and had a horrible, fatal accident. When he passed, I had two much-younger sisters to take care of."

"How old were you?"

"Twenty or thereabouts. My relatives helped us out some, and neighbors too, of course," he explained with a satisfied smile. "Anyway, I sold the farm since it wasn't something I'd ever been good at. Like I said, I was much better at fixing things and building things like benches and tables. I got a job with a furniture maker and worked there for many years until my sisters were grown and married."

"And how about you? Did you ever marry?"

He glanced down at his plate and poked at his potatoes. "*Nee*. I was engaged once when I was young. But even though she wouldn't say it, I knew she really didn't want to take on the responsibility of helping me raise my sisters. So I broke things off with her." He paused for a deep breath. "By the time my sisters were leaving home to marry, I was early thirties and, I don't know, it seemed everyone my age had already gotten on with their lives. So I concentrated on work instead."

"Do you have any regrets?"

"Yeah." He leaned back in his chair and grinned. "I regret that I've been talking a blue streak. Though somehow I've managed to down my steak in the process." He pushed back his plate.

"It's my fault. I kept asking questions." She laughed. "You know, I read a good Amish quote about regrets. It went something like, 'A man is never old until his regrets outnumber his dreams.' "

"That's a good one." He nodded. "Where do you come up with all of these Amish proverbs, Miss *Englischer*?"

She didn't mind his teasing at all. In fact, she could feel her eyes light up at the banter with him. "Around here you don't have to be Amish to be familiar with Amish proverbs."

"You're talking to the right person about that." He laughed, seeming to appreciate their exchange as much as she did. "Since you seem to like them so much, I have a quote for you."

"Oh, yeah?" She sat up straight to listen. "I'm ready."

He cleared his throat and his voice took on a more serious tone. " 'Regrets over yesterday and fear of tomorrow are twin thieves that rob us of today.' "

"Ahh . . . that's a good one too."

"It is. I thought of it because, well, I hope you don't mind me saying it, but I'm liking this day — or rather this evening. Actually, I like any time I spend with you. In your company. I guess what I mean is, I like you, Liz."

She could feel her cheeks heat with surprise at his words. She laid down her fork, suddenly unable to eat one more bite. "And I — I enjoy your company too, Daniel," she replied more breathlessly than she'd intended.

Luckily their waitress arrived at the table that instant and interrupted the moment. "How was everything this evening? All right?"

"It was wonderful. Really, really good," Liz gushed, far more comfortable talking about the food than her feelings. "I think maybe the sweet potatoes could've used a little less cinnamon, and the pork loin a tad more garlic. But very good, nonetheless."

The waitress straightened. "Are you the food critic from the *Budget*?"

"Oh, no." Liz waved her hand. "Nothing like that. I'm just . . . me." She smiled apologetically.

"She's a great cook," Daniel interjected.

"Well, I'll be sure to pass along your comments to the chef. So . . . any room for dessert?" The waitress looked between the two of them. "We have awesome pies."

"They do have great pies," Daniel confirmed.

"Mmm . . ." Liz winced. "I hate to pass up a good pie, but I'm feeling super full right this minute."

"Do you think you might like some in an hour or so?" Daniel leaned toward her. "We could split a piece."

It took a moment before she realized what he was really asking. And only half a moment before she knew how she wanted to answer.

"Apple?" she asked, tilting her head at him.

"Apple it is." An easy smile played at the corners of his mouth. "One piece to go, please," he told the waitress.

And Liz had to admit she was glad. The dinner she'd been so nervous about had gone by far too quickly, and so very comfortably. She realized she wasn't ready for the evening to be over.

CHAPTER TWENTY-ONE

"Seriously? You're saying there's absolutely no way I can borrow money from your bank? And that's it? That's final?" Jessica could feel her throat constricting in fear and hear her voice rising in indignation as she leveled her eyes at the young loan officer who would hardly return her gaze while he delivered the bad news.

"I'm sorry, Ms. Holtz." His shoulders rose apologetically. "But what I can do is get you into our newest program, where you'll be able to get free checking and double bonus points on certain debit card purchases." He looked almost embarrassed for her and her pitiful financial state as he delivered his best scenario.

"Look, I told you my situation. I don't need free checking or bonus points. I need thousands of dollars, and I need them like yesterday," she pleaded. "I can't default on the property taxes at my shop. The store is my only livelihood." How many times had she mentioned that to him already? "If I lose the shop, how am I going to pay the existing loan you have on the place? Have you thought of that?"

But of course she didn't know why she was even asking. No doubt he had thought of that. And of course he didn't care. It wasn't his problem — it was hers.

Every limb on her body had been shaking for the past couple of hours — ever since the afternoon mail had arrived at the shop and she'd received a final notice from the county treasurer. The notice had not only listed the sum of the shop's property taxes but also the penalty fees that had accrued from not paying the taxes on time. None of which would've been quite so shocking if she had been aware of an initial invoice before receiving a final notice. She could only guess the first invoice had somehow fallen through the cracks — gotten lost in the shuffle between her move to the Cottage and her working night and day to keep the shop running.

She also might not have been so surprised by the notice if she had ever owned property before and had been attuned to the idea of property taxes.

Tucking the bill into her pocket, she'd

sneaked upstairs to her apartment, out of Lydia's earshot, to call the county, certain she could get hold of a sympathetic ear, maybe even set up some kind of installment payment plan if she only explained her circumstances and apologized for her ignorance. But the woman on the other end of the line had apparently heard it all before. She seemed totally desensitized — even bored — by Jessica's situation. Jessica could practically feel her shrug over the phone.

That's when she'd scurried out of the Cottage and hightailed it to the bank. Yet now the loan officer seemed to be doing the same.

"Hey, if it were up to me," he was saying, "I'd help you out."

Again his shoulders rose and fell in such a dramatically sympathetic way that Jessica wondered if he'd practiced the gesture in a mirror for situations like hers. She was glad that at least he hadn't bothered to reiterate all the reasons why he couldn't help her. He'd covered that list earlier and she really didn't need to hear — or want to hear — the dire litany again. All about how she already owed on student loans, she had barely any savings, her one credit card was nearly maxed out, and her aunt had already refinanced recently to help pay for hefty —

and expensive — renovations she'd had to make on the shop.

"But it's not up to me," he added as he sat up in his chair with a degree of finality. "So . . ." he drawled out the word and toyed with the pen on his desk as if waiting for her to give up and leave.

"Well then, if it's not up to you, who is it up to?" she asked. "Maybe I need to speak to that person." She was surprised by her own audacity, but she was already pushed into a corner. What else could she do but push back?

"That's no problem. No problem at all, Ms. Holtz. I'll be happy to get our manager for you."

Jessica noticed that he didn't simply look happy — he looked ecstatic to get away from her, practically leaping from his chair and rushing out of the office.

Meanwhile, she sat tapping the desktop, staring out the window, wondering how on earth she was going to come up with the extra money she needed in the next thirty days if the bank didn't come through.

The answer was still eluding her when she heard a shuffle of footsteps at the office door. Sitting up straight, preparing for round two of pleading, she turned from the window. She couldn't have been more disheartened and discouraged when she laid eyes on the bank's manager — Denise Crutchfield. Of all her former classmates . . . and it just had to be Denise, didn't it?

"Hello, Jessica." Denise's voice was silky smooth, not to mention controlled and professional as she sat down at the desk in front of her. "I would say it's good to see you. But after being briefed on your situation . . ." She clucked. "How can I say that under such unfortunate circumstances for you?"

Of course, Jessica knew Denise was only being partially honest. Yes, her circumstances were indeed unfortunate. That part was totally true. But as far as Denise ever being glad to see her? That hadn't happened in eons — not since the two of them had become rivals in junior high, which turned into a soured relationship that followed them all through high school.

Jessica had never been sure what had turned Denise against her all those years ago. It seemed silly to Jessica because she had never thought of Denise as a competitor in the first place. They'd never had the same friends. Had never run around in the same group. But maybe for Denise that had been the point.

Needless to say, she would've gladly

turned over her homecoming princess and prom queen tiaras to Denise years earlier if only she'd known she'd be sitting in front of the woman now. But since she couldn't travel back in time to do that, she gave her adversary the warmest smile she could muster and quickly swallowed her pride.

"Denise. Don't you look nice," she said as sincerely as she could. "I love that suit you're wearing."

"BOSS," Denise answered curtly.

"Boss?" Jessica frowned, not quite understanding. Was Denise demanding she refer to her as "boss"?

"The brand of my suit. It's BOSS. By Hugo Boss?" Denise added with a condescending smile. "From Nordstrom in Columbus."

"Oh . . . I . . ." Jessica blinked. She was so caught up in her own drama of being too cash poor to pay her taxes that the designer reference had gone over her head. "Well, sure, of course it is. And it's, uh, really good-looking," she commented again. "On you." She swallowed another lump of self-dignity.

Then, rubbing her clammy hands on her jeans, she took a deep breath before launching into her final appeal. "Look, Denise, we both know why I'm here. And, well, bottom line is I would really appreciate it — super appreciate it — if there's anything you could do to help me. And I'm thinking you could, you know — being you're the boss and wearing your BOSS suit and all." She chuckled nervously, already wishing she hadn't added that last comment.

"I certainly wish I could help." Denise shook her head as if truly dismayed. But even as she said the words, her eyes glimmered with malicious satisfaction. "However, what we're talking about here are numbers. Hard, solid numbers. And in your case, the numbers just don't add up. Not for creating a new loan for you, and not for adding on to your existing one."

"But Aunt Rose — I mean, she — we — have been banking here for years, so there's just got to be a way. That's got to count for something. Some reward for our loyalty and our —"

Denise held up a hand to stop her, and Jessica was almost glad. Even she hated how pathetic she sounded.

"You know, Jessica . . ." Denise sighed. "If this were an episode of *Little House on the Prairie*, all of that might matter and things might turn out just the way you want them to. But sadly, we don't always get what we want. That's something I personally had to learn a long, long time ago." She glared at Jessica as if Jessica truly were the sole cause of all the disappointments in her earlier life at Garaway High School.

"Furthermore —" her foe leaned forward, crossing one manicured hand over the other — "you need to understand that your beloved Cottage isn't exactly a cash cow. From year to year, the net is not all that lucrative or stable. Honestly, I'm surprised you didn't just sell the place." She shook her head, appearing baffled by Jessica's lack of business savvy. "That's what you should do, you know. Sell it and let someone turn it into a pizza parlor."

Jessica nearly gasped, not believing Denise could say such a thing — and so harshly, too. The cruel words hurt her as badly as if Denise had been talking about a relative of hers — like a kid sister or brother who was never going to amount to anything and needed to be given up on.

"You might find this hard to understand, but that place — the Cottage — is a part of me, Denise." Her indignation flared. "It's a huge part of me, and it's a part of this town, too. And I really can't believe you're using this circumstance to get back at me for whatever you've been holding against me since seventh grade. It's not fair or logical and it's — it's juvenile," she sputtered.

Denise's mouth gaped open, but only momentarily. She quickly recovered, clamping it closed. "Me? Juvenile?" She spoke through clenched teeth. "I'd say you're the one who's being immature for even suggesting such a thing, Jessica. After all, it's not my fault that you didn't pay a bill on time. I have nothing to do with the situation you're in."

"And you're certainly not doing anything to help me out of it, are you?" Jessica hated how her face heated, surely displaying every ounce of her frustration.

Denise clasped her hands upon the desktop and pursed her lips into another tight faux smile. "Is there anything else I can help you with today, Ms. Holtz? Any of our services you might be interested in — aside from a loan?"

"No, thank you." Jessica bolted up from the chair. "I'm sure I can get what I need at Homestead Bank up the street."

"Dream on." Denise chuckled as she sank back into her leather seat. "The most you'll get out of that experience is exercise walking there. But it is a nice, brisk day. So enjoy your jaunt, Jessica."

An hour later, after Denise's prediction

came true and the loan officer at Homestead Bank rejected her as well, Jessica practically crawled out that bank's door, her hope completely shattered, her ego more than a little bruised.

Stunned, not believing what was happening, all she knew to do was head back to the Cottage. Back to her home. Her work. Her everything — that might not be hers for too much longer.

Her mind whirling and her heart feeling like a twenty-pound weight in her chest, she worked to put one foot in front of the other to get there. Once she did finally arrive, however, she had no clue what she was going to do.

Lydia smiled as she tugged at her sewing needle, making a final knot on the toddler-size sweater she'd been working on. It hadn't taken her long to complete the secret project, and she had enjoyed every minute of it. After snipping at a few loose threads, she hung the sweater on a small wooden hanger, feeling glad that the idea had come to her and also satisfied with the work she'd done.

On the front side of the off-white sweater she'd loosely knitted, she'd used a strand of pink yarn to embroider the word *Open* across the chest and had crocheted a pink rose, which she attached at the left shoulder area. On the back side of the sweater, she'd used purple yarn to stitch the word *Closed* across the chest and had crocheted a violet rose to match.

She was so pleased with the way her sweater sign had turned out that she could hardly wait for Jessica to return from her errands so she could show her what she'd done.

Better yet . . .

A grin crossed her lips.

Why wait for Jessica to return? Wouldn't it be better for her to see it and be surprised? After all, her friend hadn't looked happy when she'd left hours earlier saying she was going out to run errands. Maybe Lydia's contribution to the Cottage would be just the thing to bring a smile to Jessica's face.

Getting up from the worktable, Lydia straightened the sweater on the hanger as she made her way to the front of the store. She'd never been bold enough to make changes in the shop, but why wouldn't Jessica be delighted with the sweater sign she'd made? It was far cuter and better suited to the Cottage than the old wooden open-and-closed sign that presently hung in the window, wasn't it?

Easily removing the wooden sign from its hook, she laid it on the window ledge before eagerly replacing it with her new sweater signage. Tugging on her creation, correcting its slant to the left, she'd gotten it hanging evenly and just right when the bell chimed over the door. Ready to greet a customer, she noticed it wasn't a customer at all. Rather it was Jessica — who didn't look pleased. She didn't sound that way either.

"What are you doing, Lydia?" she snapped.

"I, uh, I made a new sign — well, a sweater sign — for the window. Do you want to see? I got to thinking it might be a better fit for the shop." Reaching for the sweater, she took down the hanger and dangled it from her hand, giving Jessica a better look, so sure her eyes would light up. So certain she would ahh over it and say how adorable it was and how great it would look in the window.

But Jessica's reaction wasn't anything like the one Lydia had been imagining every minute she'd spent working on the knitted sign.

"So, my aunt Rose's sign — the one that's been there forever — you just took it down?" Jessica narrowed her eyes. "You decided it's not good enough anymore; is that it?"

"Not good enough? Oh, *nee,* Jessica." A sick sensation crept into Lydia's stomach. "I'm sorry. I, uh, I should've talked to you about the sweater sign first. I didn't know the other sign meant so much to you." She reached for the wooden rectangle on the ledge. "I'll put it back up right away, right where it belongs."

"Forget it, Lydia. Forget the sign. Put the sweater up if you want to," Jessica said, spouting out the opposite of what she'd just said. "It doesn't matter. None of it matters. None of it at all."

Lydia hugged both the wooden sign and the sweater sign to her chest, not sure what move to make next. She'd never seen her friend in such a state before. Had never heard her speak quite so harshly to anyone. There had to be something she was mighty upset about. "Jessica, is something wrong?" she dared to ask in the most delicate way she could.

"Ha." Her friend smirked. "When isn't something wrong?" she answered, shaking her head at Lydia as if she were an inexperienced child.

Hours earlier, when Jessica had run out of the shop, Lydia had detected that she seemed flustered and in a hurry to get somewhere. But now that she'd returned,

Jessica seemed even more agitated. Her eyes had a hollow, bewildered look to them, and her lips were taut, as if she was a long way from ever smiling again. Standing next to her, Lydia could feel something negative and angry coming from her — nothing like the Jessica she was used to. "Is there anything you might want to talk about?" she probed gently.

Jessica opened her mouth as if she wanted to say something, but then after staring at Lydia for a moment, she shook her head. "No, Lydia. I don't. I don't want to talk about anything. My head hurts and I —"

So that's what was wrong? Jessica wasn't feeling well?

"If you want to go upstairs and lie down, I can take care of things in the shop and close up," Lydia offered.

"Lying down sure isn't going to help," Jessica snipped, confusing Lydia even more.

"Well, maybe some of your aunt's tea would be *gut*?" It was the only thing left she could think of. "I can get some for you," she said as the bell rang out over the door again.

"You need to take care of the customers, Lydia. I'll take care of myself and everything else, okay?" Jessica said before stomping to the opposite side of the shop.

Taken aback by Jessica's unusual and unexpected harshness, Lydia forced herself to swallow her hurt. Doing just as she was told, as she made her way over to the customers, she tried to focus on her friend instead of herself. Lifting up a prayer for Jessica, she hoped whatever her friend was dealing with would pass quickly — or that she would open up about it soon. Because whatever was going on with Jessica was making her look awful miserable. Seeing her friend that way, Lydia realized how much it pained her heart. How miserable it made her feel too.

Trying to get a moment's peace from her long day, Jessica had only meant to lie down in bed for a minute. Just time enough to gather her strength before doing all her nightly chores. To maybe find an answer to her money problem somewhere in her quiet nest, as a harvest moon shone through her bedroom window and cast a soft glow that seemed otherworldly — without problems or cares, and oh so comforting.

But then without warning, the tears came. And the sobbing.

The only thing was, she wasn't sure what she was crying about most. There were so many things causing her mind to reel — and her heart to break.

Was it the fear of her situation that shattered her most? The sorrow of possibly losing the Cottage? The anger at herself for being so naive and careless, so unorganized?

Or was she feeling bad for the way she'd treated Lydia? What a brat she'd been to her friend all afternoon, hadn't she? But every time she'd looked at Lydia, all she could think was how she might have to let her go soon. And, oh, how she didn't want to disappoint her friend! How she didn't want to turn Lydia's life upside down when she'd just gotten into a routine and seemed so comforted by it.

As it was, Jessica had already been wondering how she would afford to keep Lydia when business slowed down after the holidays. She'd been stewing about that, trying to come up with possible solutions. But now with the extra bill . . . it might be even sooner that she'd have to let her go. And then what would she do? If she lost Lydia, she still didn't know enough about knitting and quilting to run the shop herself. Not to mention, the Cottage wouldn't seem the same without Lydia and her smile lighting up the shop each day.

And then, Derek. She'd tried to act like all was good when he'd called earlier in the day, but somehow — someway — he knew otherwise. He'd kept asking if she was all right. She wished he'd just quit asking because there was no way she was going to load him down with her troubles. He couldn't be her go-to guy forever. He had a life of his own to live.

And she needed to carry on with her life as well.

Whatever that meant . . . whatever that looked like . . . however she was going to do that.

Her brain was such a jumble of thoughts and her heart such a mess of emotions that at first she barely heard Cole's voice calling to her in the dimness of the bedroom.

"Mom? Mommy?"

Feeling like she'd been caught, she hurriedly wiped the tears from her cheeks. Sitting up in bed, she saw Cole standing in the shadow of the doorway.

"Cole, what are you doing up?"

"I couldn't sleep," he complained, even though he rubbed his eyes sleepily with his fist.

"Did you have a bad dream?" She thought he'd gotten past that phase for the time being. But maybe not . . .

"No." He leaned forward, poking his head into the room. It seemed as if his eyes had adjusted to the dark and he was seeing something he hadn't noticed before. "Mommy, were you crying?"

"No, I wasn't." She sniffed. "I, uh, I just have a little cold," she lied as she plucked a Kleenex from the box on the nightstand and blew her nose as if to validate her words.

Even so, all four feet of him leaned against the doorframe as he stood staring at her.

"Cole, you need to go back to bed and go to sleep. In fact, we both need to go to sleep."

"But you don't have your pajamas on," he countered.

She imagined she did look odd to him, lying in bed, wearing the same clothes she'd had on all day.

"I was taking a rest before I sleep." That was the truth at least.

"Oh."

"Cole, if you didn't have a bad dream, what are you doing up?"

"You forgot to say my prayers with me again."

"I did?" Jessica bit her lip. She wasn't doing much of anything right lately, was she?

Cole nodded. "Did you forget to say your prayers too?"

"Well, I, uh . . ."

"We can say our prayers together," he suggested, a hint of hopefulness in his voice.

Her lips twitched at the sweetness of his suggestion. If one thing was certain in her uncertain world, she could always count on her son to bring out a smile in her. "Yes, I suppose we could."

She flipped back the covers the rest of the way, ready to get up and take him to his room. But he took her act as an invitation and flew into the room, hopping straight into bed with her. Sitting alongside her, he pulled the blanket up to their waists, tucking it around them.

"Should we say our prayers now before we forget again?" he asked.

"That sounds like a good idea."

He put his hands together and pointed them upward. Then he glanced over at her to make sure she had followed suit. She quickly clasped her hands, holding them to her chest. Eyeing her, Cole nodded his approval.

"Ready?" he asked.

"You start."

He giggled. "No, you."

"All right." She drew in a breath and was about to acquiesce when he stopped her.

"No," he blurted. "I changed my mind. We should say the words together."

"Okay, on the count of three. One."

"Two." He smiled.

"Three."

"Now I lay me down to sleep. I pray the Lord my soul to keep," they prayed, their voices blending together in the dark. "Let angels sleep by my side, and bless the day when I rise."

"God bless Mommy," Cole said.

"And God bless Cole," Jessica said.

"Amen." As they finalized the prayer in unison, quick as a rabbit slipping underground, Cole slid down and snuggled deeper under the blankets.

"Cole, you can't sleep here tonight."

He popped open one eye. "But you sleep with me when I'm sick or scared."

"I'm not really *sick* sick, and I'm not scared. Everything's fine, sweetie," she fibbed again.

But he closed his eyes tight and lay perfectly still, which she knew was no easy feat for him, and pretended he hadn't heard her. Pretended that he had already drifted off to sleep. Glancing down at him, she didn't have the heart or the energy to budge him.

Instead, she looked at her hands, still folded together, still pointed to the heavens. Oh . . . Cole was right, wasn't he? She had been forgetting to pray for a while now. Well, not forgetting exactly. She just hadn't wanted to. Didn't know what to say to God. Didn't feel close to Him. Not when He kept taking things that she loved away from her.

Although . . . She squeezed her already-clasped hands. Maybe this would be a good time to start a conversation with Him after all.

Closing her eyes, she bowed her head and waited. Waited for thoughts. Waited for some kind of feeling — for anything to come. But all she felt was the emptiness inside her. Somehow, like always, He felt distant from her. Way too far away.

Chapter Twenty-Two

"I'm sorry to call you so early in the morning, Liz," Lydia said as she stood shivering inside the unheated phone shanty, trying to control her chattering teeth.

In the past few months, she'd walked across the street to the shanty to make calls more times than she ever had in the entire eight years she'd lived on Quarterhorse Road.

Most of the calls had been to one of the town's driving services to secure rides to work. None of them had ever been to Liz. Even though her friend had given her a number to call a while ago, Lydia had never had a reason to use it. Actually, she still didn't know if she had a good reason for calling Liz. She'd been debating that fact all through her restless night of sleep.

"No problem at all, Lydia," Liz replied, sounding completely awake and even glad that she'd phoned. "What's going on?"

"I'm not sure —" her voice quavered mostly from cold, but from worry as well — "but something doesna seem right with Jessica."

There was a silent pause on the other end of the phone. "Not right? Do you mean you think she might be sick or something?"

"I really can't tell." Jessica's physical well-being had been a concern of Lydia's from the start, especially from the way she had been acting. Seeming so out of sorts, as if she'd gotten bad news that she hadn't been expecting. "All I know," Lydia explained, "is that ever since she went out to run errands the other day, she hasn't seemed the same. She came back to the Cottage in the worst of moods, as if something had gone *verra* wrong. She wasna too pleased with me, neither, and had some sharp words to share."

Of course, Lydia never expected that Jessica wouldn't ever have problems with the work she was doing. Nothing about her or anyone else was perfect; that was for sure. But generally if Jessica did have an issue with anything — as she'd had with the sweater sign — she had an easygoing way of letting Lydia know what she needed to do or change.

"Are you sure you're not being overly

sensitive?"

It was a fair question, and something Lydia had wondered as well. She sighed as she pondered the idea again. "Well . . . *nee. Nee,* I really don't think so. I've got a feeling inside me that she's dealing with something upsetting. And it's not just with me she seems distant and preoccupied. It's with the customers too. Oh!" She remembered the other peculiarity she'd noticed. "She keeps getting out Post-it notes to write things down, then after she does, she crumples them all up and sticks them in her pocket."

Lydia had been wishing, of course, that Jessica would toss a few of those yellow squares into the wastebasket so she could retrieve one and see what was written on it. But so far, Jessica had kept her scribblings to herself.

"Do you think she might be having a problem with Derek? Maybe she was — I don't know — writing out what she wanted to say to him?" Liz sounded as if she was grasping at straws.

"Nee," Lydia replied readily. "I don't think it has anything to do with Derek. When he stops by the shop I can see how she tries to act as normal as normal can be. But then when he leaves, it's like she lets down again

and gets more withdrawn."

"Hmm . . ." was all Liz had to say.

"*Jah.* That's what I've been thinking to myself too — hmm." She paused as a slight wind rattled the tiny window of the shanty. "The truth is, Liz, I didna want to ask her about anything by myself. I sure don't want her to think I'm being nosy about her or her business. But I am worried about her, and I was thinking that, well, maybe —"

"We could talk to her together?"

Liz's response brought on such a surge of relief that Lydia immediately felt like a weight had been lifted from her chest. "*Jah. Jah.* That's exactly what I've been thinking. Since we're supposed to get together for a knitting session later today, I thought it would be the perfect time," she said, hoping Jessica didn't back out of their plans. "That's why I called you."

"That's a great idea, Lydia. When we meet, we'll have plenty of time to get a feel for things with her and plenty of time to talk. I'm glad you gave me a heads-up."

"Hopefully we can find out something and be of help."

"Absolutely," Liz said, and Lydia could practically feel her friend nodding affirmatively over the phone. "So I'll see you later at the shop."

"*Jah,* you have a good day, Liz."

"And you get back inside your house. I can hear your teeth chattering all the way over the phone."

"I will for sure." Lydia smiled. She definitely needed to finish getting ready for work. Her ride would be at her house any minute.

"And, Lydia?" Liz said before Lydia could say good-bye.

"*Jah?*"

"You're not being nosy at all. You're being concerned and a good friend."

"*Danke,* Liz." She instantly warmed. "So are you."

Even though Lydia had felt relieved after sharing her concerns with Liz earlier in the morning, she'd struggled all day being around Jessica at the shop. Trying to act normal when Jessica wasn't acting that way at all, and when Lydia knew that she and Liz were going to approach Jessica, made for an uncomfortable day on the job.

She thought she'd feel better when Liz arrived at the Cottage. Yet as she sat alongside Liz at the worktable, knitting and chatting — and plotting some too — while they waited for Jessica to get Cole settled with Marisa, her stomach was still churning in anticipation.

She didn't know whether to be glad or even more anxious when Jessica finally made her way down the stairs with her knitting bag.

"Are you two talking about Mrs. Grisham's accident?"

"Virginia had an accident?" Liz's needles came to a halt. Lydia looked up in surprise as well.

"That's what Marisa was just telling me," Jessica confirmed with a nod. "She overheard some ladies at Hair and Now talking about it. Apparently Mrs. Grisham fell down a flight of steps at her house and —"

"She fell — or someone pushed her?" Liz interrupted, then quickly put a hand over her mouth. "Oh, did I just say that? I'm sorry. That's terrible of me."

Lydia pretended she hadn't heard Liz's comment. "Is she all right?" she asked Jessica.

"Thankfully she didn't hit her head." Jessica laid her tote on the table. "But it sounds like she broke her left wrist and sprained her right one."

"Oh, that's not *gut* at all," Lydia replied.

"I guess she won't be doing any knitting for a while," Liz added.

Jessica's brow creased. "No, I suppose not."

Lydia thought after sharing the news, Jessica would settle into a chair and get knitting on her scarf, but instead she remained standing. "I feel like we should make a Secret Stitches run," she said, placing her hands on her hips.

"For Virginia Grisham?" Liz looked shocked. "Really, Jessica? After what she pulled on you?"

"Liz, I'm the one who initially made the mistake with her," Jessica easily admitted, to which Liz shook her finger.

"And the woman could've been more forgiving about it."

"Well, but . . ." Jessica stammered. "I don't need any more bad karma."

"*More* bad karma? What do you mean? Is something wrong?" Liz spoke up and Lydia's heart beat faster, waiting for Jessica's reply.

Jessica gave a quick shake of her head, her hair swinging back and forth. "Did I say *more*? I didn't mean to say *more*. I'm just thinking Mrs. Grisham's got to feel lost not being able to knit and —"

"Yeah, not being able to knit and manipulate other people's lives," Liz quipped.

"Look, Liz, I know you're just being

363

protective on my behalf, and it's really sweet of you, but —"

"And on your aunt's behalf too." Liz arched a defiant brow. "Rose always gave Virginia great discounts on everything in the shop."

"Because she was a loyal customer," Jessica countered.

"But I guess her loyalty only goes so far, huh?"

Feeling like she was caught between the forces of two opposing winds, Lydia had kept silent while her friends bantered, but now she spoke up. "Actually, I was hoping we could get some knitting done and catch up with each other tonight."

Although she felt mighty bad about Mrs. Grisham's accident, she was far more concerned about Jessica at the moment. She didn't want another day to go by without having the chance to speak to her — with Liz by her side, of course. Liz, who with a sideways glance let Lydia know she hadn't forgotten the pact they'd made earlier in the day.

"I think that sounds like a good idea," Liz chimed in.

"But, Liz —" Jessica held up her hands — "you're the one who got me started on the secret missions. You've got me hooked and now you're bailing? Plus, call me crazy, but I do feel bad for the woman."

"But we don't even have anything to take to her house," Liz contended. Yet even as Liz said the words, Lydia could hear how her tone was already beginning to soften. How she was beginning to wane, not protesting as staunchly as she had before.

"Actually, I remember seeing a really pretty greenish-blue prayer shawl in Aunt Rose's treasure chest," Jessica said, and Lydia knew just the one she was speaking of. "I thought we could bring that. Unless — well, if neither of you truly want to go, I can run to her house by myself." Jessica glanced between the two of them. "She doesn't live far from here."

Watching Jessica stand there, tapping her foot, Lydia knew there was no way her friend was going to settle in and knit. It was almost as if Jessica knew that Lydia and Liz had an intervention in store for her, and she wasn't about to sit down for it.

Which made Lydia give in before Liz did.

"*Nee,* Jessica. There's no way you're going on your own. I made a pair of slippers the other day and haven't put them out on display yet. They come up over the ankles and have decorative buttons on them. They're also a nice blue and very cute. We can add those to the package," she said as she turned to Liz, giving her an apologetic shrug. So much for their plan, she wanted to say.

Liz conceded with a shrug of her own. "Hmm. Well, I guess Virginia Grisham is in luck then, ladies. I just happen to have a box of Godiva chocolates in my car," she said with a tight-lipped smile. "I bought them for a coworker's birthday tomorrow, but whatever. I can always pick up another box."

Fifteen minutes later, after putting away their knitting and gathering up their gifts of hope, the three of them were in Jessica's car, headed for Virginia Grisham's house. Lydia had scooted into the backseat as usual, letting Liz sit in the front in case she needed to help Jessica navigate. But as they headed out on Route 39, Lydia noticed Jessica seemed comfortable with where she was going. However, she didn't seem all that relaxed about the rain, which all at once had begun to turn to slush and ice.

"Maybe this wasn't such a good idea after all." Jessica sighed, and Lydia's heart went out to her. Here she was trying to do something nice in her time of stress, and the weather surely wasn't cooperating.

"Do we have much farther to go?" she asked.

"Not at this point," Liz spoke up.

Jessica glanced at her copilot. "But we still have to get back home," she said, sounding anxious. "I hope the weather doesn't get much worse."

Against the silence in the car, the flecks of ice seemed almost deafening as they pummeled the windshield, making Lydia feel as uneasy as Jessica had sounded. She was wishing she could think of something funny or heartening to say to put them all at ease when their talkative friend came through.

"I have some good news for you all," Liz announced. "I was going to tell you both during our knitting session tonight."

"I could use some good news about now," Jessica muttered.

"Me too," Lydia agreed.

"Well, then, guess who Daniel and I saw when we were out driving through the park the other day?" Liz chirped.

"Who?" both Lydia and Jessica asked together.

"Ryan Fletcher with his dad, sitting on a park bench."

"Jah?" Lydia smiled, thinking Liz had picked the perfect moment to share with them.

"So he's home from overseas?" Jessica asked. "Did he look all right?"

"He had a bandage wrapped around his head, but it looked like he and Norm were enjoying the time together. I noticed they were both smiling over something."

"Oh, that's great to hear. It really is."

Lydia noticed a happy lilt in Jessica's voice that had been missing for days.

"And, girls, just to let you know," Liz further reported, "Ryan was wearing the scarf we left on Norm's doorstep."

"Aww . . ." Even with her coat on, Lydia could feel goose bumps popping up on her arms. "That was quite an adventurous night for me." She laughed.

"For all of us." Jessica gave a quick glance into the rearview mirror and grinned at her. "I thought for sure we were going to get caught that night with all of those lights bursting on every few seconds and —" Suddenly she straightened in the driver's seat. "Wait! Did you hear that?"

"Hear what?" Liz asked.

"Like a smack or a thump or a —"

Jessica didn't have to describe the noise any further. The clunky sound reverberated through the car as the vehicle began to shake and wobble, leaving their driver with no choice but to pull over to the side of the road.

"You've got to be kidding me," Jessica sighed after bringing the SUV to a complete stop. "A flat tire? Really? Tonight of all nights?"

"I hate to tell you, but that's what it sounds like," Liz confirmed.

"Does it feel that way too?" Lydia asked.

"I'm afraid so. But just to be sure . . ." Jessica unsnapped her seat belt, got a flashlight out of the glove box, and proceeded to get out of the car to check the tires.

Within a minute, she was back in the car, giving them her report. "It's the left rear tire," she said as she brushed ice crystals from her hair.

"I'm sorry to say, honey, I haven't changed a tire in eons," Liz said.

"And I've never changed one," Lydia admitted. "But I could try."

"No — there's no way we're changing a tire in this weather and in the dark, too." Jessica shook her head. "I'm calling AAA."

With that said, Lydia and Liz sat quietly while Jessica made the call for help. As the ice continued to pelt the windshield, Lydia hoped they wouldn't be stuck where they were once the tire was fixed.

"Obviously they have a lot of people needing roadside assistance tonight," Jessica told them once she hung up and shifted around in her seat to face the two of them. "We could be sitting here for quite some time. I certainly hadn't intended to spend this much on babysitting tonight." She sighed. "I need to start cutting back."

"Well, at least we're dry," Liz offered.

"And warm," Lydia added in.

Despite their positivity, Jessica let out a disgusted grunt. "I'm sorry I even suggested this outing, ladies."

"Jessica, it's not a big deal." Liz reached over and patted their friend's shoulder. "We'll get the tire fixed, get to the Grishams', and be home in no time."

"Yeah, hours from now," Jessica replied glumly. "I don't even know if I have a decent spare. Oh, I hope I don't have to buy any new tires." She groaned. "Just one more thing I don't need right now."

"One more thing?" Liz asked. "Have there, uh, been other things lately?"

Noticing how Liz had taken Jessica's comment as an opportunity to get Jessica to open up, as they'd hoped to do earlier in their knitting session, Lydia followed her lead. "*Jah,* because we're really good people to share things with," she said and even boldly clicked on the overhead dome light — which unfortunately caused all of them to squint and blink until their eyes adjusted. "If you need to talk, that is," she added.

"And there are lots of times we need to talk things out," Liz joined in.

"*Jah,* definitely, and I have to say this could be a mighty good time since it seems like something has been going on with you lately, Jessica. Something you might want to share," Lydia prompted. "Of course, you can tell us it's none of our business, but —"

"You are our business, Jess," Liz said sweetly but firmly.

"*Jah,* you are." Lydia nodded.

The entire time she and Liz had been speaking, their friend's mouth had been gaping open as if she was speechless. But now she pursed her lips together and waved a finger between Lydia's spot in the back of the car and Liz's seat in the front. "Have you two possibly been practicing this back-and-forth thing you have going on? Because it really sounds like you have."

"Oh . . ." Liz hemmed as she held up her thumb and forefinger, pinching them together. "Maybe just a little bit."

"*Jah,* when you were upstairs getting Cole settled in with Marisa," Lydia confessed.

"Hmm. I see." Jessica bit her lip. "Well, I

have to say . . ." A grin began to slowly show itself, lighting up her face. "I think this is the first time I've truly smiled in days. You're both so sweet. But really, guys, though it's nice of you to ask, I don't want to talk about what's going on. It's something I need to work out for myself, and no one else can help," she said, to which Liz instantly clucked.

"You never know unless you open up and spill the beans." Liz crossed her arms over her chest.

"*Jah,* spilling beans can be a *gut* thing."

"And since we're going to be sitting here for a while . . ."

"A long while from the sounds of it," Lydia added to Liz's comment.

"During which time you two are going to keep badgering me?" Jessica snickered.

"Uh, yes. Something like that." Liz gave her an assured smile.

"Well, knowing how relentless the two of you are —" Jessica held up her hands — "I suppose I give. But I'm telling you, my situation is not anything you can help me with because the thing is I, uh, messed up. Big-time. I received a bill a few days ago. Well, it's worse than a bill, actually. It's a final notice on the property taxes for the Cottage and —"

"Oh, thank You, Lord." Lydia's hand flew to her chest. "That's such a relief!"

"It is?" Jessica appeared understandably confused. "How can you say that?"

"Because we thought you might've received bad news about your health. That you might be sick," Lydia explained. "We were worried when you were acting so different."

"But it's just a money problem?" Liz asked.

"*Just* a money problem?" Jessica sounded slightly indignant.

"Oh! I didn't mean to say it like that," Liz backpedaled. "Trust me, I've had some financial issues recently and they've been very worrisome and stressful. But maybe, well, let me think. Maybe I can figure out some way that I could lend you —"

"No." Before Liz could even finish, Jessica halted her suggestion with a wave of her hand. "Thank you, but no. I just need to come up with a few thousand dollars by the middle of next month to make things right, and I'm going to figure it out," she said, sounding confident. At least until she added the last part of her thought. "I just don't know how yet. So, anyway . . . if I've seemed like my mind has been on something else this week, it has. I still can't believe how I messed up. How I was so unaware of all the costs involved with the shop."

"Don't be too hard on yourself," Liz admonished. "You're just starting out in the business, and it's a huge undertaking. Something totally new to you. Why, I've been selling real estate for years and years and lately, I'm barely having any success with it at all — which has been completely puzzling to me," she said, tugging at a spike of hair at the back of her head. "Not that this is about me, of course. It's about the Cottage."

"Which is my responsibility," Jessica replied firmly. "I own it and the problems that come with it."

"You're mighty right," Lydia told her. "You do own the Cottage, but it's a very special place where I feel blessed to be spending my waking hours each day. It's become like a second home to me. And if the shop is in trouble, I don't want to stand by and do nothing. I want to help."

"She's right, Jessica," Liz joined in. "The Cottage is too special to us. You're too special to us. No ifs, ands, or buts about it," she said with a degree of finality. "You have to let us help you."

"I can't tell you how much hearing that from both of you means to me. You really can't know." Jessica's voice croaked. "But honestly, beyond being moral support for me, I don't know what you can do."

As they all sat silently considering the situation, Jessica's phone buzzed in her hand.

"It's AAA," she said, glancing down at the screen. "They'll be here in fifteen to twenty minutes."

"Yeah?" Liz shifted in her seat, sitting up straighter. "Well, good. I'd say that's just long enough for us to come up with a plan for the Cottage."

Jessica tilted her head, appearing touched but doubtful. "Liz, really, like I said, I appreciate your concern — and yours, too, Lydia — but if I haven't come up with a plan in the last few days, then I —"

"I'm thinking I could teach some extra classes," Lydia interrupted her, scooting forward till she was hugging the back of the front seats. "More classes would bring in more money."

"And when could you possibly do that, Lydia?" Jessica asked. "In your sleep? You already do so much at the shop."

"I don't mind, Jessica. I'm sure I could find the time."

"It's great of you to offer, Lydia, and I know our customers enjoy your classes, but the other part of the problem is I need the money more quickly than that."

"I know!" Liz snapped her fingers. "We could have a sale. It could be soon after Thanksgiving when people are buying things like crazy. It could be . . . a sidewalk sale."

"In December?" Jessica's forehead crinkled.

"It's the perfect time to have one," Liz said, her enthusiasm boundless as usual. "We have an endless stream of tourists visiting town then. Oh!" She raised a finger in the air. "And we could schedule the sale on a day when there's a busload of women coming from a senior facility. You know the buses will be coming to Sugarcreek nonstop all during the weeks before Christmas."

Lydia thought Liz's suggestion was far better than hers. A special sale could make extra money in a day — not weeks. But she was uncertain about the sale being held outside, which Jessica seemed to be having a problem with as well.

"I don't know, Liz. It'll be cold and it could be icy like tonight," Jessica wavered. "That may not be the best idea when it comes to the elderly ladies and their walkers."

"Could we have the sale indoors?" Lydia suggested. "And maybe call it . . . I don't know . . ." She tried to think.

"How about Santa's Cottage Sale?" Jessica said, seeming to get into the spirit of things. "But then, what would we sell to make extra money? I mean, besides the regular things we sell," she asked, which happened to be the same thing Lydia was wondering too.

"Well, we could . . ." Liz paused, tapping her finger to her lips. "Sell things we've made," she volunteered, which caused Jessica to snort.

"Maybe things you and Lydia have made," Jessica said. "Maybe even some of the hand-knit sweaters and vests Rose had tucked away in her cedar chests. But as far as anything I've made, I'm fairly certain there won't be too many prospective buyers."

"That's not so, Jessica," Lydia spoke up. "What about your scarves?"

"My lumpy, bumpy scarves? You've got to be kidding." Jessica shook her head.

"No, I'm not. With the pretty sparkly bows, they're adorable." Lydia turned to Liz. "What did you call them?"

"Shabby chic, and I couldn't agree more." Liz clapped her hands. "And while you're making more scarves, Jessica, now that my kitchen is back in order, I'll start baking my famous red velvet cakes and freezing them.

They look so very Christmassy, and I'll have you know, the cake won a baking contest at church one holiday season. Oh, and that reminds me — Christmas cookies!" Liz's eyes widened. "We can sell cakes and cookies, too, by the box or individual ones for a dollar apiece. I love making Christmas cookies."

"We can also sell quilts," Lydia suggested.

"Oh, that's a great idea, Lydia." Liz gave her a thumbs-up. "Quilts are huge moneymakers. Huge."

"Okay, you two were beginning to sell me on Aunt Rose's sweaters and cakes and even scarves, I suppose, but quilts?" Jessica asked dubiously. "Now we're also going to whip up a few quilts? I really don't see that happening."

"Not us." Lydia shook her head.

"Then who?" Jessica frowned.

"Don't you worry about it," she told her friend. "I know just the 'whos' who can do the job." She smiled.

"And if anyone knows how to advertise the sale online, you do, Jessica. Which means you've got to let us make a go of this," Liz insisted.

"We have to at least try." Lydia nodded at Jessica, hoping against hope she'd say yes.

"Well?" Liz cocked her head, waiting for

Jessica's final approval. "What do you think?"

"Well, I . . . what I think is . . ." Jessica glanced at Liz, then at Lydia, then back to Liz and Lydia once more, while the two of them waited for her answer. "Honestly, I don't know how to say this."

"Don't say no to the sale, Jessica. Please," Lydia implored her.

"Oh, it's not that. It's just . . ." Jessica took a deep breath. "It all just hit me right now."

"What just hit you, honey?" Liz leaned closer. "The money? The situation?" she asked, her voice more subdued than usual.

"No." Jessica shook her head. "The two of you. Your kindness. And your caring. The way you love Aunt Rose's Cottage like I do." Her voice quaked with emotion. "For the longest while, I've been so caught up in myself and my hurt, hating that God kept taking things — the people I loved — away from me. I haven't been praying to Him or talking to Him at all. I just haven't felt like He was there. Or that He cared. But now . . ." Jessica looked down at her hands, then back up, and Lydia knew she was trying to get control of herself before speaking again. "Like I said, it just hit me that all the while I wasn't thinking of Him, He was thinking of me. I know He was because He sent you — both of you — into my life. Giving me a new family, new people to care about, just when I needed them most."

As the tears trickled down Jessica's cheeks, Lydia tried to control her own. Reaching out, she patted her friend's shoulder, knowing that despite what any of them might think at times, *Gott* was always present, always at work in their lives. That was His promise. "You mean the same to us, Jessica," she said. "*Verra* much you do."

Liz wiped at her eyes. "So, I'm guessing —" She paused to clear her throat. "I'm guessing that this, uh, means you'll agree for us to do the sale with you?"

Jessica chuckled faintly. "Oh, definitely. Yes. Now I see the light."

As she said the words, eerily, a soft light began to filter into the car. A light that grew brighter and whiter with each passing moment, until finally it filled the car from back to front.

In sync with one another, they turned their heads to see exactly what Lydia expected to see. The AAA truck had pulled up behind Jessica's SUV, its headlights gleaming through the rear window.

"Actually, I think we've all seen the light," Liz quipped and Lydia couldn't have agreed more as the three of them laughed through their tears.

CHAPTER TWENTY-THREE

Lydia was feeling quite sheepish as she stood holding open her front door for Jonas. But she was also feeling very much appreciative as he carried yet another one of his chairs into her house and placed it on the periphery of her sitting room.

"That's the last of them, Lydia." He stood in the center of the room, brushing his hands together. "I wish I had more chairs for you to borrow, but even if I did, I don't know where you'd put them."

He was right, of course. He'd placed a few of his chairs in the extra bedroom, where her pedal sewing machine was set up. He'd added a couple to the chairs she already had in the kitchen. At that point, they'd decided to leave the rest of his wooden seats in the sitting room, so the ladies from church could rearrange them however worked out best for their quilting session.

"*Jah.* It's a bit of a tight fit in here, isn't

it?" she agreed, glancing around the room.

Tight — and much too warm.

She'd made a huge fire in the fireplace a half hour earlier, hoping to make her home as cozy and welcoming for her guests as possible. Jeb and Kit certainly seemed to be enjoying the heat, curled up together in front of the hearth. Yet she was fanning her face with her hand as she turned to her neighbor to thank him. Once again.

"I cannot say it enough, Jonas. I'm mighty indebted to you," she said sincerely. "Here I remembered to gather up all the material and threads from the Cottage for the quilts. And I remembered all the ingredients I needed for my potato soup and for the friendship bread I made. But then I forgot all about chairs." She put her hands on her hips and shook her head. "I sure don't know where I thought everyone was going to sit to quilt and eat."

Jonas's eyes twinkled as he laughed, not seeming concerned by her oversight at all. "*Jah,* well, there you go. Sometimes we forget the big things when we're focusing on all the little ones," he said.

"You know, you're exactly right."

"You can relax now." He took a pair of work gloves from his coat pocket and held them in his hands. "All looks *gut* in here,

Lydia, and smells *verra gut* too." He turned and sniffed toward the kitchen. "Friendship bread, eh? I thought I smelled cinnamon."

"Can I get you some? A little thank-you for your help? I can spoon out soup for you to eat later too," she offered, happy to have a way to repay him — though she realized what a small payment it would be. After all, not once that morning had he ever made her feel he'd been inconvenienced or put out by helping her. In fact, he'd acted just the opposite.

As she started for the kitchen, eager to put a nice parcel together for her neighbor, he reached out and touched her arm, stopping her. "*Nee,* Lydia. You have guests you're going to need to be feeding and a long day ahead of you. Save what you have for the ladies. You women need all the nourishment you can get."

"Oh, and you don't?" She put a hand to her waist and grinned. "Especially after hauling every chair you own from your house to mine?"

"Don't ya worry." He laughed. "Big strappin' guys like me don't get worn out from carrying a couple of chairs."

She chuckled at his description, having become more accustomed to his teasing. After all, in reality Jonas Hershberger was not exactly the big and strapping type. Rather, he was muscular and fit-looking, and strong, but a few inches shy of six feet. He had a presence when he walked into a room but didn't seem to feel the need to dominate any person in it. To her way of thinking, if anything was big about her neighbor it was his heart.

"Well, that's good to know. But I have to tell you, it was more than a couple of chairs you moved."

He shrugged off her reminder.

"You're *verra gut* to me, Jonas," she said, suddenly overwhelmed with gratitude. "I hope you know I've thanked the Lord for your kindness many times."

All at once she felt embarrassed that she'd said too much. She hadn't known those words — the truth — were going to come out of her. But they had, and now she wondered if she'd made Jonas feel awkward as well. She was relieved when he gave her one of his relaxed smiles.

"Some people make it easy to be nice, Lydia," he said simply. "That's how it is for me with you." He looked into her eyes as though he didn't have anything to hide. Before she could even think of a way to reply, he took a step forward, toward the fireplace. "C'mon, Jeb." He clapped his hands. "We've got to get going, boy. We need to get out of here before the woman work begins."

Jeb rose slowly, then took a moment to stretch out his hind legs. As he sauntered toward his master, Lydia had to smile at the way the well-trained dog kept glancing back at Kit as if he wished he could stay.

By the time she walked Jonas and his pup to the front door, a horse-drawn buggy was making its way up her drive.

"Good timing," Jonas said. "It looks like your first buggy of quilters is just arriving."

"*Jah,* you're right. That's *verra gut* timing."

"Have a great day with the ladies, Lydia." Her neighbor tipped his hat.

"You have a great day too, Jonas. I'll get the chairs back to you as soon as I can."

"No need to think about it now." He waved as he and Jeb descended the porch steps and headed toward his house. "We'll work it out later."

"Okay, *danke.*" She waved back and then folded her arms over her chest, bracing herself against the chilled air and for what was to come.

Ever since the night she'd sat in Jessica's car and they'd come up with the idea for the sale, she'd been preparing for this day

— first in her mind, then for real.

Her initial task had been to approach the ladies from church to see who might be willing to share their talents. Naturally, she felt timid about reaching out to them since she hadn't been friends with them for all that long. But she needn't have been anxious. After she explained about the Cottage's situation, they'd all been willing, even eager, to help without question or hesitation.

The next item of business had been to name a date, and then to gather all the materials they'd need for such a large number of quilters. After that, planning out the snacks and sweets was a must, as she'd mentioned to Jonas, and took some doing. She'd never entertained such a large group in her home before except for the few times she and Henry had been designated to host church.

She'd spent so much time organizing the get-together that she hadn't thought what it would be like actually hosting it. Now that the first buggy was arriving, she felt a twinge of nervousness tighten her stomach. She hoped she'd thought of everything that would make for a comfortable, productive day for the ladies. She hoped she could say the right things to let them know how much they were appreciated.

Standing on her porch, she rubbed her shoulders and all at once remembered another time when ladies were making their way up her driveway. Jessica and Liz. Sneaking up the gravel path on foot in the dark of night. How the memory made her smile! How much had happened in her life since then.

"Thank You for bringing me this far, Lord," she whispered. "I truly don't think You brought me this far to leave me now, did You?" The thought made her relax as she watched her church friends spill out of the black buggy.

"Lydia!" Ruth Keim waved up to her.

"Hi, Ruth! Hi, Abigail!" She waved. "Oh, Sarah, it's so good to see you, too."

As the Keim buggy emptied, several other carriages caravanned up her driveway. Soon over a dozen women and just as many puffs of breath in the cold air could be seen as the ladies greeted her and each other in the warmest way.

A few of the women carried plates of baked goods, others a covered dish or two. Between the ladies and the extra snacks, her modest home and kitchen filled up quickly.

"It was so nice of you to bring things," Lydia said as she bustled around the kitchen trying to organize all that they'd brought to share.

"I don't think we'll starve as we're quilting, do you?" Abigail spoke up. "It looks like we could be here for days."

"Ain't that the truth?" Lydia laughed. "Would anyone like some friendship bread or sweets?" she asked, glancing around, going into the sitting room, trying to make sure everyone heard her over their individual conversations. "Or I also have coffee or tea?"

"We should probably get down to business instead. Don't ya think?" Ruth suggested. "We can always visit and snack in between getting our work done."

Lydia looked over the group of women, who all seemed to be nodding in agreement. "Well, *jah*. We can do that for sure," she said.

"You just need to tell us what you want us to do," Sarah said. "Or more like how you want us to do it."

At the Cottage, the largest class Lydia had ever been in charge of contained seven knitters. This time she had fourteen faces looking to her for direction. The good news was, they were all adept at their quilting craft.

"First, ladies, I just want to say *danke*. *Danke* for coming today." She looked out at the women, some standing, others sitting, around her living room. "As I mentioned to you all previously, the Cottage is in a bit of financial trouble. We really hope and pray that the Santa Cottage Sale will be a way to get the shop on its feet for the new year. Your quilts could mean all the difference in making that hope a reality." She paused before adding the rest that Jessica had asked her to say. "But I have to tell you all, Jessica doesna want you to go unpaid for your kindness and help."

She noticed many confused expressions and furrowed brows upon the delivery of that message. "She would like you and your families to share in any money the quilts bring in."

With that, feet shifted, backs straightened, and there was a lot of glancing at one another before Ruth spoke up. "We're just here to help a neighbor, Lydia. You know that."

"*Jah,* it's not for us we're doing this," another woman said, to which a dozen heads nodded assent.

"Well . . ." Lydia tilted her head at the group. "What about discounts? Would you consider a discount on Cottage purchases as a repayment for your work?"

"There's no need for discounts neither," Sarah said. "Or any kind of repayment. We wouldn't be here if we didn't want to be."

"I know." Lydia's voice came out in a hush as she found herself wishing she hadn't missed out on so many years of friendship with these women. But at least she knew them now, and she was grateful for that in many ways. "Everything you've said —" she smiled — "it's all exactly what I told Jessica you would say."

"You can also tell her we'll be there to check out her Santa Cottage Sale," an older woman affirmed.

"We sure will," Abigail said. "But right now we better get cutting instead of just chatting. I can't wait to see the material you picked out."

"With so many of us here, I think we can manage to come up with three quilts," Ruth added. "What do you ladies think?"

Heads bobbed and lips muttered *"jah"* all around the room.

"Do you have enough material for that many?" a lady standing in the back asked.

"Actually, I do." Lydia had imagined that working on two quilts wouldn't be a problem, but when so many women offered to come and help, she'd hoped for three quilts and had brought home enough material to make that many and more.

"Which pattern do you think Jessica

would like us to use on the quilts?" Ruth asked, causing Lydia to smile.

"Jessica will be happy with whatever design you choose," she answered, deciding not to tell on Jessica, who wouldn't know the difference between a log cabin pattern and a lone star one.

"Well, I guess we can get started then," Ruth said as all the women around her nodded.

"*Jah,* definitely," Lydia said, looking around the room and taking a deep breath.

Of course, with these women she knew exactly what getting started meant. Before dividing into groups, before picking out material, before getting a cup of tea . . . each one of them bowed her head and clasped her hands together, first taking a moment for silent prayer.

CHAPTER TWENTY-FOUR

"It's a pawnshop, Miss. You didn't really expect to get top dollar for your earrings, now did you? Haven't you seen the shows on TV?"

Jessica's cheeks burned as the bearded shop owner peered over the top of his wire-rimmed glasses, seeming annoyed by her attempts at bargaining. But not so irked that he was about to give in to her. "Either you want to turn your rubies over to me at that price or you don't. Simple as that," he said succinctly as he held up her earrings in his hand while she held the worn, empty jewelry box in hers.

"But they mean so much to me," she moaned. All through her ride to the shop, her mind had been flooded with fond recollections attached to the ruby and diamond teardrop-shaped gems. From the moment her aunt had given the jewels to her nearly ten years earlier, they'd claimed a treasured place in her heart. Even wearing the sparkling earrings on her date with Derek recently had somehow made her outfit and the night feel more special and complete. "My aunt Rose gave them to me when I graduated from high school and —"

The owner didn't hesitate to interrupt her. "Like I said —" he held up his hand — "you either want to sell me your earrings at that price or you don't."

Well, of course she didn't want to relinquish her beloved earrings to the man at any price. And especially not at the super-reduced appraisal he was set on. But what was she going to do? The earrings were the only thing of value she owned. She wouldn't have brought them to the pawnshop in the first place if she didn't feel she needed to.

"I, uh . . . guess I . . . Oh, all right," she surrendered with a sigh. *You win,* she wanted to say.

The transaction with the owner was quick, but not at all painless. As she left the pawnshop and trudged down the sidewalk toward her car, she couldn't recall a time in her life when she'd felt more heartsick about having extra cash in her wallet. But it was a sacrifice she'd had to make, wasn't it?

After all, Lydia and her buggy team, as her friend was calling them — a group of

Amish women Jessica didn't even know — were sacrificing their time and talents to make quilts for the sale. Liz was spending a huge amount of energy and days to make all kinds of Christmas cookies and cakes to sell.

Besides working social media to incite interest about the sale — and knitting as many lumpy, bow-covered scarves as she could up until the sale date — Jessica felt like she had to do something more. Not only for the Cottage, but she had to think of Cole, too. He would be expecting gifts from Santa under the tree come Christmas morning. And with it being the first Christmas without his Grand Rose, Jessica knew he'd be missing his great-aunt's love and thoughtful gifts as well. They both would.

I still miss you every day, Aunt Rose!

Burying her glove-bare hands in her pockets and nestling her chin into the collar of her coat to ward off the cold, she strode over the last blocks to her car, lost in thoughts of past Christmases with her aunt. She was so caught up in the past that she practically leapt off the sidewalk when the ear-piercing sound of a police siren screeched behind her.

Her hands flew out of her pockets and up to her ears. Luckily the jarring noise lasted all of a few seconds, after which she turned to see where the sound had been coming from.

Although she should've guessed.

There was Derek behind the wheel of his sheriff's car. He slowed, keeping an even pace with her stride as he rolled down the passenger window and called out to her, "Hey, Jess. What are you doing in this part of town?"

Startled to see him, she tried to maintain her cool. "Me? What are you doing here?"

"Uh, the sheriff's building is just a few blocks west." He pointed over his shoulder. "Remember?"

"Oh, yeah." How could she forget? She'd been so wrapped up in what she was doing, she'd completely forgotten about the possibility of bumping into Derek near his workplace. Not to mention needing to have an explanation ready for him as to why she was in his territory and so far from the Cottage.

Luckily it was close to lunchtime and he seemed to have his mind on other things. He leaned as far into the passenger side of the car as he could, giving her a hopeful look. "Want to get some lunch or something? You look hungry."

"How could I *look* hungry?" She laughed.

"I'm thinking you sound hungry."

"I am. So you want to grab a bite?"

"I shouldn't, Derek. I should get back to the shop."

"You sure have been avoiding me lately." He gave her his most pitiful expression.

"How can you say that? We just went to the tree-lighting ceremony in the park with Cole, didn't we?"

"And with a lot of other people." He jutted his teeth, gazing at her with thoughtful consideration. "I don't know . . . I might have to arrest you just to spend some time with my friend."

She giggled. "Arrest me for what?"

"Uh . . ." He hesitated momentarily. "How about jaywalking?"

"Do they really arrest people for that? And if they do, I haven't even crossed the street yet. Who's to say I'd jaywalk anyway?"

"Well, if that doesn't stick, how about arguing with an officer?" he tried.

"Really? I could get arrested for that, too?"

"Do you really want to find out, ma'am?" he said in his best deep-toned, authoritarian voice.

"I give up." She chuckled at his antics. "I would love to have lunch with you, Deputy. Where's a good place to eat around here?"

"Where's your car?"

397

She pointed up the street, only half a block away. "Right there."

"I'll meet you by your car and then you can follow me."

"Yes, sir, Deputy, sir." She saluted.

"Now you're getting the hang of how these things work, little lady," he teased as he straightened behind the steering wheel and rolled up the car window.

As she retrieved her keys from her purse, Jessica found herself shaking her head at him. Oh, how he could bring out the happy in her. Ever and ever, the man could always make her laugh.

It had been quite some time since Jessica had been to Mick's Diner, but the place didn't seem to have changed at all. Resembling an old, nostalgic diner from the fifties, its neon sign still beckoned in a dazzling way even in the middle of the day, and the structure's high-gloss, candy-apple-red coat of paint shone as it always had. Inside, the oversize black-and-white squares of linoleum flooring also gleamed like the eatery was brand new, as did the metallic soda fountain countertop.

As she and Derek sat on opposite sides of a red vinyl booth, Jessica was actually glad that he'd made the suggestion to come there. Not only did Mick's have the best burgers and fries in the entire country — which she could easily attest to, since she'd downed the first half of her burger in record time — but the diner held a lot of fond memories for her too.

"I need to bring Cole here," she said, smiling at the jukebox in the corner and the high barstools she used to swivel around on. That is, she'd swivel until Aunt Rose would make her stop or her stomach would begin to churn — whichever came first. "I haven't been here in forever. I forgot what a treat it was to come to Mick's as a kid."

"The only time I got to eat here was with you and Rose." Derek smiled as he dragged a fry through a mound of ketchup.

"Oh, yeah. You loved their root beer floats, didn't you?" She nodded toward his ice-filled glass of water. "I'm surprised you didn't order one."

"Too much sugar while I'm on the job. I was afraid I'd fall into a sugar coma." He picked up his glass and took a sip. "But I have to say, those floats were incredible. Almost as incredible as you. I mean, when you're all here — and not distracted by whatever has been going on with you lately," he added.

Her eyes grew wide and her grin did too

as she sat shaking her head at him. "That had to be one of the strangest segues I've ever heard. From root beer floats to me? Interesting . . ."

"Yeah. I guess I'm not as slick as I used to be, am I?" He managed a halfhearted grin himself. "But seriously, Jess, are you going to stop pretending all's well and tell me what's been going on with you? Or are you going to make me guess?"

"Derek, like I told you the other day, I'm fine." She pushed back her plate, unable to look him in the eyes as she answered. Which, of course, he picked up on.

"Mmm." He slid aside his plate as well, then reclined against the back of the booth, crossing both arms over his chest. "I get it, Jess. I know it's been a long time since we've been around each other. But I'm still the same me." He dipped his head toward her. "You can trust me with whatever is going on with you. Unless of course you don't want to share it — and if that's the case . . . well, it doesn't make me feel very good, but I guess that's something I'm going to have to get used to." His jaw tensed right before his brows drew together in an agonized expression.

"Uh-uh-uh, Derek Reeves." She wagged a finger, giving him a knowing smile. "Don't you be doing that to me."

"Doing what?" His expression flipped like a switch, from dejected to innocent. Although he couldn't keep the mischievous twinkle from sparkling in his eyes, proof that she'd caught on to him.

"You know very well what." She cocked a brow and folded her arms on the tabletop, leaning in closer. "That thing where you make me feel like I'm hurting your feelings just so I'll share with you."

"What?" His eyes lit up even more as he gave her a tight-lipped grin. "You're saying I'm trying to manipulate you?"

"Uh-huh."

"By saying I'm here for you?"

"Uh-huh. Because that's the thing, Derek. If I tell you what's going on with me, then —" She caught herself midsentence, cupping her hand over her mouth.

"So there is something going on? I knew it. I knew it," he repeated. "So what *is* up, Jess? You may as well tell me now."

She felt like she'd been acquiescing to men all morning. First giving in to the owner of the pawnshop, and now to Derek. But at least she knew the man sitting across from her cared about her well-being in a way few people did. His eyes appeared non-judgmental and kind as he steadied his gaze on her, making it easier for her to admit her blunder.

"The quick version is, I have a huge bill that needs to be paid, and if it doesn't get paid, I could lose the shop," she said matter-of-factly. "But the good news is, everything is going to be all right because Liz and Lydia came up with the idea of a sidewalk sale."

"At this time of year?" He frowned.

"Well, not really a sidewalk sale." She waved her hand. "It started out as that but morphed into an indoor Santa's Cottage Sale, where basically we're going to be selling everything under the sun. Sweaters, scarves, cakes, cookies, quilts."

Listening to what she had to say, he paused to rub at his chin. She could feel her optimism sinking a bit as he seemed to be taking his time to reply, trying to choose his words carefully. "That sounds like a lot of extra work without being sure of a return," he said finally. "You could've just borrowed the money from me, Jess. You still can."

"No," she said flatly, rearing up in her seat, working to keep her voice calm. "Thank you, Derek. Really, thank you," she said sincerely. "I know you're trying to be a friend, but I can't do that. That's exactly why I never wanted to say anything to you. It's my mistake, my headache. I didn't want to come to you begging for money."

They may have been teasing a few minutes earlier about him pretending to be hurt, but now she could tell he really was. "Begging?" His face caved and his tone changed. "Is that how I make you feel? Like you'd have to beg me for my help?"

"Oh, no. Not at all. You're always so good to me about everything. I just — I didn't want to use you like that," she sputtered.

"*Use* me?"

"No, not use you. Well, not exactly." She could see by the look on his face that she was only making things worse. "Oh, Derek, I'm sorry!" She covered her cheeks with her hands. "I'm saying all the wrong things here, aren't I? And I don't mean any of it the way it's coming out. It's just, I made a mess of something, and I didn't want you to have to get involved with my mess."

"People make messes of things, Jess. They make mistakes."

"Well, living in my skin, sometimes it feels like I make more than my share."

"Trust me," he said softly, "you're not the only one who feels that way at times."

He laid his hand on hers, squeezing it consolingly. Even though she knew he'd probably only meant it as a friendly gesture, she could feel the sensation of his touch all the way up to her cheeks. Reminding her she needed to be honest with him about something else too. She needed to tell him she couldn't keep seeing him so much. Only because every time she was with him, she wanted him more and more. And one of these days she was going to embarrass herself and shock him when she couldn't stop herself from kissing him.

She was relieved when his cell buzzed and he removed his hand from hers, apologizing as he retrieved the phone from his chest pocket. "Sorry, it's work. Gotta get this," he said before answering the call.

"No problem. I'm going to the restroom," she whispered as she gathered up her coat and purse. "Meet you at the cash register when you're finished." She pointed toward the front of the diner, and with one ear already attached to the phone, he nodded in reply.

As she made her way toward the glossy red restroom door, Jessica had to admit to herself that she was glad he'd gotten the call. Even though there was no question she needed to speak with him, she wasn't ready for the conversation. At least not today. But soon. Very soon.

CHAPTER TWENTY-FIVE

Liz gripped the collar of her wool jacket, protecting her neck from the wind, as she crossed the hardware store's parking lot with Daniel at her side. They'd been in and out of stores all day, Christmas shopping for his nieces and nephews and for her grandkids as well. The temperature had kept dropping all afternoon.

As he always seemed to do, Daniel clued into her, noticing she was cold. Taking a broad stride to get to the door quickly, he opened it for her.

"Brr . . . thanks!" She acknowledged his gallantry with a grateful smile.

"No problem." He rubbed his bare hands together once they were inside. "I'm going to head over to the plumbing area. Need to get a few items for my leaky sink."

"You'll know where to find me when you're finished," Liz told him, pointing toward the paint department.

"Pick out something good for your kitchen. Something pretty, like its cook."

His light, teasing comment encouraged her to continue their banter. "Are you trying to flatter me so I'll bake another pecan pie for you?" In between her red velvet cake baking, she'd taken some time to make Daniel his favorite pie.

"Or pumpkin is fine too." He winked at her in reply.

As Daniel headed to the left side of the store and she veered to the right, she couldn't help but eye — and covet — the beautiful kitchen cabinets on display. Along with the fashionable new sinks. Maybe somehow . . . someday.

As things stood, Daniel had finished up her ceiling weeks earlier, and at the risk of never having the chance to enjoy his company again, she'd had to be frank with him about her finances. With Christmas in the wings and things quieter than ever at work, there was no way she could move forward with any other improvements to her kitchen. The most she could afford to do was paint it. On her own, which she planned to do sometime after the Santa Cottage Sale, coming up soon, and before Amy and her family arrived for the holidays.

But of course, Daniel being Daniel, he'd

offered to help. In fact, after their dinner at Annabelle's, they'd been helping each other in many ways and spending much time together nearly every day. She enjoyed the hours in his company so much that during a few instances, she'd even lost track of time. Like the evening she'd arrived half an hour late to a session with Jessica and Lydia at the Cottage.

Fearing she'd been in an accident, they were ready to call the police when she hadn't picked up her phone. When she finally got to the Cottage and told them she'd been with Daniel, they'd teased her relentlessly, as if she were involved in some hot, torrid romance. But what she and Daniel had wasn't like that. Goodness, Daniel had never done more than squeeze her hand in parting, which suited what they had between them. Which was . . . well, comfortable and enjoyable. Uncomplicated and easygoing.

She smiled, thinking once again about Jessica and Lydia's reaction, or rather over-reaction. But then sobered as soon as she lit in front of the display of paint samples. There was a one, two — she turned her head, scanning the array — at least a five-foot section of color samples.

"How overwhelming!" she sighed, staring

at the rows upon rows of colors.

"Isn't it though?" a female voice answered beside her.

"It truly is." Liz could practically feel her eyes glazing over. "I mean, I have a hard enough time just deciding between chocolate chip ice cream and butter pecan."

The lady next to her laughed out loud. "For me it always comes down to raspberry chocolate chip and — Liz? Liz Cannon?"

Liz looked up from the bins of color strips. "Belinda! Oh, my goodness! I haven't seen you since . . . well, I'm trying to think how long it's been."

She reached out to hug her old friend, then stepped back to take a look at her. Petite, with curly red hair that seemed to still have a mind of its own, Belinda Sears looked just the way Liz remembered her, though a little more tired around the eyes. But 'twas the season . . .

"It's been at least two years," Belinda informed her. "Ever since John and I moved to Millersburg."

"I can't believe it's been that long. What a treat, bumping into you!"

"A nice surprise, considering I don't get to Sugarcreek too often. I happen to be in town today picking up a few Christmas items I ordered, and I stopped in at Rose's

Cottage too. Actually, I was glad to see that it still was Rose's Cottage and that Jessica had taken over the shop. What an undertaking!" Belinda shook her head, visibly awed. "And what a wonderful Amish woman she has working there as well."

"They're both sweet gals," Liz agreed. "I've been meeting with the two of them at least once a week since the fire at the church, just to visit and knit and, well, do a few other things," she added vaguely.

"Oh, Liz." Belinda's forehead creased in sympathy. "I was horrified to hear about Faith Community burning down, and about Rose, too, of course, God rest her dear soul. I can't imagine how you all must've felt . . . and are probably still feeling."

The lump that formed in Liz's throat was immediate. "Yes, Rose truly was the sweetest, wasn't she?" she said hoarsely. "Her passing was incredibly shocking. And as far as the church, well, that's been an adjustment too. Right now, there's a candlelight ceremony scheduled for the week before Christmas, which I'm looking forward to. We're also hoping rebuilding will begin in January, but that will depend on the weather, of course."

Liz raised her hands in the air, not having any other facts about the church to share.

"So tell me about life in Millersburg, Belinda," she said, anxious to hear some happy news. "Have you been enjoying your new home there?"

Belinda's face clouded, and Liz hated to see that, hoping there was nothing serious going on in the Sears family. Although she and Belinda hadn't stayed in touch after the move, she still felt they'd shared a special bond of friendship. For years, the two of them had served on numerous church committees together, cooking countless meals for church events and members of the congregation.

"It's been great, Liz, it really has. Until recently anyway." She exhaled heavily as each one of her features collapsed into a sullen, grim expression. "If you would please keep John in your prayers . . . He was diagnosed with MS, and for the longest while the symptoms seemed to be manageable and not so life-altering. But recently, they've gotten much worse. It's been very difficult."

"Oh, Belinda, I'm so sorry to hear that." Liz reached out to touch her friend's arm.

"He gets so worn out but doesn't want to succumb to the fatigue. It helps him mentally if he has a project to work on a little each day. He's painting our mudroom now

410

and wanted me to look for colors for our bathroom."

"I will definitely be praying for him, Belinda."

"Thanks, Liz. A lot of people at our new church are praying for him too, which is such a comfort. You know, come to think of it, you might actually like our church. I mean, until Faith is up and running again. Although it would be somewhat of a haul for you."

"For a good sermon, I sure wouldn't mind the drive," she replied, thinking a visit to the church in Millersburg would be a good way to show Belinda her support as well.

Belinda pulled her phone out of her jeans pocket and thumbed through screens till she found the spot she was looking for. "Here you go." She handed the phone to Liz. "Why don't you put in your cell number, and I'll text you the details?"

"That'd be great, Belinda." She punched in her number and then handed the phone back to her friend. "You know what's funny? I rarely ever make it to Millersburg, but just recently I went to a restaurant all the way out there. The food was very good. A little too much cinnamon in the sweet potato casserole, and they could've added a tad more garlic —"

Before she could finish her sentence, Daniel strode up the aisle toward them.

"Belinda, I want you to meet my, uh, my friend Daniel Kauffman. Daniel, this is Belinda Sears. We used to go to church together before she and her husband moved from Sugarcreek."

"Nice to meet you." He reached out his hand, which Belinda started to take. Until her phone buzzed, distracting her.

"I'm sorry. I'd better see who this is." She glanced at the screen. "Oh, dear, it's my sister. I need to get this. It was nice to meet you, Daniel," she said as she clicked on her phone and started to walk away. "And really great to see you, Liz." She waved with the phone at her ear.

"Hmm," Daniel mumbled as they stared after Belinda.

"Hmm, what?"

"She looks familiar, but I can't seem to place her."

Liz blinked at him in surprise. "Maybe it'll come to you later."

"Maybe." He shrugged. "Have you decided on a color?"

Liz shook her head. "Not even close. I think I'm just going to grab a bunch of color samples and take them home. I've had enough shopping and deciding for one day."

412

Besides, as much as she enjoyed seeing Belinda, the news about her husband's illness had made painting her kitchen not seem as direly important at the moment.

"I'm not going to fight you on it," Daniel replied, suddenly looking tired himself.

In fact, Liz noticed Daniel barely spoke the entire drive to her house, keeping his eyes fixed on the country roads. But after being together most of the day, Liz didn't have much to say either. Plus, the first snowflakes of the season had arrived and she was mesmerized, watching as they danced and swirled in the air and skipped over the windshield. By the time they arrived at her neighborhood, the whimsical white flecks had seemed to tire, finally catching hold, making picturesque landings on the limbs of the maple trees that lined her street.

As Daniel pulled into her driveway, she was enchanted once again by the cozy, merry way her house looked. As if Christmas had already arrived at 1031 Trellis Lane. White lights twinkled from every eave and gutter of the house and all around her front door. And two glimmering reindeer, which Daisy was still getting used to, stood majestically on her front lawn.

She hadn't had her home looking so festive in years, and it was all because of Daniel. And all because the day they'd worked in her kitchen together, he'd actually heard what she'd shared about her family and her last Christmas with Karl when he'd lost the battle for his life. That November, she and Karl had learned that Amy was pregnant with their first grandbaby, and Karl had known he'd never live to see the child. At that time, he'd made Liz promise that his passing at that time of year wouldn't steal the joy from the season in the future — not from her, or Amy, or their grandchildren yet to come into the world.

Knowing her grandkids were indeed coming for Christmas, and being the great guy he was, Daniel had shown up at her house one Saturday with extra Christmas lights, extension cords, and a very tall ladder. He hung more lights than she ever had before. Even hooked them all up to a timer, conscious of her efforts to save money.

"I know I keep saying it, but thank you again for making the house look like something from the North Pole. Ellie and Jack will love it, Daniel."

"I told you, Liz, it wasna anything." He sloughed off her thanks as he grabbed her larger shopping bags from the trunk, leaving her the smallest ones to carry. Daisy was already at the door when Liz opened it, wagging and poised to greet them.

"You can just set the bags on the bench here. I'll get to them later." Liz motioned to the wooden seat in her entry, then took off her coat and tossed it there too. "Would you like some hot chocolate? And maybe grilled cheese sandwiches for dinner?" she offered as she bustled into the kitchen and opened the refrigerator door. They hadn't stopped to eat anything since their midmorning breakfast together. "If you want, we can eat while we finish watching the movie we started the other night."

"Aw, I probably shouldn't," he called to her from the other room.

"It's low-fat cheese. Not too many calories." She bent over, perusing the refrigerator's shelves, seeing what else she had to offer. "Or I could make you a turkey sandwich and soup if that sounds better — and healthier — to you."

"No, I didn't mean that, Liz. What I meant is, I don't think I should stay."

It wasn't just his words; it was the seriousness in his voice, the dull tone, that made the hairs stand up on the back of her neck. Straightening, she slowly closed the refrigerator door, searching her brain, trying desperately to imagine why he was saying such a thing.

He rarely just dropped her off, and certainly not without a prior explanation. He always came in and stayed awhile. In fact, she'd thought he'd already settled onto her sofa. But when she walked back out to the family room, he remained standing in her entrance. With his coat on.

"Do you have work to do? Are you still finishing up that special order for Christmas you've been working on?"

"Yes," he said, the answer terse for him. His tone foreign to her.

She searched his face. Stared into his eyes. And felt a tension between them she'd never felt before. "But I'm suspecting that's not the reason you've decided not to stay. Am I right?"

He exhaled deeply. "You would be right."

"Is it anything I can help with?"

He looked away. "I'm not really sure."

"Do you want to try me?"

"I think I should." His jaw tensed as he spoke through pursed lips. "What's going on with me has to do with you, Liz. With us."

Her heart felt as though it stopped beating in her chest. His answer was so unexpected. She thought they'd been getting along so well, enjoying each other's company. Had he been trying to tell her something and she hadn't gotten the message? Her stomach sank to her toes. "In, uh . . . in what way?" She was almost afraid to ask.

"Well, I keep going back to the way you introduced me to your friend in the hardware store, that Belinda lady, and, uh, I'm not sure what to think about it."

She could feel her face heat as if she'd been caught at something. "I introduced you as my friend because, well, you are my friend, aren't you?"

"I am, but — this is crazy. I feel like an awkward teenager talking about this." He rubbed his brow, shifted on his feet. "Look, Liz, I thought I could wait. I thought I could be more patient. But once I heard you say that today, I realized the time has come. For me, at least. I need to know how you feel. And if that's how you think of me — as *just* a friend?"

She stared at him, searching her feelings, trying to find words. Oh, if she was being honest, introducing him to Belinda as a friend had made her pause. It had. But what were they, then, if not friends — the very closest of friends? And did he have to bring this up now? Get serious so soon? When things had been going so well between them?

Seeing she was speechless, he held up his hand.

"Okay. If you don't have anything to say, I do." He glanced at the floor as if to get his bearings, then looked into her eyes with an intensity that shocked her. Making her feel powerless to look away.

"Liz, I go into a lot of houses month after month, year after year, but when I came into your home, right off I could feel it was filled with something special. And also, right off, I knew that something special is you. I know we haven't known each other very long, but after all the years of being on my own . . ."

When he spoke again, his voice was filled with a new earnestness and a sweet softness as he gazed at her. "Liz, I like the way you think. The way you look. The way you laugh. The way I feel when I'm with you. I even have to admit I like the way you can't keep from talking when I'm watching the news. That has become endearing too. But only because I've come to realize I'd rather have you near me — above anything else."

"Daniel, what you're saying . . ." She faltered. "I mean, of course, you're special to me. You really are. And I love spending time with you too."

418

"Yeah." His eyes scanned her face as if trying to read her mind. "But I'm not sure if it's the same way for you as for me. I want more, Liz. I want a chance to have more for us." He paused. "I know I haven't exactly said anything before, but I'm saying it now. I'm asking you, will you take some time to think about it? About us being more than friends?"

Already her heart ached. She couldn't imagine not seeing him. He'd been there day after day. But as much as she enjoyed his company and felt completely comfortable with him, it had all happened too quickly. Had taken her by surprise, the way they so easily fit into each other's lives. It was all still so new to her. And even though her feelings ran deep for the man, being more than what they already were to each other . . . What did that mean? What would that look like?

He was right, of course. Her heart was going in all directions. She needed time, needed to sort things out. "Yes, of course. I'll think about it, Daniel. I will."

"Thanks," he said quietly and then started to go. But before he grabbed the knob on her door, he turned on his heels and faced her. "Oh, and Liz?"

"Yes?"

She thought he wanted to say something else. But apparently he was done with talking. Before she knew what was happening, he took her hand in his and swung her close to him. Closer than she'd ever been before. Against his broad chest that held his heart of gold. She couldn't resist wrapping her arms around him to steady herself.

Immersed in his embrace, she could smell the familiar, pleasing scent of him. And just as she was getting used to that, he shocked her by leaning down and covering her mouth with his. Kissing her so ardently yet so sweetly that once he released her from his arms, she stood breathless, wide-eyed.

"Daniel . . ." She touched her fingers to her lips, the effects of his tender kiss still leaving her quivering, reverberating all the way from her mouth to her toes. "I thought you said you wanted me to *think* about things."

"I did say that," he replied, his voice low and intimate. "And when you do, Liz, I want you to think about that kiss, too."

CHAPTER TWENTY-SIX

On most days after work Lydia preferred to have her usual driver, George, drop her off at the bottom of her driveway. That way she could get her mail along with a little exercise by walking up the drive to her house. But today she was thankful when George stopped his car a foot from her mailbox and was intent on waiting for her. Between working nonstop with Jessica to get the shop ready for the sale and helping her Amish friends finish up quilts, she felt as spent as a plow horse ready for retirement.

"You get out and get your mail, Miss Lydia. Then I'll drive you up to your front door," George suggested kindly. "A woman your size could blow away in this wind."

Truly it had been a gray, gusty day in Sugarcreek. Hour after hour, the wind had howled mercilessly as if wanting to prove that winter was there to stay, causing her weary bones to ache even more than they already did.

Not about to turn down George's offer, she dashed out of the car and back in just as quickly, not even bothering to look at the few envelopes in her hand. It wasn't until she was in her house and kicking off her boots at the front door that she began to thumb through the mail.

"Oh, Kit, there's a letter from *Maam,*" she informed her nearly domesticated stray. The cat rarely ventured outdoors nowadays. Instead, Kit was there to welcome her home at the end of most days, circling her furry self between and around Lydia's ankles in greeting.

"It's a long letter too," Lydia added, as if Kit understood everything she was saying.

The envelope bearing her mother's handwriting was noticeably thicker than any she typically received. *Maam*'s response was much quicker than usual too. All of which had Lydia's heart thudding dully in her chest as her limbs grew even heavier and more tired.

She'd been concerned when she'd mailed the letter to her *maam,* fearing she'd said too much. Now, receiving such a lengthy and fast response, she knew for sure her emotional outpouring must have had an effect on her mother. Something she had never meant to do and instantly felt sorry about.

Letting go of a sigh, she turned on both lanterns in the sitting room and sank down onto the love seat. As she gently tugged open the envelope, Kit mewed at her feet, protesting the change in their daily routine.

"I know, Kit, I know. Don't worry. I'll get your food in a minute," she promised.

As if to make certain Lydia wouldn't forget her, Kit jumped onto the love seat, curling up next to Lydia's hip. Stroking her fluffy companion, Lydia let out a deep breath. "Oh, Kit, I'm not even sure I want to read *Maam*'s letter. I hope I didn't worry her too badly." But even as she said the words, she drew the bulky letter from the envelope and began to focus on her mother's writing.

Dear Lydia,
    In all the years that you've been gone from home, I may have wished there weren't so many miles that separated us. I know for a fact, though, that I have never said that to you. But I am saying it now because this is certainly one of those times when it would be better if we were sitting across the kitchen table from one another. If we were, then I

could be there to steady you as you read all that I have to write to you.

Her mother's words were far more sentimental than usual, but sounded oddly ominous, too, causing Lydia to pause and take a deep breath as she clutched the paper more tightly.

First off, I know you aren't imagining the distance between you and your husband that you talked about in your letter. I only know this because of a conversation — a very difficult conversation — I had with Henry's grandmother Miriam after his passing. She came to me with a grieving heart. But she wasn't only grieving Henry's death, she was also aching over what he'd been through in his short life. In her words, it was a secret she — and only she — had been carrying in her heart for decades and just couldn't bear to carry alone any longer.

I have to be honest and say Miriam shared things that I certainly wished she hadn't. Things that made me feel mighty uncomfortable to hear — and I sure didn't want to repeat them to you. I suppose I didn't think you needed to hear them. At least that's what I thought until I received your letter. When I read how disturbed and confused you were about your years with Henry and your marriage, it was then that I began to think differently.

Now I'm feeling Miriam's confiding in me had a greater purpose than I ever imagined. Her sharing with me about Henry lets me share with you. As disturbing as what I have to tell you certainly is, I pray it will help you find a sense of peace with your past, my child. I also pray it will help you move on with the life ahead of you . . . just as I pray that Henry has finally found rest and peace in eternity.

Lydia had never received a letter from her *maam* that made her hands shake, but her hands were certainly trembling now. Kit, seemingly sensing her sudden onslaught of tension, hopped from her snuggly spot on the couch to the floor, busying herself with a self-cleaning. Meanwhile, Lydia, like her mother, wished there weren't so many miles that separated them. Oh, how she'd much rather hear what her mother had to say firsthand instead of sitting and reading her message all alone.

But that was a useless wish to make, and nothing she could do anything about. Instead, she braced herself as best she could and read on.

Twenty-four hours after opening her *maam*'s letter, Lydia was still having a difficult time processing all that she'd read. She was just thankful for an extremely busy day at the Cottage in which she could go through the motions, helping customers and making preparations for the Santa sale in between. The busyness masked the fact that she was stunned beyond words about her husband's past. And didn't allow time to interact with Jessica the way she normally did.

With so much going on at the Cottage, Jessica hadn't seemed to notice her quietness anyway. At least not until the end of the day, when they were sitting around the worktable with Liz.

"Okay, girls," Jessica addressed them. "I know this is boring, tedious work, making bows for my scarves. But don't forget —" she paused to chuckle — "you two were the ones who talked me into knitting all of these lumpy things, saying how stylish they are. And now you've both gone silent on me."

Lydia looked up from stitching a baby-blue bow into place on one of Jessica's creations but still didn't have anything to say. Apparently — and atypically — Liz was short on words as well. Glancing up from cutting strips of glimmering ribbon, she simply shrugged, not offering any kind of explanation.

"Wait a minute." Jessica's dark eyes narrowed in on Liz. "You weren't even supposed to be here to help, were you? Hadn't you and Daniel planned to —"

Liz held up a hand to stop Jessica midsentence, and for the first time that day Lydia's mind shifted from her own issues to her friend's, noticing an unmistakable look of sadness in Liz's eyes. "Yes, Daniel and I had a lot of plans. For today, next week, next month. But I don't know." She shrugged again. "I don't know if any of them are going to come together now."

"Oh, Liz . . . Did you two have a fight or something?" Jessica pressed Liz more boldly than Lydia felt comfortable doing.

"Not really a fight." Liz sighed as she let go of the pair of scissors. Sinking deeper into her chair, she plucked unconsciously at the hair at the back of her head. "He gave me an ultimatum."

"Meaning?" Jessica prodded.

"He doesn't want to be 'just friends' with

me anymore."

Knowing how fond Liz was of Daniel, Lydia felt relieved to hear he wanted to see more of her — not less. "Is that a bad thing?" She leaned forward, asking her friend tentatively.

"It doesn't sound like it is," Jessica interjected.

Rarely was Liz slow with an answer. But she hesitated, picking up a half yard of silver ribbon, sliding it through her fingers over and over again, causing specks of sparkle to dust the table. "I don't know. I definitely have some thinking to do. Everything he said took me very much by surprise. One minute I think we're just that — really good friends — and the next minute he wants so much more." She glanced between the two of them. "Oh, I know what you two are thinking, and yes, you're right. I probably shouldn't have been so taken aback by what he said. Obviously I could tell we both had strong feelings for one another. Even our first dinner together was perfect, a perfect evening. And ever since that night, I've been happy with the way things were going. Slow and easy. So why does he need to complicate perfection?"

"Maybe he thinks you both can be even happier," Jessica suggested.

Liz frowned. "But a relationship like he wants — well, it's such a big step for me at this point in my life. Nothing I imagined for myself. And I guess, even today, I'm still quite overwhelmed. I mean, you think you know what's going on in a relationship, but so often you really don't." She sighed more wearily than before. "I suppose many times you're only aware of yourself, too caught up in your own reality."

"*Jah.*" Lydia's hands and Jessica's scarf dropped to her lap. "*Jah.* That is the truth, isn't it?" she said. "*Verra* much the truth," she added, unable to hide the quiet, grave tone in her voice, which made both of her intuitive friends gaze at her intently.

"Is something going on with your friend Jonas too?" Liz's forehead creased curiously.

"*Nee, nee,*" she was quick to answer. "It's nothing about him. I haven't even seen him this week, I've been so busy. But yesterday when I got home, there was a letter waiting for me. From *Maam.* Telling me about a visit she had from Henry's grandmother months ago, after his passing. Reading that letter . . . well . . . I learned things about Henry that I . . ." She looked down at her hands until she could gather the nerve to glance back up at her friends. "Lord forgive me, but the truth is, I misjudged my husband something awful."

Jessica and Liz eyed her sympathetically but kept silent, their questions voiced in their caring, pensive eyes.

"He, uh . . ." She shook her head and blinked at them. "I don't even know how to say this."

She'd been shocked when she'd read about Henry's grandmother's account of what he'd endured. Achingly sad and sick to her stomach, completely depleted of strength. The most she could manage was to feed her mewing Kit. Other than that, she couldn't eat. Or sleep. Or even pray with any clarity, her mind such a jumble of thoughts. Most of the night, she'd simply sat in the sitting room and stared out the window. Or gazed at the quilt her friends had made, recalling each shirt Henry had worn and how he'd looked in it. Or she'd fixed her eyes on her Bible, hoping to get through the dark night, too numb and vacant to even pick up the book in her hands.

She'd been glad when daylight finally came and she could get ready and get to the Cottage. But as much as she wanted to say something to her friends about what she'd learned — to clear Henry of all she'd been thinking of him and all they might have imagined him to be because of what she'd said — she still didn't know how to get the words out.

"Henry . . . ," she started again, but then stopped as she glanced over at Cole, who was kneeling by his great-aunt's bench in the middle of the store. Waiting for Marisa to arrive, he was oblivious to their talking and concerns as he played with some LEGO figures he'd put together. So carefree. So innocent. So trusting. As every child should be allowed to be.

Yet from what her mother's letter had said, from the time Henry was Cole's age, he had never been given that chance.

"Someone took away Henry's innocence," she finally said, her voice breaking in a hoarse whisper. "And I never, ever knew. He never told me. It was someone . . . someone he trusted."

Tears brimming in her eyes, she glanced between her friends, who both appeared horrified. Just as she'd been. Just as she still was.

"Oh, Lydia, I . . ." Jessica grasped for words.

"That's just so . . ." Liz closed her eyes, shaking her head in disbelief. "So awful. So heartbreaking."

When Lydia had first read that her husband had been sexually abused during his growing-up years, it had been just that — heartbreaking. Unleashing a profound maternal reaction in her that she'd never felt before — as if Henry were still alive but a small, vulnerable boy who needed her protection. And then to find out that the abuser had been an uncle on his father's side — an uncle who was a minister — brought on an onslaught of anger that raged through her veins.

Not only had the abuser robbed Henry of his childhood innocence, but he'd cheated him of so much more. It was no wonder, no wonder at all, that Henry couldn't trust in love. That he showed such little desire for intimacy. And as for fatherhood, had he maybe thought he carried the same perverse sickness in his genes?

Beyond all of that, his vile uncle — a man supposedly drawn to the Lord — had taken away a fullness of faith from Henry as well. It stood to reason why her husband had never wanted to be involved with the people at church. Or better acquainted with others throughout their church district.

"I hope whoever did this to him is in jail now," Jessica spoke up, looking at Lydia and then glancing at her son.

Lydia drew in a deep breath before she

spoke again. "That never happened. As I understand it, by the time Henry confided to his grandmother — his maternal grandmother, who I'm supposing was the only person he felt close enough to confide in and talk to — his uncle had already passed away. But even though he was dead, Henry's grandmother said Henry was still haunted by it all, of course. Why wouldna he be? Tormented day and night, as you would figure."

"But your mother never knew?" Liz asked.

"*Nee.* Like I said, not until recently. *Maam* only knew of him as a good person, and because he had so many skills, thought he'd be a good provider, too."

But after reading all her mother had written, now it did make sense that Miriam had pushed their marriage so much, and why she'd been thrilled her grandson and his wife were moving to Sugarcreek to get a fresh start together. Plus, from what Miriam had said, she thought a loving girl like Lydia would help heal Henry and give him the chance for a happier future. Most likely, she'd made Henry believe and hope the same thing — that a new person in his life and a new place void of haunting memories would restore him, make him whole again.

Make him the person he was always meant to be.

But those awful, hideous memories wouldn't be left behind. They must have followed him and tortured him each day . . . as his hope slipped away.

Because in all their years together, he'd kept himself busy, hadn't he? He'd run from her. He'd never been able to find it in himself to hold her and love her. To be close. To let her love him. All of which she now understood. Yet it still hurt.

Only now, she mostly hurt for him.

"I just wish . . ." She wrung her hands. "If only he could've confided in me. Maybe I could've helped him more."

When Henry had first passed, she'd grieved him as a partner in marriage — a protector and provider who gave shape to the hours in her days. Then she'd grieved the life she'd wanted with him and realized they'd never had together. She'd mourned the love they hadn't shared. But now her heart broke all over again, aching for him as one human to another, wishing she could've done more for him. So much more.

"After all the hurt he'd gone through, I just hope I loved him enough." She sniffed. "I hope in some small way Henry felt my love."

"Oh, Lydia." Jessica reached out and took her hand. "You're a good, loving person. I'm sure he felt that from you. Just like we do."

"It sounds like you did everything you could, honey. I'm sure he knew how you cared for him." Liz offered up more consoling words. "Why, when you think about it, I'm guessing that's why he would push you away. He might've been too afraid of his own feelings too."

More than her friends' words being comforting, Lydia hoped with all her heart they were true.

"I need to tell you both, I moved the quilt." She swiped at a teardrop sliding down her cheek. "I had to put it away. In an old trunk. At least for now. I just couldn't bear to look at it. So if you're at my house and don't see it, I don't want you to think I'm not grateful, but —"

"Shh, Lydia, shh . . ." Jessica patted her hand. "Don't you worry. We understand."

"And you don't need to be thinking of us right now, honey," Liz chimed in. "Not one bit."

Actually she didn't want to think, period. She was tired of thinking, in fact. "I'm going to get some air." She started to get up from the chair.

"Are you sure? Would you rather I drive you home?" Jessica asked. "It's not a problem at all, Lydia. Really it isn't."

"Nee." She smoothed down her skirts. "This is the place I want to be. It feels like home to me. And the busier I am, the better, honestly. But a little air would be *gut* right now. Something to cool my cheeks."

She'd barely finished her sentence and Liz had already retrieved her coat from the back closet for her. After Lydia had buttoned it up, Liz raised the collar around her neck, then reached out her arms and wrapped Lydia in a hug. A long, warm, strong hug that she hadn't even realized she needed so much.

As she slipped out the door of the Cottage, shop windows and lampposts along Main Street glimmered warmly with Christmas lights, yet the air was so brisk it took her breath away. But . . . it felt good just the same. Just as good and rejuvenating as it would be to see Rebecca and to hear her friend jabber on and on. All about her children and her wonderful life. To hear something good. And fresh. And clean. It was exactly what she needed at the moment.

Hands in her pockets, Lydia made her way toward Good for the Soul Bakery, very much looking forward to seeing her friend.

CHAPTER TWENTY-SEVEN

As Lydia stepped into Good for the Soul, the bell jingled over the door as it always did, announcing her arrival. She noticed that the bakery cases were still partially filled with cookies and a few cupcakes left over from the day, but her friend was nowhere to be seen. She waited a few moments for her pink-cheeked, pregnant-bellied friend to appear. When she didn't, Lydia leaned over the counter, trying to see past the bakery cases.

"Rebecca?" she called out. "Yoo-hoo, friend. Where are ya?"

In response to her question, a blonde-haired woman instantly appeared from the back of the shop. "Sorry about that," the lady apologized. "I was in the back, cleaning up."

Spying a dab of frosting at the corner of the woman's mouth, Lydia had to smile, wondering what she was cleaning. Maybe some icing-covered spoons? Or some cupcake crumbs?

"Can I help you?" asked the woman, whose name tag read Kimberly.

"I was looking for Rebecca."

"Oh." Kimberly shrugged. "She's not here. That's why I am. I'm her replacement."

"But . . ." Lydia could feel her smile taking a downward turn. "I thought she had a little more time before her leave."

"You're right. She did. But . . . well, I'm guessing you're a friend of hers?" Kimberly asked even though she was eyeing Lydia warily.

"*Jah. Jah,* I am."

"And you didn't hear?"

"Hear what?" Lydia could feel her chest tightening.

"She had to leave in the middle of her shift yesterday. An emergency situation. From what I heard, she had to go on immediate bed rest. They were afraid she was going to lose the baby."

"Lose the baby?" Lydia gasped, shocked. She couldn't imagine such an awful thing happening to her friend and prayed *Gott* wouldn't let it be. "But she can't. She can't lose the baby."

"Like I said, that's why she had to go on

bed rest. So that everything would be okay with the baby."

"*Jah?* They think the baby will be all right?"

"That's what I heard." Kimberly nodded.

But Lydia wanted to hear it for herself. Pushing away from the bakery cases, her head swimming, she quickly headed toward the front door.

"So, you don't want anything?" Rebecca's replacement called out to her, holding her arms in the air, looking perplexed.

"No, *danke. Nee,*" Lydia said, not hesitating a bit. She didn't want anything at that moment. Nothing at all. Except for her friend's precious little one to be all right.

It wasn't even an hour later when Lydia was saying *danke* again, this time to Jessica and Liz as Jessica steered her SUV toward Elmhurst Road just on the outskirts of town.

"Thank you for making a trip to Rebecca's house," she told the two of them, grateful they'd been quick to react to the change of plans. "I know a Secret Stitches outing wasn't exactly what we'd scheduled tonight."

"I'm getting the impression many times it isn't." Jessica chuckled. "It just sort of happens, doesn't it? And I do feel so bad for

Rebecca. She's such a sweetie."

"As sweet as the baked goods she sells," Liz chimed in. "No matter when I stop in the bakery to pick up something, she always has a big smile on her face."

"She can be a chatterbox, too." Lydia smiled fondly, recalling how listening to Rebecca prattle on could often put her at ease.

"I sure hope all is good with her and her baby," Jessica said wistfully as she slowed the car down and made a right turn. "Well, here we are already. Elmhurst really wasn't far from town at all. If you want to stay and visit with Rebecca for a bit, Lydia, just let us know."

"Yes, we can wait," Liz agreed.

"*Nee.* I don't want to intrude on her family. Not at night. I'll come back and visit in the daytime. Or after church," she said, thinking ahead. "I just wanted to drop off our surprise gifts tonight to give her a boost of hope. To let her know someone is thinking of her."

It hadn't taken long at all to put together a Secret Stitches package for Rebecca and her family. Lydia had already been busy knitting a few pairs of booties for Rebecca's new arrival, be it boy or girl. And after searching through Rose's treasure chest, Jessica had found a darling baby quilt, replete

440

with colorful farm animals. Liz had brought a yummy white-chocolate Chex Mix snack for their evening treat, which they ended up dividing into fourths. One-fourth they left behind for Cole and Marisa to enjoy. The rest they divvied up for Rebecca's other three children, placing the mix in three small tins Jessica had uncovered in her cupboards. Tying the tins up with pieces of sparkling ribbon, they placed the snacks along with the other items into a wicker basket and had been ready to head out the door to Rebecca's in no time.

"Believe it or not, I don't think I've ever been on this street," Liz said, looking out the window as Jessica cruised slowly down the lane. "The houses are very homey looking."

Lydia scooted up toward the front seat, peering through the windshield to get a look. Just being able to get out and do something was making her feel somewhat better — about Rebecca's situation and even her own.

Each and every time thoughts of Henry would come back to her, she could feel her heart sink in disbelief and sorrow. But she made herself vow to *Gott* that she would try to help others as best she could. Especially since, sadly and most regrettably, she hadn't

441

been able to do anything to help Henry through the turmoil she'd never known about.

"Are we looking for a certain house number?" Liz asked.

"Oh . . ." Lydia frowned. "I don't have an address. But her house should be easy to find. Rebecca told me their road dead-ends, and they live in a white house at the very end of the street."

Half a minute later, the road stopped, just as Rebecca had told Lydia it would. But as Jessica put the car in park and the headlights beamed momentarily in front of them, they realized there was one little item Rebecca had left out of her description.

"Hmm," Jessica said as they all stared out the windshield.

"Interesting," Liz remarked, sounding mystified.

"*Jah,* for sure." Lydia turned her head, left to right. "Rebecca never mentioned there were two white houses at the end of her street. Sitting side by side."

"Yeah, and I don't see anything to distinguish them," Jessica commented, which was completely true. Both two-story homes looked very much the same, and so did the trees and hedges surrounding them.

"There aren't any buggies sitting out."

Lydia scoped the grounds.

"Or any cars," Liz added.

"I suppose they're all in the outbuildings?" Jessica guessed.

"Oh, goodness." Liz scratched her head. "Now what?"

Jessica cut the engine and they sat in silence, pondering the situation. But when no one came up with a solution, Lydia voiced her own.

"I just need to do this myself," she said. "It's too chancy — too much commotion with three of us. I'll sneak up to the house on my own and look in the window so I can see who lives where."

"Like a Peeping Tom?" Jessica's voice had a slight screech to it.

"Who?" Lydia asked, confused.

"Never mind," her friend said. "I just don't know if it's a good idea, Lydia. Peeking into windows sounds like trouble."

"Maybe you should knock on the door instead," Liz suggested.

"But we're the Secret Stitches Society," Lydia protested. "We never knock on doors." She took in a deep breath, knowing she had to take matters into her own hands. "Don't worry, ladies. I'll be fine. Mighty fine," she said as convincingly as she could. "It'll be *gut*. I'll be back in the car before you all know it."

With that, she grabbed the gift basket, opened the car door, and skipped over the road toward the white houses. The only thing she wondered was which one she should try first.

"What do you think?" Jessica asked Liz a while later in the quiet of the car. "Does it seem like Lydia's taking a long time? Because it sure seems like that to me."

"Yeah, I thought her white *kapp* would be like a beacon in the night." Liz sighed. "But I lost track of her a while ago."

"I know. Me too. What happened to the moonlight?" Jessica wondered out loud.

"I think they call it clouds," Liz quipped, which made Jessica worry even more.

"Maybe she tripped and fell in the dark."

"Oh, dear." Liz shot her a quick glance, her features crumpled with concern. "Let's hope not, honey."

"She could've, you know." Jessica couldn't help imagining the worst. "She could've fallen and hit her head or broken her leg and —"

"Wait!" Liz reached over and clasped her arm. "I think I see something moving."

"Seriously?" Jessica poked her head over the steering wheel, anxious to see. "Oh! I think I see it too. Over there, right?" She pointed toward the left side of the windshield. "Through the trees?"

It was only a moment later that Lydia's form burst through the dark clump of trees, illuminated by the moonlight, which had broken through the clouds. Holding her long coat and skirt up with one hand, still clutching the basket of gifts in the other, her *kapp* all askew, Lydia looked like something out of a cartoon. Jessica started to laugh. Until she leaned closer and realized how terrified Lydia appeared. Her friend looked like she was running from the boogeyman.

"Oh, my . . ." Her mouth gaped open at the sight. "Oh, my goodness."

"Turn on the car," Liz yelped. "Start it up. We have to get out of here. Quick!"

Jessica fumbled for the key in the ignition. At the same time Lydia had reached the car. Groping for the handle on the door, she flew into the backseat, slamming the door shut behind her.

"Are you all right?" Jessica managed to ask as she put her SUV into gear.

Lydia's breathy heaving filled the car in reply. "I was . . ." She gasped for air. "Looking in a window, trying to see, and . . . I couldna see. Then I snuck to the back . . .

to the kitchen window and looked in there and . . . This woman . . . her face came out of nowhere," she puffed. "Nowhere. She saw me. And screamed. And I . . . I . . ." She huffed and gulped. "I got so scared, I screamed too!"

"Oh, dear!" Liz exclaimed as Jessica worked to turn the car around in the small space at the end of the lane. "We'll be lucky if they haven't already called the —"

She didn't have to say the word.

As soon as Jessica had gotten the car straightened, intent on hustling out of the neighborhood, a police car with its flashing light and low *whoop-whoop* of a siren halted right in front of her SUV. Stopping them from going anywhere and blinding them all at the same time.

"Oh, dear Lord, please don't let it be Derek. Don't let it be Derek," she whispered, blinking into the light.

Days before, she'd already leaked out one embarrassing situation she'd created. Her tender pride wasn't in the mood to be caught in another one. At least not so soon.

Shielding her eyes from the flashing light, she held her breath as the deputy sheriff got out of the car. It was easy to see it wasn't anyone but . . .

"Derek! Of course." She groaned. "Somehow this Secret Stitches thing is never very simple, is it?" Motion sensors. A flat tire. Now the police?

"Guess we'll just have to keep trying to get it right," Liz offered.

"I'm *verra* sorry, you two. I really am," Lydia apologized. "It's all my fault. I'm the one who should be in trouble."

"Nonsense, Lydia," Liz spoke up. "We're the ones who let you run off by yourself."

"Yes." Jessica sure didn't want her friend to take all the blame herself. "We've got to be all for one and one for all," she said as she watched Derek approach the car.

Even in her ridiculous present situation, she couldn't deny how just seeing him in his uniform hurried her pulse. As she lowered her car window and he peeked inside, she tried to ignore the musky scent of him tickling her nose and taunting her senses.

"Ladies." He nodded sternly. At the same time, Jessica could tell he was biting his lip, as if trying to hold back a smile. "Interesting meeting you all here tonight on Elmhurst Road. We had a call about a Peeping Tom — or should I say, a Peeping Thomasina?"

"Oh." Lydia spoke up from the backseat. "A Peeping Thomasina. Now I know what you all are talking about."

"No one was exactly peeping as in *peeping,* Derek. We were just trying to see if we had the right house," Jessica explained. "We had some gifts to deliver to a friend who lives in a white house at the end of the street, but as you can see, there are two white homes right next door to each other."

"And we didn't know which was which," Liz added.

"Ah, I see. And a knock on the front door wouldn't have alleviated that situation?" Derek said practically, raising a brow.

"Did I mention the gift was supposed to be a surprise?" Jessica said.

"Oh, well." Derek scratched his chin. "I'd say there was definitely an element of surprise involved in all of this. Problem is, Mrs. Winkleman and her family were more than surprised. They were frightened to death."

Lydia scooted to the left side of the car and pushed the window button too, poking out her head. "It's all my fault, Deputy Derek, and I'm *verra* sorry. I'm the one who was doing the peeping."

"Look, ladies." He glanced back and forth among the three of them. "I'm sure whatever you were up to is all innocent. But I hope none of you will let this happen again.

No more peeping into windows, mostly for your own sakes. You could get yourselves shot, you know."

"Yes, Deputy," they all murmured in concession.

With that, he opened the back car door. "Why don't you go drop off your package to your friend, Lydia? In the meantime I'll explain things to your friend's neighbors and get them calmed down."

At his prompting, Lydia obediently exited the car with the basket. Closing the door behind her, Derek bent down and peered into Jessica's window once again. "Jess, you and Liz can get going and be on your way back to town. I'll get Lydia home."

"Derek, you don't have to do that. I can take Lydia."

"I'm sure you can," he told her. "But then, no one has to worry."

"You mean then *you* don't have to?"

An easy smile played at the corners of his mouth. "Well, yeah. Something like that," he said, tapping the top of her car, signaling for her to be on her way.

Lydia was happily relieved to find out that Rebecca was doing just fine and had a positive prognosis when she checked in on her — at the correct white house this time, the one on the right — and dropped off the not-so-secret stitches basket.

She was afraid that Derek might grow impatient, being that Rebecca was her usual chatty self. However he didn't seem to be the least bit bothered when she finally broke away from her friend and joined him in his sheriff's car, taking a seat in the back.

She had seen Derek plenty of times when he dropped in at the Cottage to visit with Jessica. But she hadn't talked to him all that much. Getting to know him better during the ride to her house, she could understand why he and Jessica got along so well. They both seemed to have much the same outlook on things and were both easygoing.

In fact, he put her much at ease and had her laughing most of the time as he cruised over the roads leading to her home. It wasn't until they reached her house and he pulled into her driveway that she grew quieter.

"Oh, wouldn't you know it?" She worried her lip, glancing next door.

"Something wrong?" He looked into the rearview mirror.

"Uh, *nee*. It's just that Jeb would have to be outside doing his business about now, wouldn't he?"

"I'm hoping you're talking about a dog, right?"

"My neighbor's." She peered out the window, trying to get a better look. "Oh, and there he is too."

"Your neighbor?"

"*Jah.* He's right out there keeping a watch on Jeb."

A while earlier, when Derek had caught up with them on Elmhurst Road, she knew Jessica had been quite embarrassed that Derek had been the one to find them in their predicament. Now Lydia was feeling much the same way as she eyed Jonas. "I wonder if he's ever seen one of his neighbors brought home in a police car before."

Derek chuckled. "Uh, probably not one of his Amish neighbors, I'd venture to say."

"*Jah.* Don't be surprised if he comes over to see if I'm all right."

"He's a nosy neighbor, huh?"

"*Jah.* But in a *gut* way. A caring way," she said, knowing it to be true.

"That's sounds like a good thing then, especially since you're out here on your own."

"It is," she agreed.

But even so, as she watched Jonas and Jeb head toward the path through the shrubs, she knew she was going to feel a wee bit flustered seeing him. And explaining, of course, all about her ride home in a sheriff's car.

CHAPTER TWENTY-EIGHT

Liz was running a few minutes late getting to town, but it was more Daisy's fault than her own. She'd had her coat on and her car keys in hand, ready to leave the house, but Daisy had been too caught up in sniffing around the wire-framed reindeer on the lawn to come in when she called. Finally Liz had had to lure her inside with a treat, which took longer than she anticipated.

Walking as swiftly as her legs would carry her past the storefronts on Main Street, which looked much like a Swiss Christmas village these days, she hoped Belinda would be running late for their morning meet-up too.

It had been a complete surprise — and somewhat of a let-down — when a text lit up her phone late the night before. After getting home from last evening's Secret Stitches adventure, she'd quickly gotten into her pajamas and snuggled into bed to read.

Her heart beat harder in her chest when she spied the light coming from her cell, thinking she might see Daniel's name on the screen.

She missed talking to him so much she would've been glad for him to be calling, even if it was just to say hello. Or even to prod her for an answer. But disappointingly, the text wasn't from him at all. It was from Belinda, giving details about her church as she'd promised and also asking if Liz could meet for breakfast.

As Liz ducked into the Pancake House, she spotted Belinda sitting by a window trimmed with holiday greenery. Liz waved and, walking toward the table, mentally prepared herself. No doubt Belinda had asked her to meet because she needed to talk to someone about her husband and his illness. Someone who'd experienced the same sort of heartache and trauma.

"Sorry I'm late, Belinda. That dog of mine . . ." Liz shook her head.

"I'm glad you could come on such short notice." Though Belinda smiled sweetly, her face appeared tense. "But I don't have much time. I apologize if this seems rude, but would you mind if we just order bagels or something quick?"

Liz was somewhat taken aback by Belinda

asking her to breakfast then wanting to rush through it. On the other hand, she readily understood the demands of being a care-taker to a sick spouse and a working woman too. "Whatever you need to do, Belinda. I'm fine with it."

After they'd ordered hot tea, orange juice, and blueberry bagels with cream cheese, Belinda looked across the table at her, and Liz readied herself for her friend's questions. But instead, Belinda surprised her again. Leaning forward, she said, "You're right, Liz."

"I am?" Liz asked, and felt her forehead slip into a crease.

"Uh-huh." Her friend's eyes lit up. "I put two and two together and realized it was *you.* I tried what you said, and you were dead-on."

Liz blinked at her friend, bewildered. "I have absolutely no idea what you're talking about, Belinda."

"Less cinnamon in the sweet potato cas-serole, and a tad more garlic to season the pork loin."

"I'm sorry? Say again?"

Belinda was staring at her like she'd just uttered the most interesting thing in the world, but Liz was completely at sea.

"I'm sorry, Liz, I'm so excited that I'm

455

getting ahead of myself," Belinda started to gush. "Shortly after John and I moved to Millersburg, we took over a restaurant there."

"Oh, my goodness!" Liz instantly pulled the pieces together. "Annabelle's? You and John own Annabelle's? It's such a great place, Belinda, and I can't believe I critiqued your cooking! I apologize. It was such a small nuance sort of thing, a personal taste. Why, the dinner was superb just the way it was."

"And now those dishes will be even better because of your input, Liz," Belinda said as the waiter placed their bagels on the table. She waited until he was gone before she spoke again. "But even more than that, your honest appraisal reminded me of your great cooking instincts — which has led to much discussion between John and me since I saw you last. And, well, we've decided we would like to have your future input as well, Liz."

Liz took a bite of bagel, eyeing her friend quizzically. "I'm not sure I understand." She picked up her napkin, swiping cream cheese from her lips. "You want me to be what? Like a food critic for your restaurant?"

"More than that." Belinda paused, then spoke slowly and distinctly. "Liz, what we'd like — what I'm asking you — is if you'd

456

like to become a part of Annabelle's? A rather big part."

Liz's mouth gaped open. A part of a restaurant? A restaurant as wonderful as Annabelle's?

All along, people might have said that cooking and food preparation was her calling, but Liz never realized how much she wanted it to be true until Belinda said those words. Of course, she didn't yet know what Belinda had in mind exactly. Overwhelmed by emotion and caught by surprise, she tried to rein in her thoughts and listen.

"Now, I know that's a lot to take in. I know you already have a life you're used to, Liz," her friend continued, "and that you've been selling real estate for years. But John and I feel it's no accident that you and I crossed paths again. We believe God was looking out for us, bringing you into our lives right now. Obviously, we don't know what the future holds, but right now it seems John isn't going to be able to be a huge help in the business much longer." She grimaced with a sigh.

"Anyway, all that being said —" Belinda straightened her shoulders — "we've invested a lot into the restaurant, and from the beginning we had a dream to make it even more than what it already is. John had started to establish a catering side to our business that would service all the areas that surround Sugarcreek. But now with his health being what it is, we need someone to partner with us, someone to work alongside us. You and I were a formidable duo when we worked together before. It's so obvious that we would make a strong team once again."

"Belinda, I —" Her voice croaked and faltered, wanting so badly to say yes in a heartbeat. But the sad reality was, her savings were almost nil. She didn't have money to help start another leg of their business. Why, lately she was lucky to be filling her own refrigerator with food.

"You can't imagine what a gift you've given me," she said slowly, weighing each word. "Just by you offering this opportunity, believing in me so much . . . I really needed to hear this right now, trust me. But . . ." She closed her eyes, blinking back unshed tears, hating to say the words. "I don't have the funds to become a partner. As much as it hurts to say it, I simply don't."

Belinda shook her head. "I guess I made myself clear as mud, didn't I? When I said the word *partner,* what I really meant is that we'd like you to be a part of our dream." Belinda picked up her coffee cup but then set it back down without taking a sip.

"Maybe I should put it this way," she said. "We have really great cooks at Annabelle's, Liz. Cooks. Waitresses. Bussers. But with John's shaky health situation, we need a special person we can trust with this new venture. Someone who not only has a love for cooking but who really cares. A person who works hard and who's spunky and won't give up. Someone who has sales experience and food preparation experience too. Working alongside you in the past at church, I know you have all of those qualities. That's why John and I would like that someone to be you." She'd barely ended her sentence when she glanced down at her watch and half-eaten bagel.

"I'm sorry. I know it's crazy, but I have to run. I've got to get back to Millersburg. John has a doctor's appointment." She started to gather up her purse and coat. "I know I've said a lot, and I don't expect an answer until you've had a chance to think."

Looping a scarf around her neck, she continued, "My sister is staying in town through the holidays to help us. That is, if we don't strangle each other before that." She laughed. "My sister hates to cook — actually she hates to clean and do laundry too." She rolled her eyes. "But still, it was good of her to come."

"Is there anything I can —" Liz started with an offer to help, but Belinda held up her hand.

"What I'd really like for you to do is consider everything I've said, Liz. John and I were hoping you could start in January. Of course, like any other position we fill at Annabelle's, we'd be hiring you on a trial basis."

"I understand." Liz nodded. "That only makes good business sense."

"But in order to make you feel more secure about this venture — and to lure you away from your real estate profession, we're prepared to offer you a salary along with bonuses as the catering business grows. And if it does grow the way we hope it will, well then, perhaps we *could* take you on as a partner."

Liz's head jerked back in shock at everything her friend was saying.

"I'll give you a call in a couple of days for your answer, and to discuss specifics if you're interested." Belinda laid money on the table for the check. "Again, I hate to rush off, but I have to go. Thanks for meeting me, Liz."

"Are you kidding? Thank you, Belinda," she said, still reeling in disbelief at the conversation. "And thank John, too, will you?"

Belinda nodded and then was gone, leaving Liz sitting in front of her own half-eaten bagel, far too dazed to eat one more bite. Instead, feeling overcome with generosity and goodwill, she left a five-dollar tip for the ten-dollar check and grabbed her coat and purse from the back of her chair.

As she left the Pancake House and started back up Main Street, her first inclination was to run and tell Daniel all about the meeting. More than anything, she wanted to share the exciting news with him. She wanted him to be the first to hear.

But then she recalled her last conversation with him and all she was supposed to be thinking about. It was strange how she'd gone through such a long spell of not being able to fill in any blanks regarding her life, feeling vapid and lost. And now suddenly there were life-altering decisions to be made. People she needed to give answers to, including Belinda and, most of all, Daniel. And all soon. Very soon.

Her boots clicking along the pavement, her mind jumped from one dizzying thought to another. Looking up ahead, she wished her church still stood at the top of the hill. If only it were there, she'd do what she'd done so many times before in her life when there were decisions to be made. She'd go sit in a pew to quiet the noise in her head and feel God's stillness all around her.

But with no church in sight, the only other thing that seemed to stand out in the landscape was the petal-outlined sign for Rose's Knit One Quilt Too Cottage.

So clearly she could see it. Rose's Cottage. Rose wasn't there any longer, obviously. Yet the Cottage still stood. But that was only because of the two women inside, Jessica and Lydia, who'd become very special parts of her heart. They'd been given a new shape to their lives. A second chance. And they'd been brave enough to embrace that and to try to make it work.

Suddenly, her steps slowed. Her mind stopped racing. And a peaceful calm came over her as she realized all she'd been feeling for Daniel for the past months. She'd been given another chance. A second chance at love. With him.

And all at once it wasn't just her news about Annabelle's that she wanted to share with him. No, it was more than that. It was what she knew for sure. All that she felt for him in her heart.

Throughout the day, with thoughts of Daniel filling her mind and heart, Liz had barely been able to concentrate on any of her work obligations. Ironically, after suffering through months and months of a lingering dry spell, the one day when she wanted nothing more than to focus on her personal life and Daniel, she'd been booked solid with clients.

Unfortunately, the sun had already set by the time she headed for Daniel's house. As she drew to a stop in front of his home, she heard the shepherd's pie she'd made slide forward on the baking sheet she'd wedged into place on the passenger-side floor. She bent down to set it to rights before looking closer at the street outside. The houses on either side of Daniel's brick ranch were completely lit up, time for most families to gather for dinner. In contrast, his home was as pitch-black as the December sky above it.

Pulling into the driveway, noticing both his truck and his car there, she thought possibly he'd fallen asleep after work. But she rang his doorbell more than once, giving him ample time to answer. When he didn't, she assumed it could only mean one of two things. Either someone had picked him up to go out or he was still at work and had walked the few blocks to the shop that day, something he sometimes did for exercise.

She was hoping it was the latter as she got into her car and headed back toward town. But once she swung around the corner of Trader Lane and arrived at his shop, her heart sank all over again. All she could see were silhouettes of tables and chairs outlined by the streetlight shining in the store window.

Except for — She leaned over the steering wheel. Was there possibly a sliver of light glowing from the rear of the shop? She turned off the car and got out, taking her pie peace offering with her. With each step closer, the glimmer of light grew, and so did her optimism. Without a doubt, someone was in the shop.

Hoping it might be Daniel, she turned the doorknob, only to discover it was locked. She knocked. And knocked again. When no one came, she knocked a little louder, the sound echoing down the silent street.

Please, Daniel. Please be here!

Her toes were already beginning to feel the effects of the chilly temperature, but she was determined not to let another day go by without telling Daniel how much she cared for him. Suddenly feeling desperate, she knocked once again, then rapped on the glass of the door's small window. And waited some more.

All through the ride to his house, she'd had a vision of him throwing open his door and welcoming her into his arms, no matter the time of day or night. But now her mind was a crazy mixture of hope and fear, and physically her body definitely leaned toward unease. Her heart pounded in her chest. Her legs felt unsteady beneath her. Her teeth started to chatter more from apprehension than from the frigid temperature.

What if he'd changed his mind about her?

What if he'd decided she'd waited too long?

Frantic at the thought, she hit her fist on the door once more.

Finally, she saw movement. At last she saw him as he ducked out from the back of the shop, glancing toward the front door.

Nervous as a schoolgirl, she lifted her hand and waved. Even held up the baking dish in her hands for him to see.

But he disappeared. Back into the cavern of the workshop. Surely he was turning off a machine. Or pulling the plug on a tool. Maybe taking off his work gloves and brushing the sawdust from his shirt?

So Liz waited. And waited.

Until she realized she was waiting for

nothing. No reason at all. He wasn't coming to the door. He wasn't inviting her in.

Oh, she knew what Jessica and Lydia would say. They'd ask her why she hadn't tried to knock again. They'd say it might not have been Daniel she saw anyway. That it could've been someone else in the shadows.

But just as she couldn't be fooled by her feelings for him any longer, she knew in every part of her that the man she'd seen was him.

So she did the only thing she knew to do. She turned from the shop to go.

CHAPTER TWENTY-NINE

The December sun gleamed and streamed through the Cottage's front windows, its warmth and clarity feeling like a gift from heaven. It was a perfect day for the Santa sale, Jessica mused — for avid shoppers to get out and do what they did best. And the pleasure of working alongside her friends — her extremely helpful friends — was certainly another blessing to add to her list.

"It looks great in here, doesn't it?" She beamed, glancing around the shop, hoping with everything inside her that the sale would be a shop-saving success . . . that the Cottage would always be a part of her family.

Meanwhile, Lydia paused to smile as she buttoned a hand-knit sweater over a wire mannequin form. "*Jah*. It's very cheery looking."

"And so Christmassy too!" Liz added. "I didn't think we could make the place look any more charming than it already is, but somehow I believe we did just that."

It had certainly taken a lot of work and had been quite the team effort. Luckily none of them had had any major Thanksgiving plans that required their attention. Instead, during the weeks prior to the special November holiday and the week after, they spent nearly every day getting ready for the sale. There didn't seem to be an end to all there was to do! Planning, plotting, cutting, sewing, knitting, Lydia quilting, Liz baking, and Jessica tweeting, e-blasting, advertising, and sending out flyers. But most of the decorating and merchandise setup they'd done had taken place a couple of days earlier, and a lot of it the night before. Thankfully, Derek had taken Cole for the evening since it had been nearly midnight when they'd finally called it quits.

They'd started the shop makeover by adding pine garlands with white twinkling lights and red velvety bows all around the store, outlining the windows, the cash register counter, and many of the fabric bins too. Together, they'd also moved around some cubbies of yarn, making room for a Christmas tree to light up the right side of the shop. The tree sparkled with a mixture of Rose's antique ornaments and some smaller sale items, too — packages of sewing needles, threads, crochet hooks — dangling from its limbs.

Nearby, closer to the front of the shop, they'd set up quilt racks to create a prominent display of the fine-looking quilts Lydia's friends had made. They'd even brought a rocker down from the apartment to make the corner look cozily complete.

Each time Jessica looked at the quilted coverlets, she was overwhelmed. The Amish women had done so much work out of the kindness of their hearts — and what beautiful work it was too! She'd mailed letters to each and every one of the ladies to thank them since they wouldn't accept a commission or even a store discount. Lydia had assured her she could also thank the ladies in person since most of them intended to drop by to further support and check out the Santa Cottage Sale.

At least she felt far better about her own lack of crafting acumen when she came up with the idea of knitting and quilting kits. The ideal crafters' Christmas gift, she left it up to her talented assistant to take the idea and run with it. All of which Lydia was thrilled to do — and did so well.

Mostly for beginners, and for some intermediates too, each see-through package contained a simple pattern for either a small knitting or quilting project along with all the materials and tools needed for the activity. Tied up with pretty Christmas ribbon and a bow, the packets were the perfect Christmas gift for anyone thinking of trying a new craft — or wanting to pass along the love of their craft to someone else. They'd placed large baskets filled with the project packets all around the Cottage. What kits they had left over looked perfect and pretty underneath the Christmas tree.

They'd also removed skeins of yarn from the cubbies in the middle of the store, topping them with a sale sign and twinkling lights, to create a festive display for the sweaters from Aunt Rose's treasure chest and for Jessica's bow-covered scarves. And of course, the shop's regular inventory was available and on sale for anyone who had their own project in mind — any procrastinators in the crowd who might think they still had time to make something new for Christmas.

And no matter if a customer was a knitter, a quilter, or simply a browser, there was something everyone could love — sweets made by Liz.

"The Cottage not only looks like Christmas —" Jessica turned to her baker friend

470

— "you've got it smelling Christmassy too."

While the refreshing scent of pine and conifers emanated from the right side of the shop, the deliciously combined aromas of peppermint, chocolate, and cinnamon wafted from the left. That's where Liz had set up what looked to be a mini holiday bakery.

All along the red linen tablecloth covering the long oak worktable they'd moved from the middle of the store — with much strain and huffing and puffing — were goodies made by Liz's very hands. Cakes topped with Santas, reindeer, jingle bells, and holly-shaped leaves. Individually wrapped cookies of every shape and every kind. All displayed on white porcelain cake stands and on tiered dessert stands as well.

"Is Cole up and about yet?" Liz asked as she tastefully dotted the tablecloth with gold star-shaped ornaments and glimmering white snowflakes. "I put together a box of Rudolph cookies just for him."

"Actually, Derek must've worn him out last night. Cole ended up falling asleep on his couch," Jessica said, still surprised even as she said the words at how comfortable Cole must've been at Derek's condo. "So we decided to let him sleep there, rather than pick him up after we'd finished our

471

decorating."

"Maybe I'll hide his stash behind the cash register counter when I get finished with these stars," Liz told her. "I'll put his name on the box too."

"That's really sweet of you, Liz." Jessica almost felt guilty. "But you didn't have to make something special for Cole. You've already done so much."

"Well, it's not like I haven't had more time on my hands lately." Liz frowned. "A lot of extra time."

"So you haven't had any word from . . ." Jessica paused, almost hating to ask the question.

"Daniel? No," Liz said glumly. "Nothing at all."

"Are you sure you shouldn't give it one more try?" Jessica suggested.

"Oh, I don't know. I really don't." Liz sighed as she moved one cake holder to a different spot and stepped back to look at it before placing it in its original spot again. "I don't know what I should do."

Days before, Liz had told Jessica and Lydia how she'd stopped by Daniel's house and, when she couldn't find him there, went to his shop, where the light was on.

Jessica shook her head. "It still seems odd, Liz. And if it's true that he saw you, there must be a reason why he didn't come to the door."

"Well, I sure don't know what it would be." Liz's voice rose. "There I was, standing in the doorway, all ready to hand him the shepherd's pie and my heart, too. But obviously he didn't want either." She winced as if she were reliving the humiliation and hurt all over again. "I just wish I would've taken the pie home instead of dropping it off at my elderly neighbor's. But honestly?" Liz glanced at Jessica and at Lydia, who was also listening in. "I couldn't stand to look at the thing. However, it would've been a lot healthier for me than all the sweets I've been gorging myself with since that night." She tugged at her sweater, pulling it away from her midline. "But, ladies . . . today is a new day. A big day. And I'm going to focus on all good and positive things. As for matters of the heart, well, I just have to believe things will work out the way they're supposed to."

"*Jah,* but if you help them along, they're certainly more sure to," Lydia spoke up.

Liz turned to Jessica. "Do you remember how quiet she used to be? Oh, whatever happened to our shy, demure Lydia?"

Lydia grinned, not seeming to mind being

teased at all. "Sometimes even I wonder too."

As they stood in different areas in the shop, laughing over the same thing together, the bell jingled over the door. Caught off guard, they all turned toward the entrance, eyes wide with alarm. It was too early and they still had way too many loose ends to tie up before entertaining even the thought of customers, let alone real, live ones.

Thankfully, it was Cole and Derek who came through the door, each carrying a box, prompting sighs of relief all around.

"Well, if it isn't my two favorite guys." Jessica put aside the sweater she was pricing and walked toward them, eager to give her son a hug. "I missed you last night, Colester." She bent forward to kiss the top of her son's head.

But Cole couldn't have cared less about her show of affection. Instead, he was busy turning in every direction, eyes wide, taking in all the decorations. "This looks just like a place Santa would like."

"It really does look great in here, ladies." Derek nodded in agreement. "And I'm sure it took no time at all." He winked, causing them all to smile.

"When is Santa getting here?" Cole asked.

"Uh, well . . . ," Jessica stammered.

"Unfortunately, he's, uh, not going to be able to make it. He's too busy with his own stuff to come today, if you know what I mean," she added in a stage whisper. "But we're calling it Santa's Cottage Sale anyway because who doesn't like Santa, right?"

"Oh." Cole nodded, looking confused but assuaged.

"So what are you two up to?" She changed the subject quickly, turning from her son to Derek. "And what's in the boxes?" She gestured to the cartons they were carrying, Derek more easily than Cole, who kept shifting on his feet from the weight.

"We've got stuff to sell," Cole informed her.

"Oh yeah? You do?"

"But not exactly along the same lines as the items in your shop," Derek let her know.

"But just as good, Mom."

"Well, let's see, then. You guys want to set the boxes on the counter?"

Smiling and curious, she waved them toward the cash register counter, where Derek set down his box and then helped Cole relieve his arms of his.

As Jessica peeked inside the cartons, it only took a moment for her to register what she was seeing — all the beautifully framed and perfectly photographed pictures she'd admired on the walls of Derek's condo.

"Derek, I can't sell these." She sifted through the box, eyeing one incredible landscape shot after another.

"Why? You don't like them?"

"Like them?" She gawked at him. "I love them. But they're yours and they're your memories."

"And I can make more prints of them if I ever want to." Derek shrugged indifferently. "But honestly, I don't think I'll want to. I believe I'm ready for new pictures in new places. I, uh . . . I think it's time."

As he looked into her eyes, she thought she saw something there, heard something in his tone. Some underlying double meaning that she was supposed to catch. Or was she just imagining it? Hoping for it?

"You're really serious, Derek?"

"Absolutely. It's my small contribution. To Rose. To the Cottage."

His words tugged at Jessica's heartstrings, and unable to stop herself, she reached out to hug him around the neck. "Oh, Derek, thank you," she murmured as he reciprocated her touch, wrapping his arms around her waist, holding her close, in a place she never wanted to leave.

But of course, she had to. She stepped back and, not knowing what to do with her arms after that, crossed them over her chest. "Well, they'll make great Christmas gifts for people. I may even buy one for myself."

"How about you just take whatever you want that's left."

"They are a mighty *gut* idea," Lydia said as she and Liz came over to check out the sensational prints. "Now we have everything — stitcheries, sweets, and scenic snapshots at Sugarcreek's Santa's Cottage Sale."

"Try saying that five times fast," Liz said to Cole, who began trying to do just that but without much success.

Meanwhile, just as Jessica was trying to figure out how she was going to display Derek's work, he let her in on his plan.

"I brought the wall easel from my condo, so if you'll let me know which wall you want me to use, Cole and I will get these hung up in no time and then be out of your way."

"Hmm." She tapped a finger to her lip. "I'd say . . ." She swung left and right and then back again. "You know, how about right here, actually?" She pointed to the blank wall at the left side of the cash register. "There's enough space and the pictures will be right up front, where everyone can see them."

"Perfect." Derek gave her a thumbs-up. "You ready, Cole?"

Jessica had to smile at how eager Cole was to keep up with Derek and help him out. In fact, Derek was practically tripping over her son, that's how close Cole was sticking to his new mentor. It seemed he was taking his assisting role seriously.

Liz had tuned in to his behavior too. "It looks like Cole really enjoys being with Derek."

"Yeah, he definitely took an instant liking to him."

Since the very first time Derek had been around Cole at Halloween, he'd won Cole over. Easily. Cole always seemed disappointed when Derek couldn't join them in whatever they had going on. Jessica wanted to think the three of them shared something very special. But then . . . she'd remember that Derek had experience with kids through his volunteer work. Perhaps Cole was just another young, fatherless boy to him. A kid who Derek thought could benefit from a male figure in his life.

"You haven't said anything to Derek yet, have you? About how you're feeling?" Liz asked as they both watched the guys at work. Cole holding tools for Derek, ready and willing to help. Derek encouraging Cole, guiding him through the hanging process.

Jessica shook her head.

"And you're bugging me about trying to contact Daniel again?" Liz shot her a wry smile. "Girl, you need to listen to yourself."

"I know, I know. I've just been busy. . . ."

"Uh-huh."

"And I've had other things on my mind."

"Oh, yeah. Like your mind can only handle one thing at a time."

"I plan to soon, though."

"You need to, honey. You need some resolution."

"I know."

She did need to stop torturing herself and talk to Derek, but since she'd put it off this long, she decided not to have that conversation until after Christmas. The holiday was going to be different and difficult enough for Cole — and her — with Rose gone. She didn't want anything else to change the equilibrium that she and Cole and Derek had been enjoying together.

Besides, as long as she could control herself, did it really matter when she talked to Derek? It wasn't as if he was waiting for her to profess her love to him. Not like Daniel was wishing for with Liz. In fact, her confession might even scare Derek off. Leaving her and Cole without their new, old best friend.

"I'm going to tell him soon," she said again.

Her moment of truth with Liz was interrupted when Lydia called out from across the store, where she was making up a few more last-minute packets.

"Your phone buzzed over here," she said.

"I was wondering where I laid it down. Can you see who it is?"

Lydia picked up the phone, eyeing the message. "It's Marisa. She's almost here and is wondering if you need her to stop for any last items. Marshmallows? Paper plates?"

Jessica turned from the shelf of sweaters she'd finished tagging, glad that she'd hired Marisa to fill in around the store during the sale, to help out in any way she could. But since she wasn't in charge of the sweets, she readily deferred to Liz, who was now busy setting up the hot chocolate machine she'd had stored away in her basement.

"What do you think, Liz?"

"Tell her thank you, but I think we're in good shape for now."

Jessica walked over to retrieve her phone and thumb in the message to Marisa. By the time she was walking back toward the cash register counter, the wall easel was in place, the pictures were hung, and Derek was snapping his toolbox closed.

"You guys work fast," she said.

"It's what you call teamwork. Right, Cole?"

Cole replied with a huge grin.

"I'll let you name your price on the photos, Jess."

"Really? Because I don't know what to think . . . They seem kind of priceless to me." She hated to be the one to decide. "You do know there might not be one of them left by the time you guys get back."

"Yeah, well . . . nothing would make me happier." He grinned, sincerity lighting his eyes. "Anyway, like I said, I'm ready for some new favorite spots. Starting with this morning." He turned to Cole and ruffled his hair. "Cole, what do you say we head out? We're scheduled for a horse-drawn wagon ride in an hour, and I sure don't want to miss it. And we need to get some breakfast first, don't you think?"

Still holding a level in one hand, Cole slipped his other hand into Derek's free one, tugging him toward the door. "I'm ready."

"Don't forget to wear your ski hat, Cole," Jessica called after her son. "And your gloves."

Cole nodded without looking back. It wasn't until Derek stopped in the entry to say his good-byes that Cole turned too.

"Good luck and sell big, ladies!" Derek wished them well.

"Yeah, Mom, sell big," her son said, mimicking the man she'd never stopped caring about.

Jessica blew a kiss to her son — and if truth be known, in her heart of hearts, she'd sort of meant the gesture for Derek, too.

As the two guys were walking out of the Cottage hand in hand, Marisa happened to be traipsing in. Wearing red tights and a long green sweater under a white ski vest, she stopped in the entry, her eyes as wide as Cole's had been as she gawked at all the changes and decorations.

Marisa spun from side to side. "It looks so, so awesome in here. I really do feel like one of Santa's helpers now. Like an elf come to help," she proclaimed. Then, unzipping her backpack, she pulled out a red-and-green felt elf hat, looking more than a little jolly to plunk it over her head of curls.

An hour after Derek and Cole left the Cottage, Jessica officially turned over the sweater sign to Open with a hope in her heart and a prayer on her lips.

But it was the screech of brakes and the hiss of the huge charter bus from Columbus coming to a stop right outside the Cottage door that was like a starter pistol going off, getting the Santa sale rolling. Evidently the flyers announcing the sale had been well received at the nursing home. Even the ladies with walkers and canes came flocking into the shop.

But the elderly bunch weren't the only ones to show up. It seemed the flyers they'd distributed around Sugarcreek and nearby towns had gotten much notice too. As well, her social media and online marketing brought in visitors from many of the surrounding communities, who made quite a few purchases. Then there were the tourists who'd come to Sugarcreek for a quaint, nostalgic holiday weekend to do a little shopping and maybe take in a play. Many of them were curious about a Santa Cottage Sale too.

Once the stream of traffic began, it never seemed to slow up. Meaning Lydia was answering every question imaginable for customers. Liz was busy boxing and bagging sweets nonstop. Their very own elf, Marisa, was scurrying in every direction, helping out in any way she could. And Jessica didn't dare venture far from the cash register.

"I have to tell you, I just love these kits,"

an older woman was telling her as Jessica rang up three of Lydia's knitting kits and three quilting kits the woman had laid on the counter. "I'm getting them for my great-granddaughters, and we're going to set aside a day — well, a few days, I'm hoping — to work on these projects together," the lady informed her. "The kits will be an easy way to start them out. And it's something I've been meaning to teach the girls before I leave this earth."

"Oh, ma'am, I'm guessing that's not the only thing your grandkids have learned from you," Jessica countered as she gave the woman her change and placed the kits in a large shopping bag. "But I'm sure it'll be a memorable day, crafting with your girls. You enjoy your time together."

"I know *I* will," the woman stressed.

"I'm sure the girls will too," Jessica assured her.

"I do hope you're right," the woman said, taking the bag. "If so, I'll be back for more kits. You have a merry Christmas and God bless."

"Same to you, ma'am." Jessica gave a slight wave and realized the woman had been the end of the line. At last! She could finally take a breather — for a moment, anyway. Grabbing her water bottle from under the counter, she was taking a sip as Lydia came around the back of the counter.

"Your kits are such a hit, Lydia," Jessica told her friend excitedly. "We've sold dozens of them already."

"You mean *our* kits," Lydia stressed.

"Okay, yes, *our* kits." Jessica nodded.

"Oh, *gut.* I also put a few more sweaters out, and I noticed the log cabin quilt is already gone from the rack." Her brows raised with happy delight.

"Yes, the biggest sale of the day."

"So far."

Jessica smiled at Lydia's positivity. "Yes, so far. Actually, it's been so busy, I haven't been able to get out from behind this cash register and help at all."

"And that's a *verra gut* thing." Lydia chuckled.

"Oh, and I got a chance to meet some of your friends when I rang them up, Lydia. They're all so nice and far too generous. I'd hoped to get around and meet more of the women and let them know firsthand how much I appreciate their help."

She'd glanced up once or twice from the register to see Lydia hugging several other ladies in *kapps* and long dresses, strolling through the shop.

"Trust me, Jessica, my friends already

know how grateful you are. They've all been telling me the thank-you notes you sent couldna have been any sweeter. If you really want to meet more of them, though, I'll be happy to take over the cash register while you make your way around the shop. There's also someone by the front door who asked to speak to you," Lydia told her, her eyes twinkling.

Glancing in the direction of Lydia's gaze, Jessica was more than surprised to see a woman who had only been in the shop once since she'd taken it over. A woman she'd definitely started off on the wrong foot with. Mrs. Grisham.

She didn't know if she should be worried or pleased, but she slid out from behind the counter anyway and headed toward the front of the store. The closer she got, she realized why Mrs. Grisham probably didn't feel very comfortable coming any farther into the crowded shop. A purple cast stuck out from the left armhole of the brown wool cape she was wearing, and a black brace on her right arm poked out the other side. Jessica also instantly recognized the greenish-blue prayer shawl from her aunt Rose's treasure chest, wrapped around Mrs. Grisham's shoulders like a scarf.

Taking a deep breath, Jessica stepped in

front of the formidable woman and nodded a hello. "Mrs. Grisham."

"Hmph," Mrs. Grisham grunted. "I would think you could call me Virginia by now — now that you've been to my house."

"Your, uh, house?" Jessica pretended to be confused.

"It's all right, Jessica." A slight smile began to tug at the other woman's lips. "Your secret is good with me. Just as your aunt's secret was good with me too."

"Well, I . . . ," Jessica stammered and tried to steer away from the Secret Stitches, not sure what to say. "How are you doing?" she asked instead. "I was sorry to hear about your fall."

"I'm doing well. It's just a matter of time before this all heals," the woman said stolidly, straightening her shoulders. "But actually, the reason I'm here is that I thought I'd feel even better if I came and apologized to you."

Jessica had expected the woman to speak staunchly, assuredly. To pull back her shoulders and act as if she could handle anything that came her way. What she hadn't expected was for her to offer up an apology. That left her completely stunned. "Apologize for what?"

"For giving up on you so quickly. For not

showing you grace. It wasn't fair of me."

"Mrs. Grisham, really, an apology isn't necessary." Jessica waved a hand, then looked down at her feet before she glanced at the woman again. "Remember? I was the one who messed up your order to begin with."

"Yes, you did. But anyone can make a mistake," she replied, repeating the words Derek had uttered to her recently. "Even I made a mistake by judging you the way I did. Why, just because you don't have your aunt's knitting and quilting knowledge —"

"Oh, I know. It's quite apparent, isn't it?" Jessica halfway grinned, almost feeling better that she was finally learning to accept her shortcomings and work on them, rather than keep berating herself for them.

"Yes, dear, I'm afraid it is." Mrs. Grisham didn't try to soften her reply in the least. "But that's exactly what I came here to tell you. Because one morning I woke up, and lo and behold, I found something on my front doorstep. A little package of hope, would you believe it?" She tilted her head, and Jessica could tell by the way her eyes brightened that the package had been most appreciated. "And that's the day I learned you have something even more important about you than your aunt's craft knowledge,

Jessica."

Puzzled, Jessica frowned. "I do?"

"Yes, you do. You have your aunt's caring heart. And that's a big part — the biggest part — of making a shop like the Cottage successful, my young friend. It's something that will have women wanting to come back to your shop, time and time again."

Once again, Mrs. Grisham had taken her by surprise. Jessica found herself blubbering, "I don't know what to say. You'll never know how much it means to hear that from you, Mrs. —"

The other woman held up her hand. "Virginia," she insisted.

"Virginia." Jessica smiled. "It truly means a lot. It does."

In the middle of all the chaos and worry, Virginia Grisham's words calmed her and touched her like nothing had in a long, long while. To be told she was anything like her aunt Rose — any special little part of her, and especially her caring heart — made her feel like she was giving a gift back to the aunt who had raised her, had mercy on her, and loved her unconditionally like a daughter of her very own.

"I do have to tell you, Virginia," Jessica confessed, "I'm not the only one trying to follow in my aunt's footsteps to keep the

Cottage going. Lydia Gruber is a huge part of that too." She nodded at her Amish friend, busy at the cash register. "And Liz Cannon has been an incredible help. As you already know, my aunt left some big shoes to fill."

"But together you're filling them, and I'm here to promise you, I won't be driving all the way to Coshocton anymore for supplies. My ladies' group is coming back to the Cottage. That is, if it's okay with you."

"It's more than okay," Jessica told her new customer, who was actually beginning to feel like an ally and friend. "I'd be honored to have you all, Virginia, whenever that may be."

"Well . . ." Virginia's face broke into a full-fledged smile. "Some of the ladies are here today. There's Joann." She nodded to a woman studying the items hanging from the Christmas tree. "Then Vicky and Debbie are over there looking at the prints on the wall. And then Lucy —" She paused to chuckle. "It looks like she might have her eye on one of the quilts. She'd so much rather buy one than make one any day of the week. Knitting is more her thing.

"I figure you may as well get to know their names," Virginia continued, "because you'll be seeing a lot of them. And me, too, once I get back on my feet — er, well, back to using my arms and hands. In fact, I'd really like to knit one of those scarves over there." She nodded toward one of Jessica's creations. "The ones with that pretty, sparkly ribbon."

"Oh, that? That's probably far simpler than you're used to." Jessica waved her hand. She couldn't even begin to imagine how she'd show someone how to make such a lumpy, bumpy thing. "But I appreciate your vote of confidence, Virginia."

"Will you thank the rest of the gals for me? Lydia and Liz? For the prayer shawl and chocolates and slippers?"

"Uh . . ." Forcing herself to stay straight-faced, Jessica arched a brow and cocked her head sideways. "Hmm. What prayer shawl, chocolates, and slippers?"

Virginia laughed out loud. "Oh, you're right. You'll have to excuse me. The fall I took still has me a bit daffy. I have no idea who was kind enough to deliver a prayer shawl, chocolates, and slippers to my doorstep." She winked. "Absolutely no clue at all."

The sun that had poured through the shop windows first thing in the morning was beginning to give up its reign in the sky by the time the last customer left the Cottage. It had been one busy and tiring day.

But a successful one, as well.

In fact, Jessica thought the shop looked as if a winter storm had blown through the place, leaving the quilt racks bare, half the Christmas tree ornaments missing, baskets and bins totally empty where kits and sweaters and scarves used to be. The cake stands and dessert trays held nothing but a few crumbs. And only one photo was left hanging on the wall. A shot of a flower garden at sunrise, which Jessica planned to keep for the shop with Derek's permission.

"You don't mind if the hot chocolate machine sits here until tomorrow, do you?" Liz asked as she and Marisa were gathering up their things to leave. "I'll drop by and pick it up then."

"Or I can run it over to your house," Jessica offered.

"Whatever. We can see what the day brings."

"Are you sure neither of you wants to stay for a cup of tea? And to rest your feet for a minute?"

Still wearing her beloved elf hat, Marisa zipped up her vest, ready to go. "I'm already too full. This little elf drank way too much hot chocolate." She groaned, patting her belly.

"Honestly, it was a fun day, Jess, but I'm pooped," Liz told her. "All I want to do is go home, get in my pj's, and eat some red velvet cake."

"But I thought you sold all the cakes," Lydia spoke up.

"All the ones I brought to the sale." Liz gave a sheepish smile. "But I kept one cake at the house. One just for me. Ho, ho, ho." She jiggled up and down, making them all laugh.

"Well, ladies, I couldn't have done this without you," Jessica said as she walked them both toward the front door.

"Oh, pshaw. Sure you could've." Marisa waved a hand at her.

"But if you had, I would've missed out on a lot," Liz said as she pulled on her gloves.

"Just to tell you, from a quick tally of the sales, it looks like you helped to save a life today. The Cottage has been revived and can remain open for business."

Jessica tried to sound businesslike as she gave them the brief report, but she could feel the emotion rising inside of her. And what did it matter anyway? More than anything else, these women were her friends.

"I really . . . really can't thank you all

enough." Her voice warbled on the verge of tears as she eyed each one of them. What an unlikely group the four of them were. Yet somehow they worked together and cared about each other in such a perfect way. "Without you . . ." A tear slid slowly down her cheek. "I know I would've lost something that's very precious to me. And something that was so precious to Aunt Rose, too. But now . . ." She sniffled, and before she could get anything else out, Lydia was by her side, patting her shoulder.

At the same time, Liz's gloved hand reached out to touch her cheek. "It's all good, honey. It's all good."

"It's really good," Marisa piped up. "Because there were a lot of women today asking if we'd be doing the same thing next Christmas."

"Really?" Lydia sounded unusually curious. "What did you tell them?"

"I said yes, of course." Marisa twisted the end of her hat around her finger, tinkling the bell there. "This time next year I'll be home from college for a long stretch, and I'll be looking for something fun to do."

"You think working at the Cottage is fun?" The idea of Marisa thinking so warmed Jessica's heart all over again.

"Sure." Marisa shrugged, glancing among

the three of them. "I mean, why wouldn't it be? You guys are all nice, the shop is great, and it's a whole lot better than cleaning the toilets at my aunt's hair salon," she said, causing all of them to break out laughing.

"Well, there you go." Jessica held her hands in the air as a chuckle dissipated her tears. "An honest woman. I knew there was something I liked about you, Marisa. Actually, there are many things I like about you." She hugged the teenage girl, who smiled shyly.

"At least we have a year to rest up," Lydia said wisely.

"Yes." Liz paused to cup a yawn. "And that's just what I intend to do."

After a round of hugs, the bell over the Cottage door chimed farewell as Liz and Marisa left the store.

Without waiting a beat, Lydia started in with her usual endless store of energy, picking up wayward skeins of yarn and knitted items that had been shuffled around. Jessica had to stop her in her tracks.

"Uh-uh-uh." Jessica approached her friend, shaking a finger. "No more straightening up or cleaning up, Lydia. The day is done. Time to rest. We'll get the mess another day, another time," she said, taking sweaters and knitting needles from Lydia's arms and laying them aside. "How about something to drink before I take you home? Something cold? Or hot tea? Or —"

"Hot chocolate?" Lydia asked.

"That does sound good, doesn't it?"

Each grabbing a cup of hot chocolate, they settled onto Rose's bench in the middle of the store. Jessica reached into the pocket of her Cottage apron and brought out a baggie containing two candy cane–shaped sugar cookies, frosted with green icing.

"Oh! I didn't think there were any cookies left." Lydia happily took one.

"I hid them before we got started this morning."

"*Verra* sneaky. *Gut* thinking."

"Actually, I believe my best thinking was in hiring you, Lydia. I really couldn't have done any of this without you. And I have to tell you, I'm amazed. I mean, you've had a very rough, emotional week, and you still went above and beyond. You really should take a couple of days off. I mean it. And with pay, of course."

"*Danke*, Jessica. *Danke* for your kind words, but *nee.* I don't think I want to have *verra* much free time right now, if you know what I'm saying. It's been *gut* to be as busy as I've been with the Cottage and the sale. It's been a saving grace, to be sure, with all that's been going on. I think that's true for Liz, too."

"She's just not her usual high-spirited self right now, is she?" Jessica hugged the warm cup. "Even though she keeps pretending all is well . . . which breaks my heart."

"*Jah.* Sometimes that's what we have to do, I guess. Isn't there an *Englischer* saying about that?"

"You mean 'fake it till you make it'?"

"*Jah,* that's the one." Lydia nodded.

"I just wish she would try to reach out to Daniel again." Jessica sighed. "Actually I wish he would've come to the door the night she went to his shop. I wonder why they're both being so stubborn."

"I don't know." Lydia shrugged. "But I was thinking there might be something we could do about that."

"Yeah? Well, whatever it is you're thinking, all I can say is, I'm in, sister." Jessica lifted her cup and started to take a sip, then stopped with the cup at her lips. "Oh, goodness. I just called you 'sister,' didn't I?"

Lydia smiled. "*Jah,* you did."

"That's funny. I've never had a sister before."

"Well then, I'd say you're in for a mighty *gut* treat." Lydia raised her cup in a salute, making Jessica laugh.

"Liz is right," Jessica mused. "You have opened up quite a bit, Lydia, which, as you would say, is a *verra gut* thing."

CHAPTER THIRTY

Liz had been surprised to be greeted by a note on Lydia's front door, inviting her to come right in and saying she'd had to run next door to help Jonas with something and would be back real soon. In much smaller print, there was also a reminder for Liz to park her car up near the barn. Out of the way. That request, Liz already knew, was to make room for buggies, just in case some of Lydia's Amish friends joined them later in the evening to make peanut butter spread.

Having followed Lydia's directions to a T, Liz stood in the kitchen, waiting for her return, wondering how the woman managed to do all that she did.

Although Liz had told Lydia several times that she didn't need to come home from work and make dinner for the two of them, her friend wouldn't hear of doing anything but. She had also insisted, more than once, that Liz needn't bring a thing.

Seeing what a pretty table Lydia had set for the two of them, complete with lovely butter-colored plates and a hurricane candleholder surrounded by a wreath of pinecones, and after peeking into the oven at the roast and vegetables that looked delicious and ready to eat, Liz wished she wouldn't have listened to Lydia.

She could've at least brought a dessert. Not that she needed any sweets these days. Since the sad chain of events with Daniel, she'd been bingeing on any sugary thing she could get her hands on. As if that could fill the void she kept feeling deep inside her. At least she wouldn't have any trouble coming up with a New Year's resolution when January rolled around. She just hoped she could muster up some resolve by then regarding Daniel.

Sighing, she stood in the middle of the kitchen with her arms crossed over her chest, rubbing at the sleeves of her sweater. She seemed to be doing that a lot lately too, she'd noticed. As if Daniel's departure from her life, and the lack of his warmth, had left her with a permanent chill.

Maybe her friends were right after all. Maybe she should try to contact him once more. But then, if she did, would she only regret it? Only get hurt all over again?

Glancing out the kitchen window into the darkness, she weighed the situation and her possible options, just as she'd done a hundred other times before. She still hadn't settled anything in her mind or heart when she heard a creaking sound coming from the front door. Not wanting to be a downer for her friend — especially not after all the trouble Lydia had gone to — she did her best to hide her angst and put on a cheery face.

"Hey there, girlfriend," she called as she started for the door. "You sure went out of your way to make things ni—"

Her voice faltered at the same exact time her feet did. Halting in her tracks, she gazed at the figure standing in the entry, who did not look one bit like Lydia.

And not one bit happy to see her.

In fact, the very man she'd been thinking of, stewing about, yearning for, and eating way too much chocolate over stood staring at her, a scowl taking hold of his entire face.

"Liz? What — what are *you* doing here?" Daniel's brow furrowed and his lips weren't curved upward in their usual sweet way — the way she'd remembered him by. She was hoping he was simply as shocked at seeing her as she was at seeing him. That one of his embracing, tender smiles would surface any moment. But instead, he grimaced. And frowned some more.

Hurt by his greeting, and tired of hurting, she drew herself up, put her hands to her hips, then haughtily tossed her head.

"Well, hello yourself, Daniel. I could say the same thing about you, you know. What are *you* doing here?"

"Sorry." His chin jutted outward. "But you're the last person I expected to see."

"You mean the last person you wanted to see."

"Did I say that?"

"Not so much with words, no. But if the expression on your face is any indication . . ."

"Look, I'm confused, is all." He glanced around the sitting room and over her head toward the kitchen, avoiding eye contact with her. "Jonas asked if I'd meet him here. He said he needed help fixing his neighbor's plumbing. Then, just as I'm pulling in the drive, he calls from someone's cell and says he's running late, but to come in anyway."

"That's strange." Liz was just as puzzled. "I didn't know Lydia had a plumbing problem. I was supposed to be meeting her here twenty minutes ago for a bite to eat. Then we were going to spend the evening making peanut butter spread with her friends. But when I got here, there was a note on the door saying she had to help Jonas with something, and . . ." She scratched at her head, trying to make sense of it all. "What do you think they're doing? Do you think they're all right?"

"I have no clue." Daniel blinked at her. "All I know is that Jonas said his neighbor left a note for me in the kitchen, describing the problem, so I could get started looking at things."

"Well, he's wrong. There was no note on the table, Daniel. I can attest to that."

"Not on the table." Daniel shook his head, still not meeting her gaze. "I was told it'd be on a kitchen counter, in her stationary basket. Do you know what on earth a stationary basket looks like? Is it a basket that stays put?"

At a former point in their relationship, Liz would've laughed and thought Daniel's silly comment was cute. She might've even laughed right then if he still didn't seem so put out to see her. "I doubt it." She crossed her arms over her chest. "I would guess the basket contains Lydia's letter-writing materials — as in *stationery,*" she answered smugly.

"Oh . . . yeah. Right." He shrugged. "Well, I'll take a look and then be out of your way so you can have that dinner you're looking forward to."

He began to stride toward the kitchen, but somehow she couldn't let him go. Not again. Before his broad shoulders could disappear around the corner, she had to say something. She was tired of the puzzle, tired of wondering. Seeing him again, unable to deny all that she felt for him, she couldn't hold her feelings in any longer.

"Daniel, I —"

Her heart pounded as she boldly reached out to touch the arm that she'd hoped would hold her again. He stopped and turned, his serious eyes leveled on hers. Her legs were as shaky and unsteady as they'd been the frigid night she'd gone to see him. Shocked by her own audacity, she knew what she meant to say, what she had to say, but she had no idea how to get started.

"Daniel . . . I — I came to see you." She stumbled over her words. "At your shop." She closed her eyes for a moment, not wanting to ask the next question but needing so much to know the truth. "You — you knew I was there, didn't you? That was you, wasn't it? Who wouldn't let me in?"

"It was dark. . . . I didn't think you saw me. . . ." His voice drifted. Like a convicted man, he bowed his head and looked away from her.

Just as she'd suspected. Her stomach grew sick and heavy, and her legs weaker, as she swayed on her feet.

Removing her hand from his arm, she couldn't stop shaking her head. "I don't understand, Daniel."

"Oh, come on, Liz. Can you blame me? For not wanting to be that guy?" His accusing voice stabbed the air, his eyes glowering as he finally looked at her.

"That guy? What guy?" Her mind reeled with confusion. "I don't know what you're talking about."

"Really? You *really* don't understand?"

"I — I —" She wavered, trying to comprehend what she was hearing. "I'm sorry, Daniel, but I don't."

He stared at her for a moment. His jaw clenching. His eyes glaring. Then he sucked in a deep breath and seemed much calmer when he spoke. "Look, it's really nice what you do. How you keep a list of people in need. People who are sick, people who are hurting. You take time — when no one else does — to make them a meal or bake something special. And I get it; I understand it. I know you truly want to make people feel better about their situation. To help them through whatever it is. You want to let

505

them know someone cares. Which is great of you, Liz. It is. But . . ."

He paused and Liz stiffened, still so bewildered by what he was saying. Still so frightened of losing him all over again.

"I don't need that from you, Liz," he finally continued. "That's not who I wanted to be to you. Not a person on your list. My feelings for you . . . Well, I wanted to be *the* person. I told you that. And when I saw you standing at the shop door, at first I was thrilled to see you. But then I saw the casserole dish you were holding, and I . . . It made me angry. Angry that I was like everyone else to you . . . that you'd made it and brought it along to soften the blow. And when I didn't hear from you after that night . . ." He shrugged. "I figured either you hadn't seen me in the shadows of the shop or — honestly? — I assumed I'd fallen off your to-do list."

Her mouth gaped at his bluntness. "Actually, Daniel, if you only would've opened the door, you would've learned it was a shepherd's pie." She hated the way her voice was shaking as she tried to explain. "My version of humble pie because I was there, at your shop, wanting to humbly ask for your forgiveness."

"My forgiveness for what? Because you

506

don't feel the same way I do? Don't worry, I'm not going to hold it against you. I just want some distance from you right now." He glanced down at his feet before meeting her gaze again. "And, no offense, I'm sure your shepherd's pie was great, but I really didn't need a consolation prize."

Hearing the sting in his voice, she reached out to touch his arm again. "Oh, Daniel, that's not what I meant for it to be. Not at all," she pleaded, wanting so much for him to understand all the things she'd had a hard time comprehending herself. "I was hoping you could forgive me for taking so long to realize what I was feeling for you. Even my friends could see it in me from the very beginning. But I was scared and so surprised. I didn't know how to react because I just didn't think it was possible to feel this way again."

"Not possible because of who I am? Or what I do?" He cocked his head. "Because those things aren't going to change, Liz." He spoke quietly but she could still detect a note of bitterness in his voice. She hoped he could hear the sincerity in hers.

"Daniel," she said softly, "I don't want them to. I don't want to change anything about you. You're an incredible man. Every time I'm with you, I find more and more things to like — to love about you. What I'm having such a hard time saying is, I didn't think my feelings for you were possible because I've already had so much. A good life. A good marriage."

He frowned, looking as if he was trying to understand. "And you didn't think you deserved more?"

"Not that I didn't deserve it. Why, I never even imagined it. I thought my life was all that it was going to be. I kept busy at it, filling the hours and days. Then I met you, and I never stopped to truly acknowledge how you were filling my heart. I still can't believe it," she croaked, an overwhelming sense of gratitude welling up inside her.

She fanned her face, trying to stave off the tears, so determined to explain to him, to share everything in her heart. "It seems amazing to me that God would give me a second chance. And a first chance to build a new life with you."

He took his time to scrutinize her face, and she knew he was weighing her words. She only wished she knew what they meant to him. The moments of waiting for his reply felt torturous, but how could she blame him? She'd certainly taken her time to consider her feelings for him, hadn't she?

Finally, he reacted. He crossed his arms

over his broad chest and arched a lone brow. "So . . . ," he drawled, sounding duly serious. "I guess what that means is . . . you do want to be more than just friends?" A slight smile crept over his lips.

She didn't know whether to laugh or cry at his response. So she did both, choking on her laughter. "Oh, so much more."

"Jah?" His grin broadened as he dropped back into the vernacular of his childhood.

"Yes."

He held out his long-awaited arms to her, and in two steps, she was right where she wanted to be, locked in his embrace. A place she knew she belonged. And this time when his lips caressed hers, she gave in to the heady sensation of his kiss. More than that, she answered him with kisses of her own, wanting him to know the yearning and fervor she had for him.

When they finally came up for air, she looked into his eyes. Though she wanted him to reclaim her lips, there was more she had to say. "Besides being right about us, Daniel, there's one other thing I need to tell you. Another thing you were right about."

"My head is going to be too big to fit through the door if you keep this up," he joked.

"But you need to know you were correct.

God also had a plan concerning my job."

"You made a sale?"

"Even better. I had breakfast with Belinda — the day I tried to see you, actually — and the reason she looked familiar to you is because she and her husband are the new proprietors of Annabelle's."

"Ah." Daniel nodded. "That's where I've seen her."

"When I met with her, that's when I really came to recognize my feelings for you, too, Daniel."

He frowned, pushing a stray hair back from her forehead. "I'm sorry, Lizzy, but you're losing me."

"Well, as soon as I spoke to Belinda, I wanted to share my news with you and only you," she confided. "I mean, I love my girlfriends, and I tell them absolutely everything. But you're the one I wanted to tell first because I knew it would mean so much to you."

He stared at her, baffled. "What would mean so much to me?"

"Belinda and her husband want to hire me to run the catering part of their business. Can you believe it?"

"Annabelle's?" He stepped back, pure joy bursting from every feature on his face. "Liz, that's incredible!" He gripped her shoulders, almost shaking her in his delight. "Fantastic! And much deserved after all the meals you've cooked for people over the years."

"And I don't have to give that up either." Her words came excitedly. "Their restaurant works in partnership with the local food pantries, so I can even help distribute meals for them."

"What great news!" he exclaimed. "We need to celebrate you!"

She stood on her tiptoes and brushed a kiss upon his cheek. "I'd much rather celebrate us."

"Yeah? Me too." He smiled languidly, gazing into her eyes.

"Anyway, I have a feeling Lydia and Jonas aren't showing up."

"I have that same feeling."

"Do you think there's really a note in the stationery basket?" she wondered.

"I don't know. We can sure look and see."

Arms wrapped around each other's waists, they strolled into the kitchen. Right away, on the counter next to the bread box, Liz spied a wicker basket she hadn't noticed before.

"That has to be it." She broke away from Daniel's embrace to peer inside. The basket was filled with loose sheets of pale-blue paper, and right on top she discovered a small envelope, also blue, with black print on it.

"Hmm." She picked it up, eyeing the words there. " 'For a special couple,' " she read. " 'Liz and Daniel, that means you.' "

She laughed and Daniel chuckled as well. He peeked over her shoulder while she opened the envelope and pulled a piece of folded stationery from the sleeve.

"A-hem." She cleared her throat. " 'Roses are red. Violets are blue. Look in the oven to find dinner for two. Share the meal, and share the time, and everything will work out fine.' " She looked fixedly at the words for a moment longer, digesting the message. "Well, it's confirmed, then. We've been —"

"Set up," he finished her thought. "But it seems we were a step ahead of them. We didn't even need dinner to work out our differences."

"But we did need our friends' help to bring us together." She spun around to face him. "We're lucky we have such special people in our lives. Friends who care so much."

"True." He took her hands into his. "We're even luckier we have each other."

"Oh, Daniel. I've missed you so much." She sighed, leaning her head against his solid shoulder. "So much has happened since I saw you last."

"You mean more than your job offer?"

"So much more."

"Like what?" His fingers sifted gently through her hair.

"Well . . ." She paused to think and couldn't come up with a single specific answer. "I don't know exactly. All I know is that every day that went by without you, there would be things I'd want to tell you about. Times I wanted to laugh with you. Thoughts I wanted to share."

"We can get started now, talking over dinner. That is, if I ever let you go." With that, he tightened his embrace, pulling her even closer, causing her to giggle in his arms.

"Oh, but we really should eat, shouldn't we? Lydia went to a lot of trouble for us. And Jonas, and Jessica too, I'd imagine."

"You're right." Stepping back slightly, he raised her chin with the crook of his finger. "It's time for dinner for two." He smiled into her eyes. "To share with one beautiful, incredible woman . . . mine." Then he bent to kiss her once again, his lips warm and sweet on hers.

"I love you, Lizzy," he whispered. "I've loved you for some time now."

"Actually, Daniel," she felt thrilled to

admit, "I believe I loved you first."

"Oh! Oh! Oh!" Lydia squealed happily. "It's working. Our plan is working!" Standing at Jonas's kitchen window, holding Jessica's binoculars over the bridge of her nose, she peered into her own kitchen across the way. "We did it, Jessica."

"Yes!" Jessica thrust a triumphant fist into the air. "I was hoping things would turn out all right for those two."

"But I mean to tell ya, it's *really* working between them. Liz and Daniel are kissing and hugging and everything over there."

"Kissing?" Jessica's eyes widened. "You've got to let me see," she said as she stole the binoculars from Lydia's hands.

"I'm so *verra* happy for them." Lydia sighed. "And so glad for Jonas, too. He was a bit nervous duping his uncle the way he did."

"Is that why he scooted Derek and Cole out to the barn to meet his new goat so quickly?"

"I'm sure it was."

"Ah . . . nothing can stop true love." Jessica came away from the window looking dreamy-eyed as she laid the binoculars on the table. "I'd say we make a pretty good team, Lydia."

Lydia laughed, both delighted and relieved by their successful plan. "*Jah,* we do. A pretty *gut* team, for sure."

"You know . . . I've been thinking." All at once Jessica seemed unsettled, rubbing her hands together.

"*Jah?*" Lydia frowned. She couldn't imagine what had her friend suddenly stewing so.

"It's about the Cottage." Jessica's tone turned more serious. "I think I've figured out a way to make the Cottage more profitable all year round. But my idea — well, it's going to take a lot of groundwork and grunt work. And I know I can't do it alone. It's something we'd have to do together. You and I."

"How so?" Lydia's curiosity piqued.

"Well . . . the idea came to me when I heard about Liz's new catering position. And then it really began to feel like more of a possibility when we came up with those quilting and knitting kits for the Santa sale." Jessica's eyes began to glow brightly. "Oh, Lydia, with e-commerce we can cater to our clients year-round," she said excitedly, "and we can develop so many more new customers too. And the kits — those packets — are a perfect way for us to get started. Every month we can offer a project to customers online, and seasonal projects, too, for anyone from beginners to seasoned vets."

Lydia didn't want to throw cold water on her friend's idea, but listening to what Jessica was explaining, she had reservations about her own abilities. "But, Jessica, I don't know anything about computers. Not that I wouldn't try to learn if you wanted to teach me, but —"

"But that's the point, Lydia. You don't have to know. You'd be the creative and crafty part of the business, and I'd handle all the marketing, offline and online. We'd be partners."

Lydia's cheeks flushed at the very idea of the word. "It's all *verra* exciting, Jessica. But you don't have to make me a partner to do all of that. I'd do it anyway."

"But it only seems fair." Jessica shrugged. "And anyway, I'd be doing it because I want to. Not because I have to."

"You may want some more time to think about it," Lydia graciously told her friend.

"I have thought about it, Lydia. A lot. And I wouldn't have said so if that wasn't the way I wanted it to be."

"Well then . . . if you're sure . . . I do have one suggestion," Lydia said shyly.

"Really?" Jessica's expression quickly turned serious. "A suggestion already?"

"*Jah.* I do."

"Okay then. Shoot." Jessica wriggled beside her, then stilled and narrowed her eyes, waiting to hear.

"Partners or not, I don't think we should ever change the name of the shop. We should always keep it as Rose's Cottage. Rose's Knit One Quilt Too Cottage. I never met your aunt, but I feel like I know her. And, in a strange sort of way, I'd miss her if her name wasn't there."

She hadn't meant to bring up anything to upset her friend, but she could see Jessica's eyes grow misty. "See —" Jessica's voice broke. "That's exactly why I want you to be a part of the Cottage, Lydia. You just get it."

"*Jah,* but you have to know it doesn't only work one way, Jessica. The Cottage, and you, have been great blessings for me too."

Jessica stepped closer to hug her, but before Lydia could even reciprocate, her friend rocked back on her heels.

"Uh-oh."

"What's wrong?"

"The guys." Focusing her gaze out the window, Jessica pointed at the two men and her son, straggling back from Jonas's barn. "They're going to come in here any minute, hungry and wondering what there is to eat."

"*Jah,* you're right." Lydia rubbed her chin thoughtfully. "I suppose when we were making dinner for Liz and Daniel, we shoulda been thinking about dinner for ourselves, too. I was already getting kind of hungry myself, peeling those carrots and potatoes."

"And your pecan pie . . . oh, it smelled so heavenly," Jessica moaned. "You did leave a note in one of the napkins, didn't you? Letting Liz and Daniel know that the pie was in the refrigerator for them?"

"Just as we'd planned." Lydia nodded, thinking how her stomach had growled hours ago as she blended the pecans and brown sugar.

"Personally . . . I think we've cooked enough for one day. I say we go out to eat and celebrate." Jessica raised a brow. "What do you think? Der Dutchman?"

Lydia's mouth watered at the mention of her favorite restaurant. "Perfect," she said because it was. A perfect way to end a mighty *wunderbar* day.

CHAPTER THIRTY-ONE

Jessica had just finished zipping her knee-high black boots and straightening her gray turtleneck sweater dress when she heard footsteps coming up the outside stairs, followed by a knock on the door. Derek's knock — a recognizable *rat-a-tat-tat* that he'd been using ever since she'd known him.

Striding in her heeled boots toward the door, she was breathless from hurrying to get herself ready and Cole, too. Or at least that's what she told herself. But seeing Derek standing in the doorway in his black wool coat and newsboy cap, she knew without a doubt her rushing around was only a part of her shortness of breath.

More and more lately, no matter when she saw him, or what the occasion, her body betrayed her in so many ways. Either with a catch in her breathing, an extremely dry mouth, flushed cheeks, or sometimes every symptom at once. And each time, she hoped the man who'd always been her closest friend wouldn't happen to notice.

"Hey, you're early," she greeted him, trying to sound light and breezy.

"Yes, I am," he said as he wiped his shoes on the outdoor mat and stepped inside. "I hope that's not a problem."

"No, not at all. It's so sweet of you, Derek. Going with Cole and me tonight. I appreciate it so much."

She couldn't have felt more thankful when Derek offered to escort her and Cole to the candlelight service at Faith Community's church grounds. Obviously he knew it would be an emotional night for her, and it comforted her greatly to know that he'd be there, close by her side.

The service wasn't meant to be any kind of groundbreaking ceremony. That was scheduled for January. Since the *Farmers' Almanac* was predicting a mild winter, it was hoped construction crews wouldn't face too many bad weather interruptions in the months that followed.

But not wanting to let Christmas go by without some kind of observance, Faith Community's pastor had invited congregants — and any and all townspeople, too — to meet at the church grounds on this evening. To come and remember, to come worship and sing, and to celebrate their Savior's birth as they looked forward to the rebirth of their church in the new year.

"There's no way I wouldn't want to be with you two, Jess." His eyes shone with sincerity. "Where is that little guy anyway?"

"He's in his room, taking pictures of toys. He's been obsessed with the camera you got him. He carries it everywhere."

Derek smiled, looking pleased. "Good, good, I'm glad he likes it. I'm also, uh, kind of glad he's occupied because I . . . well, there's a reason I stopped by, you know, a few minutes early. . . ."

It was so unlike self-assured, talkative Derek to stumble over anything he was saying — and he was fumbling quite a bit. Suddenly concerned, Jessica felt her heartbeat quicken. "Is everything okay, Derek?"

"Yeah, I, uh, just wanted to . . . you know . . ."

She nodded reassuringly, as if that might help him get the words out.

"Well, first . . ." He shook his head, seeming to change tracks. "I, uh, I brought you something you may want to wear tonight."

Instantly self-conscious, she glanced down at herself. "I know the dress seems sort of plain, but I do have a plaid scarf I'd planned to wear with it, and I think that might —"

"Jess." Derek stopped her. "You look great. You always look great."

She looked up at him, questioningly.

"Seriously, you do."

"Well, thanks, but then . . . ?"

All along he'd been standing with his hands behind his back, but she hadn't thought to ask or reason why. Now he drew both hands forward and held out a tiny crimson gift bag for her.

Definitely too small to hold a blouse, a pair of gloves, or even earmuffs. Jessica stared at the bag. Her breathing became shallow all over again as she glanced at him, puzzled.

"Go ahead. There's nothing in there that will bite. I promise."

Taking the teensy bag from his hands, she used two fingers to pull out the equally petite box inside.

A jewelry case. Of course. She knew that's what it had to be. What else would be so small?

Hands trembling at the very sight of it, she set the empty gift bag on the coffee table and held the case in her hands. Again, she looked up at Derek, baffled.

"Like I said, it's something I thought you'd want to wear tonight."

She'd barely opened the box halfway when

she gasped. Opening it all the way, she let out a cry. "Oh, Derek, I can't believe this. I can't."

Tears of joy clouded her eyes. Even so, she could still see the earrings so clearly. The earrings her aunt Rose had given her so long ago. Rubies and diamonds, sparkling with a sentiment more priceless than their value could ever amount to. A piece of her heart she thought she'd lost forever.

"I don't understand. How did you find them? How could you possibly know?"

His features began to relax, his voice sounding more normal and almost amused as he explained. "When we were at Mick's Diner for lunch, remember? I got a call and then you got up to use the restroom. I noticed a piece of paper had fallen out of your coat onto the floor. I picked it up and put it in my uniform pocket, meaning to give it to you. But then I forgot." He shrugged.

"It wasn't until later that night," he continued, "that I came across the paper again when I was emptying out my own pockets. When I saw it was a receipt from the pawn shop for your ruby earrings, I knew I had to do something, Jess. I knew how much they meant to you."

She stared at him in disbelief. In wonder

at how well he'd always known her. In awe of how much he'd always cared. "I went back for them, you know," she told him. "After the sale, when I had some extra money. But they weren't there, and I was so sad. I didn't think I'd ever see them again."

"I'm sorry. Maybe I should've brought them by sooner. But I thought —"

"That tonight would be the perfect time for me to have them back? Oh, and it is. It's the best time ever." She threw her arms around his shoulders, hugging him as tightly as she could. "To be able to wear them tonight . . . I can't think of anything more special than that."

Letting go, she stepped back, wanting so much for him to see the gratitude in her eyes. "Thank you, Derek. Really, thank you so much. Having the earrings feels like having Aunt Rose close again."

As he gently brushed her cheek with his thumb, a corner of his mouth curved upward. "Anything for you, Jess."

Slowly and reverently taking the earrings from the case, she put them on, one by one. Then, tucking her hair behind her ears to allow the rubies and diamonds to glimmer and shine, she grinned. "I bet this plain old dress looks better already, doesn't it?"

"Like I said before, Jess, you always look

great to me."

She warmed at his compliment but tried to dismiss the way it made her feel. "I can't believe you were able to keep the earrings a secret. That's so unlike you," she teased. "You never said a word."

"Yeah, well . . ." Derek took off his hat and ran a hand through his hair. "Actually, Jess, there's a lot I want to say. Even at Mick's that day, there were things I wanted to say . . . but it wasn't exactly the place I wanted to tell you what's been on my heart for years."

On his heart . . . for years? Oh, there went the catch in her breath again!

"For too many years." Derek shifted on his feet. Turned the wool cap in his hands, over and over again. "That day, at lunch, you were talking about mistakes you'd made. Well, what you don't know is, I made a huge mistake too, the day I came to visit you at Ohio State."

As she tried to think back to that time in her life, she frowned. "But . . . you never came to see me at college."

"I did. You just never knew about it. You weren't in your dorm when I got there. You were out doing laundry or something, and a guy answered the door. He introduced himself and told me how the two of you were headed to Las Vegas the next week to get —"

"Oh . . ." She closed her eyes. "Sean."

Derek nodded as he continued. "I was on my way up to Wisconsin, but I'd made a detour to Columbus first, to see you. I wanted to spill out my feelings for you. To tell you how much I'd always loved you."

Had he really just said those words? He loved her? She reeled on her heels, not sure she was hearing right. "But all those years, Derek . . . and you never let me know . . ."

"It's not like I didn't want to, Jess. I was just waiting."

"For what?"

"I wanted to be able to offer you something." His eyes glimmered with proud determination. "I wanted to know I had a future. When my aunt and uncle suggested I come live with them in Milwaukee and offered to help me get trained in the police academy there, I finally felt like I was on my way. That I could be a whole person for you. Not just some down-on-his-luck, broken kid."

"But you never seemed like that kid to me, Derek. You were my best friend. You filled up my world."

"You were my world too, Jess. But . . . I wanted more for myself than what I had, and I wanted to be able to give more to you. To be more for you."

Seeing the heartrending tenderness of his gaze, she opened her mouth to protest again, but he held up his hand. "I gave up too easily. And I've regretted it for a long time. That day I came to OSU, I took no for an answer before I'd even asked you the question. And months ago, when I finally moved back to Sugarcreek, I didn't say anything to you about how I was feeling because it didn't seem like the right time. Not after all you'd been through. And I also knew there were Cole's feelings to consider. I didn't know how he'd respond to me." He shifted on his feet. "But I think things have been going pretty well with him and me, don't you?" He raised a brow, seeking her response.

"I'd say really well, Derek." She smiled. Better than she could've ever hoped. "I think you had Cole at 'hello.' As in 'hello, Spider-Man.' "

Seeming pleased, he smiled at her answer, but just as quickly his face grew serious again. "So I guess what I'm saying is, Jess, if you have any feelings for me, any at all, I . . ." He held out his arms as if he didn't know what else to say.

In her mind, he'd said it all.

As though his words had released her at last, she took his hat from his hands and tossed it aside. Then, flinging herself against him, she locked herself into his embrace. Lifting her chin to meet his, he kissed her gently at first, feathery strokes of his lips, delightedly exploring. A series of slow, shivery kisses that left her quivering at his sweet tenderness.

But after all the years of waiting for each other, wanting each other, those light kisses just weren't enough. Derek pulled her even closer, his lips caressing hers, over and over . . . every touch the delicious sensation she'd always imagined it would be.

"Oh, Derek, do you know how long I've wanted to do that?" she said as his kisses ebbed into soft wisps of his lips again. "Ever since we were kids, going to prom. Jumping in Manor Lake. Dancing in the snow. Ever since the day you came back to Sugarcreek and walked into the Cottage and back into my life." Happiness poured out of her in a giggle. "And you never picked up on that, Deputy?"

He laughed at her implication. "I thought I felt something from you. But then, I wanted to believe it so much that I couldn't be sure."

"So you didn't notice my red cheeks every

time I saw you?"

"Oh, maybe once or twice." He tenderly kissed one cheek and then the other. "Actually they're looking pretty pink and flushed now."

"Happily flushed, I'd say."

"So, Jess, if you're feeling what I'm feeling, maybe, uh . . . well, what I mean is . . . I was thinking . . ."

There he was, stuttering all over again. There she was, nodding, encouraging him to say whatever was on his heart and mind.

"So, well, maybe . . . ," he finally started as he pulled another box from his coat pocket. "This isn't too much, then?"

It was a tiny jewelry case, as diminutive as the one before. Far too small for a bracelet, but just right for a necklace. At least that's what she assumed. What she expected. Until she peeled open the box, revealing something altogether different.

A mist of tears sprang to her eyes, clouding her view of a ruby-and-diamond ring. "It's so beautiful, Derek, so beautiful," she gushed. "And it matches the earrings perfectly."

"I had it designed to match. That's another reason why I didn't give you the earrings before now. I was waiting for the jeweler to have this ready for you."

"Is it — is it possibly what I think it is?"

"It's whatever you want it to be. It can be a ring that completes your set, along with the earrings. Or . . ." He paused a beat, gazing at her longingly. "I'm hoping it's a ring that completes my life — our life together. A family for the three of us." His voice broke with huskiness. "But, uh, I know all of this is a surprise, Jess, so if you need more time . . ."

"I think we've already wasted enough time, Derek. The only time I want is with you."

Her certainty triggered a smile that spilled over his face. Not hesitating a moment, he took the ring from the box and placed it on her offered finger.

"I love you so, so much, Derek."

"Ah, Jess. I'll love you forever. I already have. You know that, don't you?"

"I do," she said softly. "Now I do."

His mouth captured hers once again, leaving them both so caught up in one another's kisses that they startled at the sound of Cole's voice.

"Smile!" her son shouted out.

All at once, their lips broke apart. Still locked in each other's arms, they turned to see Cole, half of his face hidden behind his new camera.

"Smile!" he commanded them again.

But he didn't really have to.

Neither she nor Derek could contain their joy. They couldn't stop smiling or laughing as Cole clicked away, documenting their special event — the start of their lifetime together.

And as sure as there was a heaven above, Jessica knew her aunt Rose had to be looking down and smiling too.

CHAPTER THIRTY-TWO

At the sound of her cell phone, Liz looked up from her rows of knitting and noticed Daisy's head poked up curiously as well. Until then, the pup had been napping undisturbed beside the hearth under the string of Christmas stockings hanging from the mantel, looking like something out of a Norman Rockwell painting.

Being that it was Sunday and early evening, Liz was anticipating Amy's call. But she wasn't expecting to hear her grandkids' voices the moment she picked up the phone.

"Mare-wee almost Christmas, Nana!" The two of them shouted their sweet garbled greeting, warming her heart and making her laugh out loud.

"Merry almost Christmas to you, too!"

"Do you have kisses for Nana?" Liz could hear Amy saying, to which Ellie and Jack both made smooching sounds in the phone, and Liz readily returned the love with smacks of her own. But of course, once Ellie and Jack had started, they didn't want to stop. And didn't, until Amy chimed in. "Okay . . . that's enough kisses. Off to baths, you two. Daddy's waiting for you."

Liz could hear them scampering away in the background and moaned into the phone. "Oh, they are so precious. I can't wait for you all to get here so I can cuddle them close."

"It won't be too much longer now. How's everything on your end, Mom? What are you up to?"

"Just sitting here enjoying my beautiful Christmas tree." Well, *beautiful* might be a stretch. She and Daniel had made a trip north to a Christmas tree farm, determined to find the perfect tree for her family room, something grand the whole family could admire. But then they spotted Pat, the name they'd given the pathetic, skinny eyesore of a tree with nothing much symmetrical about it. Instant pushovers for the endearingly sad thing, they'd brought it home and decorated the scrawny, lopsided limbs the best they could. Unfortunately, the layer of tinsel hadn't improved its appearance much at all.

"You're just sitting there?" Amy suddenly sounded concerned. "Are you feeling okay?"

"I feel great! I'm knitting while I'm sitting. And not a vest this time. I'm knitting a sweater."

"Oh, something new! One of your argyle vests *with sleeves.*" Amy snickered, and Liz couldn't blame her daughter for ribbing her. As she'd mentioned to the gals at the Cottage, over the years she'd worked from the same pattern so many times she could recite it backward. Even sideways if that were possible. She felt completely comfortable with the tried-and-true design and knew it would always turn out. Just so. But like everything else in her life, she'd known it was time for a change.

"Okay, I deserve that." She grinned. "But I'll have you know I've found a brand-new pattern. Something I've never tried."

"Mom! After all these years!" her daughter teased more. "I'm so proud of you. What's it like?"

"It has cables, and I'm using a nice, subtle olive-green yarn." A color sure to bring out the green flecks in Daniel's hazel eyes.

"Cables and no crimson, gray, or white yarns?" Amy chuckled. "Well, that is new and different. You're branching out."

"Geez, Ames, I can't believe you called just to ridicule your dear old mother." Liz smiled. "And after all that I've been going through to plan a special Christmas for you all, shame on you."

"Oh, you know I'm only kidding. We love everything you knit for us," Amy insisted. "And, Mom, about our visit: I seriously hope you're not going to a lot of trouble. We're only going to be in Sugarcreek for four days."

"Trust me, celebrating Christmas with my darling grandchildren is no trouble at all."

After accepting the job offer from Belinda and John, she'd had a few loose ends to tie up at the real estate office. Then, when she wasn't visiting the Annabelle's kitchen to get a feel for the daily operation there before her official start in January, she'd been in her own kitchen — baking Christmas cookies and bars galore. Daniel had complained he couldn't taste-test any more sweets or he was going to have to diet before Christmas even arrived.

"Have you taken the kids to see Santa yet?" she asked Amy.

"We're going a night this week so it's not as crowded. But tonight, once they're bathed and in their pajamas, we're planning to take a ride and look at Christmas lights."

"That was always so much fun to do with you," Liz sighed. "I'm actually going to the outdoor candlelight service at the church grounds tonight."

"Oh, you told me about that. Sounds chilly."

"Ha, yes. I'm sure it will be. But they promised it won't run too long, and it's a way of joining together for Christmas before they start the reconstruction in January. It'll be an emotional night, for sure. But overall, a good one, I think."

"Are you going by yourself? And meeting people there?"

"Uh, no . . ." She stumbled over her words. "Actually, my, uh, ride should be here any minute."

"Is Jessica picking you up? How is she doing?"

"Jessica? She's doing well. But no, that's not who's taking me. I'm going with . . ." She paused and instantly her heart sped up a few beats at the knowledge of what finally had to be said. She'd kept putting off telling Amy about her feelings for Daniel, not sure how she'd react. But she couldn't put it off any longer, not with Amy and her family coming to town. Her ear felt like it was on fire, pressed against the phone. "I'm going with someone very special, Amy. With Daniel."

There was a moment's lull on Amy's end. "Daniel? Your handyman? But I thought . . . Well, I'm confused. I thought you said he was just a friend."

"I know, Ames," Liz said ever so softly. "For a while, I thought that's all he was too."

Her daughter went silent, and Liz wished she knew what was going on in her mind. As much as Amy didn't want her to be alone, was she ready to see her with someone else? Especially now, right at this time of year, when she'd surely be remembering her father's passing? Would she be hurt? Disapproving? Embrace the idea? Or fight it like Liz herself had?

She sat silently, hoping and praying their Christmas together wouldn't be spoiled because of her disclosure. The seconds felt like minutes before Amy spoke again. "Well, all I can say is —"

Liz closed her eyes and held her breath.

"I was wondering when you were going to realize how special he is to you, Mom."

"What?" Liz squealed. "You knew too?" Just like Lydia and Jessica had. Liz sure felt slow on the uptake.

"Are you kidding? I could hear it in your giddy voice every time you'd talk about your 'friend.' So we'll be seeing you *and* Daniel when we get there on Christmas Eve?"

"Yes! I mean, that's what I was planning."

"Good. I can't wait to meet him, Mom."

"Oh, Amy, I can't wait for you to meet

him either."

"And, Mom . . ." Amy faltered, and Liz could detect the emotion in her daughter's voice in the way only a mother can. "I want you to know, I'm really, *really* glad for you."

"Oh, honey, thank you." Tears brimmed in Liz's eyes. She was so relieved . . . so appreciative of the support, understanding, and love in Amy's words. "I love you, Ames."

The doorbell rang just as Liz was finishing her call and swiping the tears from her eyes. Knowing it was Daniel, she quickly hid the beginnings of his sweater under a sofa pillow and turned off Pat's tree lights before answering the door.

He stood in her doorway, grinning as if he were seeing her all over again for the first time. And she knew just how he was feeling. Seeing him, her heart swelled the same way it had the first morning he'd stood on her doorstep with a bag of muffins.

"Hey!" He leaned forward slightly and she stretched up to meet his kiss hello. "I left the car running so it would be warm for you. Are you ready?"

Gazing into the face of the man she'd come to love, she sighed. "Yes!" she said without hesitation. "Yes, I am."

It had taken a while for her to get there, but she was definitely, definitely ready.

Open for any and all blessings to come her way. And it dawned on her at that moment that in many ways her life was a lot like her knitting. She'd learned lessons, acquired a few skills, and then had settled into a way of doing things she was comfortable with, sometimes expecting nothing more. It wasn't until recently that she'd realized the real depth in life — as in knitting — came in being brave and trying out new colors and patterns. Being open and accepting of the new situations and new people God had brought into her life.

Obviously, she had no way of knowing what the end result would be. But if she only kept trusting in His love — and herself — she was sure to discover more some-things and someones pleasing to her heart. More than she'd ever imagined, just as she already had.

"We'll be back soon, Daisy," she said over her shoulder to her pup, then picked up her coat and purse from the nearby bench and closed the door behind her.

The air was crisp. The sky was clear. And she knew without a word being said, as she joined Daniel on the porch, that his heart like hers was full of promise. He held out his kind, solid, gentle hand. She took it. Warmed by each other's touch, they walked that way, into the starlit, glittering Christmas-light night.

CHAPTER THIRTY-THREE

A draft of cold air sneaked its way into Lydia's house as she opened the door to let Jonas inside.

"I can't promise the buggy will be *verra* warm for the trip into town tonight," he said, briskly rubbing his hands together.

"Oh, I know. Just feel that air." Shivering, she hurriedly closed the door behind him. "Flora is lucky I'm not the one driving. She can stay cozy in the barn. As for us, I thought a few blankets might help."

She nodded toward the love seat, where she'd already stacked an assortment of wool lap covers to take on their ride to the Faith Community Church grounds.

"*Jah,* those blankets will help some. But the backseat of a sheriff's car would sure be a lot warmer." His eyes twinkled merrily.

Putting a hand to her hip, she pretended to be disgruntled. Though hard as she tried, she couldn't hold back a smile whenever her neighbor got to ribbing her. "Really, Jonas Hershberger, are you gonna tease me about that forever?"

"*Nee*, not forever. Just a little while longer. Maybe till next year this time." He laughed. "Our friendly Deputy Derek is coming tonight, isn't he?"

"*Jah*, he's bringing Jessica and Cole."

"I talked to Uncle Daniel again the other day. He mentioned he'd be at the candlelight service with Liz."

"I believe the Keims and some of the other families from our quilting circle are coming too."

"That's what I'd heard from a few of the men down at work." Jonas nodded. "It's *gut* the pastor made such a point to invite nonmembers too. Though I keep wondering, Lydia, how you're doing. I know it's gotta be mighty hard for you."

Once she'd finally gotten answers that helped make better sense of her marriage, she'd still lain awake many a night crying. She'd drifted through many a day in a fog. Until one morning, *Gott*, in His goodness and mercy, brought her just the comfort she needed.

As she'd sifted through a bottom dresser drawer in search of thicker stockings to ward off the cold, her fingers came across something she had tucked away there a year or more ago. A tissue wrapped around a rose, so old the flower was nearly void of any pink color. So dry, many of its petals had broken loose. But still, the rose had been precious to her the day she'd hidden it away. And its specialness hadn't faded at all. Neither had the memory of the afternoon Henry had given it to her — a most perfect summer day that the two of them had shared.

Instead of heading their buggy homeward after church, that Sunday Henry had veered off onto a back road and into a meadow she'd never seen before. There, they spent hours sitting under a shade tree, snacking on apples he'd brought along and dipping their toes into the pond. And her heart had melted as he plucked a wild rose from a bush and tucked it into her *kapp*. That night, too, he had held her closer than he ever had before.

But by the next morning, he acted as if none of those things had ever happened. All that she had left as proof was the pink wild rose.

Rediscovering that flower brought her solace. But it was also a harsh reminder of how the evil one had racked Henry's soul, tortured his life — and she couldn't let him do the same to hers. She made up her mind right then that she wouldn't let the devil get his way any longer. She simply wouldn't let that happen. If she did, it felt as if she'd be dishonoring Henry's memory.

So her pouting and pondering turned into prayers. She kept busy crafting and working. And she vowed to *Gott* to help anyone she could, knowing from experience how healing kindness and encouragement could be. Life on earth was not easy for anyone, for sure. Everyone was going through something at one time or another. But a stitch of hope, as she'd been told Rose used to say, was just the thing that could help get a person through hard times more easily.

"I'm just thankful for so many friends who are coming tonight," she told Jonas. "A friend can make all the difference, ya know?"

Jonas stared at her longingly, like there was something more he wanted to say. Something perhaps to comfort her?

She placed a hand on his forearm, consoling him instead. "Don't you worry, Jonas. I'm going to be all right." A promise she'd made to herself as much as to him.

"I know you will." He clasped his warm hand over hers, patting encouragingly. "Knowing you as I do by now, I have no doubt about that, Lydia."

He squeezed her hand gently before she broke away from him. Taking a deep breath, she tried to lighten the moment with a smile. "We still have some time before we leave. This morning, I defrosted the pecan pie that your uncle Daniel and Liz didn't finish. Do you think you'd like a piece and some *verra* hot tea before we go?"

"Pecan pie?" His eyes lit up. "It's my favorite."

She raised a brow as they walked side by side into the kitchen. "Hmm . . ." She started to grin. "Really? I thought sugar cookies were your favorite."

"Ah, did I say that?" He scratched at his chin.

"Yes, you did."

"You have way too good of a memory. I'll have to watch what I say around you."

Laughing at his honesty, she gently chided him, "Yes, you certainly will."

As always, it was easy making small talk with her neighbor as she placed wedges of pie onto plates and poured steaming water into both of their mugs. Going from one topic to the next, they chatted about work, the weather, their pets, and even her excitement over the upcoming visit from her mother and sister.

"How long did you say they're staying again?" he asked once he'd savored his first bite of pie.

"Oh, just for a week or so, though I wish they could visit a lot longer. I haven't seen them in forever. Or at least it feels that way."

"It'll be a nice way for you to end the year, for sure."

Lydia could feel the delight bubbling up inside her as she thought about the approaching day of their arrival. "I'm also *verra* glad they're coming soon so they can stay at my house. Especially since I'm not sure how much longer I'll be here."

Jonas's fork halted in the air. It hovered over his plate as he narrowed his eyes on hers. "Well, if not here, Lydia, where on earth would ya be?"

"Oh, I can't believe I didn't tell you the news!" She leaned closer. "Derek confided to me that he's proposing to Jessica tonight."

"Jah?" Jonas blinked, looking even more bewildered than before. And slightly put off as well. "That's wonderful *gut* for the two of them, but I don't understand what it has to do with you."

"Well . . ." She picked up her mug, cupping it in her hands. "If Jessica says yes, and I'm guessing she will, I figure they'll be moving into Derek's place. And then, who knows? Maybe I would move in over the Cottage. That way, I'd save money on transportation, and I'd be *verra* close to work."

"But, Lydia . . ." Jonas's chair squeaked as he sat back to look at her. "If that happened . . . if you lived close to work, well then, you'd be far from me."

His concern showed in his eyes as they met hers. But there was something else in his warm gaze as well. A longing. A fondness that she'd seen before . . . whenever Daniel glanced at Liz. And when Derek looked at Jessica. The way she'd always hoped someone would look at her . . . would see her. A way no man had ever regarded her before.

As a flash of warmth coursed up her neck, she was too stunned to speak.

When she didn't readily reply, he quickly began to apologize. "I'm sorry, Lydia. That wasna right of me. I probably shouldn't have said that."

Setting her mug on the table, she took a moment to find her voice. "*Nee,* Jonas, it's okay that you did. I've learned in this life that it's a *gut* thing when people say what they feel," she told him. "A *verra gut* thing."

They sat staring at one another in a silence that was foreign to them. Until finally Jonas spoke again.

"I'm guessing we should get going to town, don't you think?"

"Jah." She took a deep breath. "I do."

As they both got up, he helped her clear the table, placing dishes in the sink.

"There's still some pie left," she let him know as she tore off a piece of foil. "Since it's your favorite —" she smiled — "do you want me to wrap it up for you?"

"Nee. I'll be back soon enough," he said as he scooted in their chairs. Then he paused and slowly dipped his head toward her. "I mean . . . if that's still all right with you, Lydia."

"Jah, Jonas. *Jah,* of course it is," she said to her kindly neighbor.

As she covered the pie for safekeeping, she surprised herself by thinking how much — how *verra* much — she hoped what he said was true.

As Jonas rounded the last bend in the road and slowed the buggy at the base of Main Street, Lydia gasped, feeling like she'd never seen the town before. And she hadn't — at least not like this.

"It's a beauty, ain't it?" Jonas read her mind.

"*Jah,* it sure is," she whispered in agreement.

White lights glimmered on both sides of the streets, outlining frost-covered shop fronts and roofs all the way up to the hilltop. Every shop window, doorway, and lamppost was adorned with greenery and red bows, leaving nothing left out or exposed. Horses and buggies parked along the way added a nostalgic feel. All making Sugarcreek look like exactly what it was — a Christmas village of the quaintest kind.

And it wasn't just the town that shimmered in the night. As she looked to the top of the hill, where Faith Community Church used to stand, even that area appeared to be glowing.

All the grime, the ashes, the remnants of the scarred, charred church had been taken away, completely removed from the scene. Now there was only light where darkness used to be. Now there was life where death had had its ugly hold.

Faraway stars twinkled like diamonds overhead, helping to illuminate the life-size manger scene with real people and farm animals. As a slight dusting of snow continued to cover the grounds in bright whiteness, townspeople — *Englisch* and Amish alike — were gathering together to give

549

thanks and praise.

And it came to Lydia as Jonas's horses clip-clopped leisurely up the hill — a memory of a rare buggy ride she'd taken with Henry, when they'd come to town on a spring day. Right away her eyes had been drawn to Faith Community's steeple. How pretty it had looked to her, gracing the landscape the way it did. Reaching up, into the clear blue sky. The highest thing for miles around with sheer strands of the purest white clouds drifting by.

Yet now, as her eyes settled on the hilltop, she saw everything so differently.

For the first time in her life she felt a part of something — something bigger than herself. A town and people she'd come to know. So much more to care about in her life.

Now she was looking forward to the day the steeple would be raised over the town again. Not for any beauty it would hold. Or any elegance it would add to the horizon.

But for the reminder it would always be.

Letting her never forget that she and all the others were being watched over. Cared for. And loved.

In that, as she'd come to know, she could trust. In that, she could always find her strength.

DISCUSSION QUESTIONS

1. Jessica could barely knit, Liz could knit one or two things well, and Lydia was accomplished at both knitting and quilting — yet they all find a haven in Rose's Knit One Quilt Too Cottage. What does the shop mean to each of them? Do you have a special place that's a haven for you? What makes it so special?

2. Liz, Jessica, and Lydia are different from one another in many ways — life experience, age, faith walk, and culture. Yet they become like sisters — sisters of the heart. Do you think it's common for women to bond that way? Why or why not?

3. Early in the story, Jessica stares at Lydia's house in the dimness of night, thinking there is no place safe from things that tear your world and heart in two. Has your sense of security ever been shattered as

Jessica's was? Where do you turn to feel safe?

4. As members of Rose's Secret Stitches Society, Liz, Jessica, and Lydia traipse around in the dark of night, hoping to bring encouragement and hope to townspeople going through trouble. Yet in each act of kindness, something goes just a little haywire. Does this ever seem to happen to you? How do you respond when your good intentions run into obstacles? Can you think of a time when such mishaps made you laugh?

5. Which Secret Stitches Society outing was the most enjoyable for you? Could you see yourself doing something like that?

6. As Lydia becomes more accustomed to Liz and Jessica and the world around her, she begins to realize that her marriage had many problems. Do you think if Henry hadn't passed, if they'd always stayed married, that those issues would have come more to light in later years? Or do you think Lydia would've remained satisfied with the sort of relationship they had?

7. The darkness in Henry's past comes as a

complete shock to Lydia. Yet that sickening and sad information helps her better understand the puzzle of her husband and their marriage. Henry never shared the horror he lived through, so there was no way Lydia could've known. But too often, in everyday incidents, do we also look at the surface of a person's life and make assumptions we shouldn't? Can you think of a time when your first impressions were proven wrong?

8. Jessica tells her new friends, "All the while I wasn't thinking of [God], He was thinking of me. I know He was because He sent you — both of you — into my life." Do you believe God sends people into our lives when we most need them? How was this true for each of the women in the story?

9. Having Daniel enter her life the way he did comes as a surprise for Liz. Why do you think she has such a difficult time understanding her feelings for him? Has there been a time when a new door unexpectedly opened in your life? Did you welcome it? Fear it? Both?

10. At times, as with the fatalities from the

church fire, it is difficult to imagine any good can come from such a devastating event. But did some good come from the fire? In overwhelming situations in your own life, have you been able to, with time, look back and see evidence that God was there and that He cared?

11. Rose certainly had an enormous impact on many people she left behind — her family, friends, even customers. How do we know this? What made her so special?

12. Coming into town for the Christmas candlelight service, Lydia remembers a time when the church steeple pointed to the heavens, and she looks forward to when it will be raised again. How do her feelings in this final scene reflect her relationship with God? How do her thoughts bookend the beginning of the novel, when she is recalling her mother's advice?

ABOUT THE AUTHOR

Cathy Liggett is the American Christian Fiction Writers' prestigious Carol Award–winning author of *Beaded Hope,* her debut women's fiction novel, which was also a nominee for *Romantic Times'* Reviewers' Choice Awards' Best Inspirational Novel. Besides women's fiction, she enjoys writing sweet romances and has been honored to be recognized in her hometown for literary and artistic achievement by the public library of Hamilton County.

Cathy knew writing fiction was for her after reading aloud a junior high English assignment and watching the class — at least the girls — well up with emotion. Yet it wasn't until much later in life that she seriously tried her hand at storytelling again. First came years of advertising copy writing, gift product development, and the publication of a nonfiction book for NAL.

Cathy and her husband, Mark, live in

Loveland, Ohio, and spend most of their free time walking and spoiling their boxer mix, Chaz. They are always happiest when their greatest blessings — their two grown children and most delightful son-in-law — are home for a stay. Visit Cathy's website at www.cathyliggett.com.

The employees of Thorndike Press hope you have enjoyed this Large Print book. All our Thorndike, Wheeler, and Kennebec Large Print titles are designed for easy reading, and all our books are made to last. Other Thorndike Press Large Print books are available at your library, through selected bookstores, or directly from us.

For information about titles, please call:
  (800) 223-1244

or visit our Web site at:
  http://gale.cengage.com/thorndike

To share your comments, please write:
Publisher
Thorndike Press
10 Water St., Suite 310
Waterville, ME 04901